MOTYA

MOTYA

Unearthing a
Lost Civilization

Gaia Servadio

VICTOR GOLLANCZ
LONDON

First published in Great Britain in 2000 by Victor Gollancz
An imprint of Orion Books Ltd
Orion House, 5 Upper St Martin's Lane, London WC2H 9EA

A CIP catalogue record for this book is available
from the British Library

ISBN 0 575 06746 2

Printed and bound in Great Britain by
Butler & Tanner Ltd, Frome and London

This book is dedicated to
Giuliana Saladino Cimino

Contents

Acknowledgements

I would like to thank the Whitaker Foundation, and in particular its President, Aldo Scimè, and its Secretary-General, Maria Enza Carollo. Signora Bice Gozzo was an exemplary and dedicated archivist who helped me a great deal. I would also like to express my thanks for the Foundation's permission to quote from the material in the archives and to reproduce some of their photographs. I wish to thank Ben Whitaker and Raleigh Trevelyan, Miss Honor Frost and Dr B. S. J. Isserlin. My grateful thanks also to Professor Vincenzo Tusa and his wife Professoressa Aldina Tusa, to Dr Maria Luisa Famà, Giuseppe Pugliese and his family, Vincenzo Arini and his family.

Most of the chapters have been seen by the people quoted above, but any remaining mistakes are my own, as indeed are the opinions expressed.

I wish also to thank Dr Pietro Alagna at the Stabilimento Pellegrino for letting me look at the Whitaker papers – he keeps 93 volumes of Ingham/Whitaker accounts and business letters; to Dr Renata Zanca for her chronology of the Whitaker family; and to Professor Salvatore Nicosia for his invaluable advice. I owe to his authority (he holds the chair of ancient Greek at the University of Palermo) the liberty of calling the Kouros a *kouros*.

My thanks also to Hugh Myddelton and his wife for ever-patient collaboration; to Christopher Sinclair-Stevenson for his intelligent participation and for being a wonderful agent-cum-editor.

I owe a special debt of gratitude to Doctor B. S. J. Isserlin for casting a scholarly eye over the work of an intruder.

I want to thank the following publishing houses for allowing me to quote from their books: Thames and Hudson for *The Israelites* by B. S. J. Isserlin; Cambridge University Press for *The Phoenicians and The West* by M. E. Aubet; Penguin Books for *The Aeneid* by Virgil, translated by David West; Random House UK for *The World of Ulysses* by M. F. Finley; RCS Libri for the essays by Professor Bondì and Professor Tusa from 'I Fenici' and for *Memoire del Mediterraneo* by Ferdinand Braudel; and Prion Books Ltd for *The*

Bourbon of Naples by Harold Acton. Thanks also to the periodical *Antiquity*, for allowing me to quote from two essays by Doctor B. S. J. Isserlin, and the *Journal of Nautical Archaeology*, for quotations from an essay by Honor Frost. The details and dates of publication are in the Bibliography and Notes. Other works quoted belonged to the author or were out of copyright. I have made every effort to clear permission. In those cases where I have been unsuccessful, I will make corrections to future editions.

Photographs are reproduced by kind permission of Enzo Sellerio Editore, Palermo; RCS Libri; the Louvre Museum; the Fondazione Giuseppe Whitaker, Palermo; the B. and H. Isserlin Collection and Gualtiero Malde. All these photographs retain their copyright.

As usual the London Library was a surprisingly rich source of books on the subject, and I want to thank its helpful assistants and Alan Bell, a more than welcome new Chief Librarian. My gratitude also goes to the wonderful Bodleian Library.

My total gratitude, finally, to my dearest friend Giuliana Saladino Cimino, who encouraged me so much and helped me in many ways but who died before this book was published without knowing that it was dedicated to her. Sicily for me is for ever linked to her and without her it is another Sicily, not a better one.

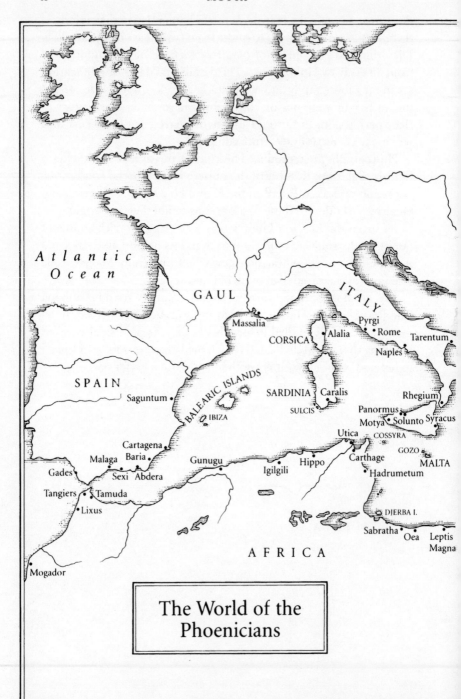

Atlantic Ocean

GAUL

ITALY

CORSICA

SPAIN

Massalia

Pyrgi
Rome
Alalia
Tarentum
Naples

BALEARIC ISLANDS

SARDINIA

Saguntum

Caralis

Rhegium

IBIZA

SULCIS

Panormus
Motya • Solunto
Syracus

Cartagena

Utica

COSSYRA

Malaga Baria

Gunugu

Hippo

Carthage

GOZO

MALTA

Gades

Sexi Abdera

Igilgili

Hadrumetum

Tangiers • Tamuda

Lixus

DJERBA I.

Mogador

AFRICA

Sabratha

Oea

Leptis Magna

The World of the Phoenicians

Black Sea

THRACE

PHRYGIA

MACEDONIA

LYCIA

GREECE

• Sardis

Ephesus

CILICIA

Karatepe

Tarsus •

• Alalakh

• Ugarit

• Arados

• Athens

Biblos
• Beirut
• Sidon
Tyre

CYPRUS

CRETE

• Joppa
• Jerusalem

• Gaza

Mediterranean
Sea

Alexandria
Naucratis

• Retabe

Memphis •

Cyrene •

LIBYA

• Arae Philenorum

0   100   200   300   400

Miles

Illustrations

I

RETURN TO MOTYA

The myrtle was still in bloom, although a low fire had swept through the fields leaving the ground scorched. After many months of dry weather, the rain was finally bathing the trunks of the vines, now old and tired and long since barren. That is why the fields had been burned: to finish off those poor old vines which had once produced the best Marsala, a wine offered in a tiny chalice, dry as the fields outside and just as powerfully scented.

It was easier to walk among the fields now than it had been earlier that summer, when my progress had been hampered by dried bushes, thistles and randomly sprouting corn. The rain was encouraging intensely coloured flowers, mauve primulas and wild orchids as well as the myrtle, brighter than ever in their need to attract insects quickly before their season was over.

While I walked, I inhaled the smell of the sea and the scorched vegetation; a pungent mix which evoked in my imagination scenes I had never witnessed. Sitting on those ochre stones cut some 2,500 years earlier, I watched with my mind's eye and I saw shadows; I fantasized. There was so much conjecture about this ghostly island and about Motya, the fallen Punic city, the walls, the steps, the remains of the temples, the necropolis, the sacred area for human sacrifice; they all evoked a power which I remembered experiencing during my very first visit, thirty years earlier. Then, I had been lucky to have my eyes opened through the knowledge and passion of an archaeologist who had dedicated most of his life to the study of Motya and of its long-dead citizens. Now, sitting by the ancient gate, on the north side of the city, I tried to imagine life unfolding in Motya. Although there was much known about its fall and the fate of its inhabitants – the screams, the fires, the looting and the rape as the city was sacked – there was little knowledge about how the

Motyans had actually lived. So many of those everyday details were still buried under my feet, but the ground that had been excavated had gradually unfolded its secrets, revealing the story of an ancient city and a lost civilization.

Looking south from the gate, my back to the lagoon and to the Sicilian mainland beyond it, I faced the remains of the two main watch towers, each with a small adjoining temple containing votive altars. Incoming carts laden with goods had left deep marks on the paved road here. Metals, wool and pottery arrived by sea, but food was brought in over the road built by the Motyans to link their city with Birgi, a settlement on the mainland just one and a half kilometres away across the lagoon. So the carts probably arrived carrying agricultural produce to sustain the population of Motya; but they left carrying corpses because, as the city developed on the island, there was little space to bury the dead.

On the other side of the island the lagoon flowed into the open sea: the Mediterranean at its narrowest, across which, a mere twenty-four hours by sailing-ship, was Carthage, Motya's mother-city and the centre of the Punic world.

How did these people live, how were they governed, how did they think? The odd thing about the Phoenicians and their Mediterranean offspring the Punics is that, although they invented the alphabet, they wrote little. Their writings are limited to a few names jotted on their funerary stelae, dedications to gods and letters to identify stones for building.[1] They were, after all, primarily traders and navigators; they left the arts to the Greeks, from whom they bought artefacts and who recorded their story.

One of the few written stelae found in Motya, for example, reads: 'Hammon on behalf of Hanno son of Adonibaal because he heard the voice of God, that He may bless him.' What information can we glean from this? Only that Hammon, who was an Egyptian deity, had at a certain stage – probably around 700 BC – been adopted by the Punics and that the Punics were religious. Adonibaal was one of a group of names, like Hannibal and Hasdrubal, that were derived from the name 'Baal', the Phoenician word for 'Lord', and mean 'son of Baal' or 'protected by Baal'. Minimal though this information is, it is more than can be gleaned from most of the Motyan funerary stelae: although more than a thousand were unearthed, only forty were inscribed. Women's names do not appear on them: as with most Bronze Age civilizations, Punic history seems to have been made by men, with a few notable exceptions, like Dido, founder of Carthage, or Europa, the Phoenician princess raped by Zeus.

Early Punic statuary probably depicts male and female human sacrificial offerings, for these people feared God and they feared representing God; after all, they were Semites, close in origin and in language to the Jews. The Bible tells us a lot about the Phoenicians, who are referred to as Canaanites, but the name by which history knows them first appears in the Homeric period and in Greek: Phoinikes, 'the red ones', a designation conferred in acknowledgement of their ability to dye cloth in shades of red or purple, from violet to lilac. Phoenicians from the Levantine coast travelled widely across and beyond the Mediterranean, founding many settlements where they traded and mingled with the local populations, buying from them, selling to them, living with them. These descendants of the Middle Eastern Phoenicians are those we know as the Punics – the word is the Roman rendering of the Greek name – famed for their mighty cities of Carthage and Gades (Cadiz). At first the Greeks and the Romans did business with Punic settlements in North Africa, Sicily, Sardinia and Spain rather than making war against them. In fact, from its very establishment as a city in the eighth century BC, Motya was home to a mixture of Phoenicians, native Elymians, Sicans and later of Greeks. Before they came to regard the Phoenicians/Punics as their enemies in the struggle for control of the Mediterranean, the Greeks admired these travellers and traders: they adopted their alphabet, borrowed their gods and copied their ships.

The Punics had in fact developed a different culture from their Phoenician forebears who had thrust out from the Middle East, first to the heart of the Mediterranean and then onwards beyond it, pushing their vessels out past the Pillars of Hercules into the unknown. In search of metals, Phoenician ships reached Cornwall where tin was mined; they also sailed down the Atlantic coast of Africa as far as Mogador, where archaeologists have found traces of their presence. To those among whom they landed these people must have seemed odd, even ugly, with their guttural speech and swarthy appearance. They had much in common with their cousins the Hebrews, and in a way the ancient world considered them as the

new world regarded the Jews: clever, but too clever by half; necessary at times, but a nuisance to be crushed when they became too
cocky. They were terrific navigators, these Phoenicians and the
Punics after them, and impressively efficient in their organization
of affairs aboard ship. The Greek scholar and soldier Xenophon
puts the following words into the mouth of a Greek sailor:

I think that the best and most perfect arrangement of things that I ever
saw was when I went to look at the great Phoenician sailing-vessel; for I
saw the largest amount of naval tackle separately disposed in the small-
est storage possible. For a ship, as you well know, is brought to anchor
and again got under way, by a vast number of wooden implements and of
ropes, and sails the sea by means of a quantity of rigging and is armed
with a number of contrivances against hostile vessels, and carries about
with it a large supply of weapons for the crew and, besides, has all the
utensils that a man keeps in his house, for each of the messes. In addition, it is laden with a quantity of merchandise which the owner carries
with him for his own profit. Now all the things which I have mentioned
lay in a space not much bigger than a room that would conveniently hold
ten beds. And I remarked that they lay in such a way that they did not
obstruct one another and did not require anyone to search for them; and
yet they were neither placed at random, nor entangled one with another,
so as to consume time when they were suddenly wanted for use. Also I
found the captain's assistant, who is called 'the look-out man', so well
acquainted with the position of all the articles, and with the number of
them, that even when at a distance he could tell where everything lay, and
how many there were of each sort, just as anyone who has learnt to read
can tell the number of letters in the name of Socrates and the proper
place for each of them. Moreover, I saw this man, in his leisure moments,
examining and testing everything that a vessel needs when at sea; so, as I
was surprised, I asked him what he was about, whereupon he replied:
'Stranger, I am looking to see, in case anything should happen, how
everything is arranged in the ship, and whether anything is wanting, or is
inconveniently situated; for, when a storm arises at sea, it is not possible
either to look for what is wanting or to put to right what is arranged
awkwardly.'[2]

At the beginning the Phoenicians built mere settlements beside
natural harbours. Only Carthage became a real city in the sense

that it was conceived as such from the start and was self-governing. Having become rich and powerful in its own right, it was the turn of Carthage to found colonies. One of these was Motya, closer to Africa than to mainland Italy. From the Phoenicians' point of view this island was set in the best possible position: it was one day's navigation from Carthage; its lagoon was a natural harbour; it had drinking water, fuel and salt: like the great Punic city of Gades, its low basin, in the strong wind and sun, could be made to yield salt-pans. At Motya ships could revictual and sail on to the sister cities of Panormus and Soloeis (modern Palermo and Solunto), and thence to Sardinia, the Balearics and the coast of southern Spain. At times they called on Phocaean or other Greek harbours, but only for trading. So these clever and adventurous people settled in Motya and remained there for around four centuries.

Once, the entire perimeter of Motya, two and a half kilometres in circumference, had been protected by high walls punctuated with watch towers. By the seventh century BC it was an established city, not just a settlement, and by the sixth century BC probably one of the most flourishing Punic cities in the Mediterranean, richer than the harbour of Palermo; as early as the fifth century BC it had its own mint, a sure sign of financial independence and prosperity.

I wondered where that mint was. Somewhere under that rubble in the centre of the island near the main road, perhaps. If the archaeologists were to discover it, we would learn much more about life in Punic Motya. I moved away from the north gate and walked back through the fields, their blackened stubbles and scorched rubble reminding me once again of the final days of Motya.

In 397 BC the city was attacked by Dionysius I, ruler of the Greek city of Syracuse in eastern Sicily. During the long siege catapults were used for the first time, perhaps hurling missiles from the very site where I found myself standing. Dionysius built his siege towers six storeys high; from their vantage points upon these fearsome engines the aggressors could both fire at the defenders and engage in hand-to-hand combat. When Dionysius eventually stormed the city, there was frightful slaughter, the inhabitants were overrun and put to the sword. According to the Greek historian Diodorus, who recorded the battle in detail, the Motyans had 'fought like people who were desperate and prodigal with their lives, knowing too well the cruelty of the Greeks'.

I could imagine the groups of screaming women with their children as the Greeks and their mercenary troops fell upon them. I could even hear their screams. I could hear the wailing wind.

I was hungry.

I decided to return to the little house, called with self-conscious dignity the Missione Archeologica, where the young Roman archaeologist Pamela Toti was preparing a bowl of spaghetti. Pamela came to Motya twice a year and lived on the island, helping with the study of the archeological stratifications and any digging that was going on. She was large and serious, not particularly friendly but brave and skilful. Next to the Missione stood the museum and the house that had belonged to the Englishman Joseph Whitaker, who played such a crucial role in the rediscovery of ancient Motya. It must be under those buildings that the most important Punic edifices were to be found: on the opposite side of the island from what is now referred to as 'the industrial district', which I was now leaving, where woollens and linens were dyed. Linen arrived by ship, but wool was provided by the local sheep, while the huge quantities of murex shells which are still found ground up at Motya, as also in ancient Phoenician factories at Tyre and Sidon, produced the many shades of purple. The process of dyeing was very smelly, so it is logical to imagine that the mint and the government buildings would have been located as far away from the stinking factory as possible: the other side of the island, where there was a little hill, seemed the obvious location for the Punic civic centre, the most important buildings of the thriving community.

The Phoenicians were famous for dyeing cloth which, before the discovery of the attributes of the murex, had always been white. How dull it must have been to dress in monochrome white, day and night! Having discovered how to derive the colour purple from a shell which inhabits the Mediterranean in vast quantities, in effect the Phoenicians started the art of fashion, producing and selling variety as well as vanity. You could say that Baal is the patron saint of Armani and Dior. The Phoenicians could turn out all sorts of shades; they stencilled white cloth with designs and embroidered them with coloured threads. Punic women became skilled at weaving wool and linen together and, for very special clients, even silk, which was already available from China. They could produce patterns not only by weaving but also by block printing. Only the rich could afford coloured clothes, and white remained the colour for mourning, poverty and penitence through Greek and early Roman times; during the Roman Republic and later, in the empire, only senators, kings and despots wore purple. Even today cardinals are still called *porporati* in Italian, after the purple robes that they wear; and purple remains the colour of might, of kings' mantles.

The only difficulty with Motya as a site for dyeing works – apart from the stench it caused, to which the inhabitants no doubt became accustomed – was that there was not much water on that flat island, and supplies had to be transported through pipes from the mainland, where there was plenty – as I could tell from the reeds which grew around the lagoon. Now I understood why the Punics eventually decided to abandon Motya and move to the more westerly Sicilian settlement of Lilybaeum (modern Marsala), which Thucydides tells us was named after the miraculous source of gushing water that springs from a cave close to Cape Boeo.

The Motyans also manufactured urns and ewers for carrying oil, water and wine. What did they use for heating the kiln? I asked Pamela, as we ate her excellent spaghetti seasoned with fresh basil. I could see no trees around the lagoon, the Stagnone as it is known, and the forests must have been quite a long way away, behind Eryx and Selinunte. They dried huge quantities of the seaweed from the lagoon, she told me – the *Posidonia oceanica*, unique to this environment. The lagoon is also home to another rarity, the alga *egagopili* (*Rityphloea tinctoria*), which you can see rolling in the swell of the shallow waters. Both plants, when dried, served to fuel the Motyan furnace, while the algae also made it easier to beach boats by protecting their keels. By harvesting the seaweed, too, the Motyans kept the Stagnone free from excessive vegetation, which in turn increased fish stocks. Because of its position, sheltered within a lagoon embraced by a fertile mainland, the low, warm sea-basin is in effect a fish nursery. Consequently Motya was always well stocked with food and able also to export salted fish.

The Punics' maritime power was celebrated – and envied – all over the Mediterranean; but in Motya there was neither space nor wood to build ships, the triremes for which the Punics were famous and without which a city like Motya would have been unable to survive. Therefore Motya was totally dependent on Carthage, not only for cargo transport but, as we shall see, for its defence as well;

indeed, it paid a yearly tax to its mother city. One suspects that its own skills were developing in a different direction from the usual Punic emphasis on trade and navigation. The city was described by the Greeks as rich with temples and high buildings; and in 1979 a magnificent statue was unearthed depicting a young athlete, probably commissioned from one of the best Greek sculptors of the day. The Punics understood that the Greeks were great interpreters of aesthetics, whereas their own chief expertise lay in trade: so they bought Greek vessels, Greek mosaics and probably Greek furniture as well. Those Greeks who lived in Motya are likely to have been mainly artisans. Dionysius had them crucified when he won the siege of 397; he considered them traitors for their loyalty to the Motyans against their Greek brethren. In fact the Greeks were probably far happier living in the comparative freedom of a Punic city like Motya than in the terror of Syracuse, a city ruled with cruelty by a succession of tyrants.

While Pamela returned to her work, I walked away from the house. The Stagnone had turned dark, reflecting the trees and salt-pans around it, a landscape in black and white. The wind was sweeping the lagoon carrying sand from the Sahara, rippling the shallow waters into white crests. In the background, on the mainland, mounds of salt ready for collection sketched larger waves of glittering white against the sky. Salt had been one of Motya's sources of wealth for centuries, and the industry had been maintained up to the present day by the Greeks, Romans, Arabs, Normans, Swabians, Spaniards and Italians who followed the Punics in exporting *il sale di Sicilia* – in effect, Motya's salt.

Today we can find salt anywhere, from a small shop in a mountain village to an oasis community in the desert. In the past, this all-important mineral which our bodies crave was a rarity. In order to carry it, caravan routes and new ways of navigation were devised; some people died, others became rich. It was so extensively traded that it became a means of barter. The wages of some Roman soldiers were paid in salt; hence our word 'salary'. The salt-pans were one of Motya's main resources, and it was partly in order to preserve fish for consumption and export that the island's inhabitants developed salt production into an industry. Today there is no longer a salt-pan on the island itself, but those around the lagoon remain active: though they bear the name of Ettore Infersa, they belong to a local tycoon called D'Ali, a name that echoes the Moorish past.

The manufacture of pure salt is not as easy as it may seem, but Motya's lagoon provides the ideal conditions. The water is very salty and very shallow; the salt dries quickly in the stifling heat, aided by the parching wind which also moves the sails of the picturesque windmills still used to crush the salt and propel the water from one basin to the next. These windmills, built by the Spaniards in the eighteenth century, project the world of Don Quixote on to the Punic past. The salt-making cycle starts in April and ends with the approach of winter when the white mounds are covered with large terracotta tiles to shelter them during the rainy season. When the salt is 'gathered' (strangely enough, salt-making follows the calendar and vocabulary of agriculture), workers chant Moorish songs whose words describe the process in an ancient Arab dialect.

The Isola Lunga, too, the long island that separates the lagoon from the open sea, is spotted with salt-pans and huge salt mounds; flat and green, it served as a look-out post, while the neighbouring island, Santa Maria, was used for extra housing and storage. Both should be excavated, of course, and never have been.

Why did I find Motya so special, so mysterious?

Motya is unique in having been destroyed suddenly, leaving the inhabitants just enough time to hide their treasures. Its ground therefore still conceals what individuals buried as their best objects, thereby saving them from the Greeks but not from twentieth-century archaeologists. In one instance the fragments of a dish were found still lying on the ground where they had fallen from the hand of its fearful owner just as he was struck down by the sword of a victorious Greek. Possibly most of what had been hidden was looted by the vanquishers; but nevertheless a wealth of artefacts has surfaced, objects which the frightened population hoped to recover one day. This, for me, is one of Motya's main attractions: the slow unveiling of a mystery, of a way of life which has been erased by time and by defeat, but civilised enough to leave behind many clues.

I knew that under my feet lay the secrets of an entire civilization which hitherto had been described only by hostile pens. I knew that only 4 per cent of the island – only 4 per cent of the entire city, therefore – had been excavated. I knew that every time one scratched the earth of Motya, something of interest would inevitably emerge. The Punics had been hidden; but their stones talked. They had first talked to Schliemann, the father of contemporary archaeology, the man who had discovered Troy and 'Priam's' treasure, and who paid a visit to Motya. Then they called to Joseph Whitaker, an English gentleman living in Sicily, dilettante turned passionate archaeologist and scholar. They had talked to the archaeologist Vincenzo Tusa, to Marisa Famà, to Dr Isserlin; and now they were shouting in my ears. In my imagination I went on seeing ghosts, armies, crowds of citizens, women carrying water . . .

As the night was drawing close, I called the boatman who gave me the last passage to the mainland. The little boat was called *Tanit*, after the Punic deity of Carthage and of this part of the world. As we pushed out from the shore, my mind went back to my first visit to Motya.

2

THE FIRST VISIT

'What? You have never been to Motya?' Professor Tusa asked me reproachfully. His voice was a bombardment of vowels. Not only I had never been but, what was worse, I had never even heard of it. 'You must come.' So it was decided – by him: Tusa always took decisions. It was 1966.

When I first stepped on to Motya, more than thirty years ago, I was entering private property: at that time the island was still in the hands of the Whitaker family. My visit was arranged by Vincenzo Tusa, who was in charge of all archaeological sites in western Sicily. He had worked at Selinunte (Greek Selinus), the city which had been at loggerheads with the Punics until it fell to the Carthaginians in the fourth century BC, and had been responsible for the discovery of many extraordinary artefacts. Diodorus Siculus recounts that the conquerors of Selinunte paraded themselves with chains of severed arms around their necks; but maybe that is an exaggeration to justify the cruel revenge wrought by the Greeks a few years later in Motya.

I was flattered by the invitation and attention of a respected man of culture – and something of a Sicilian hero. Vincenzo Tusa was then in his late forties, a passionate man from the countryside near Catania. A broad figure with big brown eyes in a dark face and a penchant for open, enthusiastic gestures, he was a forceful personality; he was also a Communist in days when to be a left-winger meant to be a fighter against the Mafia, and was rumoured to have had unpleasant clashes with some important mafiosi. I had first met him some years earlier when, with the boldness of the very young, I had simply called on him without introduction while working on a documentary for the BBC.[1] He was then the director of the stunning archaeological museum in Palermo, one of the finest of its kind, which he progressively enriched with his discoveries (the metopes from Selinunte are some of the finest Greek sculptures to be seen anywhere). His wife Aldina was a scholar in numismatics and had studied the coins which had been found in Motya and elsewhere, showing the extent of the city's commerce with other communities. These coins bore Greek letters and featured the Carthaginian horse and the dog, a symbol of Phoenician dyes. Although I was a complete stranger, Tusa had been most welcoming and showed interest in my work. A coffee was ordered from the café downstairs – in Sicily a sign of acceptance, almost of friendship; and now, a few years later, I did indeed count Vincenzo Tusa as a good friend.

Around the time we met he was experiencing his first serious encounter with corruption, which in Sicily invariably means Mafia corruption. An island without decent roads, Sicily suddenly became the focal point for tenders to build motorways, many of which were unnecessary. Huge viaducts looped across remote villages supported by gigantic columns said to contain more corpses than cement. One such motorway was to be built almost on top of the temple of Segesta, an enchanted spot and one of the finest and best-preserved Doric temples in the world. When the project was submitted to the Soprintendenza alle Belle Arti, it was denied a permit by Tusa, who imposed stringent conditions to be met before the construction could go ahead, stipulating a large detour and a tunnel to avoid impairing the view, cut the noise of running cars and prevent the danger of subsidence. As a result that motorway was much more expensive to build, but the temple was saved. Tusa had been brave: disagreeing with the Mafia can be fatal.

Nor are the dangers over now. In 1998 Serafina Buarnè, who works at the Soprintendenza in Partinico, a town with a strong Mafia presence, turned down a project for real estate development and was the subject of death threats. After a bomb blew up her garage she called the police. As she persisted in being faithful to her job and duty, she knew that the death threats were for real. 'I began to be really scared,' she told me; 'now, wherever I go, I have to be followed by the carabinieri. So I am the prisoner.' She is a woman alone, thin and fragile and almost unique in her firmness in a world which has been flooded by a newly aggressive Mafia.

Back in the 1960s, reaching Motya was not easy. The island,

which is flat and only 45 hectares in area, is in the centre of a lagoon
near the north-western tip of Sicily, south of Trapani, and is protected from the open sea by a long island. I took the road from
Trapani to Marsala which wound slowly past flaming bougainvil-
leas, vineyards and palm trees. The little white houses with plots
enclosed by prickly pears suggested that I was in north Africa.
Leaving the main road, I found myself on a dusty track beside the
Stagnone, the lagoon, flanked by reeds and mounds of salt. That
was a good sign; Tusa had told me to watch out for the salt. He was
already on the island ahead of me, temporarily abandoning his big
excavations at Selinunte. He had instructed me to wave a white
handkerchief from the shore and wait; a boatman would come and
collect me.

So I waved, sat on the jetty and waited.

There was no sign of life from the other side. But which was the
other side? There were several islands, flat and wooded, all of them
embraced between the mainland and a long island which stretched
along behind them like an arm, parting the lagoon from the open
sea. That was Isola Lunga, as it is popularly called, or Isola Grande,
to give it its official name, where I could detect a few buildings and
several palm trees. In the distant past Isola Lunga had been linked
to the mainland. It was a captivating prospect, where land and sea
intertwined and one green island ended where a stretch of green
lagoon began. The light had changed into a flat, mournful yellow
and white. Lagoons are always sombre, the light always magic.

Again I waved my handkerchief towards the sea. Which one of
those islands was Motya? The nearest to the jetty was capped by a
building embraced in thick vegetation. Could that be Motya? The
long flat island, Isola Lunga, seemed to end opposite Cape
Lilybaeum, now called Cape Boeo, the headland of Marsala's harbour. So the tiny island with three semi-destroyed buildings could
not be Motya; that must be Scola, where slaves were sent to die,
according to Cicero. It was probably also used later as a place to
house those arriving by sea dying of the Black Death or cholera in a
rough form of quarantine. More recently it was written that Cicero
kept a school there – a *schola*, hence the island's name; but it is most
unlikely. Why should Cicero, one of the most powerful men of his
time, choose to set up a school on an island consisting of a few
rocks, remote and without water? Behind it, Santa Maria was in

private hands; so probably the island facing me, now called San Pantaleo or San Pantaleone, was my destination, where the city of Motya had once stood in all its splendour.

Suddenly, from the island which I had correctly identified as my goal, a boat appeared, heading towards the jetty where I had now been sitting for half an hour or so. A mere kilometre separated us, but the oarsman took twenty minutes to reach me. He helped me on board and, without saying a word, began to row again.

'Il Professore l'aspetta,' the boatman finally said in a strong Sicilian accent, his handsome face weathered by wind and sea. He then fell back into silence, gazing at the water as he tugged at the oars. Sicilians do not speak if they can help it; especially the western Sicilians, who are quite different from those in the east. Here they are of Punic–Arab stock, while the people on the other side of the island are descended from the Greeks. Western Sicilians call the east Provincia Babba, the stolid province; but the Provincia Babba had been clever enough to avoid the stranglehold of the Mafia clans for centuries. It is only in recent times that Mafia influence has reached eastern Sicily, aided by modern communications and funded by hard drugs. Neither easterners nor westerners spoke Latin. Sicily was the only Italian region which did not use it; its language in ancient times was Greek. When the Romans came, the Sicilians continued to speak Greek until the arrival of the Byzantines, who were Greeks in any case.

So silence prevailed in the boat, and I listened to the relaxing, rhythmic sound of the oars in the water. The Sicilians do not speak; the Punics did not write. Maybe the Punics did not mark their buildings and temples in order to preserve secrecy. Even their way of not inscribing the names of their gods, in case others might appropriate them, had been a form of *omertà*. Baal, it must be stressed, was the word for 'Lord', not the actual name of the god. The Hebrews, of course, followed the same custom; but that was out of respect, not for fear that the gods would leave the chosen people in favour of those who had stolen the secret of their names.

I broke the silence. 'Did the Professor arrive a long time ago?'

'No.'

'I am sorry I am late, the roads were difficult.'

A sort of grimace.

'What is that house?' I pointed at a building which emerged

clumsily from the tree tops, a rather simple, square, nineteenth-century tower.

'The Vitakre's castle.'

'Vitakre' was Joseph Whitaker – 'Pip' to his friends, *il Commendatore* to the Sicilians: an Englishman who, having inherited a great deal of money, set out to spend it on science and research. He bought Motya in the late nineteenth century and published the most important book on Phoenician history and archaeology, from which stemmed a new school dedicated to Phoenician and Punic studies. When Whitaker died in 1927, Motya was looked after by his second daughter, *la Signorina Delia*. Tusa had continued Pip Whitaker's excavations at Motya with a team of young archaeologists to whom he delegated the work while he was on the mainland at Selinunte.

'And that is Professor Tusa.'

There he stood smiling on the jetty, the archaeologist-*contadino*, as he was called – the 'peasant archaeologist' – barefoot and clearly happy.

On that first visit *il Professore* took me around the walls of Motya. The sea almost touched the beautifully cut ochre stones; as we walked under a perpendicular sun, he talked to me, agitating his hands and bringing the stones to life.

The Punics built differently from the Greeks and the Romans, Tusa explained, and did not create cities in the same format: they did not have an agora, a forum, a piazza like those ancient sites we have learnt to recognize from excavations. A Punic wall is easily identifiable because of its rectangular blocks of ashlar stone set at regular intervals with smaller rocks filling the spaces between. This was just one of the many differences that set the Punics apart from those who subsequently came to colonize Sicily. They were people from the east, strange in their customs and appearance and disliked on that account; but Tusa's sympathy was clearly on the Punic side.

Had the Romans destroyed Motya? I asked. I assumed, inevitably for one who had studied the Punic wars between Rome and Carthage at school, that the Romans had been the only enemies of the Punics. We had all been told how Cato used to appear at the Roman Senate every day with a basket full of fresh figs, saying that they came from Carthage. Figs have to be eaten very fresh, and so this was Cato's way of indicating how near Carthage was to Rome:

too close for comfort. Rome had been victorious, but Carthage was rebuilding itself as a centre of revolts against the northern power, and Cato foresaw the danger of a Punic revenge. Usually the Senators were not eager to provoke expensive wars against mighty Carthage, which in the past had been an ally of Rome; but the Consuls and the plebs were urging action. Waving his basket of fresh figs Cato used to add, monotonously, every day: 'Delenda est Carthago' – Carthage must be destroyed.

Not so, Tusa told me. Motya had been destroyed by the Greeks who had settled in Syracuse, for a time the most powerful city in the western Mediterranean. Its ruler, the tyrant Dionysius, wanted to unify Sicily under his control, and in order to do so had to defeat the Punics and evict them from the island. Syracuse had been built by Greeks who, as their population expanded, found it difficult to feed themselves from the meagre agricultural produce which could be gleaned from their rocky territory. 'Of course, the Greeks were highly cultivated, they brought knowledge with them, their *koinè*. They gave everything to the Mediterranean and therefore to us, but when they arrived in Sicily they found the Punics already here, holding the best harbours and controlling the seaways.'

We had lunch on a wooden table, simply and invitingly laid in the shade under the huge trees outside the Whitaker 'castle'. The meal had been prepared by Giuseppe Pugliese, the caretaker of the house, and his wife. Nicknamed Zio Peppino, Giuseppe had first come to Motya as a boy, helping Joseph Whitaker on several of his digs. Lean and tall, he had the characteristics of a very private man; he sparingly used a captivating smile and seemed to hold Tusa's trust. Of all the people now on the island, the gentle, handsome Giuseppe was the only one who had actually met Joseph Whitaker.

The basil leaves on the pasta gave off the scent of paradise; the Marsala wine, dry and golden, had been made by Peppino himself with grapes from Motya and he was proud of it. 'It's strong and it goes to your head; this one is twenty years old,' he said, looking at it through the light that made it glitter. 'Even *la Signorina Delia* drinks it, she likes it. But she is ill now.'

The 'Vitakre castle' turned out to be a house surmounted by a crenellated block conceived to echo the appearance of the Punic defensive towers before they were destroyed. *La Signorina Delia* was Delia Whitaker. Zio Peppino and his wife used to expect her in

Motya for a month every spring, before the mosquitoes arrived in force. They described how *la Signorina* would arrive dressed in pink, wearing gloves, followed by her dogs and her staff: a maid, a manservant, her chauffeur and a cook. When speaking to her directly, they called her 'Voscienza', the mode of address Sicilians use for princes – and Mafia bosses. 'We wait for her lined up on the jetty and she shakes our hands, she is very kind to us.'

But *la Signorina Delia* had not been seen for the past few seasons. 'She used to come every May, but she has been poorly,' Tusa explained.

The house – the 'castle' – was amusingly English. In fact, it couldn't have been more English: every piece of furniture, print, book and tile had been shipped down the Channel and into the Mediterranean via the Pillars of Hercules in order to furnish the house where Joseph Whitaker had chosen to set up his home, on that remote little Sicilian island. There were neat, small bedrooms and bathrooms, a dark drawing room and a sitting room adorned with yellowing Penguin books and framed photographs, prints of horses and reproductions of dull Gainsborough portraits. It was an interior designed to mimic the customs of an Edwardian upper-middle-class family, a dwelling conceived for life near Cheltenham rather than on Sicily; outside, the glaring light relentlessly burned the already scorched earth, reminding one with a shock that we were nearer to Africa than to the English midlands.

Zio Peppino looked after the 'castle' when it was empty. It was he who had collected me on the boat; now, seeing that Tusa was a friend, he became more talkative. He was a passionate gardener and had learnt most of his horticultural secrets from Joseph Whitaker, 'who had green fingers, a real English gentleman he was, although he spoke Italian with a Sicilian accent!' These days Peppino produced a smaller quantity of wine than in the past: most of the vineyards had had to be removed, he told me, because they had been planted on areas of archaeological interest. But he was still passionately enthusiastic about it: 'In September we gather the grapes and it is *festa*, you should see it, Signora!'

Tusa echoed Peppino's words describing the wonders of wine-making in Motya. The carts laden with grapes left for Marsala from the north gate across the underwater causeway which had been built in Punic times. 'These carts look like miraculous vehicles, ships without sails, carts navigating,' he said, because most of the wheels were underwater and so the carts seemed to be sailing, or flying on the lagoon. After the grape, it was the turn of the sheep, he continued. Year after year, the same shepherd arrived from the mainland with his herd on a raft and left the sheep to graze the last grass of the summer. As they approached the shore of Motya, the sheep jumped off the raft on to the island as if they had been accustomed to do so since the dawn of time. 'It is probably what the Punics did; they had grapes and wool, they made wine and wove cloth.'

After lunch Tusa escorted me to the little museum that Joseph Whitaker had built. It was a bit disorderly, he said, in the sense that it contained objects not only from Motya but also from Lilybaeum. There was some confusion, he went on, about which items Whitaker had bought from local farmers and dealers and what had been found in situ. As Whitaker's curiosity and knowledge grew, so did the size of his collection, with the result that his daughter Delia, *la Signorina*, had to add an extra rectangular pavilion to the museum. Tusa showed me finely coloured unguent bottles of vitreous paste – the Phoenicians were masters at producing coloured glass – coins, lucky charms, weapons, domestic ceramics and many other items. Some of the Egyptian artefacts bore witness to the commercial ties Motya maintained abroad, while a ravaged metope showing two lions attacking a bull was clearly Semitic in style and might have crowned the north gate of the city. It was found in 1793 by a certain Father Airoli and sold to a local nobleman, Baron Alagna. But sadly, sighed Tusa the archaeologist, Joseph Whitaker did not leave notes on where some important items had been found. Of course, he added, archaeology was in its infancy then, and Whitaker did his best under the prevailing circumstances, seeking the advice of professionals and surrounding himself with scholars. There were similar Punic exhibits to be seen in Marsala, Tusa added, and I should go and inspect them.

After they destroyed Motya, the Syracusan Greeks sold most of its inhabitants into slavery, leaving behind only a small garrison. The following year, Carthage took the territory back, the harbour being vital for their trade and navigation, but they built an entirely new city, Lilybaeum, on the promontory, Cape Boeo. Motya itself was abandoned and forgotten. The water level of the lagoon rose so that the causeway the Motyans had built to connect their island to the mainland disappeared; the surviving stones of the high defensive walls were either taken away for other purposes or vanished under the encroaching wild vegetation. The island became known as San Pantaleo; people forgot the name Motya and where the city had stood. When Cluverius, a Dutch traveller, stopped on the island in the seventeenth century AD and declared it to be the ancient Motya, nobody believed him. Motya was merely a figment of the imagination of some ancient historians, it was alleged; it had never actually existed.

As Professor Tusa related all this to me my head began to buzz with questions: the more he told me, the more I wanted to know. We were walking a little south of the house, over the remains of a villa that Whitaker had excavated around 1910. It was a grand villa, and had probably belonged to a rich merchant. Motyans employed Greek artisans, and this house was conceived and built on the Attic model, Tusa explained, apart from the mosaics: made out of pebbles, not tesserae, and representing a panther attacking a bull and a griffin pursuing a deer, these were typically eastern, Semitic, Punic.

Near the south gate, with its two towers, there was 'a surprise', Tusa warned me, 'something beautiful and perfectly preserved. A colleague of mine from Leeds University worked here a few years ago. Pity he is not in Motya, he could tell us a lot about this cothon – but cothon is the wrong word: it means harbour, in Greek. We, including the Greeks, thought it was an artificial harbour, but Isserlin dug it out and found that the very centre of the basin has been excavated to fit the keel of a ship. In short, it is a dockyard where ships were repaired.'

The canal running to the sea was beautifully paved. 'There are similar places in Carthage and Tyre.' Tusa's big hands gesticulated vigorously.

'Isn't the whole of Motya an archaeological gold mine?' I asked him as we picked our way through the stones of some ancient edifice just visible above ground. Even an unprofessional eye like mine could detect the presence of ruins under the humps and mounds. Of course, Motya was a paradise of possible discoveries, he said, leading me to the tophet, a sacrificial enclosure sacred to Baal-Hammon. In this place hundreds of urns, masks and stelae were amassed in layers, easily detectable in the reddish soil. Half buried inside the sloping wall of beaten earth were grinning terracotta masks, spherical urns with flat lids, elongated vases and other odd artefacts.

Tusa bent down and, scraping some earth away, took the lid off a vase and handed it to me. I held the strange object reluctantly, without the excitement that such a relic from the past should have communicated. I didn't know why, but there was something repulsive about it. I almost expected a rat to emerge from that dark shape, and my hesitation was clearly apparent. 'Don't drop it!' warned Tusa.

Inside the receptacle was a kind of bundle, like a gift; a sort of damaged parcel. In the parcel were the small bones of a child. 'They sacrificed the first-born,' Tusa explained.

Turning to a mound of stones, he went on: 'You can see that the walls were built in great haste, here.' He showed how the line of the defensive city walls had been hastily built, dividing the tophet in two. 'They were in such a hurry to rebuild them that they cut into the tophet. This happened at the time when the Greeks first attacked Motya.' He told me that as early as 580 BC a Cnidian called Pentathlos, at the head of a Greek army, landed at Cape Boeo, opposite Motya, wanting to start a new city and aiming to evict the Punics; but he was defeated by a local force of Motyans and Elymians. Thirty years later, in 550, Carthage interfered in Sicilian affairs for the first time, sending its best general, Malchus (a name which in Phoenician means 'king') to fend off the new Greek colonists; and it was at this time, Justinus tells us, that Motya built its defensive walls.

Malchus's expedition was intended to baulk the expansionist ambitions of the Greek cities Acragas and Selinus (Agrigento and Selinunte) to gain a position on the Tyrrhenian Sea, which was then controlled by the Punic cities of Palermo, Solunto and Motya. At stake was access to the sea routes linking Sicily with Sardinia, rich in tin and silver, the Etruscans of central Italy, who had iron and silver, and the Phocaeans in northern Italy and southern France; so that Malchus's expedition, although he headed a terrestrial army, should be read as a first clash for the control of the sea.

In 510 BC, Tusa went on explaining, the Spartan Doriaeus attacked Carthage itself: he was pushed back, but sailed on to Sicily where he collected a larger army and renewed his colonial ambitions near Mount Eryx. Once again the alliance of the Motyans and their neighbours the Elymians won the day and Doriaeus was killed. Immediately after this episode, in 509 the Carthaginian government saw fit to make an alliance with the growing power of Rome; as part of this treaty the Punic hegemony was recognized in 'a sector of Sicily which the Carthaginians keep in their possession'.[2]

By now the sunset was flaming across the lagoon, turning the salt pink and the sea orange. Tusa warned me that we had to hurry; there was no electric light in Motya, and he did not want to spoil the Puglieses' dinner. But he still managed to underline a few details which I would have not noticed. Explaining that the main water supply in ancient Motya was brought to the island by pipes laid along the sea bed, Tusa showed me some cisterns which were used for collecting rain water. That was the city's problem, he told me with his large hands: water, as everywhere in Sicily. He also inspected and showed me various layers of pots which were buried horizontally. 'There are not just human bones here,' he added reassuringly. 'You are lucky to see all this; one day it will be kept in a museum, I hope this one in Motya. All these vases will be numbered and studied. You won't be able to touch any of this, it will be behind glass. Anything left outside will be protected by fences. Motya will be closed to the public for a long time, there is a lot to study before showing this place. Anyway, who on earth would want to come here and see these pieces of bones and cut stones!' He laughed. Tourist curiosity in archaeology seemed a long way off then, an almost unimaginable concept.

As we walked away from the tophet, Tusa told me that a clause was inserted in one of the early peace treaties between Rome and Carthage prohibiting the Carthaginians from practising human sacrifice. It was a great lesson in civility, he observed, in spite of the fact that, as a true Sicilian, he didn't feel any sympathy towards Rome. After Rome occupied the whole of Sicily in 241 BC, it colonized it, and from that date onwards Sicilian history became a history of exploitation.

All I could hear now were the sounds of our footsteps and the sea. Suddenly, the bells from Marsala's large baroque cathedral, its cupola visible in the distance, interrupted the peace of a hot sunset. It was the summons to Vespers: a sound that took me back to my

Italian childhood. Then Tusa spoke again. 'Near the tophet is the burial ground. We don't find so many interesting things there, but we have just started digging. On the other side of the lagoon, there, at Birgi,' and he pointed at the mainland, 'there are many more tombs, but the farmers get rid of them, they throw them into the lagoon and they never warn us because they fear that otherwise we would stop them from farming.'

'And they might have a point . . .'

'Yes, because when they plant new vines and plough with these new mechanical machines, they destroy everything underground, so we do stop them. We should start work at Birgi soon.'

Why, I asked, did the Motyans bury their dead in Birgi?

'As Motya grew, this cemetery became too small. In effect there are only archaic funerary stones here, so we come to the conclusion that the Motyans would bury their dead over there when they stopped incinerating corpses and there was no room left on Motya for inhumation. The city was growing larger, so they only kept the tophet here and the tophet was considered to be holy, like a temple. They built the road for the carts to bring foodstuffs to the city and for their funeral processions to go back the other way.'

I could see no road.

'It's underwater, but only just under the surface.' I discarded my sandals and found the stones which paved a road about half a metre below the level of the lagoon. Outside the main north gate there was a slope leading to it and a paved platform where the carts stopped, waiting their turn to pass through the city gates. When the city came under attack, and the Motyans saw the strength of the Greek force on the mainland, Tusa told me, they damaged the road to prevent the infantry from using it; between then and modern times the water level has risen so that the causeway has become invisible. In 1917 Joseph Whitaker started to study it. He established that it had been 1.7 kilometres long and wide enough for two carts to pass side by side. On a scrap of paper he jotted down on the spot, the freshness of the discovery and his enthusiasm tamed by his strict English upbringing:

This morning we have taken some soundings here and examined this road between Motya and the mainland. My chief objective in sounding here was to ascertain, if possible, what might have been the depth of the

Stagnone in this part in the time of the Phoenicians, when this causeway or mole was made. According to what I've been able to make out, the stones of which this road is constructed do not extend to more than 30 to 40 centimetres below this present level ... Apparently the construction of the road was a primitive and simple one, slabs and pieces of natural rock, probably sea rock ... No squared blocks are to be found ... the sandy bottom is fairly hard but, on piercing this, there is a soft stratum ... [3]

The water of the lagoon was full of weeds, slimy crabs and small fish. 'Careful,' warned my companion, 'some of the crabs can bite.' I saw a few scamper from under the stones, huge dark creatures, some as big as my foot.

Tusa had to return to Selinunte and I had to go back to London. Before parting, we had a cool drink. *Latte di mandorla*, milk of almonds, is a Moorish legacy made with almond paste, deliciously refreshing and perfectly fitting: after all, the Arabs had been in Motya and had started the conquest of Sicily from nearby Lilybaeum; they had changed its original name into Mars-Allah, Marsala, the Harbour of Allah.

It had become dark.

'We know so little about these Punics,' Tusa lamented as we said goodbye. 'But Motya is going to talk. Come back in a few years, and you will see.'

He was right. Since that distant day, back in 1966, discoveries on Motya have revolutionized our knowledge of the Punics, of the Phoenicians and of the Mediterranean. English archaeology has been central to this knowledge, starting with Joseph Whitaker. Others had continued on his path: Vincenzo Tusa, Dr Isserlin, Honor Frost and Marisa Famà. But still, stubbornly secretive, Motya has guarded its magic.

3

THE MAGIC OF MOTYA

For centuries – nearly twenty-seven centuries in all – the dust of time settled on Motya. Before brushing away some of that dust, I want to reinvoke the myth of Motya, because it is in the myth that the magic begins.

Ancient legends express history, the distillation of years of human deeds. The older the saga, the dimmer the remembrance of what actually was, so that characters become symbols, metaphors. That is why we never tire of recounting and studying myths – especially since Schliemann reminded us at Troy that behind the legend there is history. 'Myth serves admirably to provide the necessary continuity of life, not only with the past but with nature and the gods as well. It is rich and vivid, it is concrete and yet full of symbolic meanings and associations, it explains institutions and rites and feelings, it is instructive – above all, it is real and true and immediately comprehensible. It served the early Greeks perfectly.' So wrote the great historian M. I. Finley.[1]

According to mythology, Heracles (in Latin, Hercules; Melqart to the Phoenicians) reached Sicily in his wandering adventures, and here his flock of sheep was stolen while grazing on the green pastures near Lilybaeum. 'The field of Heracles' is a location near Lilybaeum mentioned by Thucydides. The hero suspected that Eryx, king of the Elymi, had stolen his sheep. As he searched frantically for his flock, a nymph or sibyl called Motya told him where it was hidden. In gratitude Heracles/Melqart founded a city bearing the nymph's name. When he continued on his travels, he bequeathed his flock of sheep and the city to the Punics as a gift.

A slightly different version of the story, which is told by the Greek Hecataeus, excludes the figure of the nymph or sibyl. In this version Melqart is challenged to single combat by Eryx, whom he already suspects of having stolen his sheep. When Eryx, who is the son of Poseidon and Aphrodite/Astarte, loses, he surrenders his kingdom to Heracles/Melqart and his descendants after him (the Punics).

'The function of myth', Robert Graves wrote, 'is to justify an existing social system; it also solves the question which every human asks: where do we come from, who made us?' [2] Analysing this myth, we can identify the prehistoric events which took place around Motya. Melqart, whom the Greeks recognized as Heracles and absorbed into the figure of one of their archaic heroes, was to the Phoenicians both god and king, a symbol of the monarchic institution, an incarnation of the state and a founder of colonies. The Tyrians called him Lord of Tyre (Ba'al de Sor). His name, *melek-qart*, means king of the city (MLQ, in Phoenician, means king). Some ancient authors, like the second-century AD Greek historian Arrian, have hinted at a direct link between two spectacular pillars of the temple dedicated to Melqart in Tyre, as described by Herodotus, and the Pillars of Hercules at the other end of their world.[3] Strabo recounts that to the Libyans and Iberians the pillars were not the capes either side of the straits at the entrance to the Mediterranean, but two bronze stelae that the Phoenicians had placed in the temple of Melqart at Gades.[4] Next to another famous temple in Eryx dedicated to Astarte, the Phoenician goddess of renewal, procreation and love, stood an earlier temple dedicated to Melqart.

This adventurous god voyaged to the Black Sea in search of gold (in the Greek myth, the Golden Fleece). He then sailed westwards, symbolizing the Phoenician search for tin and silver. Having vanquished the perilous straits which marked the end of the ancient world, Melqart founded Gades, where he settled for a while. Here a most spectacular temple was built in Melqart's honour; we know that Julius Caesar made a special voyage there to sacrifice and to enquire about his future from a sacred sibyl.

The Punics were particularly keen on magic, devising curses and reading the future. The classical world was scattered with sibyls, holy figures to whom the devout made pilgrimage to consult their oracle or ask for divine favours, as we today use our several Madonnas of Lourdes, of Fátima, of Loreto and so on. They were priestesses who delivered prophecies, oracles, on behalf of the god:

thus there were oracles of Heracles/Melqart at Achaean Bura and several of Asklepios/Eshmun (the god of Sidon).[5] At Lebadeia the suppliants purified themselves and sacrificed to Demeter/Europa; at Delphi, Didyma and Cumae to Apollo. Originally the sibyls spoke through the guts of Mother Earth (Gaia), but then male deities stole the power of prophecy. The 'theft' of knowledge from the sibyls, the Pythian priestesses, marks the very ancient passage of the social order from matriarchy to patriarchy. With their quixotic behaviour and their shrieked and often ambiguous pronouncements (they were probably epileptic or heavily drugged), the sibyls remained quintessentially feminine figures in the imagination of man. The oracle, an expression of the god who is willing to tell the future to the questioner, was of eastern origins, even those in Hellas, for instance at Dodona, Delphi and Olympia, where the cooing of doves was interpreted by priestesses.

On his way to Gades, seeking tin and silver, Melqart would naturally stop at Motya, where he would need food and clothing; a flock of sheep would provide both. The Elymians, symbolized by King Eryx (the mountainous city of Eryx – modern Erice – overlooks Motya) are hostile to the new arrival, even though they themselves are of Asian stock, from Troy, according to Thucydides. The local Sicilian tribes, who are weaker (hence represented in the myth by a female, the nymph Motya), ally themselves with Melqart, representing the Punics, and with him fight the Elymians. The locals intermarry with the Punics, who then build a proper city with a civic administration and a harbour. The Punics bequeath the herd, leaving the care of agriculture to the locals, because they themselves were not shepherds but navigators, traders and manufacturers.

The Punics called their new city MTWA, the Greeks Motie, the Romans Motia; Italians today call it Mozia. The derivation of the name is still a matter of conjecture. The root is Phoenician and could mean 'slime', referring to the seaweed and mud of the site where it was built. Others have seen a connection with another word signifying 'weaving' or 'loom' (in Hebrew, *motua*) because of the Motyans' skill in textile production.

Motya was defended by a fortified wall 2.5 kilometres long around the entire island. Much of it can still be seen, although some sections have totally disappeared – including, probably, two gates on the east and west sides of the city. Crenellated watch towers to which the guards had access through stairs and ramps stood at regular intervals and flanked each gate. The north gate, which faced the mainland and through which goods vehicles and embassies alike arrived, was grander than the others and built at an oblique angle. Archaeologists have come to the conclusion that the walls were built no earlier than the sixth century BC, when the Greeks began to attack the Punics in Sicily, starting with an expedition led by Pentathlos in 580. Pentathlos, who founded Acragas (Agrigento), used the Greek colony of Selinus (Selinunte) near Motya as the base for his assault. His aggressive mission failed but set an example which was soon to be followed.

Once again I go back to the founding myth of Motya, in which the Phoenician/Punic god arrives, marries a local girl (Motya), gives the city he has built to her (the local tribes) and makes peace with those Elymians who at first had been troublesome and hostile to the Punic settlement (Eryx stealing from Melqart). There is no element of rape and piracy in the myth – unlike, say, the legend of Troy – since the Punics had no appetite for territories. They had learned how to develop good relations with whatever indigenous tribes they met, so that they could exploit the natives' knowledge in finding and quarrying metals which they would then sell back to them in the shape of ingots and artefacts: a 'modern' form of colonization.

'We have found unmistakable evidence of pre-existence of what may be called a large fortified town covering apparently the entire area of this island,' Whitaker jotted down in a note in 1914. 'This is shown by the ruins of fortifications completed round this island, except for about 150 m on the west . . . such ruins have disappeared . . . other important constructions, not fortifications, and by the necropolis found on this island which was evidently abandoned for that on the mainland, the town growing so large as to necessitate such a step.'

More damage to the walls of Motya, always on the same side, towards the mainland, occurred in violent battles with the Spartans under Dorieus later in the sixth century BC. The wall remained in ruins for several years until eventually, as noted above, the Motyans decided to scrap the necropolis and bury their dead on the mainland where there was more space.

At the necropolis across the end of the causeway one day I looked through the layers of sandy soil eroded by the sea and uncovered several stratifications of simple sarcophagi excavated in tufa. Occasionally, one bore the sign of Tanit, the main female goddess of the Carthaginians, but most were bare: not a scratch, not a name. Death was eternal fogginess and did not remember individual identities. Behind the shore, the fields cultivated with rampant vines vomited pieces of sarcophagi and broken-down tombs were gathered in heaps. But it was the ones by the sea, released from the sandy banks, that moved me – empty shells, witnesses of a populous city.

The Punics of Motya relied entirely on their neighbours for food supplies other than fish, so it is obvious that they needed to keep on good terms with their trading partners. After a few initial skirmishes, the Motyans became firm allies of the Elymians and Sicans.[6] Carthage apart, the first Punic colonies were settlements planted where there were abundant marketable commodities. Cyprus was settled by the Phoenicians for the sake of its copper mines and timber; Thasos for its gold mines; Salamis and Cythera for their abundant supplies of murex on which the dyeing trade depended; Sardinia and Spain for their metals. Pliny went so far as to declare that 'the Phoenicians invented trade',[7] though he was exaggerating, since trade was the first manifestation of an organized society. In return for metals the Punics supplied metal utensils and arms, linen, wool and textiles, and a variety of pottery including dishes, jugs, amphoras and vases. Their best vessels, though, were of Greek or Siceliot manufacture; these the Punics either bought or had made by Greek or Siceliot artisans resident in their cities – as in Motya's case, where many dishes with a variety of lovely fish designs have been found.

A colony like Motya would export bronze arms and cooking utensils, and then develop its own specialities, for example, in Motya's case, salt, preserved fish and dyed cloth. Carthage sold tin from Cornwall to its colonies, where it was manufactured with copper into bronze for resale. The Phoenicians certainly used local know-how to produce the bronze in the form of ingots which could be carried by their ships. To some extent they trained the indigenous populations of their colonies in the art of metal quarrying; but the actual transformation of ingot into artefact took place in Phoenician and Punic factories. There was an enormous demand for tin, since bronze was used universally for all forms of metallic goods, including weapons. The secret of where tin or silver was quarried was so jealously guarded that one Punic captain preferred to run his ship against a rock rather than let the Roman ship which was following him discover the secret of the source of the metal. Once back home, the Carthaginians leaders praised the captain and refunded him the value of his lost goods and ship.[8]

Less than a century after the foundation of Motya, the Greeks began to emigrate from their various city-states. The population of mainland Greece had grown beyond the point where its mountainous terrain could support all the inhabitants; so, having already founded colonies in Asia Minor, which they in essence occupied, the Greeks moved on to build large cities in Sicily like Syracuse, Acragas (Agrigento) and Himera. These cities were not in the least dependent on their homeland, nor did they feel bound by national loyalties, because there was no such concept as a Greek nation; but the Greeks or Hellenes (or, before that, the Achaeans) were bound together by a common language and a common culture. On the other hand, while rivalries between the colonial settlements occasionally impelled them to ask their mother-cities for help against competing colonies, ties with the city of origin were few and rarely called upon unless serious strategic or economic problems arose. This was in contrast to Carthage, which maintained strong links with its subordinate colonies like Motya. The Motyan Punics, more tolerant than the Greeks of different religions and customs, had merged easily with the local tribal groups, although they used diverse languages. Already part of a diaspora and without any attachment to a specific cultural root, they were inclined to intermix with the populations they found, adapt their languages and adopt their gods. However, the Motyans paid a yearly tribute to Carthage, on which they relied for military help.

In Sicily the Greeks built temples, roads and defensive fortifications. They also brought with them that sense of aesthetics which expressed itself through music and theatre, sculpture and painting, and because of which a cooking vessel became a work of art, a dwelling architecture. In short, they brought Culture. They also brought wine: although vines and wine-making were originally Middle Eastern,[9] it was the Greeks who introduced them to Sicily. The Punics described wine in writing as YN (*yayin* in Hebrew, *wo-i-no* in Mycenaean and *oinos* in Greek). The Punics, a practical

people but with little artistic talent, recognized the superiority of
the Greeks as designers and creators; the Greeks, for their part,
admired the Punics' ability as traders but also – rather like English
gentlemen – considered 'trade' a bit below their status. They looked
down on the Punics, describing them as oily and short, too cunning
and solely interested in making money. Unlike the Greeks, the
Punics had no interest in historical events or cultural transmission.
They preserved scant written accounts of the deeds of their
ancestors, and their gods were hideous monsters, inhuman and
rarely represented. Astarte was utterly unlike her beautiful sister
Aphrodite, and the handsome Heracles looked quite different from
Melqart. No opportunity for Phidias to emerge in that world! In
short, the Greeks considered the Punics mere Semites, barbarians,
beneath them; and the Punics, while admiring the Greeks for their
ability to create beauty, judged them wasteful and aggressive.
However, for a time at least they coexisted: many Greeks lived in
Punic cities, and we know of Punic districts in Greek Syracuse and
Selinus.

When the Greeks first colonized Sicily, Thucydides tells us,

> there were also Phoenicians living all around Sicily, who had occupied
> promontories upon the sea-coasts and the islets adjacent for the purpose
> of trading with the Sicels. But when the Hellenes began to arrive in con-
> siderable number by sea, the Phoenicians abandoned most of their sta-
> tions and, drawing together, took up their abode in Motya, Solunto and
> Panormus, near the Elymians, partly because they confided in their
> alliance, and also because these are the nearest points for the voyage
> between Carthage and Sicily . . .[10]

Accurate historian that he was, Thucydides states that the
Phoenicians were in Sicily before the Greeks, and identifies those
peoples which preceded both. His account clarifies several points
about the state of affairs in and around Sicily at this time. The
Elymians, a non-Greek population from Asia, were 'historical'
allies of the Punics. The two newcomer groups – the Punics and the
Greeks – were at first able to share the territory of Sicily without
animosity. But the island was a coveted prize, and although the land
was rich and could initially provide for everybody, when cities
began to grow, greed sharpened hostilities between the different

populations. The Greek cities understood that any territory they won could be held only if their forces could match those of their competitors at sea, as indeed the Romans were to understand later, when they also came into conflict with Carthage; for trade and any kind of exchange took place exclusively by sea.

When the Carthaginians came back to this area of Sicily the year after Motya's fall, they took everything they could find of its contents that remained and established a new harbour at Lilybaeum, still visible today north of Marsala; and they discovered that the few Punics who survived had already adopted Greek for writing and possibly even in speech. Following the Roman conquest of Sicily in 241 BC, the new rulers prospered in Lilybaeum, which they took the same year and transformed into a formidable military naval base; Cicero described it as *splendidissima civitas*. By contrast, the Romans ignored the ruins of Motya, which they probably despised (Punic architecture being crude, not monumental) and, as we have said, allowed its history to fall out of memory. How thoroughly the Romans forgot Motya can be gathered from the fact that Polybius does not mention it once in his long and detailed account of the events that occurred in and around Lilybaeum. Not even Tacitus, who described every important site in Sicily, alludes to the existence of Motya. Silence fell, and Motya, described by Diodorus as a city of 'embellishments of the highest level with several fine houses' became a haven for migratory birds on their way to Africa – even flamingos stopped there – and a few tenacious vines, the only plants that would grow in its stony ground. Nothing else could thrive on the site of the dead city.

Christianity came late to this part of Sicily, between the fourth and fifth centuries. Despite the claims that the Apostle Paul landed at Lilybaeum, it is doubtful that he even set foot in Rome on mainland Italy, let alone Sicily.[11] It is also doubtful whether St John the Evangelist left Patmos for Sicily, but his cult did overlap with that of the sibyl. Even today, during the days of his festival, 23–25 June, the fresh waters in the sibyl's pool are said to become miraculous and whoever bathes in them can shed even the most horrible disease. And until the nineteenth century, drinking from the spring at its source in the name of St John was said to enable one to predict even whether one's husband's would be faithful.

As already noted, in the ninth century AD the conquering Moors changed the Punic name of Lilybaeum to Mars-Allah; they also renamed Motya variously as Zizaretti and Zizareth, Guzizet and also Gisira-Melbugi, using it for pasture. A few Christians moved to the island and as they spoke Greek, they renamed it Panteleimon, 'All-Pitiful'. When in the eleventh century the Normans took Sicily back from the Moors, the name of the island changed yet again and it became known as San Pantaleo or San Pantaleone. Count Roger Hauteville, governor of Sicily, presented the territory to two Byzantine generals; later, having become King Roger, he took it away from them and presented it to the Roman church, together with the other islands on the Stagnone and the immediately adjacent mainland.[12] The Norman king wanted to keep the Holy See on his side since his mandate to liberate the south from Islam had been granted by Rome as a concession only; in the event he had actually seized the crown and made himself king of the whole territory, while the papacy still looked upon the Hautevilles as mere feudatories.

On 16 May 1131, in Palermo, King Roger signed the following document (the original text is in Latin):

Roger, king in Christ, powerful monarch and defender of the Christians, being in Palermo together with his counts and princes hereby gives to Bartolomeo Abbot of the Basilian monastery of St Mary of the Grotto in Marsala the privilege that His Mother Adelasia had [previously] indicated ... In addition Our Authority has given the aforementioned sacred monastery the hamlet of S. Pantaleone which is located on the island towards Libriges, called Guzizet Ezzobugi and the island and the salt-pans located on this same island. And then also Our Authority gives to the aforementioned sacred monastery some land, a garden, a fountain and the sheep cot called Muddid located on the site called Heraclia.

As this text (and later excavations) reveal, a hamlet was built at Motya on top of the original Punic city, using the same roads and water supply. The monks retired to Motya, where they built a small basilica with an apse in the area near the former Punic 'industrial' site. It was destroyed by the archaeological digs in 1930, but a drawing of it made by Thomas Ashby of the British School in Rome shows its simple structure.

In 1196 the Basilian order in Marsala and that of Palermo were put under the same administration by Queen Constance, the mother of the Holy Roman Emperor and king of Sicily Frederick II. From then onwards the island and its surroundings were administered from Palermo. In the second half of the sixteenth century Charles V, not only Holy Roman Emperor but also independently king of Sicily, gave San Pantaleo and its surroundings to the Jesuits, whose order had just been established by Ignatius Loyola. For two centuries thereafter the Jesuits had a virtual monopoly on education among the Sicilian aristocracy, and as a result accumulated enormous power and possessions. The backlash, when it came, was sudden: 'At nightfall on November 3, 1763,' wrote Harold Acton, 'every Jesuit home in the Kingdom was confiscated by Royal officials.' In the same year the Society of Jesus was expelled from the Kingdom of the Two Sicilies. The ruling Bourbons seem to have realized that the Jesuits owned 82 per cent of Sicily, more than the monarchy itself. So the religious order was not only expelled but suppressed, and all its possessions, including Motya, were sold through the French consulate.[13] 'The Jesuits, condemned without a trial or any proof of guilt, left calmly and quickly, and saw their life's work destroyed with Christian resignation. They had educated the flower of Neapolitan youth, and their schools had been free, without any expense to the state. Tanucci [minister of state of the Bourbons] crowed over his easy victory; still he would not rest until the Order was abolished.'[14]

Thus the island and its surroundings came into the possession of the town of Marsala, whose authorities divided it into smallholdings which were sold to various families. This remained the case until Joseph Whitaker, with great patience, labour and tenacity, succeeded in buying it all back. Before that, many stones from its once proud towers and most of the rocks which made up the defensive walls were removed to be used for building elsewhere. I wondered how many barges left Motya laden with finely cut stones from the Punic city that were to reappear as walls in some modest farmhouse or concealed in the grand baroque cathedral of Marsala. Joseph Whitaker remarked that farmers were using rectangular slabs of unmistakable Motyan provenance to shore up the walls of their orange groves. They still do.

As I opened this short appraisal of Motya's history and geographical situation with a legend, let me end it with another myth which describes the deeds of Melqart, a god who will accompany us throughout this story. This time we find Melqart not in Motya but in Tyre, at one time Phoenicia's mightiest metropolis: the mother-city of Carthage and hence indirectly of Motya. Pliny described Tyre as 'famous once for its noble descent, having given life to the city of Leptis, of Utica and of that notorious rival Carthage, greedy for universal dominance, and yet of Gades found-ed on the other side of the inhabited world'.[15] Like Motya, Tyre was a city of high buildings, because, like Motya – or indeed Manhattan – it was an island city; therefore it lacked space and built upwards. As the traveller approached Tyre or Motya, he would contemplate the tall towers with awe and admiration.

According to the myth, Melqart wooed a nymph called Tyre, but she resisted his advances. While walking by the sea, the nymph had noticed the beautiful colour purple exuding from a mollusc shell, and refused to sleep with the god-king unless he gave her a mantle of this same colour. To win her over, Melqart revealed the secret art of dyeing cloth purple.

Purple figures as a theme in the story of Melqart, and of Motya, not just as the colour of the cloth but as the colour of blood. Besides being a navigator, a king and an adventurous explorer, Melqart sac-rificed himself with the changing seasons; he shed his blood in order to renew himself, but exacted human blood in the process. Much blood was shed at Motya to placate the god or to win his attention; the memory of human sacrifice still seems to linger over the lagoon, which retains an eerie atmosphere. One field on the island where some of ancient Motya has been excavated was called Cappiddazzu by Joseph Whitaker's daughter, after the ghost said to haunt it, a figure wearing a Sicilian beret, a *cappiddazzu*. Zio Peppino insists that Cappiddazzu was merely a scarecrow; a hat atop a stick, set there to scare the thousands of migratory birds away from the maturing grapes. Seen in the dusk, against the flaring sunsets on the lagoon, the black Cappiddazzu looked like a ghost, he claimed. But when I was walking alone over the stones of the Punic temple, I felt a shiver. The phantoms of Motya dissolved into the ground. Only the ghost of Cappiddazzu remained, smiling threateningly.

4

THE FALL OF MOTYA

It was daytime, but the sky on the lagoon was darkening. Day was changing into night, it seemed; suddenly the heavens took on the shape and colour of a blue mantle, through which electricity discharged brief, luminous, zig-zagging stripes, almost in a pattern, each burst followed by rumbling thunder. The whole Stagnone seemed to have been affected by the startling change in the weather and the surf grumbled like the entrails of the monster Charybdis – or like the entrails of Etna, a sound which always frightens me.

Nature was behaving like history, unpredictable, threatening and changeable. Giuseppe Pugliese's sister Rosina dashed out of her little house next to the Missione Archeologica carrying a large empty basket which, a few minutes later, was laden with the drying laundry. Vincenzo Arini, her son and Giuseppe Pugliese's nephew, had become Motya's caretaker, inheriting the job from his uncle, who was too old now to be in charge, but still lived on Motya with his wife, remembering and recounting tales of Joseph Whitaker. Rosina, or Rosa, a rather stretched version of Giuseppe and, like her brother, handsome and kind, had lost her husband when he was only thirty-four. Her son was the only person in two millennia to have been born on Motya: Rosina had been caught waiting for the boat to take her to the mainland. So that baby Vincenzo – no baby now – was a true Motyan.

'It would happen today!' Rosina's olive skin had taken on a darker shade from the indigo sky. Looking above her, she grimaced at the heavy black and blue clouds. 'Come in, Signora, you'll get wet. And beware of the lightning, it is dangerous here, with all this water everywhere.'

But I didn't want to go straight in; instead I walked away, towards the north gate, making a gesture which signified 'I'll come back, but

not right now.' I wanted to witness the frightening spectacle of
nature unleashing its energies on Motya. Fighting the wind, I
reached the north shore where the causeway begins, opposite the
white gleam of the salt mound on the mainland. The black water of
the shallow lagoon echoed the lowering heavens: gloom hung over
the island, which still retains the tragic secrets of its fall and the
bloodbath which followed.

Perhaps I had chosen the wrong day to be in Motya. I felt
exposed on my own so near Trapani and Marsala, in the Mafia
heartland. There were no archaeologists on the island this time:
only old Giuseppe Pugliese, Zio Peppino, and his wife Rosaria,
besides Vincenzo and Rosa.

The overbuilt coastline of the Sicilian mainland had disappeared
into the darkness; the cement cubicles had become mysterious
objects, catapults and machines of war. Rushing, impetuous rain
slashed the stones of the main gate through which Motya had seen
the arrival of goods, people and, finally, death. It was almost
refreshing, that drenching rain, cold against my body and falling in
rivulets through my hair. Earlier that day it had been stiflingly hot.

Suddenly I became aware of a lean, proud figure walking
towards me, fighting the wind and the rain. It was Giuseppe, Zio
Peppino, his old eyes still capable of admiring a landscape he had
known for eighty-odd years. His fragile body was bent into the violence of the wind, so that he had to lean against one of the ruined
walls while he shouted: 'Signora, even the lagoon gets angry, move
away from the sea.'

So I joined him against the Punic stones, which had lost that
golden tonality given by the sun and had instead, impregnated by
the rain, turned the colour purple. We winced at an extravagant
outburst of lightning, followed almost immediately by a guttural
thunderclap. Angry Zeus with all his might was probably con-
demning Dionysius, tyrant of Syracuse, for his deeds of long ago.

'Peppino,' I asked – no one ever called him Giuseppe – 'Do you
remember when the Commendatore Whitaker excavated here at the
north gate?'

Peppino looked around, at the steep steps which led nowhere,
towards what had been a high tower, and then turned his gaze to the
deep marks on the paved road.

'When I arrived the Commendatore Whitaker was no longer

young, but I was. He had finished excavating here; I helped in other areas, but I remember that we still found arrow tips around here, many, many. Hundreds of them. *Il Commendatore* said that they were both Greek and Punic arrows but that probably they all came from the same source.'

Yes, I thought, the Phoenicians, the Punics were the ones who smelted metals and sold bronze to anyone who cared to buy it. They were probably killed by the very weapons they had themselves made.

'Here they fought like madmen,' Peppino continued, his hands indicating the spots where the Motyans and the Greeks had clashed, as if he himself had been present at the slaughter. 'The Motyans realized by then they had to fight for every inch of land, that no one was coming to their rescue, they had no hope.'

Many had probably hidden their treasures in cellars or buried them in the earth in a hurried attempt to hide them from the Greeks and their mercenary troops.

'The mercenaries had been waiting a long time,' Peppino went on. 'The siege had taken weeks if not months and they were hungry for loot. The struggle for Motya had been a long one.'

I was not surprised that Peppino knew so much about the fall of Motya; after all, he had been living on that island, walking over those stones and the secrets they occasionally yielded, for decades; he had lived those events of many centuries ago.

There were many secrets we did not know about the Motyans, but the riddle of the city's fall had been explained by a historian. Diodorus Siculus lived around three centuries after the events he described, but his source was a contemporary, Timaeus, who saw Motya with his own eyes. Diodorus was one of those indefatigable historians who, following in the footsteps of Herodotus, had recalled political and historical events. Herodotus, known as 'the father of history', was a 'reporter', a researcher in the best sense. Almost every time his words have been doubted or his tales dismissed as exaggeration or make-believe, archaeology has come to his rescue – just as the reliability of Homer's descriptions of heroes and the locations of their deeds has been supported by recent excavations at Sparta, or at the royal palace of Pylos, or at Troy itself. Diodorus wrote from the point of view of the victors, and maybe he exaggerated at times; but, as Professor Tusa stressed to me, 'We are finding that those historians were precise. For a long time they were not believed, like Homer or the Bible. Now we have scientific proof that writers like Herodotus, Thucydides or indeed Diodorus were real historians.' Not everybody agrees with him; but Tusa's view demands respect, for he is not only a renowned archaeologist and historian but also held the chair of Punic studies at the University of Palermo for twenty-four years.

The Phoenicians and Punics did not produce poetry and did not recount their own story; they have remained mute, allowing the Greeks, their bitter enemies, to tell of their terrific naval achievements. We should, however, remember that Carthage's library was burned down; and we know that it was rich in volumes of history and literature.

Across the Mediterranean from Carthage stood Motya, the pride of the Punics, a beautiful walled city of high towers and temples. At its feet, in the lagoon, ships lay at anchor, barges delivered goods to the cothon or, if in need of repair, found safe haven and craftsmen to nail new planks, renew ropes and mend tackle.

Peppino's profile was just visible in the rain. He was shaking. I nudged him. 'You are cold, we'd better go back.'

It was while preparing for his war on the Punics and on Motya that Dionysius' artisans developed the catapult, a mighty war machine which was to change the tactics of battle and siege warfare. Diodorus writes: 'On that very occasion, since all the greatest artisans were assembled in the city, the catapult was invented in Syracuse. Every day Dionysius visited the workers, talked kindly to them, presented prizes to those who were the most active and welcomed them to his table.' [1]

'It is as if I saw them,' Zio Peppino whispered against the thunder.

'Saw whom?'

'Sometimes I see ghosts here and there.'

'In this kind of weather, ghosts are everywhere.'

'No: their ghosts.'

'So, it's true.'

'Not just the one of the Cappiddazzu ...'

Peppino had altered in his attitude towards me. He was no longer the distrustful boatman who back in 1966 had collected me from the mainland shore when Tusa had been waiting for me and who had prepared the lunch table under the shade of the trees – trees planted by *il Commendatore*. At that time, *la Signorina Delia* was still alive and Motya was respected. Now, everything had changed; new people had arrived, money not science made Motya attractive, and he himself was getting old.

We walked back, following the shore rather than cutting across the fields. Then, facing the cape where Marsala had disappeared among the low clouds, we stopped – or rather, Peppino stopped, looking and listening. I too, halting alongside him, watched the sky, the open sea, the lightning and the grand scenery.

He might have been a Punic Motyan, standing there by the canebrake. He might have been looking beyond the lagoon towards Cape Boeo, where suddenly the indigo sea had become animated by the Greek fleet. And then, turning towards the mainland, he might have seen the assembly of Greek cavalry, 8,000 strong. The infantry, 45,000 men, were dragging the new war machines which Dionysius was bringing into action for the first time in his war against the Punics. Perhaps the same scirocco wind which was blinding us that afternoon, coming straight across the sea from the Sahara and filling the air, the vineyards, my nostrils, my eyes with yellow sand, had also swept the island of Motya as it faced the assault.

There he stood, gaping at the awesome sight: but what had been his name? There were so few names carved on the Motyan stones; nothing had been written by these inventors of the alphabet about the battle that destroyed their city. The tale had been left to a Greek who painstakingly described the chessboard of the battle, the position of the adversaries and the moves they made, and by what chance one side won, but disclosed few names of the participants.

Realizing that we were wet through, Peppino made a tiny gesture indicating the way home. Hard though it was to leave that fascinating natural pandemonium, we walked back towards Joseph Whitaker's Motyan residence, which the locals called the Castle; right beside it was the Puglieses' house, where Rosina was waiting to welcome us back.

'I was beginning to get worried,' she said.

There was no electricity because the mains did not work at night, so not only it was cold but, she added, 'We cannot watch television.'

Vincenzo looked for his best Marsala while we dried our heads with a towel and sat around a table in the tiny room.

Vincenzo poured the golden wine in small glasses. 'It is one of our best, 1964.'

'That was two years before I came to Motya for the first time,' I said.

'But I don't remember you,' said Peppino.

'It was you who served the lunch to Professor Tusa and your wife cooked it.'

Rosaria smiled. She spoke little to me, because, she said, she could not speak Italian properly, and indeed she used a difficult local dialect. I could manage Palermitan but not this one. There was a lot of North African in it and maybe Punic as well.

The windows lit up and the thunder shook the house.

'That one was right on top of us,' Rosaria began to tremble, and they all speedily made the sign of the cross.

There was little to do, apart from listening to the wind and the rain crashing on the roof.

'Professor Tusa must have told you a lot of stories about this island,' I said.

'*Il Professore* was amazing,' replied Giuseppe. 'He tells us because he knows that if we know about those stones, the stones will speak to us and we will look after anything that wants to converse with us. We are only ordinary people ...'

I had rarely seen anybody looking and sounding more distinguished than Giuseppe/Peppino, Vincenzo, Rosina or Rosaria, I thought, observing Peppino's regular profile in the half-darkness of the room.

'Perhaps you could tell us more,' he added.

'Me?' I asked. It seemed incredible to me that they could want me to tell them about their own island; but it was evidently a genuine request, so I looked for a candle and opened my notebook full of scribbled pages. Rosaria announced that she was going to heat a bit of soup; she distributed some dishes around the table and lit more candles as I extracted from my bag another two books: the fourteenth and fifteenth volumes of Diodorus' history.

'I shall start a bit earlier, two or three years before the battle for Motya,' I announced. 'This is straight from Diodorus.

'It really started when the inhabitants of the rich tip of southern Italy began to be suspicious of Dionysius, the Greek tyrant of Syracuse, who was cutting down the forests all around Etna in order to build a powerful new fleet. He was recruiting mercenaries everywhere and had already captured cities like Naxos and Catania which are near Syracuse. Because he was extremely cruel, many Greeks fled and went to live in areas controlled by the Carthaginians ...'

'The Punics?'

'Yes, places like Motya and Palermo – although the latter, which the Greeks then called Panormus, was a long way from here. Selinunte had been captured by the Carthaginians after a blood-bath, and had also become Punic. That was a few years before the times we are talking about ... '

'The Greeks were afraid, then, because some Greek cities were taken over by the Punics,' Peppino said; he must have heard Professor Tusa talking about Selinunte.

'Selinunte, that is Greek Selinus, was built on a Punic area,' I answered.

'Were they always at war, the Greeks and the Punics?'

'Not really; they needed each other. Previously, in fact, Selinunte had become rich because Motya and Carthage bought food and wood from them. But I also think that the Selinunte Greeks built such vast temples and so many just because they were in Punic ter-ritory, to show off, to demonstrate how superior they were, richer, stronger and better architects . . . There was a sort of agreement by which they divided the island of Sicily and most cities prospered as a result. But more and more Greeks arrived and the new colonies multiplied into yet more colonies. Even Selinunte itself was the out-come of one of the earliest Greek colonies in Sicily. As they expand-ed, they had to increase their trade and they required more land. But the sea was the sole property of Carthage, which was a very powerful maritime power. We have forgotten or we have been made to forget how mighty it was. That is why, only a century after these events, the Romans clashed with Carthage and its colonies. But, at the time we are discussing, they were allied to Carthage, as indeed were some of the mainland Greeks themselves. Athens had just asked Carthage for a treaty ...'

The soup was ready, hot and peppery. We all started to eat; the thunder had begun to move away and the rain no longer lashed against the windows.

'At least the cisterns will fill up.' Rosaria lit a candle in front of a hideous reproduction of the Madonna.

'Dionysius knew that a terrible disease, the plague, had hit Carthage and so he decided that this was the moment to attack. Beforehand he wanted to prepare his army and fleet, "since he would have to fight against the most powerful people in Europe",' [2] I said, quoting Diodorus. 'Strange that Diodorus uses the word "Europe", don't you think? Because Carthage wasn't in what we think of as Europe today; but the ancient writers obviously did. They meant the European basin, the Mediterranean, the heart of culture and activity ...' I read on: 'So, "without losing any time Dionysius summoned to Syracuse all the artisans he could find, paying them huge salaries and causing the city to buzz with activity." At this time, Syracuse and Acragas were ruled by tyrants. But great poets and playwrights such as Pindar and Aeschylus visited Sicily because it was part of the Greek world. Empedocles, the greatest philosopher of his day, died in Sicily about one century before the events I am describing; and Archimedes was to be born in Syracuse a few years later. The whole civilised world sang the praises of a city which is still immensely beautiful but which was then the most populous and powerful in the Mediterranean.'

I opened my notebook and read from Pindar:

Great city, O Syracuse, precinct of Ares
that haunts the deeps of battle; nurse divine of horses and men
who fight in iron,
from shining Thebes I come, bringing you
this melody, message of the chariot course that shakes the earth,
wherein Hiero in success of his horses
has bound in garlands that gleam for Ortygia. [3]

'Hiero was another tyrant, earlier than Dionysius.'

'Were they all autocrats? were they all cruel?'

'Most Greek Sicilian city-states were governed by tyrants, a word which did not have such an unpleasant meaning as it does today. Sometimes aristocratic families would stage a revolt and rule for a while, but it was always a single man who emerged as king, as tyrant. Mainland Greece had its tyrants as well.'

'And the Punics?'

'As far as we know, and we don't know much, there were officials called suffets who were elected every two years; there was an assembly and senators. Earlier there had been kings, but they were kings who were elected by the aristocratic families and ruled for a span of time. Those kings were venerated, regarded as gods.'

They all crossed themselves. 'Go on.'

'Dionysius then took trouble to ally himself with the most powerful cities in the south of Italy. For instance, he sent ambassadors to the city of Locri asking for the hand of Doride, the beautiful daughter of one Seneto, head of a prominent Locrian family. Simultaneously he married Aristomache, the most respected of Syracusan women.' [4]

'He married them both?'

'Yes, and at the same time. He gave huge banquets to which he invited all the population and he seemed so generous that many Greeks came back to Syracuse, thinking that he had changed his ways. This was the year 397–396 BC. Soon after the marriage celebrations, Dionysius summoned his assembly and declared war on the Carthaginians: they were the real enemies of the Greeks, he claimed, against whom they were always plotting. It would be impossible for Syracuse to consider itself safe as long as the Punics remained so powerful. The mob reacted enthusiastically and sacked the Punic districts of Syracuse and, having stolen their cargoes, burned the Punic ships at anchor in the harbour. Other Greek cities which were in Punic territory rebelled and killed their Carthaginian garrisons.'

'How cruel!' said Rosaria, serving the hot soup.

'But the Punics were cruel as well; they were despised by the Greek world because among other things they went on sacrificing human beings; crucifixion was a Carthaginian "invention". Any Punic general who returned home as a loser was crucified publicly. That is why most Punic generals preferred to commit suicide.'

They recoiled. I read on.

'"Dionysius, leading an army of Syracusan soldiers, mercenaries and allied troops, left Syracuse heading towards Eryx. Not far from this hill lay the city of Motya, a Carthaginian colony which they used as a base for operations against Sicily. He hoped that by taking Motya, he would derive several advantages over his enemies. During this journey he continually encountered men from the Greek cities whom he fully armed; all joined his army with enthusiasm because they loathed the harsh Phoenician rule and wished to procure their liberty once and for all ... He had 80,000 foot soldiers as well as 3,000 cavalry and almost 200 warships. Also with the fleet there were at least fifty cargo ships loaded with many machines of war and supplies. Because Dionysius' army was so great in size and ready for war, the inhabitants of Eryx were terrified and because they hated the Carthaginians, decided to join the Greeks."'

'Traitors even then ...' Donna Rosina clearly did not like people from Eryx. Naturally she was on the side of the Punics; indeed, she was probably as pure a Phoenician as one could find.

'"On the other hand,"' I continued reading from my book, '"the inhabitants of Motya, who were expecting help from Carthage, were not overawed by the army of Dionysius and prepared themselves for a siege. They were aware that the Syracusans would seek to destroy Motya first because it was totally loyal to the Carthaginians. This city was built on an island, six stadi [about 174 metres] from mainland Sicily, and had many attractive houses built in a supremely artistic way because its inhabitants were rich. The city also had a narrow man-made causeway which joined it to the Sicilian coast. On that occasion the Motyans destroyed it so that their enemies would have no access route by which to attack them."'

'Ah, that's when it happened ...' Peppino was thoughtful. 'I never knew, I thought it had collapsed on its own accord because when I drive the cart, I take a little detour where I know that the road under the sea is broken. I can't see it unless the sun shines ...'

'At that time the sea level was lower,' Vincenzo told his uncle. 'I heard that Vitakre used to say that in the old times, when there was this battle, it was 50 centimetres lower so the causeway showed above water. It was a road.' Then, turning towards me, he asked if I was tired of reading aloud; I, in turn, asked them if they were getting bored. They all pleaded with me to continue, so I went on:

'"After having reconnoitred the area with his engineers, Dionysius began to construct dams against Motya; he dragged his warships across the land along the mouth of the harbour, then beached the cargo ships along the coast, leaving Leptines [Dionysius' brother], the admiral, to supervise the operation while he, together with the infantry, advanced against those neighbouring cities allied to the Carthaginians. All the Sicans, fearing the might of his army, joined the Syracusan cause, only five of the other cities retaining their friendship with the Carthaginians; these were Alicie,⁵ Egesta, Solunto, Panormus and Entella.

'"Dionysius laid waste to the territories around Solunto and Panormus, as well as those of Alicie, and he felled trees; he encamped with huge forces around Egesta and Entella where he launched continuous attacks, intending to take them by force. This was the situation in which Dionysius found himself.

'"Himilco, the Carthaginian commander, personally involved himself in raising troops and other preparations for war. He sent the admiral with ten triremes and orders to sail in secret and as fast as possible towards Syracuse to enter the port at night and destroy the ships lying in the harbour. He decided on this action in order to create a diversion and to force Dionysius to dispatch part of his fleet back to Syracuse. The admiral sent on this mission rapidly executed his orders and reached the port of Syracuse at night without being spotted. He launched a surprise attack, ramming the anchored fleet and sinking almost all of the ships before returning to Carthage."'

'So they win!' Rosina was ready to rewrite history in order to see her team get the better of the Greeks.

'Steady on, I fear not,' I cautioned her, and read on. '"Dionysius having laid waste all Carthaginian territory, having forced the Punics to retreat behind their walls, led his entire army against Motya. He hoped that, having destroyed it, the other cities would surrender immediately. He quickly filled in the gap in the causeway between the city and the Sicilian coast, employing a large number of men in the works and so, bit by bit, as the jetty was lengthened, he placed his siege-machines closer to the Motyan walls."'

'These were the ballistae or catapults which his artisans had just invented,' said Peppino, who remembered what Joseph Whitaker had recounted to him.

'Imagine what it must have been like for the poor Motyans to see these huge machines being dragged towards them,' I said. 'Now we start the fifteenth chapter of Diodorus' account, which covers the actual battle for the city of Motya. It is so complicated that I don't think anybody could have made it up. Perhaps it sounds a bit too much like the description of what happened at Tyre when it was captured by Alexander the Great, maybe Diodorus was a bit influenced by those events—'

'Which events?'

'Was Alexander on the side of the Punics? Who was he?'

'No, no, I was just being confusing, let's read on: "During this time Himilco, the Carthaginian admiral, realising that Dionysius had beached his ships, quickly armed his hundred best triremes since he thought that if he took them by surprise he could easily overcome the beached ships, thus becoming master of the sea. This action, he thought, would raise the siege of Motya and transfer the initiative of the war directly against the city of Syracuse itself. He set sail with 100 ships, reaching the area of Selinunte during the night, and, having rounded the cape of Lilybaeum, was in Motya the following dawn. Suddenly, falling upon the enemy, he destroyed some of their anchored ships and burnt others while Dionysius' men were unable to defend them. Next, having approached the main harbour, he organized his fleet as though he intended to attack the enemy's beached ships. Dionysius concentrated his troops at the entrance to the harbour, realizing that his enemies were guarding the exits; he hesitated about allowing his ships in the harbour to put to sea because he knew that, the mouth being narrow, he would find himself in a position of confrontation with a much more numerous enemy against only a small number of his own ships. That is why, having a large number of soldiers available, he transferred, overland and without difficulty, the ships to the open sea, taking them outside the port and thus saving them."'

'I don't understand this,' said Rosaria.

'Don't interrupt,' said her husband. 'It's clear: he had his ships transported by his soldiers overland, that's what he did. Maybe with stones and rollers. The writer says that there were many men, so they pushed the ships across dry land.'[6]

Since this was indeed the explanation, I continued: '"Himilco attacked the first triremes but was repulsed by a cloud of arrows: Dionysius had manned his ships with a large number of archers and javelin throwers while, on land, the Syracusans killed many of their enemies using the catapults which threw very sharp darts (this new weapon caused great fear because it had just been invented at that time); thus Himilco, not succeeding in his plan, returned to Libya, not judging it advantageous to continue the battle because the enemy now had twice as many ships.'

'Traitor!'

'Coward!'

I went on: "'Dionysius, having completed a road on which to drag the ships overland thanks to the abundance of manpower, placed siege machines of every type against the walls. He attacked the towers with battering rams, he suppressed the defenders on the battlements with his catapults, he also made his own siege towers of six levels on wheels with protruding bridges. These were pushed against the city walls to which they were of equal height. The inhabitants of Motya, even at this dangerous moment, were not at all frightened by Dionysius' army, even though by that time they had no allies. Seeking glory even more than their besiegers, they first lifted their men on platforms by means of ropes hanging from the trees higher than the ships, and from that elevated position threw burning torches and burning tow on to the war machines of the enemy. The flames quickly devoured the wood and precipitately the Greeks rushed to put them out. By continuous blows with battering rams they breached part of the walls. As the two sides massed together, a violent battle developed. Believing themselves masters of the city, the Syracusans attacked everything in revenge against the Phoenicians because of the blows that the Carthaginians had inflicted on them in the past. The inhabitants of the city, faced by the dreaded prospect of slavery, and seeing that they could not escape either by land or by sea, nobly faced death. Realizing that the defence of the walls was lost, they crowded in the narrow streets and fought from house to house; therefore Dionysius' soldiers found themselves in great difficulty. Hampered within the walls and although thinking themselves now masters of the city, they were in fact being hit from above by defenders on the rooftops. Nevertheless they moved the wooden towers against the first houses to gain access to the others. Because the machines were of the same height as the houses, the fighting had developed hand to hand. The Greeks launched their bridges and by this means attempted to assault the houses.'"

My little audience was silent, hanging on every word of the dramatic account. As I paused to take a sip of water, an unnatural crash followed by a blinding flash lit up all our faces. They crossed themselves again, even Vincenzo who was not very religious, and Rosa exclaimed: 'This must have hit the tower!'

'The castle?'

'Do you think so?'

There was a commotion as the two men decided to go and see. The rain was still lashing the tree-tops and, as Peppino with his nephew Vincenzo opened the door, a gust of wind swept the room and the flames of the candles trembled; but mine survived the blow. Outside it was still dark. Maybe this was the storm's final flourish.

'Shall we go on?' the women said.

'What about Peppino? Won't he want to hear it too?' I asked.

'He knows it already, he was told by those English and those important people he dug for.'

'And Vincenzo?'

'Peppino tells him everything.'

So I continued reading from Diodorus: '"The Motyans, considering the gravity of the situation and fearing for the women and children who were with them in the houses, struggled all the harder. Some men with their parents beside them, the latter begging not to be abandoned to the violence of the enemy, blinded by sorrow, risked all; others, hearing the cries of their women and children, sought a noble death rather than see their children enslaved. Flight from the city was impossible because it was surrounded by sea which the enemy controlled. The fact that the Phoenicians had treated their Greek prisoners with cruelty made them expect the same treatment themselves, so that they felt panic-stricken and without hope. The only thing left to them therefore was to fight to the death.

'"As a result of the desperate courage with which the besieged struggled, the Greeks found themselves hard pressed. In fact, fighting from bridges hanging in thin air, they did not achieve great results because there was little room for manoeuvre, and their enemies risked all as only those who despair of life can; so that some fell in hand-to-hand combat giving and receiving wounds, others repulsed by the Motyans lost their lives falling to the ground from the ladders. The street fighting lasted for days, but Dionysius always took cover towards evening, recalling his troops with a trumpet signal. After a while the Motyans became used to this, so Dionysius waited for both sides to withdraw and then sent Archilus from the city of Turi forward with some chosen men. It was by now night and he put ladders against the ruined houses, climbed up and occupied a favourable position to allow the main army inside the city. The Motyans, aware of what had happened, immediately

rushed towards them and, even if they arrived late, they none the
less contained the danger. The battle grew in violence as many more
Greeks climbed the ladders. Finally, thanks to their number, they
overcame their adversary.

'"Immediately, also using the causeway, the rest of Dionysius'
army surged into the city and corpses were piled everywhere. The
Greeks, wishing to avenge cruelty with cruelty, killed everybody,
one after the other, sparing neither girls nor women nor the elderly.
Dionysius, who wished to take slaves for money, at first tried to stop
the slaughter of prisoners. But since nobody listened to him, and
seeing that the fury of the Syracusans was unstoppable, he placed
heralds who shouted to the Motyans to seek refuge in those sanctuaries which were also sacred to the Greeks. So the soldiers ceased
the slaughter and fell to looting; they found much silver, quite a lot
of gold, luxury clothes and other objects of value in large quantities. Dionysius allowed them to sack the city in order to maintain
their morale for future battles. Then he gave 100 units of money to
Archilus, who had been the first to climb on the wall. He honoured
all those who had distinguished themselves according to their
merit, sold the surviving Motyans as booty, and ordered the crucifixion of Diomenes and of all the Greek residents who had been
allies of the Carthaginians. He then stationed a garrison in the city
under the command of the Syracusan Bito. He ordered Admiral
Leptines to blockade the passage to Carthage with 100 ships . . .
And then, as it was the end of summer, he returned with the army
to Syracuse."'

'And then?'

'That is all Diodorus wrote about this battle.'

'The crucified bodies lined the causeway, from here to the mainland,' said Rosina. I could not believe that there would have been so
many Greeks living in Motya, and in any case, who had seen this
horrible spectacle? I suspected that Rosa had found inspiration
from a film by Cecil B. De Mille.

We all fell silent.

Diodorus' account is so evocative that the tragedy of Motya is
still alive on the island. Few battles in antiquity have been so thoroughly described and the words which recount the carnage ring
true. The sense of loss reminded me of the fall of Troy, or how I
imagined it. Whenever I had looked at that silent mound near the

Dardanelles, to my shame, tears would accumulate in the corners of my eyes which not even the wind which Homer describes, and which still sweeps the hill of Ilium, would dry up.

Diodorus was no Homer. I suspect that Homer, although Greek, was more on the side of the Trojans than Diodorus was on that of the doomed Punics, the underdogs.

'In the following year a powerful Carthaginian fleet of 200 ships carrying an army of 100,000 men entered the harbour of Palermo. That city had remained in Punic hands. Then they advanced on Motya and Himilco took it back; by then the city was a pile of burnt stones. So the Carthaginians, who needed a harbour in this area, built Lilybaeum.' Thus Diodorus concluded his account.

At that moment the two men came back to the house and, since it had stopped raining, we all went out to look at the light on the cape. 'What an awful story,' Rosina remarked.

'I think all those battles were horrible, either for one side or the other,' Rosaria added.

'Maybe Motya is under siege again,' Zio Peppino murmured, thinking that nobody would hear him. The surf of the sea, now calm, reflected a vermilion sunset.

5

MOTYA FEVER

With its great harbour, Lilybaeum flourished; darkness shrouded Motya, and its name was gradually forgotten. After the Roman and the Moorish conquests, and then the arrival of the Normans, the Punics too were largely forgotten. Their achievements in particular were erased from the fickle memory of the victors, and the victors were Aryans. For a long time history regarded the Punics as barbarians and relegated them to a marginal role, so that we knew little about them apart from the fact that they had been the enemies of Rome and that Carthage 'had to be destroyed'. Until the Renaissance, antiquity was despised; and in any case, the Renaissance never reached Sicily.

The Renaissance was all about the rediscovery of Greek and Roman aesthetics, the glories of their architecture. Its prophets were Vitruvius,[1] Alberti and Piero della Francesca, and it was the Greek and Roman statues and frescoes that inspired Brunelleschi, Donatello, Mantegna, Bramante and the rest with feverish excitement. The Baroque period rejected antiquity once again, but Neoclassicism was astonished anew by the accomplishments which emerged from Herculaneum, Pompeii, Cumae and other sites. Goethe, in his *Italian Journey* (which included Sicily), concentrated on the purity of Greek shapes and ideas, rejecting Roman monumental architecture as gross. In his ardent and doomed search for perfection, Goethe's Neoclassicism verged on the Romantic. But the subject of archaeology as a source of knowledge about our past was still some way ahead. Although Homer remained popular, nobody would have read the *Iliad* and the *Odyssey* as sources of historical information. Christianity had condemned anything that was not part of its evangelical mysticism and destroyed it in the same way as the Muslims burned down the library of Alexandria because of the religious claim that all knowledge was contained within the Koran.[2] In some respects both the Renaissance and the age of Neoclassicism, the Enlightenment, can be considered as periods of agnosticism, of rebellion against a given cultural tendency resulting from religious intolerance. In any case, these were moments lived and caused by a minority. Not only did Christ stop at Eboli, He stopped wherever there was no knowledge.

The Christians tried to destroy the heathen past (the equestrian statue of Marcus Aurelius was only saved because it was believed to represent Constantine, the first Christian emperor); and the past exercised no widespread appeal. For the most part, people had no nostalgia towards times gone by which they regarded as burdened with hardship. Stones from old monuments were used to build new churches. But in Sicily poverty was the great preserver. The temple of Artemis in Syracuse was turned into a church dedicated to the Virgin Mary merely by walling it up; the cella and the Doric columns have remained intact since the time of Dionysius. The majestic Doric temples in Agrigento are still extant because, in the absence of enough money to build new places of devotion, they were turned into churches.

Punic buildings did not benefit in the same way as those of the Greeks and Romans because they were quaint, almost exotic, and too puzzling, distant from our sense of aesthetics. Indeed, most had been erected with a view not to monumental grandiosity but to a defensive purpose or the maintenance of some cult that seemed weird to later generations, later cultures. Apart from these considerations, they belonged to a culture which had been vanquished. Losers do not make history; they don't set standards or dictate fashions. Had the Persians won at Salamis, or the Turks at Lepanto, we would probably dress differently, inhabit a different style of architecture and speak in other idioms. Herodotus thought likewise – although he did not talk of Lepanto, of course.

The Phoenicians were erased as an influence in the development of civilized history and for centuries we knew next to nothing about Motya, one of their wealthiest cities. So, for a long time, there was no Motya fever, no driving curiosity to discover, to excavate. Besides, the Punics were Semites, they did not spring from European stock. Phoenician culture and Punic technical knowledge were annexed by the ancient Greeks, the Achaeans.

The Romans, who had copied the Punic warships in order to vanquish the Carthaginians, displayed their regard for the Punic world through the words of their greatest poet. Virgil described Dido, queen of Carthage, as a grand, dignified woman; but a woman who finally loses her heart. She may be a queen, but she is a mere female. The passage of power from Carthage to Rome is thus described as the work of destiny, given legitimacy in the *Aeneid* as something desired by the gods, a Greek concept.

But the queen had long been suffering from love's deadly wound, feeding it with her blood and being consumed by its hidden fire. Again and again there rushed into her mind thoughts of the great valour of the man and the high glories of his line. His features and the words he had spoken had pierced her heart and love gave her body no peace or rest.[3]

When she died, Dido's anger expressed itself in the wish to be revenged on the Trojan hero who, in Virgil's poem, is the ancestor of the Julians, the imperial family of Caesar and Augustus.

'We shall die unavenged. But let us die. This, this is how it pleases me to go down among the shades. Let the Trojan who knows no pity gaze his fill upon this fire from the high seas and take with him the omen of my death.' So she spoke and while speaking fell upon the sword. Her attendants saw her fall. They saw the blood foaming on the blade and staining her hands, and filled the high walls of the palace with their screaming ...[4]

The Phoenicians and Punics, the losers, the weaker, are repeatedly embodied in the character of a woman: Motya the nymph, Europa the princess who is raped, Dido the suicidal queen.

Although written about eight centuries after the events it describes, Virgil's account used real characters. Even if we have no historical notion of Aeneas, we know that Elissa–Dido existed and that, having fled from Tyre for political reasons, she founded Carthage. Herodotus, not only a historian but a widely travelled man, believed that Dido and Heracles had actually lived in the distant past and identified parallels between the latter and the Phoenician god–king Melqart. Maybe there are more links, too. The Trojan hero Aeneas, like the demigod Heracles, was the son of a divinity; his mother was Aphrodite, a goddess who was born in a Phoenician colony, Cyprus, and who can be traced back to

Astarte, the Phoenician Mother Earth.

Knowledge that Motya had existed remained, but its actual location was forgotten. The name of the city was repeated by writers such as Polybius, Diodorus and Thucydides, but little consideration was given to their regard for historical accuracy. In any case, it was argued, some of them were writing centuries after the events they described. Who in the nineteenth century could believe that the Punics had lived in houses six floors high? Or that the Syracusan Greeks had invented the catapult? For real progress, we had to await the arrival of a romantic dilettante, Heinrich Schliemann, a man with enough imagination to understand that the writers of the past told real stories.

In the seventeenth century Cluverius, a Dutch geographer, came to Motya because he had read about it in ancient texts. He was an erudite man and also a historian. Realizing that in those days the only source of knowledge was the Society of Jesus, Cluverius, himself a man of the church, a Benedictine, sought their counsel. In a sense the Jesuits had inherited the role of the Carolingians as conservers and keepers of knowledge. When he visited the island of San Pantaleone in 1619, Cluverius found much more visible vestiges of the city than we can see today. The entire circuit of the walls and many of the crenellated towers were still extant. Thrilled by his discovery, Cluverius was in fact convinced that he had found the lost city of Motya. 'Nullum jam dubium esse potest, quin haec illa sit, quae olim Motyam Carthaginiensum urbem sustinuit' ['There can be no doubt that this was once the city of the Carthaginians, Motya'].

Although at the time few were interested in the site of the Punic city, nevertheless murmurs of dissent welcomed Cluverius' declaration. One century later, also seized with Motya fever, and having read Cluverius, the French geographer Jean Houel visited the island and produced a sketch of the north gate. But it was by no means accepted among the scholars of the day that the island known as San Pantaleo or San Pantaleone was the ancient Motya. Historians disagreed with each other as well as with Cluverius. In the first place, few believed that Motya had ever existed; furthermore, the island designated as the Punic city was small, too small. Some scholars thought that ancient Motya had been situated nearer to the other Punic cities of Palermo and Solunto; that it had been built on what is now known as Isola delle Femmine, near Cinisi. Others wrote that the ancient Punic harbour was located near Mazara del Vallo, south of Marsala. As late as 1875 – the year of Schliemann's visit to Sicily – Giovan Battista Caruso, who published several volumes on the history of Sicily, dismissed the notion that San Pantaleo was the island where Motya had once flourished.

But in 1883 a student named Ignazio Coglitore demonstrated in his thesis for the University of Palermo that Cluverius had been correct. Coglitore had studied under the guidance of Professors Antonio Salinas and Adolfo Holm, respectively head of archaeology and head of ancient history at the university. Even earlier – twenty years earlier – a much more important man than the student Coglitore had become inflamed with Motya fever. He was none other than the internationally famous archaeologist Heinrich Schliemann, and he was convinced that San Pantaleo and Motya were one and the same.

On 24 July 1873 Schliemann wrote to Professor Fiorelli, director of antiquities in Italy, then working at Pompeii, that, 'offended by this ungrateful country [Greece] . . . I'd prefer to come and live in Palermo or Naples'.⁵ Two years later, in autumn 1875, he arrived in Palermo. By then he was the most celebrated of all archaeologists, famous for having discovered Troy, the treasure of Priam and what he called the tombs of Atreus at Mycenae. In spite of the fact that he made many mistakes and that he dated his findings several centuries too early, Schliemann correctly identified Mycenae as a city-state of great power in existence long before the glories of Hellas; and he also located Tiryns, the city-state of Diomedes with its Cyclopean walls.

Schliemann was the first man who, reading Homer and believing that the *Iliad* and the *Odyssey* were more than mere tales, had come to the conclusion that the great era of Athens and Sparta had flourished out of an earlier period of historical development, that human history was stratified like the humus of archaeology. Motya, Schliemann thought, had been destroyed like Troy. It had probably been razed to the ground and all its inhabitants killed or sold as slaves, like Priam's daughters Cassandra and Polyxena and old queen Hecuba. In Homer, this persistent German had found many clues about the overwhelming Phoenician presence in early Mediterranean culture, prompting him to attempt to resolve the puzzle of where those rich merchants had lived.

For instance, in the *Odyssey* Schliemann would have read that Ulysses himself, returning to Ithaca incognito, tells his swineherd Eumaeus that he had been kidnapped by Phoenician traders. Asked for his own story, the old swineherd tells his visitor that he was born a prince, but that he too suffered the same fate. One day, Eumaeus says,

Some Phoenicians came, notorious sailors, rogues, bringing all kinds of rubbish in their black ship. Now in my father's house there was a Phoenician woman, large and comely, who knew how to work well. The crafty Phoenicians led her astray. First one made love to her when she went to wash our clothes, and seduced her by the empty ship – which makes women lose their heads however honest they are. Then he asked her who she was and where she came from, and she at once named the high-roofed house of her father: 'I am proud to come from Sidon, the town rich in ore, and I am the daughter of Arybas, who is very rich. But robbers carried me off as I returned from the fields and sold me to the household of this man.'

Her lover, says Eumaeus, persuaded her to kidnap the king's son (Eumaeus himself). 'There was the swift ship of the Phoenicians. They climbed aboard at once and, after they had taken us in, sailed off across the water.' But on the sixth day 'Artemis the Archeress struck the woman and she plummeted down into the hold. And they threw her out to be carrion for the seals and fish. I was left alone in my misery. The Phoenicians travelled on through wind and water and came to Ithaca, where Laertes bought me in return for goods.'[6]

Schliemann found so many references to the Phoenicians that it is no wonder he became set on finding Motya. The son of a Protestant pastor who created scandals because of his womanizing, Schliemann was a man of small build with a reddish face and round spectacles who, in 1868, had arrived at the hill of Hissarlik overlooking the Dardanelles. He immediately decided that the site was exactly what Homer had described: the lost city of Troy or Ilium, the Mecca of illustrious men like Caesar, Alexander the Great and Byron. Even Xerxes, king of the Persians, stopped at Troy before invading Greece; he climbed to the old citadel and ordered his priests to pour wine on the old walls to honour the heroes who were thought to have died there. Moved by the Homeric drama, the 'king of kings' sacrificed a thousand sheep to Athena. Herodotus commented that the Trojan War was the first chapter of the bloody war which developed between the east and the west. In this instance Xerxes embodied the champion of the east, the king who would take revenge on behalf of Priam and his dynasty. But he did not; his invading army went on to be defeated by the finally united Greeks as resoundingly as the Carthaginians in Sicily had been vanquished by Dionysius. Antiquity saw in this double aggression a grand design, a coalition of eastern forces against Greece.

Motya was not the only ancient city whose location had been forgotten. When Schliemann began to search for the site of Mycenae, his Corinthian guides had never heard of it; only a boy from a local farm knew how to lead him to 'the fortress of Agamemnon'. In Mycenae and Tiryns, Schliemann found bronze arrows of Phoenician manufacture; so for a time he thought that the Mycenaeans were of Phoenician stock. The Mycenaeans, it was later established, bought their arms from the Phoenicians who had a de facto monopoly on commerce in metals and arms production. In 1885 Schliemann published a history of Tiryns in which he outlined the Phoenician presence in ancient Greece and argued that Heracles, 'solar god and hero', had been born in Tiryns. Schliemann was soon to understand how far-reaching was the Phoenician and Punic trade in metals and specifically arms.

At the time of Schliemann's arrival in Palermo, Joseph Whitaker was twenty-five. Although no social meetings are recorded, it is inconceivable that the most celebrated archaeologist in the world would not have been entertained by the Whitakers or by one of the aristocratic Sicilian families who, bored by their uneventful existence, were trophy-hunting for any celebrity who happened to pass through the city. The shy Joseph Whitaker would probably have met him or at least heard of his arrival. He was undoubtedly aware of Schliemann's achievements, even though they had already begun to attract criticism from those who resented his mistakes. Through insensitive excavating practice he destroyed layers of knowledge; but he opened up a new field of imagination in archaeology. By the time he arrived in Sicily he was regarded as a hero; his name was more famous than that of Garibaldi and he was equally lionized.

Travelling from Palermo, Schliemann arrived at Motya in the autumn and straight away began his excavations. The records of what he did at Motya have survived, 'though until now', says Dr Benedikt Isserlin, 'they do not appear to have attracted much notice'.[7] Dr Isserlin, who was head of the Department of Semitic Languages and Literature at the University of Leeds from the early 1960s, found five pages in Schliemann's diary dated 19–22 October 1875, written in English and modern Greek rather than German.[8] It was Hilda Isserlin who had the idea that those papers might be found in Athens. 'My wife suggested I write to a descendant of Schliemann living in Athens,' explained Dr Isserlin. 'We were told the papers had gone to the library of the American school. On my writing to them, they kindly provided a copy of papers of Schliemann's diary dealing with Motya.'

As soon as he arrived in Motya, Schliemann engaged workers (whom he declared utterly unsatisfactory) and on 20 October started digging. He was accustomed to do everything in a hurry, although he was often frustrated in his efforts. Searching for a Phoenician connection to the Mycenaeans, the man who had unearthed the Greek Bronze Age started work on the south-east side of Motya at a point 4 metres above sea level. By this time he had become an experienced archaeologist and he was right in thinking that the 'acropolis' of Motya would have been sited on a location higher than the surrounding terrain, or at least on a mound which might have been formed from the debris of important monuments. Moreover, Schliemann was right in thinking that most of the island had subsided; the sea level has risen by 50 centimetres since the time of its destruction. From aerial photographs it is clear that the space between the north gate and the beginning of the causeway, now submerged, was a proper piazza in which carts could queue up or unload before entering the city. In several letters written from Castellammare del Golfo, Schliemann stated that Motya had been founded in the fifth century and that there was no archaic pottery to be found there. 'Nothing but arrows and copper coins.' Of course he was wrong.

Having survived life in the Dardanelles, he was accustomed to enduring discomfort, including the hazards of scorpions, malaria, heat, insects of all kinds and wind 'that fills you up with dust', but he found Motya worse than Troy. At 2.5 metres below the Motyan topsoil he unearthed remnants of a pavement which had belonged to a house with four quadrangular columns 2 metres high, he jotted in his notes. Two of these columns (which are no longer in situ) were monoliths. The pottery he found on this dig belonged to the fifth century BC. Then, 'not having found anything at all' of what he expected, he next moved to the highest part of the hill, where he dug a trench 24 metres long and 3 metres wide in which he turned up arrowheads and a terracotta tablet with a sphinx in bas-relief; but, when he struck natural soil, he concluded that there was nothing of earlier origin to be found on that site. He therefore tried to dig another big trench on the north side, 'just through the ancient gate which faces the dam or dike which once connected the island to the coast'. He discovered some copper coins and other small objects, but nothing that could date Motya earlier than the fifth century BC. 'There being nothing to find and no historical riddle to solve, I shall not continue the excavations.'

The impatient archaeologist then moved on to work for a few hours 'on the top of the hill', and Dr Isserlin wonders whether Schliemann meant the Cappiddazzu. But he only dug to a depth of half a metre, and we know now that the deposits lay much deeper. He was equally unlucky, Schliemann wrote, when he moved together with his eighteen labourers to the west side of the island. After this last failure, Schliemann left the site, but we don't know whether this was out of disappointment or for some other reason. His departure had nothing to do with the Mafia or brigandage; Schliemann was well accustomed to bandits in the Dardanelles, Mycenae, Tiryns and other places and said that the threat of Sicilian brigandage had been exaggerated. He even stated that the locals were good people, although they spoke 'only the local dialect which makes one have greatest difficulty'. He also described how the nineteen families that lived on the island had intermarried, each of them living off a tiny property which enabled them to feel economically independent. This was the reason, Schliemann concluded, for their bad workmanship.

He had undertaken his work in Motya, he wrote, 'according to the wish of the most learned Mr Bonghi, then the Italian minister for Pubblica Istruzione [education], one of the most enlightened figures of the Risorgimento', which suggests that Schliemann was actually invited to dig in Sicily. It had been rumoured that

Schliemann started working at Motya without a permit, but he was in fact granted formal permission by the Italian authorities. This does not therefore explain the mystery of a telegram full of insults which Schliemann sent to Prince Trabia, the regional authority in charge of Sicilian fine arts. Prince Trabia had been taken by surprise when he was told that Schliemann was already digging in Motya. Since the archaeologist had not warned him personally of his work on the island, Trabia went to visit the famous German. There must have been a horrible scene. Prince Trabia, bearer of the most aristocratic name in Sicily, had a keen sense of his own status and was not fully aware that Sicily was no longer ruled by the Bourbons and that Schliemann had been granted a permit from Rome. Moreover, the authorities were suspicious of the international celebrity because of the artefacts he was known to have taken away with him from his earlier excavations at Troy. Prince Trabia probably told Schliemann to get out of Motya. Insulted by the little (literally) Sicilian who had never heard of him and was oblivious of the achievements linked to his name, the archaeologist-writer was furious. According to Professor Tusa, Schliemann's telegram in response to the order was so rude that it was decided not to publish it if only out of respect for the great archaeologist.

Whatever the precise circumstances of his departure, what is certain is that Schliemann left Motya precipitately, his fever for Motya having turned to nausea. Why? He was certainly disappointed to discover – as he thought – that Motya had been founded only in the fifth century BC. In fact, his conclusion was incorrect; Motya's story had started three centuries earlier. Yet even the eighth century would have disappointed Schliemann, who was trying to solve the riddle of the Phoenicians' role in the Bronze Age and had expected to find evidence which could testify to Motya's existence at the time of Mycenae and Tiryns (1500–1200 BC). But of course that was not the case.

In any event, the field was now left open to Joseph Whitaker, an Englishman born in Sicily who was aware of Schliemann's work and knew Motya because he was in the habit of shooting ducks and wild geese on and around the lagoon. In the preface of his book *Motya: A Phoenician Colony in Sicily*, published in 1921, Whitaker wrote:

Although the exploration so far made has been confined almost entirely to the fortifications and to the outskirts or fringe of the old Phoenician city and the greater part of the area which this town probably occupied still remains untouched, the work that has been accomplished has undoubtedly revealed much which was previously unknown to us, and has thrown light on several points hitherto more or less obscure.

On no other Phoenician site, perhaps, are so many ruins of an important fortified city still to be found standing in situ at the present day as in Motya. Once overcome and destroyed, as it was, by the elder Dionysius, Motya apparently ceased to exist as a town and such of its ruins as were allowed to remain, first by its Greek conquerors and later by the Carthaginians themselves when founding the new city of Lilybaeum, were covered up by the protecting soil and debris, and have probably thus remained, untouched by the hand of man, until the present day. In this lies the great archaeological interest and importance of the site.

Whitaker – like Schliemann at Troy – had been struck by the Motya fever.

Schliemann had taken care to buy the site before starting excavations, and Joseph Whitaker decided that he should buy up the island before excavating systematically; and – again like Schliemann – Whitaker was using his own money. In this account, which also appears in the preface of his book, Joseph Whitaker – 'Pip' to his friends, il Commendatore for Peppino, Voscienza for the many labourers who worked for him – reveals how the urge to dig at Motya, in other words, the Motya fever, came to him around the time of Schliemann's visit to Sicily.

The idea of excavating the buried remains of Motya first occurred to me some forty years or more ago, but it was not until many years later and after overcoming innumerable obstacles and difficulties that I became sole proprietor of the little island, and was finally enabled to give effect to the project that I had for so long cherished in pectore, and commence the work of exploration. During the first few years fair progress was made and much of interest was brought to light, but with the outbreak of the Great War work was arrested and has since been at an almost complete standstill.

Also infected by a severe attack of Motya fever was Professor Vincenzo Tusa, who passed this contagious disease on to many others, including myself. A fellow sufferer is Marisa Famà, a pupil of Tusa's, who was in charge of the site. I had caught the disease earlier as a result of that first visit to the site described in chapter 2, which took place in the mid-1960s when Delia Whitaker was alive and Motya was still the private property of the Whitaker family.

As my own study could not include archaeological investigation, I looked into an aspect of Motya's history which had hitherto gone unexplored. The Jesuits had owned what had become known as San Pantaleo for just over two centuries. Although they never inhabited it, they must have studied it; their scholarly minds must have pondered the significance of those stones which emerged from the salt-pans, from the sea and the vineyards. They would have seen more traces of the ancient city than are visible today and might possibly have recorded them. Perhaps they had contributed to the despoliation of the walls, of the heathen temples, allowing the finely cut stones to contribute to the construction of dwellings for the labourers who worked their land. Maybe there would be much to learn about ancient Motya from the Jesuits' famously rich archives – if I could gain access to them.

I therefore wrote to the chief archivist of the Society of Jesus in Rome asking him whether he, as curator of the records, knew of any reference in them to Motya or San Pantaleo. I duly received an answer in French addressed to Mr Gaio Servadio – the possibility of having to deal with a mere female being perhaps too remote to grasp – saying that my question was odd, that he knew nothing about Motya; indeed, he neither knew what it might be nor understood what I was talking about. He would, however, investigate the matter further. I wrote back saying that I was grateful and waited.

I waited in vain. Maybe he had finally understood that I was a female and the realization had been too much for him. I asked a senior Vatican monsignor to help, but nothing came of it. So I took the Sicilian route. Professor Salvatore Nicosia, who holds the chair of ancient languages at the university in Palermo and is a valued friend, suggested that I speak to the former curator of the archives at the Casa Professa headquarters of the Society of Jesus in Palermo. Father Francesco Paolo Rizzo, reader in classical history, had left Palermo in order to teach at the Gregoriana, the Vatican's university in Rome. When I found him, Father Rizzo told me that he was aware that San Pantaleo had been a Jesuit property until the end of the eighteenth century and that I had good reason to investigate this period of its history. His successor as curator of the Jesuits' archives in Palermo was Padre Salvo, 'who is one of those people,' sighed Father Rizzo, 'who thinks that archives are to be kept under lock and key and that his task is to prevent anybody from probing'. Alas, not all Jesuits were enlightened! Most Italian libraries and archives were kept by people of that kind, I consoled him – despite being inconsolable myself. One thing Father Rizzo did tell me, though, was that all archives concerning San Pantaleo were kept in Sicily, not in Rome, because all the Jesuits' property in the island had been granted to them by the Emperor Charles V in his role as king of Sicily (at that time there were 750 Collegia in Europe, 35 of which were in Sicily). Therefore all these assets came under the jurisdiction of that division.

So I began my investigation. I rang up the Casa Professa and asked to speak to Father Salvo. Father Salvo was ill, I was told. My first call was followed by several others which received no proper answer, so I decided to pay a visit to the Casa Professa in person. The side of Palermo where the headquarters of the Sicilian Jesuits stood had been heavily bombed in the Second World War; while the Baroque church had been spared, the fury of the Allied attack had hit the Jesuit headquarters, which had been replaced by a horrible cement building. The back of the church betrayed an earlier shape, with a graceful Aragonese archway and traces of Angevin Gothic. All along the narrow road which led to it there were little shops selling coffins, plastic flowers and wreaths: all the southern Mediterranean paraphernalia of death. The polished brass of the coffins echoed the polished metal of the dingy coffee-houses from which emanated a strong scent of espresso mingled with decaying tuberosa. The owners of the shops sat chatting outside on broken chairs while they waited for clients, who came in all shapes and colours. In one of the chairs sat a young African woman who was being injected by two men, I suspect with heroin. The rite – in a way appropriate to the mortuary – was conducted openly, without any attempt at concealment. The shallow square in front of the church and the Casa Professa was full of the symbols of death. Funerals are an important industry in this part of the world, where so much is in any case decaying. Triumphantly, a black car covered with wilting wreaths was waiting in the shadow for the bier to leave the church, its bored chauffeur leaning against it in top hat and white gloves like a surgeon's. Other black cars waited to take death's clients to one of the vast Palermitan cemeteries. Even Motya reminded me of the rites of death, which somehow seemed to be ever-present on the island of Sicily. Modern Palermitans are of course of Phoenician stock, and it shows: there is a strong contrast between the originally Punic side and the Greek side of Sicily, in appearance, behaviour and speech.

I entered a gate and pushed a glass door which led me into the courtyard of what could have been a nursing home, a private clinic, and a dirty one at that. When I found an official I could question, I had to wait: a large lady in front of me had come to purchase a Mass for her dead husband. 'I would like to see Padre Salvo,' I declared to the porter, who looked at me with infinite hostility from behind a thick partition, as if he were a bank clerk.

'Father Salvo is in hospital.'

'Then I could see the person who has taken his place and is in charge of the archives?'

'No one has the key of the archives except Father Salvo.' He was quite loquacious for a Sicilian.

'Then I could talk to Father Salvo?'

'He is in hospital.'

'I could ring the hospital.'

'He is in pain, he is to be operated on today.' That was clearly a fib.

'What for?'

'Father Salvo is eighty.'

'That is no disease. Plenty of people are eighty.'

'He has to have an operation on his femur. He fell and broke it. Do you know what that means? Terrible pains.' The porter was looking at me as if a creature from hell were interfering with the holy business of death and disease.

'When will he be out of hospital?'

'How am I to know? But do you think that Father Salvo is likely to be in a condition to work at the archives after his operation?'

'Then somebody else will be appointed.'

My insistence seemed to be achieving nothing until, in a moment of impatience and perhaps in order to be rid of me, the porter added: 'Ring Father Patti, then.'

I left several messages for Father Patti, who lived and worked at the Gonzaga Institute of the Istituto Storico dei Gesuiti. I told him why I was seeking his advice. I also mentioned the name of Professor Nicosia who, in spite of being a left-winger and a layman, was the respected head of the university. Father Patti, a learned man, was delighted that I wanted to look into this unknown side of Motya's history. He told me that the island of Motya was linked to the Collegium of Marsala, Trapani and Mazara, and that the papers concerning this Collegium were at the State Archive in Palermo and totalled 500 volumes in all, although most of them concerned the management of the property.

'In fact, you will not need to study them all as they concern our thirty-six Collegia. The ones you are interested in are probably no more than ten or fifteen. But you will have to check them all in order to find which ones you need.' It was an imposing documentary record, he added. With his high nasal voice and turn of phrase he sounded like a theatrical parody of a Jesuit, the kind that Rossini loved to make fun of. 'We owned the island. You should look it up in the compendium by Professor Renda and in the volumes by Tanucci [the Bourbon minister responsible for the expulsion of the Jesuits], where you will find listed all our properties in Sicily.'

A vast knowledge, an immense quantity of words emanating from a tiny body: Professor Renda was a real danger. Once he had started to talk no one, not even Dionysius and his catapults, could have stopped him. I had known him for some time and, in a burst of courage, I rang him up. He was interested in agrarian reforms, he immediately informed me, not in the Jesuits as such; although of course he had studied volume after volume on the subject. 'The island of San Pantaleo belonged to the Collegium Maximum of Palermo,' he stated. 'The property extended to thirty thousand hectares, of which a total of twenty-six thousand was let to small tenants – this was in 1769 when Giuseppe Di Piazza bought it with a notary act drawn by G. Fontana – I am afraid you will have to look his first name up as it is not stated in this document ...'

I tried to interrupt, saying that I was not specifically interested in this side of the situation at San Pantaleo but more in what the Jesuits noticed about antiquities in Motya. From Renda's viewpoint, which of course contrasted with that of Father Patti (and with that of Harold Acton; see chapter 3), the Tanucci reform had

been the fruit of the Age of Enlightenment. Following the dissolu-
tion of the Jesuit Order in the Kingdom of Naples and Sicily, Sicily
had been the first region to open free, lay schools, removing control
over knowledge from the hands of the church and placing it in those
of the Bourbon administration. In my opinion the Jesuits were better teachers than the Bourbon officials; but I did not want to begin
an argument that would have led to a battle of words which I would
have certainly lost. In any case, my quest was for information about
Motya.

Had my Motya fever been quenched by Renda, Patti and Rizzo?
Well, not really. The numerous volumes through which I trawled in
the archive revealed pages of bureaucratic detail written in Latin.
Yes, stones had been removed from San Pantaleo to build houses
and walls elsewhere, and yes, there was neither knowledge of nor
respect for antiquity. Cluverius had indeed sought help from the
Jesuits before visiting their island, and they knew that in antiquity
the Isola Lunga had been a continuous strip of land: thus the mouth
of the lagoon towards Cape Boeo was the only one, and the
Stagnone provided a superbly safe anchorage. In the 1980s a British
marine archaeologist had come to the same conclusion. This
explained the manoeuvres of the Greek and Carthaginian fleets,
which might otherwise have appeared somewhat far-fetched.

A tiny riddle had been solved with the help of the Jesuits, who for
their own part had not shown much curiosity about the Phoenicians
and Punics, the original inhabitants of Motya. I, on the other hand,
had become increasingly engaged by these obscure people. Before
my fever could be cured, I had to try to understand them.

6

WHO WERE THE PHOENICIANS?

Yes, who were the Phoenicians? And where did they come from? Not much was written either about them or by them in classical times, and modern archaeology has disclosed only a little more. When Motya is really able to speak to us, when its 4 per cent of excavated area has expanded to 40 per cent or even 90 per cent, we will have a clearer picture. Unfortunately, much of what we know about the Phoenicians, including their name, comes from their enemies: the Greeks and the Latins. The authors of classical times were rarely objective about the Phoenicians, who were branded as cunning traders or held responsible for introducing greed and luxury into Greece. The Romans spoke of 'fides Punica' for their proverbial cunning and lack of ethics.

In fact they did not call themselves Phoenicians at all, but Can'ani. They were Canaanites and their land was Canaan. In the Book of Genesis, Canaan is the son of Ham and the father of Sidon, that is to say the father of the Phoenicians. In Hebrew *cana'ani* also means 'merchant'; hence Canaan is the land of merchants. Alternatively, if the word comes from the Akkadian *kinannu, cana'ani* would mean 'purple', 'the red people': the same epithet that the Greeks used. Phoinikes (from the Greek *phoinos*, indicating red, blood, to stain with blood, death or crime) can be translated as 'those from the land of purple' or 'the red people' – a slightly sarcastic allusion to the purple textile industry for which the Phoenicians were famous. But to their face or in official terms, the Greeks named them after a Phoenician city, as Sidonians. Homer, for example, often uses that nomenclature even when writing about the people of Tyre.

Pliny the Elder tells us of a shepherd who lived near Tyre and

who had a dog which accidentally bit one of the small sea-snails
that are found in most warm seas, a murex, and as a result stained
itself red. The dog was brought before the king, who adopted the
colour red as a sign of royalty. The legend has traceable Phoenician
origins: some of their coins – those found at Motya, for example –
bear the image of a dog.

The murex shells were captured in large quantities with baskets
like lobster-pots, made of reeds attached to long ropes, with an
opening that yielded easily to pressure from the outside and made
escape impossible. These baskets were baited with mussels or frogs.
There were different ways of obtaining the dye. With the bigger
species, the *Purpurae*, a hole was made in the shell and the mollusc
removed. Then the sac containing the colouring matter was carefully extracted while the mollusc was still alive so that the dye
would not be impaired. With the smaller kind, the entire shell was
crushed and salt added; three days were needed for the maceration.
Heat was applied and the dye was left in a liquid state at the bottom
of a vessel made of lead. In order to fix the colour and make it
permanent, the Phoenicians probably used an alkali derived from
seaweed mentioned by Pliny.[1] The actual tints ranged from blue,
through violet and purple, to crimson and rose. The violet was
extremely fashionable during the time of Augustus.

Fernand Braudel wrote of Canaan: 'There it was, a tiny country,
independent, condemned by its limiting mountains, by its neighbours and by its own customs to make do with a meagre territory, a
few fields of wheat, beautifully tended orchards, forests and some
grazing meadows. The overpopulated cities had to buy abroad
those foodstuffs which they did not have in order to compensate for
such an imbalance.'[2]

The Phoenician workshops became famous for the production
of sumptuous articles of carved ivory, and jewellery in gold, silver
and bronze with filigree and granular decoration – luxuries which
archaeologists found mainly away from Phoenicia or Canaan in
royal tombs and the palaces of the east.

Scholars in Phoenician studies have many different theories
about their subject, some of them revolutionary ones. Some say
that the Phoenicians became skilled navigators because the Sea
People invaded their land. Other scholars think that the Hebrews,
or even the Trojans, pushed the Canaanites towards the open sea.

They do, however, broadly agree on the date at which a vast tribal shift took place: around 1200 BC, the time of the Trojan War. The war between the Achaeans under the overall command of Agamemnon, king of Mycenae, and the Asiatic outpost of Troy has convinced most that those so-called Sea People who invaded part of Asia Minor and brought terror to Egypt were none other than the Mycenaeans.

Because there were steep mountains immediately behind the coast where they settled after migrating from the Negev desert, the Phoenicians were forced to look seaward across the Mediterranean in order to find the food which they could not obtain from their warring neighbours, and other essentials for survival. Thus the sea became their motorway, through which they could find their raw materials and sell their wares. In a way they developed the first colonial economy in history: they searched for metals (tin, silver, gold), often quarried by local labour; they bartered coloured cloth and glass artefacts, material wealth in exchange for utilitarian wares. They developed a remarkable skill in metallurgy. The metals were transported by their ships in the form of ingots, then manufactured into objects – mainly arms – which were then sold back to those from whom they had bought the metal in the first place. They were the Khashoggis of their time, selling arms to anyone; they exploited cheap labour and local ignorance. Not only did they trade in arms, but the large Phoenician mercantile fleet carried ivory, feathers, ebony, furs and precious stones which were sold to powerful and rich Egypt. Recent archaeological discoveries at Ebla,[3] dating back to the third millennium BC, reveal that in exchange for local products – metallic ores, cotton and wool, perfumes, wheat, oil and ewes – the Phoenicians of Byblos sold linen and, in particular, precious objects in gold and silver. One all-important material grew on their terrain, colouring their mountains green, and that was wood. From their astonishing cedar trees, the Phoenicians made ships; they also built houses and temples, and sold straight planks of wood. Their craftsmanship was expensive. When Akhenaten, the mystical Egyptian Pharaoh, could no longer pay for his supplies, the Phoenicians dared to give their usual shipment a miss.

Throughout their long existence, the Phoenician towns were politically independent of each other, although they shared the same characteristics. Their inhabitants were mainly navigators and traders who observed a communal law, although they fought among themselves and were in fierce rivalry on the sea routes. As a people, they appear to have been adaptable and intelligent. In modern terms those city-states could be compared to Switzerland with its cantons, independent of neighbouring states but with more political autonomy than the Swiss cantons. Their 'banks' were notorious for their wealth. Not only did all sea routes lead to Phoenicia, but a network of roads which connected Asia to Europe and to Africa converged on Aleppo, which was the great crossroads of the trade routes between the Middle Euphrates and the Mediterranean.

These Phoenicians, with their elusive name and origin, appeared quaint to the other inhabitants of the Mediterranean coasts. They must have seemed different, and difference always appears dangerous, especially to simple people. The Greeks in particular were suspicious of them. They could not understand how these Semites had assembled a sphere of influence which stretched from the Lebanese coast to the Pillars of Hercules, and established a power founded not on military strength but on trade routes underpinned by small settlements, at first just a few huts around a harbour. Later, some of these staging-posts developed into modest walled towns with storehouses, barracks and watch towers, but without the magnificent public buildings that generally indicate permanence or a desire for permanence: no marble temples, no fluted columns.

The Hellenes were aware of the efficiency of the Phoenician fleets, into which so much effort was concentrated. They admired the Phoenicians' ability to navigate even at night, using the stars and natural sea currents. It seemed to the Greeks that they understood the behaviour of the winds and the sea as if by magic, better than their own gods. The Phoenicians also knew about reading the future; they had sibyls, and cultivated magic and maledictions.

These Phoenicians, moreover, had become a familiar sight; they seemed to be everywhere. When the Greeks ventured to distant coasts in search of places in which to settle, like Sicily for example, they found that the Phoenicians had already been there for decades, if not centuries. They were Orientals. Their small, thin bodies seemed to fit their svelte ships in any number; their aquiline profiles appeared and disappeared in market streets; the Hellenes, the

Mycenaeans, the Greeks could not understand, and hence could not tolerate, their ugly and nameless gods. They arrived by sea, traded and then sailed over the horizon, the holds of their ships laden with treasure. On the occasion of the death of Patroclus, Achilles offered a large silver vase, 'a masterpiece of Sidonian craftsmanship', as a prize. This vessel, 'the loveliest thing in the world', was 'shipped by Phoenician traders across the misty sea'. It was a vase that served as a ransom for one of Priam's daughters.

The Phoenicians had footholds – not colonies – on the north African coast, the Canary islands, Mogador, the Bosphoros, Italy, Sardinia, the Spanish peninsula and the Balearics. Real settlements, conceived and begun as permanent cities, as colonies, developed later; 'but, before the time of Solomon,' writes Joseph Whitaker,

they had passed the Pillars of Hercules, and affronted the dangers of the Atlantic. Their frail and small vessels, scarcely bigger than modern fishing-smacks, proceeded southwards along the West African coast, as far as the tract watered by the Gambia and Senegal, while northwards they coasted along Spain, braved the heavy seas of the Bay of Biscay, and passing Cape Finisterre, ventured across the mouth of the English Channel to the Cassiterides . . . [4]

The Phoenicians were allied to, and traded with, another mysterious people of eastern origin, the Etruscans. They made treaties and intermarried with them. Judged as wise by other Semitic peoples, the Phoenicians provided counsellors behind the thrones of Egypt, Assyria, Babylonia and Persia. But at times they were attacked, their cities destroyed. The Phoenicians had no army to fend for themselves, nor had they a military navy; only Carthage felt the need to build and keep a permanent war fleet. They were really a trading people, 'who sailed from one end of the known world to the other, carrying slaves, metal, jewellery, and fine cloth. If they were motivated by gain, "famed for ships, greedy men" [Homer, Odyssey], that was irrelevant to the Greeks, the passive participants in the operation.' Thus wrote M. I. Finley.[5]

One can observe different attitudes towards the Phoenicians expressed in the Iliad and the Odyssey, the latter written two generations later than the former. In the Iliad, the Phoenicians are appreciated for their wares and skills, while the voice of

the *Odyssey* expresses instead the Greeks' contempt for the
Phoenicians as mere traders with piratical tendencies whose ships
lay hidden in every distant creek waiting to steal cargoes, rape and
sell their prisoners into slavery. Although the Hellenes did the same,
the Greeks did not operate as swiftly because they were not as competent sailors. Motivated by jealousy, they mocked the Phoenicians
for their appearance, for the accumulation of riches which they did
not even display and for their ubiquity. In short, I must stress,
although aware that I am repeating myself: the Phoenicians were
the Jews of antiquity.

But what were their origins? The Phoenicians were indeed neighbours of the Hebrews, being part of the Canaanite world which was
formed by earlier waves of Semitic migrations into the territories
between the Mediterranean and the Syrian desert. In Phoenician
and Hebrew legend we find similar characters and names; thus the
Phoenician Usoos is the Biblical Esau, and *kadesh* is a sanctuary in
both languages. Originally they shared a common theology: Baal,
as the Bible indicates in the episode of Aaron, was a Hebrew deity
as much as a Phoenician. Herodotus and other Greek writers note
that both cultures practised circumcision.

The Jews who left the Negev in about 1200 BC spoke a similar
language to the Phoenicians. But before that migration, there were
Canaanites already on the Mediterranean coast; so the two different tribal groups mixed, they expanded, they merged. As early as
2900 BC Byblos was already a town with stone houses and a
drainage system, surrounded by defensive walls. It may have been
destroyed by wild nomadic people. Herodotus thought that the
Phoenicians had arrived from Persia together with the Hebrews, as
an already accomplished civilisation. In the opinion of some modern scholars, the Phoenicians had always occupied the same stretch
of land by the eastern Mediterranean seaboard and had developed
their extraordinary talents through necessity and the stimulus of
surviving on a narrow littoral with little space for expanding
inland; in short, these writers hold the Darwinian theory applied to
the history of populations.

During the Bronze Age the land of Canaan had included all the
coastal territory between the mouth of the Orontes and the Nile
delta, which was the Egyptian frontier to the south. The principal
Phoenician cities were situated on the coast, either on promontories

or on small offshore islands enclosing natural harbours. Such was the case with Byblos, Sarepta, Sidon, Tyre and Arvad, several of which were located on islands close to the coast (like Motya) and therefore almost impregnable.

'Phoenicia was a land squeezed between the mountains and the sea with a great density of population from the tenth century BC onwards and with the Mediterranean as the only possible route for natural expansion,' states Maria-Eugenia Aubet in her magnificent book *The Phoenicians*. As noted above, such arable land as they had was inadequate to supply their populous cities with food, so that they were forced to look towards the sea not only for trade and commerce, but for subsistence. The salting of fish was an important industry which their settlements and future colonies, Motya in particular, were to adopt. The Phoenicians invented a salty sauce made of herbs and fish which had been allowed to rot. It was used as a salt substitute and was adopted by Roman cuisine as garum (from the Greek for 'shrimps').[6] It is still consumed on the Black Sea even today, and I came across a 'factory' making garum in all its different forms as far afield as Thailand. The best garum is made of tuna, considered a delicacy on the Mediterranean table; the cheapest from mackerel or sardine. The English *Patum Peperium* is really just a form of Phoenician garum. The salting process – and also that of producing the dye from murex shells – required fuel; hence the famous cedar forests were cut down and burnt, even in the Bronze Age. But according to Dr Isserlin, 'the cedar forests of Lebanon were diminished mainly by the long-standing tendency to cut timber for sale and requisitioning by conquerors like the Assyrians.'

The salting of the fish, the making of garum, the crushing of the murex shells were all smelly processes. Even at the time of Emperor Augustus, Strabo complained that Tyre reeked of stinking fish; but, as we know, gold never smells.

The Phoenicians' maritime supremacy guaranteed them a degree of political independence in the face of powerful neighbours such as Egypt, Assyria and Babylon, as well as Mycenae; but the Greeks eventually had the better of them not only in Sicily but earlier, when Phoenician ships formed the core of Xerxes' fleet at Salamis.

In the international correspondence archive of Egypt at El Amarna (dating back to the fourteenth century BC), which was found miraculously less than a century ago, the city of Tyre is described as a monarchy enjoying great prestige. Tyre became a most important city in the Mediterranean with the arrival on the throne of Ahizamor Hiram I (969–936 BC). Herodotus estimated that Tyre had been founded in the year 2750 BC because, when he visited it in the fifth century BC, he heard the priests in the temple of Melqart saying that the sanctuary had been built when the city was founded, about 2300 years previously. Excavations confirmed that the foundations of Tyre, whose population numbered 30,000, an immense number for those times, 'are very ancient' (Isaiah 23: 7). Institutions such as the palace and the temple were indistinguishable, and their functions complementary. The house of the king was the house of Melqart. Tyre and other Phoenician cities became the suppliers of precious metals which the monarchies of Egypt and Assyria needed to adorn their palaces. The enormous quantity of silver that Tyre had at its disposal – 'Tyre heaped up silver', says Zechariah (9: 2–3) – came from Anatolia and from the south of Spain.

Hiram, who styled himself 'King of Tyre and of Phoenicia', built three temples, one in honour of Melqart, famous in antiquity for its two great pillars of gold and emerald; the others were dedicated to Astarte and Baal. His prestige derived above all from his political and commercial relations with King Solomon, as a result of which a treaty was signed by both monarchs pledging them to engage in large-scale mutual trade. In return for advanced technology, building materials, technical assistance and luxury goods, Solomon provided Tyre with agricultural produce and 'food for the royal household' (I Kings 5: 11).

With the help of Tyre's architects, Solomon built his temple in Jerusalem. We have an idea of what the Tyrian temple looked like from the accurate description in the Bible (1 Kings 7) of Solomon's temple, which was entirely made by Phoenician workmanship. Its decorations of carved cherubim and palm trees recall motifs in Phoenician artefacts.

Later, King Ittobal (887–856 BC) created a single state, mentioned by Homer and in the Bible, which included Tyre and Sidon. Ittobal's policy consisted in consolidating diplomatic and trade relations through marriage alliances. Therefore Ittobal's daughter, the Jezebel of the Bible, was given in marriage to Ahab (874–853

BC), king of Israel, and she was held responsible for introducing the worship of Baal to Samaria. Ittobal's direct successor was Pygmalion (820–774), Dido's brother.

As Ezekiel had prophesied, Ittobal III, king of Tyre, was deported to Babylon and, after his successor, the institution of monarchy disappeared. Then the new power in the east, the Babylonian empire, began to expand. Nebuchadnezzar, after conquering Jerusalem, laid siege to Tyre for thirteen years (585–572). But only Alexander the Great succeeded in destroying it, over two centuries later.

Byblos was not only the name of a great Phoenician city; it also furnished the Greeks with their word for papyrus, *biblion*, and hence our word 'Bible'. In the fourteenth century BC, Byblos produced the first alphabet – the Phoenicians' greatest legacy to the development of western culture. This arose out of the practical requirements of the people, who needed a system of recording their trade transactions less complicated than Egyptian hieroglyphics and cursive forms or Akkadian cuneiform. Those latter writing systems had existed for a long time but were complex, derived from picture-writing which required a very large number of symbols. They could only be interpreted by experts; these experts, the scribes, thus held a monopoly on literacy and therefore on culture (like the Jesuits). The scribes wielded great power all over the known world; and indeed, not unlike the Jesuits, became a feared and dominating class.

The Phoenician alphabet, by contrast, was democratic and easily accessible, and its revolutionary concept transformed all other writing systems. We still use Phoenician names for the two first letters of the Greek alphabet: *alef* (Greek alpha) was the ox – the sign represents the simplified head of a bull turned around – and *beth* (Greek beta), the house. The Phoenician genius, stimulated by necessity, devised a system to represent the sounds of the consonants and compressed them into a writing code at first of up to twenty-eight and then only twenty-two Phonetic signs. The designation of the letters has been preserved down to our day, thanks to the mediation of the Greeks and then of the Latins. The Greeks started using the alphabet in its modified form (to which they attached a few more signs for vowels) towards the seventh century BC, a hundred years after Homer and after the foundation of

Carthage. They called it Cadmian letters, after Cadmus, the Phoenician prince who founded Thebes. If nothing else assures the Phoenicians' glory and our gratitude to them, the alphabet alone must do so.

Numbers were not so brilliantly devised: indeed, we find that the Phoenicians sometimes used letters for counting purposes, as, for example, when they made a series of prefabricated pieces of wood which, assembled, formed a ship.

What remains of Phoenician literature is scant, consisting only of some inscriptions on tombs and a number of legends. And yet it is extraordinary that, although we cannot read the inscriptions on Etruscan sarcophagi, we can interpret Phoenician writing, which is earlier and which, like all Semitic languages, is written from right to left. One of the reasons why Phoenician records are so few may be the material on which they were set down. In Phoenicia there was an abundance of papyrus, bought from Egypt or grown locally; and papyrus deteriorates. A handful of Greek sources – Lucian of Samosata's *De Syria Dea, Fragments of the Phoenician History* by Philo of Byblos and the writings of Damascius – give us an intimate glimpse of this elusive people. At times, though, their accounts conflict, and that is why archaeology is such an important source of knowledge for our understanding of the Phoenicians – and why Motya is a book waiting to be opened.

We have echoes, fragments of literary texts which have disappeared. Probably the longest inscription extant is sculpted on the sepulchre of Ahiram, which I saw in May 1998 in a crowded room in Paris, where it had been sent for an exhibition. Invoking celestial threats on us visitors as we admired the stretched muscles of carved lions and lotus flowers on the massive monolith, it read:

Coffin which Ittobal, son of Ahiram, king of Byblos, made for Ahiram, his father, when he placed him in the house of eternity. Now, if a king among kings or a governor among governors or a commander of an army should come up against Byblos and uncover this coffin, may the sceptre of his rule be torn away, may the throne of his kingdom be overturned, and may peace flee from Byblos! And as for him, may his inscription be effaced! [7]

The biblical tone of this message has the self-assurance of a prophecy and a precise poetry.

Glass manufacture was another Phoenician development; although they borrowed the technique from the Egyptians, they succeeded in creating a transparency that the Egyptians were unable to obtain. Translucent coloured glass was produced for beads and other ornaments; indeed, the huge emerald column described by Herodotus in the temple of Melqart at Tyre was probably a glass cylinder which shone at night.[8]

How were the Phoenician cities governed? We know that their system of government had points in common as well as differences. In Tyre, for example, the sovereign could not act with full political autonomy; his powers were limited by the merchant oligarchy. On the whole the Phoenician monarchy was hereditary and had priestly functions; Ittobal I was the 'priest of Astarte', and generally priests sanctioned the power of the monarchy.

The kings were advised by a council of elders, representing the most powerful families of the city. In Carthage – we know more about that city's institutions than those of Tyre or Sidon – the Council of Ten was the basis of political power, but in special circumstances, especially when danger approached, power was assumed by only two elders. The Council of State functioned in Tyre, Byblos and Carthage from the seventh to third centuries BC and dealt with questions concerning religion and taxes. Earlier, at the time of the fall of Troy, the Phoenician cities were ruled by either a single monarch or two monarchs, one of whom was a priest. In ancient times these paired monarchs were brothers, like Moses and Aaron among the Israelites, and ruled over tribes advised by popular assemblies. Later, cities (including Motya) were governed by civil magistrates called suffetes, rather than by a monarch or tyrant.

As for their spiritual beliefs, the Phoenicians predate modern thought not only in their conviction that the afterlife was nothingness, but in the belief that life came from water. God was fire, therefore spiritual essence. Because deity was fire, the Phoenicians had been unable to steal it from the gods, unlike the Greeks, who honoured Prometheus, the greatest of human heroes, for this feat. From the so-called *Fragments of the Phoenician History* by Philo of Byblos, we learn that chaos became order, as in *Das Rheingold*:

The beginning of all things was a dark and stormy air . . . from Pothos
[Desire]. Embrace with the wind generated Mot, [9] which some call slime
and other putrescence of watery secretion. And from this sprang all the
seed of creation, and the generation of the universe. And there were certain animals without sensation, from which intelligent animals were
produced; and they were made in the shape of an egg and from Mot
shone forth the sun and the moon and the lesser and the greater stars.
When the air began to send forth light, by the conflagration of land and
sea, winds were produced and clouds and very great downpours, and
effusion of the heavenly waters. And when these were thus separated and
carried through the heat of the sun, placed upon their proper places and
all met again in the air, and came into collision, there ensued thunderings
and lightning; and through the rattle of the thunder the intelligent animals above mentioned were woken up and, startled by the noise, began
to move both in the sea and in the land, and some were male and some
were female.

This is the beginning of life according to the Phoenicians: close to
what the Bible evokes and to what science recounts. And indeed,
this is also my version of the history of the Phoenicians, which is
immense and changes constantly as more clues are unearthed and
solved, thus generating greater interest in their achievements. The
notion that we derive from them as well as from other historical
routes is quite new.

The history of the Phoenicians' Punic offspring is a different
one; more is known about them because they belong to a more
modern era, but the line which divides them from the Phoenicians is
blurred. It is the Punics' history that interests me most, because
Motya came to belong to the Punic world. So I shall now recount
the story of the Punic people according to myself.

7

WHO WERE THE PUNICS?

They say that the fair Europa, only daughter of the Phoenician king Agenor otherwise called Canaan, used to walk by the sea with her young companions. They sang and played, they washed their feet and gathered beautiful shells. One day Europa was startled by the sight of a white bull which stood by the shore, and this bull was so unusual because of its shining snow-white skin and its gentleness that she approached it and started to caress its soft coat. We know now that this bull was none other than Zeus, king of gods and men, who, in order to avoid arousing the jealousy of his consort Hera, used to appear under a different disguise whenever he fell in love with a mortal. Zeus had indeed fallen in love with Europa, whose name in Phoenician could be interpreted as meaning broad-faced (an attribute of Astarte, the moon goddess) or, strangely (though perhaps more plausibly), the opposite: dark-faced, darkness, the dark – in other words, the west. Europa approached the white bull and entwined garlands around its horns. But, when finally she playfully climbed on its back, it trotted down the beach into the sea and swam away, bearing her with it. The princess's companions went crying to the king, telling him that his only daughter, his favourite child, had been abducted by a white bull. Distraught, King Canaan called his sons to him and told them to go out and look for their sister, and not to return unless they had found her.

This is how the Greeks turned the Phoenician colonization into a myth. The quest for Europa depicted all the routes of the sea: to Carthage, to the Black Sea and Cilicia, to Cyprus and Crete.

What King Agenor/Canaan did not know was that, having swum to faraway Crete, Zeus ravished Europa near Gortyna: the plane tree that witnessed this sacred union was, in recognition of this, never to lose its foliage. Europa had three children by Zeus, one of

which was Minos, future king of Crete and judge of Hades; but this
part of the myth takes us away from the focus of our attention,
which is the wanderings of the Phoenician princes.

Phoenix, Canaan's eldest son, was sent on his quest to Libya, to
Carthage, where I shall return shortly. The king's second son, Cilix,
went to Cilicia, in Asia Minor. This was the most northern limit of
Phoenicia, on the frontier with Assyria. Tarsus, the Cilician city
with which we are familiar for its connection with the apostle Paul,
had a mixed population which included Greeks, but for centuries it
was considered to be a Phoenician city. Thasos, the third son, went
first to Olympia, where he built a statue to Melqart which he named
the Tyrian Heracles, and then proceeded to colonize an island
which Herodotus describes as rich in gold mines (possibly Ibiza in
the Balearic islands).

Canaan's fourth son was called Cadmus, and he became the
father of the Greeks. First he went to Delphi to consult the oracle in
order to find out where his sister was. The sibyl (another
Phoenician inheritance), the Pythia, found in the dark cavity of her
mysterious knowledge that Zeus himself was involved in the disappearance of the Phoenician princess. Wisely deciding not to divulge
her secret to anybody, let alone Prince Cadmus, she told him instead
to go to Boeotia. Here he slew a dragon; from its teeth, which he
planted in the ground, arose companions with whom he built
Thebes. Proof of the Phoenician presence in Thebes is supported by
the recent discovery of Canaanite bronzes on the site. There is an
echo of the adventures of the Argonauts in this strange story;
indeed, the grandson of Cadmus' eldest brother Phoenix was celebrated for his knowledge of the stars and became helmsman of the
mythical ship *Argo*.

Cadmus is much loved by the Greeks because he taught them the
letters of the alphabet, which they called Cadmean after him.
Herodotus writes of 'Phoenicians of the number of those
Phoenicians who came with Cadmus to the land which is now
called Boeotia . . . [They] taught other kinds of knowledge to the
Greeks, and specially that of letters which, I think, the Greeks did
not previously possess.' Cadmus married Harmony, daughter of
Ares, god of war, and of Aphrodite, goddess of youth and beauty,
who is in origin the Phoenician goddess Astarte; his was the last
nuptial banquet in which the gods participated together with the

mortals. The same banquet was alas ruined when a golden apple addressed to 'the most beautiful of all' was thrown into its midst by an uninvited guest. The three main goddesses, Hera, Athena and Aphrodite, contested that title, and their quarrel led to the Trojan war. Here the myth gives us another clue to the Phoenician involvement in Middle Eastern commercial wars, as well as an indication of the arrival in the Greek pantheon of Astarte/Aphrodite.

Cadmus (KDM) means the east, while Europa represents the sun sinking into darkness, the west, where the sun sets. Thus in this mythology we, Europe, are a concept perceived from the east. Europa is raped by the Greeks, by their most illustrious deity, Zeus. Together they produce the king of Crete, the origin of Hellenic power. Cadmus' daughter Semele was burned alive because of her curiosity to see her lover, Zeus once again, in his full fiery splendour. The rite of burning alive, aimed at achieving purification through fire, also indicates Phoenician ancestry.

The Greeks passed down to posterity the remote traditions of their debt to the Phoenicians through their wonderful mythological language. We should not scoff at this or belittle it; when modern history is lacking in information or when we want to rewrite it, we too use mythology. It is not far-fetched to say, for example, that for most of the French Napoleon is a mythological concept; in other words, the truth has been embellished and events reimagined to the extent where his reported deeds correspond to historical reality in only a very limited way.

In any case, as the mythology tells, the four (in some versions they are three) princes searched for their sister Europa in vain. Since they could not go back to their father empty-handed, they settled here and there, giving a mythical foundation to the history of the Punics in the Mediterranean.

The term 'Punic' calls for explanation. Inevitably, there is some conflict among the various theories. Roman authors used the terms *poenus* and *phoenix*, which are transcriptions of the Greek word *phoinix* used in respect of the Carthaginians in particular. *Poenus*, along with its adjective *punicus,* alludes to the North African Phoenicians. Modern historians have made a distinction between the peoples to whom the terms Punic and Phoenician are applied: those of the east are called Phoenician, while those of the west in the Carthaginian sphere of influence are called Punic.

Herodotus, too, made a distinction between Phoenicians and Punics, whom he called by the collective name of Carthaginians, as in the following description of their method of trading:

There is a country in Libya and a nation beyond the pillars of Hercules, which the Carthaginians are wont to visit, where they no sooner arrive than they forthwith unladen their wares, and having disposed them after an orderly fashion along the beach, they leave them and, returning aboard their ships, raise a great smoke. The natives, when they see the smoke, come down to the shore and, laying out to view so much gold as they think the wares are worth, withdraw to a distance. The Carthaginians upon this come ashore again and look. If they think the gold is enough, they take it and go their way; but if it does not seem to them sufficient, they go aboard their ship once more and wait patiently. Then the others approach and add to their gold till it comes up to the worth of their goods, nor do the natives ever carry off the goods until the gold has been taken away. [1]

There is a certain 'talking down' in this passage, because by the time Herodotus was writing, the most prominent Punic cities had struck coins which circulated in most of the Mediterranean basin.

Some scholars insist on using the word Punic only in the later, Roman, context: that is, from just before the First Punic War when Carthage and Rome came into open conflict. Others use the term from the time at which the Phoenicians moved into the Mediterranean basin in order to found colonies. 'When they started to live in large cities like Motya,' Professor Tusa explained to me emphatically, 'they are to be called Punics, there is no question, and we all agree. This is because by adopting the locals' customs, they became different from the Phoenicians. Therefore they can't be called Phoenicians any longer because they have developed differently from them, so we use the word which is a Latin mistranslation of the Greek *phoinix*.'

As the heirs of Canaan moved into Africa towards the end of the ninth century BC and started building cities rather than mere settlements, so they began to intermarry locally, the Carthaginians with the Libyans and the Motyans with the Sicels, the Sicans and the Elymians. As they adopted some of the local customs and absorbed the indigenous cultures, their religion and language changed. Their hero Melqart became first Heracles and then Hercules, while new deities like Tanit arrived from the desert and merged with Baalat and Astarte.

Like the Greek cities, Carthage found its green hinterland too limited to support a growing population. As a maritime city, its army was not strong, consisting mainly of mercenaries; but in order to defend its trade routes it built the mightiest naval force ever seen, with which it paved the roads of the sea. Inland routes, after all, only led to the Sahara.

Carthage, in contrast with Tyre, developed into an aggressive power – perhaps because it had been founded by a displaced aristocracy. Instead of one king, Carthage was ruled by the oligarchy which had founded the city, and this change in governance coincided with a certain change in religion and civic attitudes. All these developments can be traced to the sixth century BC and were common to the whole Punic world, including Motya.

The Carthaginians soon found that their overall control of the trading routes of the Mediterranean basin would not be accepted by the Greeks (nor, later, by the Romans) so they had to go on strengthening their navy to defend their mercantile fleet. This navy was used to come to the aid of all those cities which paid an annual tribute, like Motya. The maintenance of a large navy made heavy demands on public funds, so people had to be taxed to support it.

The Punics were more isolated than their kin, the Phoenicians. They found themselves surrounded by alien peoples, or indeed by earlier Phoenician colonies which had developed into rivals, like Utica. Their very isolation provoked a form of insecurity which resulted in a tendency towards cruel behaviour. The practice of crucifying military leaders who lost their battles must be read in this way (the origin of crucifixion as the ultimate form of punishment is ascribed to the Punics). Although human sacrifice had been widespread in the ancient world, it was by this period generally on the wane, while the Punics continued to sacrifice their children in their religious rites in order to appease their gods.

The Punics never felt sure of their ground. Indeed, the very ground on which Carthage was built had been secured through a clever trick employed by the resourceful Elissa/Dido, the queen–goddess who founded the great capital city. She named it the New City or, in a better translation, the New Capital City: Qart-

Hadash, Carthage. Elissa, whom the natives called 'the one who wanders' (Dido), killed herself by self-immolation, thus attaining deification because, for the Punics, fire purified and made immortal.

The myth of Carthage's birth has reached us from various Greek sources (Virgil used Dido to justify a power struggle just as Homer used the figure of Helen), but there is no question about the fact that the founder of the city was a princess from Tyre called Elissa or Elisha, daughter of King Mattan of Tyre, a grand-niece of the biblical Jezebel. In the words of Virgil, Dido greets the Trojan hero Aeneas thus:

This is a new kingdom, and it is harsh necessity that forces me to take precautions and to post guards on all our frontiers. But who could fail to know about the people of Aeneas and his ancestry, or the city of Troy, the valour of its men and the flames of war that engulfed it? We here in Carthage are not so dull in mind as that. The sun does spare a glance for our Tyrian city when he yokes his horses in the morning. Whether you choose to go to the great Hesperia and the fields of Saturn, or to the land of Eryx and King Acestes, you will leave here safe under my protection, and I shall give you supplies to help you on your way. Or do you wish to settle here with me on an equal footing, even here in this kingdom of Carthage? The city which I am founding is yours . . .²

Together with the Tyrian nobility, Dido had recently arrived in that part of Africa as a fugitive. When King Mattan died in 814 BC, his son Pygmalion, aged only eleven, was made to share his throne with his sister Elissa. Their joint rule lasted seven years, after which Elissa fled because of a political upheaval.³ Elissa's husband, Acharbas or Zakarbaal, high priest of Melqart, had become the real power behind the throne. He was extremely rich and had taken possession of the city's treasury – although, being in charge of a temple which was also used as bank, this seems quite natural. Besides being Elissa's husband, Acharbas was also her uncle (probably King Mattan's younger brother). It seemed that the king had meant to leave the throne to Elissa's and Acharbas' two children, but the Tyrians rebelled; Pygmalion therefore ordered his uncle's assassination to appease the rebels. This version of the story of a Tyrian civil war between monarchy and nobility is related by several Greek authors. Maria-Eugenia Aubet writes: 'Sceptics consider that any historical reference to Carthage that predates the fifth century BC is a myth, as, too is the story of its foundation and the figure of Elissa–Dido ... But there are too many coincidences between eastern and classical sources to allow us to think that the story of Elissa had no historical basis ... From the Annal of Tyre it appears that around the year 820 BC Mattan I left the throne of Tyre in the hands of his son Pygmalion.'[4]

As the high priest, Acharbas/Zakarbaal may have been joint king of Tyre together with his brother-in-law; or it may have been that while Acharbas was the king–priest and Elissa his wife was the queen, Pygmalion was merely the queen's half-brother, the son of the late king by a concubine. Or again, Acharbas might also have been the king's son by another wife. Whatever the precise nature of these complex relationships, they could certainly have caused political strife.

A slightly different story relates that Acharbas, having appropriated his wife's riches, was going to lend them to foreign rulers, thus limiting his brother-in-law's power. Therefore, full of hatred and fearing for his throne, Pygmalion had Acharbas murdered and the alarmed Elissa decided to leave Tyre, taking with her the temple treasure and the god Melqart's sacred vessels – indications of her position as queen–priestess. The young monarch, supported by the populace, had won out against the aristocracy, who were with Elissa and her husband; in short, the lay side of Tyre had overcome the religious. The high priestess escaped with the god's insignia (Carthage would indeed become an important religious centre) while the high priest himself had been murdered. Could this have been an attempt to re-establish monotheism in the city of Tyre? Could Acharbas have been a mystic, like the Pharaoh Akhenaten? Certainly the struggle between priesthood and monarchy is not rare in the Middle Bronze and Iron Ages in the Middle East, any more than it was in the western world centuries later. I think that the Tyrian saga can be read in this way. All the signs are there. Moreover, there is evidence that the institution of god–king in Tyre was giving way to a straightforward monarchy assisted by an assembly of elders, so that the high priesthood could no longer count on the political power of a monarch with the spiritual power of a priest. But the priesthood retained its financial strength, demonstrated by many details in the story of Elissa's escape from Tyre with the city's treasure.

By this time Tyre was no longer a town but had developed into a real capital. Its social order had become complex; the king was no longer just a clan leader, related to almost everybody and seen to graze his sheep, as described by Homer. The era in which kings had to adopt the status of divinity in order to differentiate themselves from their fellow men and arrogate more authority to themselves was on the wane in Phoenicia. It was to re-emerge in Carthage which, at the time of its foundation, was clearly a very small community.

Shrewd as she was, Elissa obtained a fleet from her brother king Pygmalion by pretending that she was ready to forgive him, and sailed away together with those factions of the Tyrian nobility which decided to flee the city with her. Her companions included some of the princely names of Carthage: Barcas, for example, head of the Barcidas clan and ancestor of Hannibal the Great; and Bitias, the commander of the Tyrian fleet. Intending to found another city, Elissa stopped at Cyprus, a Phoenician colony, where the expedition, which begins to resemble the Argonauts with a female leader, collected eighty young girls destined for sacred prostitution. In this way the future of the ousted Tyrian nobility was assured. The Carthaginian adventure was about to start.

This part of the myth seems clear enough: the Tyrians abducted eighty young maidens from Cyprus and took them away on their ships in a kind of maritime precursor of the rape of the Sabine women. On the other hand, since the Phoenicians practised sacred prostitution, and Cyprus (Kition) was a famous centre of sanctuary dedicated to Astarte, it could easily be that the girls willingly followed the rich princes in their adventure. The historical Pygmalion (the name is Greek; in Phoenician it was Pummayyaton) was married to a Cypriot priestess of Astarte.

The expedition arrived on the North African coast at Utica, an older Phoenician colony. The inhabitants were hospitable and their king, Hierbas, welcomed the nobles into his territory; but he offered them only as much land as could be covered by an ox-hide. The high priestess and queen, whom the natives called Dido, 'the wandering one' – a female Odysseus – devised a stratagem. She had always thought of founding a great settlement rather than allowing her followers to attach themselves to King Hierbas or anyone else. So she cut the skin of an ox into such fine strips that it could encompass the perimeter of an entire hill. Here Dido and her nobles founded their new city; the hill was called Byrsa in Greek, meaning ox-hide.[5]

Hierbas, king of the Mitanni or Massitani, wanted to marry Elissa; but she, horrified at the thought of betraying the memory of her dead husband, opted for self-immolation by throwing herself into a pyre. By burning, Dido achieved purification and immortality; by her sacrifice she became celebrated as one of Carthage's main deities until the city was conquered and destroyed.

It must be stressed that Carthage was not founded as part of a colonization programme, because the Phoenicians had already had a harbour at Utica. Carthage was born not as a mercantile trading post but as a settlement of aristocratic refugees. 'The founding of Carthage was the work of Tyrian aristocrats who came into the possession of lands because of their status and who maintained links with Tyre for generations in spite of such an inauspicious beginning,' writes Maria-Eugenia Aubet. Every year Carthage sent a tenth of its public treasury as a tribute to Tyre and to its main temple to Melqart. Motya, likewise, sent tribute to Carthage – not immediately on its foundation, some thirty years after that of the North African city, but beginning a century and a half later when Motya itself developed into a city, the Greeks began to attack it and it had to build defensive walls and think of military strength as well as trade. These annual payments show that Carthage remained under the protection of Tyre for a long time, just as Motya remained under that of Carthage. So, in spite of the fact that Motya might in all probability have been founded by Phoenicians, its primary dependence on Carthage and its intermingling with the neighbouring tribes justifies us in calling the city and its inhabitants Punic.

The cult of Melqart was introduced to Carthage at its foundation: as mentioned above, Elissa brought with her from Tyre all the objects sacred to Melqart, who symbolized the deified monarchy and its treasury. Tanit and Baal were to become popular deities in the Punic world later on, and represented the oligarchy. The names of the Carthaginian nobility reflected their religious affiliations. Baal, as we have seen, meant 'Lord' in the divine sense, so that, for example, Baalshamen meant Lord of the Sky; other names using the same root are Baal Addir, Baaldir and Hannibal. Sid-Melqart was the son of Melqart; Hamilcar, A-melkar, was a general who, like Dido, immolated himself in the fire. Suicide by fire was an integral part of the religion, reflecting Melqart's resurrection and immortality through sacrifice.

'There was an ancient city held by colonists from Tyre, opposite Italy and the distant mouth of the river Tiber. It was a city of great wealth and ruthless in the pursuit of war. Its name was Carthage.' This is how Virgil describes the Punic capital.[6] When Dido turned down the king of Utica's proposal of marriage his people, the Mitanni, waged war on the new arrivals (was Utica ordered by Tyre to drive out the rebels? or were the rebels heretics?) But the newcomers won – in Virgil's version, aided by Aeneas, the Trojan hero.

Carthage was built on a peninsula in the Gulf of Tunis, in a location very similar to that of Tyre and of Motya, and controlled the shipping routes towards the west. Its port was in the centre of the city and consisted of two artificial harbours, the first roughly rectangular, just like Motya's cothon, but larger, and the other more rounded. The former was used as a bay for careening, the latter for loading and unloading, and both were connected to the sea by a canal about 30 metres wide which could be barred by an iron chain. When not temporarily in harbour, all the Carthaginian ships remained outside, in the shallow waters of the bay. In addition. Carthage had a naval harbour which could hold about 200 ships and was managed by the port authorities. The mercantile elite which constituted the great 'men of the city' appears to have belonged to the princely families from its very beginnings.

The city expanded to cover a huge area. There were barracks, arsenals and stables for 300 elephants and 4,000 horses. Byrsa, the fortified citadel at the initial core of the city, was enclosed by a high wall and used both as a fortress and as a bank where treasures were stored. It also contained the state archive; in short, Byrsa was the very heart of Carthage. The market was below it near the Senate House, while the huge tophet, the place of prayers and human sacrifice, was a short walk to the south at a place called Salammbo.

Both Carthage and Motya were famous throughout the ancient world for their tall houses, much admired by seafarers. There was no need to build upwards in Carthage since there was no shortage of space here, but in building up to six storeys the Punics were imitating Tyre, the model they knew. Their temples, however, could not compare with those in Tyre. The principal one was dedicated to Baal-Eshmun (the Greeks identified Eshmun with Asklepios) – which could have been another aspect of Melqart – but there were also temples dedicated to Astarte and Tanit, who was to become the principal female deity of the Punics. The construction of these temples was funded by donations and they were managed by a hereditary priesthood.

Punic culture and military power sprang from Carthage, which kept a firm control over 'its' sea and its dependencies. Two centuries after its foundation, Carthage was confronting the Phocaeans, originally of Greek stock, in the north Mediterranean; in the year 509 it concluded a treaty with Rome setting out their respective allocations of territory and political influence. Forced to develop its military power to the detriment of the original Phoenician settlers' commercial aims, Carthage had to exact money from its own colonies in order to protect them with its fleet from the waves of Greek and subsequent Roman colonists.

Agriculturally, the Carthaginian territory was rich and lovingly tended. Cereals, vines and olives were produced with such experience and skill that the Romans acknowledged the expertise of the Punics by translating the famous treatise of Mago, one of the many such texts on agronomy written by the Punics. Cultivated fields, worked mainly by slave labour, surrounded the capital. The native Libyans took care of the animals (sheep, goats, horses, elephants, etc.) but were only allowed to cultivate their own land as long as they paid tribute to Carthage.

'In Motya, the Phoenicians enjoyed a twofold geopolitical advantage: their alliance and good relations with the Elymians of western Sicily and the proximity to Carthage, on the other side of the Sicilian straits,' writes Aubet.[7] 'The fact that it was occupied without interruption from the end of the eighth to the fourth century BC makes Motya one of the best known Phoenician nuclei and one of the few in which it has been possible to analyse the whole Phoenicio-Punic cultural sequence.' On Mount Eryx, which was not strictly part of their territory, the Punics built a temple to Melqart/Heracles; another, dedicated to Astarte/Aphrodite/Venus, stood on a small plateau on the mountain's summit, just above the town. This temple became one of the best known in the ancient world not only because of its superb position but because it practised sacred prostitution. The Phoenician deities were adopted by the Elymians, the people from Eryx, and sacred prostitution continued to be practised even in Roman times. Young women from the nobility offered themselves to the goddess; they lived in a precinct which was visited by foreigners. These would pick the woman of their choice, lie with her and pay a fee to the priests of Astarte. Only then could the young woman, probably aged twelve or thirteen, go back home and start a proper family. The Phoenician Astarte, also identified as Baalat or Pene Hammon, was a powerful deity. The faithful believed that the goddess visited Africa every year and, after nine days' absence, returned home to her mountain temple. Her departure was indicated by the disappearance of the doves which were sacred to her, and her return by their reappearance. At the same time each year the image of Astarte was itself carried to Africa and brought back again.

The wanderings of Aeneas (who, according to Dionysius of Halicarnassus, is a Phoenician and not a Trojan hero, and who founded the temple of Aphrodite at Cythera in Greece), followed the same pattern as those of Cadmus. Before arriving at Carthage, Aeneas went to eastern Sicily and then on to Motya – as, in Virgil's words, he tells Dido:

At the entrance of the bay of Syracuse, opposite the wave-beaten headland of Plemyrium, there stands an island which men of old called Ortygia. The story goes that the river-god Alpheus of Elis forced his way here by hidden passages at the mouth of Arethusa's fountain. Obeying the instructions we had received, we worshipped the great gods of the place and I then sailed, leaving behind the rich lands around the marshy river Helorus. From here we rounded Cape Pachynus, keeping close to its jutting cliffs of rock, and Camerina came into view in the distance, the place the Fates forbade to move, and then the Geloan planes and Gela itself, called after its turbulent river. Then in the far distance appeared the great walls of Acragas on its crag, once famous for the breeding of high-mettled horses. Next the wind carried me past Selinus, named after the parsley it gave to crown the victors in Greek games, and I steered past the dangerous shoals and hidden rocks of Lilybaeum.

I then put into port at Drepanum, but had little joy of that shore. This was the place where, weary as I was with all these batterings of sea and storm, to my great grief I lost my father Anchises . . . [8]

Aeneas' mother was Venus, Astarte: the earth mother, the goddess of life, of youth and beauty. She had flown from Carthage in the shape of a dove, and became less pugnacious than in her Phoenician incarnation. Besides giving life, she caused death, and hence she was also the goddess of the underworld. In this guise she was later identified as the Bitter Goddess, the Greek Persephone. There were several stelae in Motya and Lilybaeum not so much dedicated to her as appealing to her as the goddess of darkness, entrusting the dead to her. Through these poetic words we can come to understand more of Punic life; they allow us to approach the people of Motya, even to imagine what they were like and how they might have lived – and died.

A husband lost his beautiful young wife; his regret and loss are made poetically plain in the stone he sculpted which proclaims his sorrow. In the Punic belief in death as eternal fog, he cannot but recommend his wife Allia Prima to the goddess (Astarte/Persephone); this apart, there is no afterlife, no eternal bliss for Allia Prima. But he pleads with Hermes, who is to accompany her (some Greek names of deities had already been adopted) and with the 'dark goddess', to appreciate his wife's youth and beauty. There are two inscribed sides to this stela. On the first is written:

I beg you Hermes who keep underground, you and many of your group who cannot see images: the gift I send you, the girl, before she arrives. I question you: I give you the girl before she arrives: a beautiful gift. I give you a beautiful girl, fine gift, ears that hear, a lovely bosom, Allia Prima who has beautiful hair, a fine face, lovely eyelashes, beautiful eyes, two smooth cheeks, two nostrils, mouth, teeth, smooth ears, neck, shoulders, extremities, I put her under the earth, that the sepulchre might be agreeable to you. I write this letter for Allia Prima.

And on the other side:

A heart. Cerberus of Allia Prima. Beautiful neck, beautiful body, lovely knees, beautiful all and her extremities. Allia Prima I give to thee as a gift so that you pass her on to the Bitter Lady. I ask you Hermes that keep them underground, you of the underworld because it is you who take away Allia Prima, a gift to Lady Persephone, I bury. [9]

The Punics were highly superstitious, and believed that they could put a curse on their enemies by engraving threats on thin strips of lead which were fixed in places where the gods of the underworld could see them. In Latin these strips were called *defixiones* from the verb 'to nail', as the horrible words were nailed inside wells or near grottoes. This fixation with written curses has been inherited by the Spanish world (which was partly Punic) and certainly by the Punic side of Sicily.

Maybe the Punics lived in awe of the future. They were not serene people; their art is not sunny, their mythology and religion are frightening; they were perpetually apprehensive, never territorially secure. They would ask the sibyl when to found a new city; the Pythia at Delphi had this very role, and that is why she sent Cadmus to found Thebes. But the sibyl never told the Punics that they were doomed, as indeed she did not tell Cadmus the truth about his sister although she knew it. The sibyls never explained that the Punics would lose their war for control of the Mediterranean so thoroughly that their memory would be almost obliterated from the knowledge of future generations.

Back in Sicily, at Lilybaeum, and in search of the Punic sibyl, I drove along Cape Boeo. Here I stopped, lucky enough to find the pretty girl who holds the key to the church of St John, a modest building standing in an open field littered with rotten banana peel, discarded papers and broken bottles. The field is partly covered by cement, which has stopped once and for all any possible search for those temples recorded on that site. The church itself is of no interest, but it was built over a place originally holy to the Punics, the Greeks, the Romans and then the Christians. It is a large natural grotto, linked to the surface by two ramps of stairs cut into the stone. These lead down to an underground room. Here, on one side, on a bed carved into the stone the sibyl could lie down, while her voice would echo inside the large cavity of the grotto and be heard from an aperture above. A large platform led to a pool which at first I judged to be empty, such is the amazing transparency of this extraordinary spring of limpid water, as fresh and abundant during the summer as in winter. This was the grotto of the sibyl.

The grotto had become a church and the spring is held to be as miraculous now as it was when this perennially fresh water, so near to the sea, was thought to indicate that some god had wanted that place to be a centre of human activity. Diodorus recounts how Hannibal, in 409 BC, camped his 200,000 soldiers and 4,000 horsemen near a well that, at that time, was called Lilybaeum and that many years later would give its name to the city. The source still gushed fresh water, from which I drank in the name of St John; earlier visitors would have drunk in the name of the Sibylla Lilybaetana or Sibylla Punica. She was supposed to have lain on the carved stone and exploded into divine paroxysms, while from above the faithful would question her and throw money down inside the grotto. Modern coins glittered under the shallow water, given to St John in some mute request. A seventeenth-century document claimed that, by drinking this water, the faithful received from St John the virtue of knowing their own future. Which St John, the Baptist or the Evangelist, was not specified; it may even have been a third one.

The Phoenicians, so Greek writers tell us, chose to rebuild Motya on the site of the sibyl's grotto not only because of its strategic position, but because 'it had a source of fresh water near the sea which sprang up the whole time'. The spring was probably marked by a simple Phoenician temple, maybe dedicated to Baal or to Tanit. Later the temple must have been rededicated to some Latin god – maybe Apollo, since sibyls and their prophecies were attributed to him.

Although it was fairly animated, the centre of Marsala seemed ghostly, with its ostentatiously rich food, shops and cafés. In contrast, a little man selling nuts which nobody bought stood alone in the main square opposite the vast Baroque church. I entered the café, where I tried three dry Marsala wines, served in differently shaped glasses and at varying temperatures according to their taste.

Maybe Allia Prima had been the victim of one of those horrible black strips of lead, the *defixiones*, I thought to myself.

But my mind went back to Carthage, the great city across the straits, where Phoenix, Cadmus' brother, had first gone to look for his sister Europa. He searched and, never finding her, settled there, since he could not go back to his father without her. He was the eldest son of Canaan, the Phoenician king, the one who was expected to find Europa. But Dido came to Carthage instead; and maybe she was Phoenix's sister in another guise. When she flung herself in the flames, she surrendered her kingdom in order to become a goddess. She made a human sacrifice of herself, setting a horrible precedent which was to claim victims for a long time to come.

8

RELIGION AND
HUMAN SACRIFICE

The most sombre aspect of the Punics' religion was that human sacrifice was carried out from the dawn of Carthage to its sunset. Although apologists for the Punics have been quick to protest that this practice has been exaggerated by the hostility of the anti-Phoenician 'press', archaeology speaks clearly, and it speaks against the apologists.

When the community was under threat, a child had to be sacrificed in order to please and placate the god. The rite was inherited from Canaanite times, when Moloch or Mot, god of the beginning and of consuming fire and the divinity who dried up springs, was a lord (Baal) who could only be satiated by human flesh. The biblical book of Jeremiah describes in chapter 35 how 'they built altars to Baal to lead their sons and daughters through the fire to Moloch' and 'to burn their children by fire as a burnt-offering to Baal'. Although this god would accept bulls and horses, children, being the most beloved possessions of their parents, were the offerings most likely to pacify him. The custom was passed on from Canaan to succeeding waves of immigrants or invaders, and continued after 1200 BC, although it probably ceased earlier in the neighbouring Judaea. The Greeks and Latins abhorred the practice but the Punics, long after the Phoenicians, continued it in spite of pressure and censure from their neighbours.

A procession would form near the house of the family whose child was to be sacrificed and would proceed towards the tophet. This sacred enclosure was usually located just beside the city centre; smaller towns did not have a tophet so they had to carry out their sacrifices elsewhere. A community like Motya built a tophet where generations of its children were offered to Baal as soon as the city was founded. The procession would be accompanied by percussion players, the loud sound and lively rhythm of the drums drowning the cries of the child. A sacrifice by fire was effective and welcomed by the god only if executed willingly, not with tears and lamentations. Parents would force a grim smile on to their faces when marching towards the tophet accompanied by their panic-stricken children. Their impassive expressions displayed an inhuman sense of discipline which was a trademark of the Carthaginian patrician stock; it was the nobility who had imposed this sacrifice on itself. When, in their decadence, the Punic nobility sacrificed adopted children rather than their own, or cheated the god by 'passing through fire' a slave child, the deity was considered to become angry and take revenge on the city.

Some writers of classical times said that the name 'Sardinia' derived from the sardonic smile which accompanied the sacrifice of infants. According to other sources, the word 'sardonic' itself derived from the smiling masks which the victims had to wear and which were found in profusion covering the stelae at Motya's tophet; many of these can be seen today in the Motya museum. These frightening masks were moulded in clay and painted in gaudy colours; their grimace has something of the spooky circus clown. They certainly have no aesthetic pretensions, but they might have been a reflection of the god's appearance. By entering the underworld wearing a god-like mask, the cherub would be accepted into the Punic Olympus. An ancient Canaanite myth said that the birth of the perfect cherub is out of the fire; that a cherub walking in fire suggested immortality. In Oriental mythology, fire and the rite of cremation symbolized immortality and purity.

The priests of Baal-Hammon would prepare a large blazing fire inside a vast bronze statue depicting the god with arms open wide. The biblical description of this image of the deity, as a human figure with a bull's head and outstretched hands, coincided with the accounts written by Diodorus. Eventually, in Carthage and Motya, Baal-Hammon replaced Moloch and Melqart. The metal statue, red-hot from the fire kindled within it, would receive the sacrificial victim in its outstretched open arms, down which the living creature would roll into the burning embers of its belly. Maybe the noble families believed that eternity was a worthwhile prize in exchange for the little victims; certainly the bereaved family was supposed to look happy at the prospect of their burning children, as their immolation would immortalize or even deify them, like Dido. 'This custom', wrote Plutarch,

was based in part on the notion that children were the dearest possessions of their parents and in part that as pure and innocent beings, they were the offerings of atonement most certain to pacify the anger of the deity; and further that the god of whose essence the generative power of nature was, had a just title to that which was begotten of man and to the surrender of their children's lives. Voluntary offering on the part of their parents was essential to the success of the sacrifice; even the first born, nay, the only child of the family, was given up. The parents stopped the cries of their children by fondling and kissing them, for the victims ought not to weep and the sound of complaint was drowned in the din of flutes and kettledrums. [1]

Mothers, according to Plutarch, stood by the burning statue without shedding a tear. If they did, they were deprived of any honour from the act and their children would die in vain.

Because Dido had secured the greatness of the capital city, in Carthage children were also sacrificed in her honour. In 310 BC, while the Greek Agathocles with his army encamped outside the walls laid siege to the city, 200 children from the leading Carthaginian families were sacrificed. After one of their victories, the Carthaginians forced 3,000 of their prisoners 'to go through the fire'. There are also examples of adults being sacrificed in Carthage, but not in Motya. A great Carthaginian general had thousands of Greek prisoners executed at Himera, in Sicily, and his successor Himilco was to do the same.

As the scholar Sabatino Moscati wrote, Motya has turned out to be our most important source of knowledge of Punic customs and religious beliefs. In the future, further excavations in the Motyan tophet should yield objects and stelae which, after study, will provide much-needed information. Archaeological evidence from both Carthage and Motya has already revealed that the shift from infant to animal sacrifice was never total, but that the bones of small animals and birds, mixed with those of infants or older children, have been found dating from the late fifth and fourth centuries BC.

We know that the Punics used hashish liberally, and it is probable that large quantities of the drug were consumed during these sacrifices in order to tranquillize both the victims and their families. Diodorus writes that small babies and children, and at times even adults, were burnt in honour of the god inside a sacred precinct – not a temple, as it had no roof and no architectural features. The fact that tophets were regarded as sacred demonstrates that the sacrificial victims were believed to attain immortality and become cherubs. Maybe, in the eyes of the believers, these cherubs personified their families and even their cities, and could talk to the god, in spite of the fact that the Punics officially believed that after death there would be quietness and rest, but not much else. The Punics' sense of reality gave these people no illusion of a life after death; nevertheless, they often buried their dead surrounded with votive offerings, although in Motya corpses were initially cremated because of the limited space available on the island. Only when the cemetery was moved to the mainland were the dead interred.

The cherub, a figure which has lingered on in our own strange pantheon, was depicted by the Phoenicians as a little sphinx, with wings and some animal features; maybe the practice of sacrificing birds together with children derived from a wish to provide wings for the sacrificed children in that hypothetical afterlife in which the Punics did not seem to believe in any case. Maybe they felt that sacrificing their children was the only way to achieve a contact with the god; it was also felt by Carthaginian society to be a question of discipline. In Carthage, the immense tophet in the locality of Salammbo inspired the great Gustave Flaubert, who turned the name of the place into that of a cruel Punic princess. The novel *Salammbô* became popular in his time (Mussorgsky based a wonderful but alas unfinished opera on it), demonstrating the fashion for Carthage and the *femme fatale* in those days.

Maria-Eugenia Aubet observes that at Salammbo there were different layers of remains, corresponding to various eras. Between the seventh and sixth centuries, for example, deposits were 'predominantly of newborn babies', while there were 'three-year-olds in the fourth century BC'. She also observes that in Motya the social hierarchy was less strict, so that offerings in this city did not necessarily imply links to nobility, whereas in Carthage human sacrifice was a prerogative of the higher castes whose ancestors had founded the city. 'The inscriptions on the stelae reveal the lineages of families who made sacrifices in the tophet for as many as sixteen generations, in certain cases.' Sacrifice here was a national practice, as reflected in one of the inscriptions, which reads: 'By decree of the people of Carthage'. In short, there was no choice about human sacrifice; it was a death sentence with no chance of reprieve.

The votive stelae found in the western tophet, of which there are thousands, usually have an inscription with a formula referring to human blood sacrifice or the substitution of a sheep for the child. In every case they are offerings from individuals intended as a gift, a promise of payment of a debt to Baal-Hammon in exchange for a favour received. The substitution would be hierarchical: the firstborn is a substitute for the king, the child for the firstborn and, lastly, the animal for the child. [2]

Although we are horrified at the frequency with which the Punics sacrificed human beings to placate their god, we should remember that the Spanish Inquisition did exactly the same, and with the same finality. The victims' immolation purified their souls, conferring immortality; people were burnt on a pyre as a sacrifice to God who could then forgive them. In the early years of the church, Christians were burned alive because they did not recognize pagan gods, just as, a few years later, pagans were burned alive for not recognizing the Christian God (this latter phase has been less advertised by subsequent history) – and Jews were burned all over Europe, including Britain, at one time or another. The recent human sacrifice of millions of Jews on the altar of German racial purity, witnessed by many and known about by more, should render us mute.

Historically (or, rather, biblically), the story of Isaac, Abraham's favourite child, gives us evidence that the Hebrews halted a practice of sacrificing their first-born; and there are many other examples of this cruel practice in the ancient world. Polyxena, the youngest of King Priam's daughters, is sacrificed on the tomb of Achilles. Agamemnon, king of kings, shows by the sacrifice of his daughter Iphigenia that the Mycenaean world did the same with their children. In this last instance Artemis is pleased with the sacrifice of Iphigenia and so the wind blows again and the Greeks can finally set sail for Troy. Only in the much later operatic version of the tale does Iphigenia survive.

After many naval successes, Carthage began to lose. The Carthaginians had taken Motya back from the Greeks in 398, and twelve years earlier had occupied and destroyed Selinus; then, suddenly, in the fourth century, the gods turned against them. This reversal was attributed to the fact that Punic soldiers had desecrated the temple of Demeter and Persephone at Syracuse. As a result, Joseph Whitaker tells us, these two deities were 'admitted into Carthage's pantheon, and not only instituted their cult among her people but entrusted the charge of their cult to Greek priests'.[3] We saw in the previous chapter how a dead Motyan woman, Allia Prima, was commended to Persephone, the Bitter Goddess, by her grieving husband. At that stage, therefore, Persephone had already effectively joined the Punic pantheon.

The Phoenician religion and the Punic faith reflected the needs of the two different ethnic communities; although one was the offspring of the other, it diverged from the original as time passed. If we consider that the Canaanites can be traced to 3000 BC, the Phoenicians to 1200 BC and then the Punics from 800 BC, it is obvious that their religion needed to reflect the varying face of political and military circumstances. It also had to evolve to suit an ever-growing and probably more sophisticated population. Indeed, after abandoning a mystical form of monarchy in favour of an oligarchy, the Punics appear to have developed a more cruel form of religion and more Spartan habits. This was because Carthage and its satellites led insecure lives from their very inception. When the monarchy fell, the influence of Melqart, symbol of monarchical power, faded away with it. Although they brought Melqart, god of colonisation and kingship, with them from Tyre, the Carthaginians finally replaced him with the grinning Baal-Hammon. A practical society like that of the Carthaginians could not in the end accept the concept of a god–king living in their midst; their ruler could no longer be god and high priest. One can see also traces of a social movement to weaken the priesthood which, as long as it was protected by a king of divine status, would have been over-powerful.

A great change in religiosity took place in Carthage in the fifth century BC with the severance of religious connections with its mother city. In Tyre, Melqart was held to have been the god who immolated himself with the changing seasons. The Egyptian Osiris and the Sidonian Adonis had the same role of renovating life with the seasons, and, by their sacrifice of death, gave life to humanity. We should note also that we celebrate the death and resurrection of Jesus Christ at Eastertime, with the coming of the spring; and that each year we bring to church flowers and branches of palm or olive trees, symbols of crops in one form or another. The similarities between the Punic and the Christian approaches to mysticism are not coincidence. Both are Asiatic religions, and two of the greatest builders of Christianity were Phoenicians: St Paul (Saul of Tarsus) came from Cilicia and St Augustine from Tagaste, near Carthage. In fact, at the time of St Augustine, the Punic deities were still worshipped. He also described how the peasants still spoke the Punic language, and noted in his *Confessions* that 'the Phoenician Moloch, under the name of Saturn, also had his temple,' though, according to Augustine, the cult of this divinity was then in its decadence.[4] And Joseph Whitaker writes that 'pagan sanctuaries were numerous in Carthage, that of Tanit ... the patron deity of the town, with its sacred groves and courts enclosed by porticos, around the central statue of the divinity occupying a considerable area.'[5]

The Christian theologian Tertullian (*c.* AD 155–220) also came from Carthage and retained some of the fanatical quality of Punic religious devotion. We have lost, he wrote (alluding to the Carthaginians, the Punic people, the Phoenicians); but we are everywhere, our ideas and their seed are everywhere. Indeed, the cross, a sombre motif of crucifixion, a punishment reputed, as we have seen, to be Punic, became the symbol of Christianity. Both St Paul (Romans 9: 16) and Augustine (*De civitate dei*) write about the concept of predestination, an eastern belief which Thomas Aquinas swept out of Christian theology, opening the doors to the modern era. Porphyrius, a late Tyrian Neoplatonist, developed a philosophy in which all gods could be assembled into one entity acceptable to everyone. On top, there would be a good, elderly and bearded father surrounded by lots of angels and saints; he would have a holy son to be sacrificed for the good of humanity. That, said Porphyrius, was a type of religion about which we could all be in agreement.

In the beginning the Phoenicians were monotheistic, and although theirs was an odd kind of monotheism, in their way they remained so. Indeed, Philo of Byblos wrote that 'monotheism reigned in Phoenicia', El or Baal (names meaning master or lord) being the only god. The same god was also known under different titles such as Melek (king), Adonai or Adonis (my master), Melqart (king of the city) and Eshmun (our appellant). Only the king knew the actual name of the god, the only god, and at times the king *was* god. The city of Sidon, which venerated Eshmun, knew that the appellation was just a substitute for the secret name that neither the Sidonians themselves nor we have ever learnt. Maybe it did not exist.

The ancient Canaanites worshipped a god called El (master), who was the oldest of the Phoenicians' pantheon and whose favourite son was Mot, the spirit of the harvest but also the god of mud, of chaos, of the beginning. El ruled the fertile countryside, while the desert plains on which it rarely rained were the domains of Mot, the divine son. At the time of the harvest Mot was sacrificed, but did not remain dead for long and was always reborn. Some Phoenician areas believed in the myth of El and his favourite son Usoosleud, whom he invested with the emblems of royalty but whom he also sacrificed when the risk of war threatened the land.

The actual names of the Phoenician divinities were not revealed. Unlike the Jews who avoided pronouncing their God's name out of reverence, the Phoenicians wanted to hide the identities of their deities from strangers lest the latter invoked them and usurped the divine powers for themselves. Care was taken not to repeat the true names of the god or goddess in public, so that eventually these names were forgotten and all the deities became known by the general words of 'lord', 'my lord', 'face of the lord', 'king of the city', 'our appellant', etc. The Earth goddess, whose real name was Astarte, became known as Baalat, 'Lady'. Tanit, Carthage's goddess who took over Melqart's kingdom of the sea, was also known as Pene Baal, 'the Face of Baal'.

The Phoenicians knew that these various names indicated the same divinity who was manifested in each city or temple in a different guise. In this way Melqart would protect his home city of Tyre, but show his face as Adonis in another centre. In some areas Adonis replaced Mot; the similarity between these two figures, and between both of them and Christ, is not casual coincidence. All these deities came from the same region, as indeed all the main religions of the book originated in the Middle East, in the same cruel cradle of mysticism. Our Christian religion is a faith in the name of which people have continued to kill each other for the sake of one version of God or another, one doctrine or another, right up to the present day. We too do not know the actual name of our main deity, since God the Father is actually nameless. In Italian the word 'Dio' is actually the genitive of the Greek word for Zeus.

Each Phoenician city developed its local pantheon and, gradually, from its monotheistic base, established a polytheism at the head of which were Baal and Ashtoreth or Astarte, the main female divinity. Christianity developed in the same way, adding saints and martyrs specific to the different nuclei of society. Baalbek, the 'sun baal' city, built a temple as large as that of Melqart in Tyre dedicated to all the sun gods, which eventually the Greeks collectivized into Zeus. In the first century AD Silvius Italicus described the temple of Melqart in Gades, still served by several priests barefoot and clad in linen. There was no image of the god, he recounts, who was represented only by an ever-burning fire.

It is almost impossible not to perceive the blood-stained statues depicting Christ, paraded in Sicily, Sardinia and Spain – the Punic world – as the heirs of Mot, Eshmun, Adonis. In the same way Mother Earth, the Virgin Mary, is carried in processions laden with the same offerings – flowers, burning candles, music – as were offered to the gods in Punic times, and in the same season. The Punics held great festivals and celebrations in honour of the gods. The most famous, dedicated to Adonis, was observed as far away as Alexandria. Women used to lament for three days and nights and then commemorate the renewed birth of the god with crops and music. According to the myth, Astarte/Aphrodite/Persephone fell in love with Adonis but, while hunting, the god was wounded by a boar and died. Adonis, as the name appears in Greek texts, is a hellenized form of the the vocative for 'my master', an appellation repeated by the women in their lamentations during the god's festivals, which were closely linked to crop growing and fertility. The sanctuary of Astarte in the village of Afka, between Byblos and Baalbek and near the source of the river Nahr Ibrahim, remained such a popular destination for pilgrims that its destruction was ordered by the Emperor Constantine. Every year the return of Adonis to the scene of his death was celebrated by hordes of pilgrims; Adonis was slain at the end of the summer and Astarte's lamentations formed the focus of an annual celebration. A phenomenon caused by particles of a substance called haematite which became detached from the rocks during the rainy season made the river appear to run red with the blood of the mortally wounded god. According to the myth, Astarte/Aphrodite set out to search for him and, finding him in Hades, used magic powers to revitalize him.

So Adonis is killed and then recalled to life in the new season. Each year the drama was repeated according to the seasonal cycle and must have been considered indispensable to the order of the world. It was and still is enacted in many regions, and reminds mankind of nature's death and rebirth.

In another version, Adonis, born from a tree, was a god of such great beauty that Aphrodite put him in a box (death) and gave him to Persephone, the goddess of the underworld. But this goddess opened the box and fell in love with the handsome Adonis, causing the two goddesses to quarrel bitterly. So Zeus/Baal decided that for six months Adonis should remain in the underworld (autumn and winter) and for the other six months he should inhabit the land of the living (spring and summer). The Greeks thought that Adonis was the actual name for Eshmun but, as we have seen, that was also a code name; we remain ignorant of the young god's true identity. As noted above, we do not know the name of our Christian God, that word being a mere designation or title; however, we know the name of his son who, during his earthly incarnation, was called Jesus Christ and sacrificed himself for the good of all mankind. In the Bible, when God chooses to reveal himself, he does so only to Moses, but entrusts to Aaron the priesthood, which thereafter becomes a hereditary responsibility. In the Bible, God reveals Himself in a burning bush because fire was sacred and divine, it expressed supernatural energy. Only the Greeks liberated their culture, and ours, from this Asiatic slavery by stealing fire, which equates to energy, from the gods and making it a human possession. This is the origin of the most significant of all myths, that of Prometheus.

The kings of Tyre set themselves up as priests and thus as the sole intermediaries between god and man. The Baal of Tyre was a solar god and also a marine divinity, known under the title of Melqart whom, as we have seen, the Greeks identified with Heracles in his role of the founder of colonies. Tyre was admired and envied all over the world; even the Egyptians, with their near-monopoly of wealth, judged Tyre a jewel among cities. But the neighbouring and somewhat puritanical Hebrews were shocked by the arrogance of a king who pretended to be god. Ezekiel thundered:

> Being swollen with pride
> you have said: I am god;
> I am sitting on the throne of God,
> surrounded by the seas.
> Though you are a man and not a god,
> you consider yourself the equal of God . . .
> By your wisdom and your intelligence
> you have amassed great wealth;
> you have piles of gold and silver
> inside your treasure-houses. [6]

Ezekiel also foretells the fall of Tyre, which did not actually take place until many centuries later when Alexander the Great laid a long and elaborate siege to the great city and razed it to the ground:

> Tyre, you used to say: I am a ship
> perfect in beauty.
> Your frontiers stretched far out to sea;
> those who built you made you
> perfect in beauty.

It must have felt uncomfortable for a prim society like that of the Hebrews to have Tyre as a friendly neighbour. When King David and King Solomon decided to demonstrate monarchical power by building a temple and a royal palace, they turned to their able neighbours, the Tyrians, for technical know-how. These provided the timber and the builders, the architects and the artisans. As a result, Jerusalem, in all its golden splendour, was actually built by the Phoenicians. Solomon sent King Ahizam of Tyre food and raw materials in payment, and political alliances were forged: Jezebel is one of the royal princesses who descended from Tyre and tried to turn the Hebrew court into a royal society.

In Tyre the temple dedicated to Melqart might have become one of the seven wonders of the world had not Alexander destroyed it. Its walls are now hidden within those of the later crusader fortress;

from the details we know, it must have been very similar to the temple which the Tyrians built in Jerusalem, apart from the famous 'emerald' column that shone at night.

As we know, Melqart travelled to Gades, echoing the myth of Hercules' expedition to the west. Melqart was crucial to Tyre. He was of course the subject of special celebration, and once again Melqart is a god who dies and is reincarnated; his immolation was to revive him and make him immortal through fire, in a direct link with human and animal sacrifice. Melqart was also known as 'fire of heaven', and at festival times the god was burnt in effigy on a pyre, after which he was resurrected and manifested himself in the time of the renewal of the crops. During the god's festival, the Tyrians chanted hymns and all foreigners were expelled from the city in case they heard the name of the god, which not even the Tyrians themselves knew. The king of Tyre himself took part in these festivities, undertaking a ritual marriage with a priestess, who was sometimes the queen herself or a close relative, the royal couple representing Melqart and Astarte.

Melqart was also patron of shipping and trade. On Tyrian coins, he appears mounted on a seahorse. Protected by its patron god, Tyre was a glittering and opulent city. The Prophet Isaiah declaims:

> Is this your joyful city
> founded far back in the past?
> Whose footsteps led her abroad
> to found her own colonies?
> Who took this decision
> against imperial Tyre,
> whose traders were princes
> whose merchants, the great ones of the world?[7]

Walking around the peninsula which was once the metropolis of Tyre with high houses made of painted wood, I could not reconcile the idea of the wealthy ancient city which had stood under my feet with the modest village of Sur as it appears today. I thought of the two busy harbours whence laden ships would come and go, and imagined the shouts of the stevedores and the commands of the seamen. I observed fishermen lazily pulling a few shells from a polluted sea. Isaiah's prophecy and Ezekiel's angry lamentations had indeed come to pass. No other city in the world, not Thebes, nor Rome, nor Athens, has been so humiliated as the fabulous Tyre and the mighty Carthage. These were cities where even the locations of the great temples were eradicated and are still in doubt.

The Carthaginian priestly hierarchy was strictly governed by rules. The high priest and two deputies were in charge of the largest temples and they presided over a staff which included book-keepers, musicians and even barbers who shaved the heads of mourners. The high priest of a community belonged to a patrician dynasty, and the priestly college was recruited from among the most influential families in the city. As we have seen, Pygmalion's sister Elissa/Dido was married to the high priest of the temple of Melqart.

Prominent Carthaginians incorporated the titles of their gods into their names, showing that the original Phoenician deities had not been forgotten: these names included Abi-baal (Baal is my father), Hithobal (with him is Baal), Baaleazar (Baal protects), Hannibal (beloved of Baal), Hasdrubal (Baal has aided) and Hamilcar, (servant of Melqart). Apart from Allia Prima, which sounds more Latin than Greek or Punic, we know of few feminine names, but it is unlikely that they were based on divine identities as the men's names were. Dido's original Phoenician name was Elissa (in Hebrew, Elizabeth). Anna, which means 'pretty', is also Phoenician; indeed, Virgil calls Dido's sister by that name. The name Anna must have been popular in the region since the Virgin Mary's mother also bears it. Joseph Whitaker gave the name Astarete to his heroine in a Punic novel he never finished, using a derivative from a divinity, but I think he invented it; women were not considered worthy of bearing holy names by this very eastern society. On the other hand, in Carthage we find Batbaal, daughter of Baal; but no first name bears that of the main Carthaginian god-dess, Tanit.

'Baal-Hammon was worshipped in Carthage. He was a dignified old man with a beard, and his head was embellished with a ram's horns. He sat on a high-backed throne and rested his hands on the heads of two rams which formed the arms of the seat,' writes L. Delaporte.[8] Adonis was also honoured in the new colonies. Bes, a frightening dwarf with bowed legs and a huge belly, made his appearance in Carthage although he is rare in Motya. He was also honoured in Egypt and Mesopotamia. Bes had something to do with good and bad luck; he was credited with magic powers and was often the figurehead on ships.

Oddly, with the growth of Carthage, Tanit – a feminine deity – took over from Baal, and her symbol is to be found in every Carthaginian territory, Motya included. Maybe the constant state of anxiety that the Punics felt was unconsciously underlined by their feminine protagonists: first by Elissa/Dido, to whom was given the historical task of foundress, and then by the austere goddess Tanit, 'the Face of Baal'. On a majority of stelae commemorating sacrifices, Tanit is represented by her symbol, a truncated cone surmounted by a disc. This could depict a human figure in outline, but its real meaning is still a mystery; we do not know what it stands for, although it is to be found on many objects in the Punic world from Sardinia to southern Spain, from Malta and Sicily to the Balearics. However, only one such symbol has been so far found in Phoenicia itself.

Another symbol representing Tanit is the open hand. In antiquity prayers were often accompanied by raising the hand, as today the hands are joined meaning that they are free of arms, that they are 'at peace'. The open hand of Fatimah could well have been inherited by the Arab world from Carthage. The same hand features as a jewel, as a mark of good fortune, and as an indicator of religious feelings with the Berbers, those North Africans who were pushed up the mountains and who still use some Phoenician words mingled in their Arabic dialect.

The Punic gods reflected a sterner religion than those of the Phoenicians; even Astarte when she became Tanit turned into an exacting goddess, a mother-earth-cum-sea-mother. The Carthaginians seemed to possess a heightened spirituality; one can make a comparison with the decadent and corrupt Catholicism of Rome and the prim reaction of Calvin. Carthaginian deities became severe and demanding. Melqart/Eshmun remained, and there appeared a pantheon of lesser deities among which were Dido/Elissa and the cherubim, i.e. the souls of those who had been sacrificed and who presumably protected the city.

Astarte survived mainly outside Carthage where sacred prostitution was practised by men as well as women within the precincts of the temples. Eryx and Cyprus (Kition) were famous for it. Sacred prostitution shocked the ancient world. It probably started in Cyprus, the birthplace of Aphrodite, and spread from there to the Phoenician colonies and on into the Punic world. In Eryx, which was to evolve into a place of pilgrimage quite like Lourdes, it was available to foreigners only and was maintained throughout Greek and Roman times. Sailors could call on the holy temple of Astarte, who became known as Venus Erycina, and could chose one of the virgins to sleep with, having made a payment to the temple. After their initiation, the girls were allowed to return home; but the less attractive had to wait for months and maybe years before they were chosen and subsequently freed. Sacred prostitution was no fun for the young Punic women, but the priesthood made a considerable amount of money from it and were reluctant to give it up. There were sanctuaries dedicated to sacred prostitution in Byblos, in Sardinia and in Spain. Herodotus suggested that all Phoenician women had to subject themselves to sacred prostitution at one time or another.

There is something extremely cruel in sacred prostitution as well as in human sacrifice; it has a similar unpleasant, savage taste to it. Together with Punic religious rites, it is still enveloped by a cloud of mystery, an enigma which one day might be solved by Motya and by revelations still to be unearthed.

9

SHIPPING

If Aphrodite/Astarte was born out of the sea, as legend has it, so was Motya: it owed its success and indeed its very existence as a city to its vital position, its safe, ample harbours, and its proximity to Carthage, which made it into a bridgehead to outer colonies and mining regions.

Nobody should be fooled by the melancholic solitude of Motya today; in antiquity the city must have been feverish with activity. I can imagine those lean and active men, talking in their guttural language, at times using Greek words or addressing their Elymian comrades in the local dialect, throwing ropes to one another and attaching them to the vessels they were assembling in and around the cothon. They were scantily dressed and their long dark hair was kept out of their eyes by a simple knot which secured it behind their necks. They were short and fast-moving, like busy little insects jumping from one ship to another. The Stagnone, the Motya lagoon, was alive with vessels of all shapes and sizes. Prominent among them would have been the privately owned merchant boats. Their owners were also their captains and could be seen sometimes working on their vessels, painting and varnishing or repairing the sails and rigging. Pliny tells us in his *Historia Naturalis* that 'The Phoenicians invented the art of navigation. They learnt from the Chaldeans the rudiments of astronomy which they applied to shipping,' and the largest vessels anchored in the Stagnone were preparing for long voyages, perhaps through the Pillars of Hercules and on to Gades, the great Punic city which could outdo even Carthage in size and wealth.[1] Many of the merchant ships lying in the Stagnone would be going further still, towards the cold north. They would be heading for the land of the Cassiterides, which was the name for the south-west part of the British Isles where the Punics had discovered huge deposits of tin. Tin was in great demand because bronze, an alloy of tin and copper, was universally used for the manufacture of weapons as well as all kinds of domestic tools and utensils. Parts of the Punic ships themselves were covered in a layer of bronze. Pierre Cintas, one of the greatest archaeologists and historians in this area, has suggested that bitumen was used in the construction of these vessels, and that the Phoenicians found it in abundance in the Dead Sea. Having reached the Scilly Isles, or Tin Isles as they were known, it was not long before the Phoenicians and then the Punics discovered even richer deposits of tin in Cornwall; so they were constantly voyaging to Cornwall and to the southern tip of Ireland, which also had abundant tin deposits. In exchange, the merchantmen traded pottery, salt and finished bronze products – weapons, tools and cooking utensils – as archaeology has revealed.

During the fair season most of the men were away and Motya became a city of women, children and the elderly. Some worked in the 'industrial district' with the murex shells producing purple dye; others were involved in the making of ceramics used as containers for wine, water and oil. The richest Motyan women stayed at home with their families.

People had changed physically from the remote day of their ancestors' first arrival from the Middle East. From studies at the local cemeteries we learn interesting facts. The average height of women was 1.55 metres and of men 1.65 metres; they had grown taller since the first Phoenicians arrived on the Sicilian shores. Many of them had suffered tooth decay, cysts, arthritis, malaria and fractures of the bones, especially in their legs. The average span of life was 34 years, but some of the dead had reached 65 years which must have been considered a great age.

The Motyans remained attached to their home traditions and their cuisine was based on eastern dishes. The women used lovely plates in which they served grilled fish that they bought at the market near the north gate. These dishes were concave towards the centre to gather a sauce of herbs and the juice from the fish. Usually three different kinds of fish were painted around the rim: octopus, red mullet and sea-bream, for example. These dishes were designed by the local Greeks, the Siceliots, and many of them can be seen in the Motya museum, fruits of the excavations of Joseph Whitaker and Vincenzo Tusa. In fact they are to be seen in all the Sicilian

museums and many are certainly still underground; lovely specimens are on show at the British Museum.

Sometimes the women would buy fresh fish directly from boats
at anchor in the lagoon; the Stagnone was not only a natural harbour but also a fish nursery, alive with the most delicious sea-
bream, grey mullet and, at certain times of the year, eels. The latter
were trapped in specially baited baskets not unlike those used in
some areas even today. The fishing boats went out in the open sea
for larger catch like tunny or monkfish, of which the Motyans were
fond. Long nets were used which hung in the deep sea water for
hours at a time. When the catch was large, some of the fish were
salted locally to keep for the months when there was no fishing, or
to be exported; some were made into garum.

The best tunny garum came from Lixus, a Punic colony on the
Moroccan coast. Even the Athenians bought it; they considered it
an expensive delicacy which gave status to the household – almost
like serving caviar today.

The Motyans did not only repair ships, but also built new ones.
Many were constructed from prefabricated wooden parts made in
Carthage, although some were made locally in their entirety. Just as
the fishing boats and the merchant vessels were privately owned, so,
strangely enough, were the warships which, when needed, were
hired or commandeered by the state from their proprietors. But
Motya did not have its own navy; the city relied on Carthage.

When Motya's vessels were at sea in favourable winds – the
Sicilian channel is very squally – the square sails typical of the
Phoenician boats would have been seen filled by the breeze. Except
in times of war, sailing was restricted to seasons of generally good
weather, so the ships would leave at the beginning of spring and
return in October. The seamen's wives and families would have
known that their menfolk would be absent often for months on end.
Sometimes, of course, they would never return.

These mariners sailed everywhere; they had designed invisible
roads on the waters, not only over the Mediterranean but reaching
out to where the Greeks and the Latins feared to tread, beyond into
the Atlantic and even around Africa to the Indian Ocean. The
Carthaginian Hanno went as far as the Gulf of Guinea. Around the
same time, in the fifth century BC, the Punic Himilco sailed along
the northern coast of Europe to Brittany and across to the

Cassiterides. Archaeological finds witness to the Punics' presence – temporarily – in the Azores. Herodotus was impressed by the voyages undertaken by the Punics and described their circumnavigation of the African continent in the seventh century BC.

If at all possible, these merchant-sailors would arrive at a market, conduct their trade and leave immediately. But at times they had to settle in a harbour waiting for a fair wind to take them home, which sometimes did not materialize for a year or more. As time passed, here and there the Punics found an excuse for staying on: perhaps a woman who bore children, or mines and quarries. Perhaps there is more Punic blood mixed in Cornish and Irish veins than we suspect.

Often the ships did not make it home, overcome by strong winds and heavy seas. Bad weather could obscure the stars so that the navigators lost their way; or they could run into pirates, of which there were many eager to plunder the valuable cargoes aboard the Punic ships. In spite of what the Greeks wrote, not all the pirates were Punics; many were Greeks themselves.

It must be stressed that trade in slaves took place on a huge scale, and these ships were also used to transport prisoners of war, or debtors who fell foul of the usury laws, sold into slavery. Phoenician and Punic merchants alike bought slaves in one market and offered them for sale in another at a large profit.

The boats lying in the lagoon at Motya were the same as those which had colonized Cyprus because of its copper mines and timber; Cilicia and Lycia for timber; Thasos for its gold mines; Salamis and Cythera for their dyes; Sardinia and southern Spain for their metals. Between Tyre and Carthage there was a continuous exchange of goods. The latter sent exotic items such as skins and horns, strange animals, leather dyed the most brilliant colours, ivory, ebony, ostrich feathers – even gorillas, gold and guinea-fowl. Luxury items excavated at Motya included an exotic ostrich egg fashioned into a drinking cup. Its owner must have been a capricious rich man.

Notwithstanding their location in the Mediterranean, Malta and Gozo were Phoenician rather than Carthaginian colonies, and were totally devoted to maritime commerce. Like Motya, Malta had a natural harbour; the science of building sea-walls and moles underwater was not yet widely understood, but the shallow keels of the Phoenician ships did not need deep waters for safe anchorage. Gozo with its wooded hills produced great quantities of timber, and became a huge ship-yard.

During the time when Motya was enjoying its maximum splendour, from the sixth to the fourth century BC, the city-states of Phoenicia had lost most of their power. Tyre alone survived, providing the Assyrians (and then the Persians) with warships in order to escape total subjugation. On the other hand, in the sixth century Tyre was still the great market of the tin trade, which meant that many of those ships in port at Motya which had come from Cornwall were bound eventually for Tyre. An inscription on the bronze doors of the Assyrian king Salmanasar's palace at Balawat includes the lines: 'I receive the tribute from the boats of the people of Tyre and Sidon.'

We can gain an impression of what the Phoenician and Punic ships looked like by observing the seventh-century BC bas-reliefs from the royal palace of Sennacherib at Nineveh, which are now in the British Museum. The oarsmen sit in the lower deck while the sailors stand on the upper behind huge round shields attached to the side of the ship. Maria-Eugenia Aubet explains: 'The Phoenicians are credited with inventing the keel and the ram and with caulking the joints in the planks with bitumen. They knew how to trim the adjustable sails and used double steering oars which enabled them to turn and manoeuvre very rapidly.' [2]

Sculpted for King Ashurnasirpal at Nineveh (859–839 BC), a procession of notables shows, among others, two noble Phoenicians, almost certainly Tyrians, as they pay homage to the Assyrian king. They look Semitic, with their long noses and curly hair loose on their shoulders. One of the princes has two monkeys on a lead, presumably pets brought from the land of Ophir as a present for the monarch. The men are wearing elaborate sandals and, if the sculptures were still painted, we would certainly notice that their robes were of the best purpura colour.

At Motya, we would probably not encounter princes dressed so elegantly; but we would have noticed dignitaries with their conical hats and pleated tunics. Rope-makers, coppersmiths, clothiers, fruiterers and fishmongers would push through the crowd, selling their wares. Not all of them would belong to the original stock who founded Motya: we would have seen tall Celts, Iberian mercenaries,

Greeks wearing light cloaks clinging to their bodies and the men from Campania who made such good soldiers. Beyond, in the lagoon, there would have been a forest of masts.

We know that the Punics were expert sailors and navigators, able to draw maps of the skies and of the coastlines. The ships used oars when there was no wind and for difficult manoeuvres; they resorted to coastal navigation whenever possible during the day, and at night sailed by the stars. The art of astronomy they had learnt from the Egyptians and the Babylonians, but the Punics were the first to apply surveying to navigation, and they understood the importance of calculation in establishing the course of a voyage. The techniques of navigation used by the Phoenicians hardly changed until the Middle Ages and the information shown by Ptolemy in his *Mappa Mundi* was based on Punic charts.

In and around the natural harbour of the Stagnone there is a cemetery of Punic ships. Over half a millennium of frantic maritime activity in those days must have resulted in many casualties. Indeed, in recent times Punic and even ancient Phoenician statues, some in stone but most in metal, have been recovered from the sea. Now that modern technology has rendered the reading of the seabed easy, what is hidden under the sea is no longer so mysterious. There is therefore clandestine underwater excavation; but fortunately Phoenician and Punic artefacts are less highly valued than, say, Greek or Roman statues, so that most are saved for study by archaeologists and historians.[3]

A statue, a stela, even a nail can reveal a great deal to a knowledgeable eye. On the other hand, many artefacts have left the Tyrrhenian and Ionian seas at night en route to museums in America hungry to assemble history and culture. The Getty Museum in Malibu recently returned some items to Italy, and a few more are expected back. But I think it is no bad thing for artefacts to end up in places as safe as the Getty Museum. I remember Professor Federico Zeri, once in charge of the Getty Museum at Malibu, showing me a little painted column that had come originally from a temple in Herculaneum. It was almost Baroque in style: not beautiful, but very interesting from the point of view of architecture and the history of art. The Getty Museum had actually bought it legitimately, but there had been a huge controversy about the column being removed from its original location. Well, in the course of forty years the other three columns which had formed the little temple disappeared, so the only example of this type of column, which bears witness to eastern influences, remains at Malibu. The museum is open to the public, so that scholars can inspect, study and ask for photographs. The danger for artefacts left in situ is that thieves, if not organized, tend to destroy what they find, and if organized, sell only to private customers. Many inscribed stelae have been lost because they had no intrinsic aesthetic value, and so they can no longer enlighten us. Had they survived, their historical value would have been enormous.

People gossip about objects that emerge from the sea around Motya, Lilybaeum and Trapani which are never acknowledged and leave by boat. Under the sea, they say, there is a museum. Under the sea there are also ships. But after centuries of waves, tempestuous winters and even underwater seaquakes the wooden relics have become scattered and the sand has covered the wrecks. In any case, if the wood is brought to the surface, it disintegrates unless lengthy and very expensive precautions are taken.

Very few ancient ships have been found in the world and even fewer have been conserved. There is the famous Viking ship in Oslo, and the superb Egyptian ship built from cedar wood by the Phoenicians of Byblos for the spiritual voyage of the Pharaoh – but that was never under water, being conserved under dry sandy soil. Of more recent origin, there are Tudor vessels and Spanish galleons. But a Phoenician or Punic warship had never been found until a few years ago. We had to rely on bas-reliefs and ancient coins in order to understand what a Punic ship might have been like. We knew none of its secrets, until the discoveries made by Miss Honor Frost, one of the most distinguished of underwater archaeologists.

In 1969 the captain of a commercial dredger reported that he had seen ancient wood off Cape Scario, outside Motya's lagoon. There were indeed many wrecks and an archaeological team went to survey them. Miss Frost relates, 'in 1971, the movement of a sand-bank exposed (thus endangering) the "Punic Ship's" exceptionally well-preserved stern-post; rescue excavation began immediately and continued during four annual campaigns.'[4] The British School at Rome appointed Honor Frost to be in charge of the underwater archaeological mission which was under the patronage of Sir Mortimer Wheeler and Dr Richard Barnett of the British Museum.

The Punic ship the investigators found belonged to the third century BC, about 100 years after the fall of Motya, and was lying in only 2.5 metres of water. It turned out to be a warship. 'The reason why no classical warship has, hitherto, been discovered on the seabed is that the decks of fighting ships were kept clear for action. Consequently, when they sank, their hulls became waterlogged, then collapsed and were covered and hidden by sand,' wrote Miss Frost.[5] It took three years to bring the remains of the ship to the surface.

'There are seventeen ships beneath these windows,' Pietro Alagna told me, pointing his finger towards the old harbour of Lilybaeum which lies under water, close to the Stabilimento Pellegrino, which he owns, and where the famous Marsala wine is still produced. I had gone to see Dr Alagna in order to look at the Whitaker commercial papers. Everything was beautifully bound and preserved, Dr Alagna included. He went on: 'There was an English archaeologist who came here and excavated one of these ships, but there are many more. *L'archeologa* was here for a long time, she is *la Dottoressa* Frost. Do you know her? She is not easy.'

Vincenzo Tusa had described Miss Frost to me as a woman of 'a certain age' who, 'when underwater, turns into a mermaid'. But I knew that dignitaries in Marsala complained about Honor Frost because the British archaeologist had been unhappy, to put it mildly, about the way her ship was displayed at the museum in Marsala. I could not take issue with her about that. This extraordinary object is kept in one room under a heavy curtain which hides it completely. When I questioned Dr Camerata Scovazzo, the Sovrintendente for the area for the past ten years[6], about the poor state in which the ship is kept and shown, she answered: 'I always tell them! They should air-condition the room.' One cannot part the curtain or catch a glimpse of the ship; nor can one buy a photograph or a postcard or even a museum catalogue describing it from which to gain an impression of its shape. If one asks whether one is allowed to take a photograph, one is insulted.

On the other side of the room, fortunately, are the items that were discovered in the hold of the ship, and these can be studied and are properly labelled – although on my last visit they had been mysteriously removed. They include pieces of rope and even branches of olive trees; some remains of hashish and a large number of amphoras which would have contained edible stores and water. The mission found quantities of tools, nails and even that basic domestic utensil, a broom.

'The Queen of England came to Marsala to see the ship,' said Alagna, interrupting my thoughts, as he showed me a framed photograph of Her Majesty, smiling and to all appearances totally confused at the sight of the Punic ship. Then Dr Alagna pointed at another photograph, this one framed in silver. 'This was taken inside the Stabilimento. She came here; it was a great day for Marsala.'

'Seventeen ships?' I asked.

'Yes, and just here under the Baglio, at the mouth of the old harbour. Out there, they say that there are remains of more than eighty ships, all of them warships; but they are buried deep in the sand and it would be impossible to bring them up to the surface. Anyway, they are better down there than up here where they would quickly decay.'

Miss Frost succeeded in saving the wood from disintegration by sending the pieces to Palermo, where Vincenzo Tusa housed them in the archaeological museum. I remember them well, in their special containers. Miss Frost specified that 'the wood of the Punic Ship was only desalinated in Palermo; it was conserved chemically in a custom-built laboratory in Marsala.' In 1978 the hull was put together in Marsala's Regional Museum at Cape Boeo. The ship in question was sunk during the First Punic War, and Miss Frost stresses that this is not a Phoenician but a Punic ship, belonging to Lilybaeum, not to Motya. But since Lilybaeum was the city founded after the destruction of Motya in 397, the wreck can tell us a lot about what vessels looked like one century earlier.

An important point made by Miss Frost is that at some stage the lagoon changed so that it was no longer navigable, 'because the rocky islets making up the reef that separated it from the sea joined together (probably owing to the enlargement of salt-pans which, here as elsewhere, were exploited by the Phoenicians). Once the reef became one long island, Isola Lunga, this blocked the flow of through-currents, so that the lagoon silted and stagnated.' Those currents which could no longer flow inside the lagoon accumulated and formed Cape Scario, which is close to the Egadi Islands.

In 241 BC the Romans vanquished the Carthaginians in a famous naval victory; 'the wreck's contents, epigraphy and Carbon 14 determinations are consistent with this period,' explains Miss Frost. The vessel was a kind of auxiliary warship which, after the naval defeat, hurried towards the nearest friendly harbour, Lilybaeum, together with a sister ship, the one which was sighted 40 metres away from the wreck in question. Because banks of sand at the bottom of Cape Scario were mobile, rescue excavation began at once. Four expeditions were dedicated to rescuing the ship. The other wreck, lay close to the site where the British expedition had excavated the auxiliary warship; but it was abandoned because 'this work plus conservation and museum display would have been unrealistic, so it was left beneath the sand for posterity,' Miss Frost relates.

The condition of the Punic ship which Miss Frost successfully raised was, she said, exceptional. Its recovery revealed a great deal about the shipbuilding techniques used by the Phoenicians, including the fact that Punic ships were assembled from prefabricated parts: wooden components made separately and assembled later. Letters – not numbers – from the alphabet were written on each section, and some parts had figures drawn on them as guidelines for the carpenters. There were also traces of an exterior lining that protected the planking. 'Study of the writing left by the builders revealed traces of two alphabetic sequences, together with the more usual incised markings; this showed the hull's design to have been preconceived, while the fact that one letter was written in several different ways suggests several handwritings, and consequently several literate shipwrights (such literacy would be surprising in the traditional Mediterranean shipyards that survived until recently),' Miss Frost writes.

The technique of assembling prefabricated parts had been mentioned by Polybius, but nobody believed his account. 'On this occasion, the Carthaginians had assaulted [the Romans] in the straits [of Messina] and a cornered ship, having driven too far in the heat of the battle, had gone aground and had fallen into the hands of the Romans. They used it as a model for building the whole fleet.'[7]

When the Romans came into conflict with the Punics at the outbreak of the First Punic War, Punic naval technology was so much more advanced than that of the Romans that it could have affected the eventual outcome of the conflict. The Roman commanders, well aware that they had to gain mastery of the sea, ordered a fleet built on the exact model of the captured Punic quinquereme. According to Pliny's evidence, they took only two months to produce a fleet of 100 ships.[8] This timespan was so short that it was doubted until Miss Frost found the evidence that the ships would have been assembled from prefabricated parts. Thus the Punics could build a fleet very rapidly – and so too could the Romans, once they had understood how to copy their enemy's system. Even before her rescue mission was accomplished, Miss Frost wrote that the wreck found off Cape Scario 'cannot fail to throw light on this technical problem, because it bears signs of preconstruction that show that it would have been an easy matter to copy the component parts. Consequently, the mass-production of ships was feasible at that period.'[9]

An extraordinary feature of the ship raised by Miss Frost's expedition was that it had iron nails, while previous Punic vessels were constructed using less satisfactory nails made of copper. She described the technique used: 'Each nail which passed through a wooden dowel, had been hammered in from the outside of the ship. Inside, the points had been turned back and hammered into the top surfaces of floor-timbers and frames.'

In 251 BC another Punic ship was captured by the Romans outside Isola Lunga, very near the spot where Miss Frost found her wreck; this second vessel was very fast and easy to manoeuvre and its commander, Hannibal the Rhodian, was recognized by the Romans to be far superior to their own men. Roman shipbuilders studied the 'Rhodian' ship, which was different from the previously conquered quinquereme, and only after having done so did they feel they could beat the Carthaginians in naval battle – and they did.[10] Until then, Phoenician shipbuilding had been superior to all its competitors; from then on the Romans were able to copy every single detail of the shipbuilding techniques which those Semites had accumulated through centuries of experience. By stealing their naval secrets, the Romans would be able to annihilate them.

Before finishing her work, Miss Frost sent pieces of the Punic wood to London to be identified at the laboratory of the Royal Botanic Gardens at Kew. The results showed that both these pieces and the 'dunnage' (or plants laid to protect it) came from various parts of the Mediterranean. The ship's longest timber was made of oak of a species common in Southern Europe; other beams were of maple, while a type of Mediterranean pine was used for the planking. Other types of wood had also been employed and shavings were found where they had been chopped by the carpenters who were still working on the ship. In their despair the Punics were churning out vessel after vessel, until their work was rendered fruitless by the final destruction of the Battle of the Egadi. Local analysts established that these shavings probably included cedar, pistachio, beech, oak and maple. Leafy olive branches had been laid down between the floor timbers to protect them from the ballast. The ship carried no cargo, only a few amphoras used for carrying liquids, and small cups for use by individual members of the crew. 'Food remains were even more unusual, for they represented fresh ingredients including various kinds of meat (attested by butcher-cut bones.)' The vessel had been launched in haste. 'The ship appears to have sunk on her maiden voyage, or at least when she was very new ... The tufa ballast stones from Pantelleria certainly indicate a port of call between Sicily and Africa.' [11] The ship was obviously hit when it was hastening back towards safety in Lilybaeum.

At some seasons the Stagnone must once have been teeming with vessels of various kinds. When Motya had a population of 15,000, it is reasonable to estimate that at least 1,000 of its inhabitants, being seafaring people, must have possessed a boat, whether a little fishing vessel for use within the lagoon or larger craft for fishing off Cape Boeo. Some of the rich Motyan merchants would have owned larger ships for trading expeditions. Often, too, the Motya lagoon would give shelter to the Carthaginian naval fleet which patrolled the high seas to keep them clear of pirates and enemies. And there would be trading ships arriving from Utica or Malta, from Solunto and Palermo, Gades and Sardinia, and from the Balearic Islands. Big and small, they came to Motya for a variety of reasons: to take on new supplies, for repairs or to change the crew. Some of the larger vessels anchored at the mouth of the lagoon, where barges could go out to them with supplies of food and water, and perhaps carpenters as well to carry out repairs. The many seamen coming through Motya from all over the Punic world would have spoken the same language, but in varying dialects. They shared a common knowledge of the sea, which they considered to be their own territory, and they worshipped the same gods.

While the Punics loved their sea, they also knew how dangerous it was and how carefully they had to tread on it. Melqart protected the foundation of their new colonies, but it was Tanit, more a Mother Sea than a Mother Earth, who had to be appeased. As the maritime power of the Carthaginians grew, gradually Tanit became their main deity. Special ceremonies were dedicated to her at the beginning of the sailing season in March. Unlike the merchantmen, warships had to be prepared to go to sea all the year round, and had to cope with the unpredictable winds of the Mediterranean.

The cargo-carrying merchant ships were called *gauloi* in Greek, meaning 'round' (in Latin, *naves rotundae*), because of their rounded hulls which provided them with cargo space. In Phoenician the word was *golah*; hence the Italian *goletta* and maybe the English galley and galleon. They were between 20 and 30 metres long; their sterns culminated in a fishtail or a spiral shape while their bows were decorated with a horse's head. (Sometimes, according to Strabo, the Greeks called these ships *hippoi*, from their word for horse). The main masts carried rectangular or square sails which, according to many Greek texts, were black. Two huge eyes were painted on the hull so that the ship could see its way across the sea. At a distance these eyes were supposed to frighten the enemy; but when at anchor in the Motya lagoon, all those Phoenician eyes stared peacefully at each other, fixing their sailors in a sympathetic gaze. They must have made an extraordinary spectacle.

These ships followed two systems of navigation. Smaller vessels, making short-haul trips from one point of the coast to another, navigated within sight of the coast. They sailed at daytime and on routes which linked known harbours via friendly promontories; they anchored in lagoons or in the lee of islands where they could find shelter from the wind. These types of trading vessels covered no more than 25–30 nautical miles a day, depending on their route and cargo. The speed of commercial shipping was only about 2–3 knots; a craft could cover more than 50 nautical miles a day.[12] Polybius tells us that Hannibal the Rhodian, mentioned above, covered the stretch between Carthage and Lilybaeum, a distance of 125 nautical miles, in twenty-four hours, averaging just over 5 knots; but that was an exceptional speed for which this Rhodian navigator became famous. Open-sea navigation was reserved for the larger ships, and even these preferred to stay within sight of the coastline on the Mediterranean routes. At night the pilots navigated using the Ursa Minor constellation, which was known in antiquity as the 'Phoenician star'.

The Phoenician fleet is the first naval power in history; from the eleventh century BC onwards the Canaanites/Phoenicians were the rulers of the high seas. From 800 onwards the Tyrian and Carthaginian navies had the capacity to blockade the Mediterranean ports and disrupt commercial traffic at will. Warships were much narrower than cargo vessels but required a larger crew and many more oarsmen. They were seven times as long as their width. The prow was strengthened and came to a bronze-plated point at water level with which enemy ships could be rammed and severely damaged. The horrible and wide-open eyes of the warships were painted on each side of the prow and it is possible to imagine that the crews of smaller adversaries might be hypnotized by their gaze. Archers and catapults would be assembled on a wooden castle raised above the main deck.

A type of ship called a penteconter carried fifty oars and was 25 metres long; besides the oarsmen it had to have a crew of fifty, which included a captain, a pilot and a team for working at the sails. The pace for the oarsmen was set by a flute player, which suggests that they were not slaves – which would make sense, for in a small boat slaves could not easily live alongside freemen. Besides, these crews, and especially the oarsmen, took marijuana; the herb was found by Miss Frost in the ship near Cape Boeo as part of the cargo necessary for a warship. This too suggests that the oarsmen were free.

The shipbuilding skill of the Carthaginians was displayed at its peak in their design of the trireme, which was the queen of the Mediterranean from the seventh to the fourth century BC. The trireme was a big ship, said to have been first used by the Sidonians. There were eighty oarsmen on each side, and the remaining crew handled the sails. All in all there might have been as many as 240–300 men on board, including a contingent of assault infantry. The trireme was quite low, and longer than most other Punic ships at about 40 metres. The innovation of the trireme (and of the quinquereme, which was the ship that fought the three Punic Wars) is that the oars were arranged along three banks, which gave the ship its name. The bireme, called *navis longa* by the Romans, sailed with two banks of oarsmen, five to a bench. It was fast and could manoeuvre swiftly.

We know that, during the Punic Wars, the crews of the Carthaginian warships were composed of those citizens who could demonstrate that they were born in the city. The Carthaginian army, by contrast, consisted mainly of mercenary troops. These included Celtic cavalry and infantry from Iberia and Africa, among whom the Numidians were famous. The elite troops were a special legion entirely composed of Carthaginian-born soldiers who, however, did not move into action unless defeat was threatened – in which case these specially equipped citizens would advance on the enemy and, presumably, scare the wits out of them. But while the Punics were unrivalled seamen, we know that they were not great soldiers. Only Hannibal Barcas mastered military tactics, because by his time the Punics' exclusive command of the seas was beginning to collapse.

Although they were masters of shipping and had devised a complicated system of harbours and docks, the Punics never made a spectacular show of their skill. While, for example, the Egyptians built the Pharos of Alexandria, one of the wonders of the world, and at Rhodes the access to the harbour was between the legs of the Colossus, another of the world's seven wonders, the Carthaginians and the Motyans erected no pompous monument to signal their unchallenged naval superiority. Maybe their ships were just that: the eighth wonder of the world.

Il COMMENDATORE: 'PIP' WHITAKER

Without Joseph Whitaker, the imagination of international scholarship would probably not have focused on Motya, its history and its treasure trove of information. Always trying to be as self-effacing as possible, Joseph Whitaker, 'Pip' to his family and friends, was happier waiting for a flight of wild duck than taking tea in the elegant drawing room of his parents' house in Palermo. Although he was born in Sicily and had lived there all his life, he couldn't have been more English. His passions were those of the Edwardian country gentleman: shooting and reading; he was not particularly interested in women, or in business – or, indeed, in human beings in general. He found small talk impossible, and preferred the company of the simple Sicilian peasants to that of the Sicilian high society that his family frequented.

Pip was a scholar at heart, but he was expected to be a businessman: specifically, a trader in the Marsala wine which had made the fortune of his family for the last three generations. The Whitakers were the heirs of the Inghams who had started the business and were at this time among the richest people in Sicily, if not the whole of Italy. In spite of the fluent Palermitan he spoke, Pip had been brought up to be English to the core; his mother Sophia was the daughter of William Sanderson, permanent consul in Marsala. She was a very proper lady, although her father was in trade as well. Pip's father (1802–84) was Benjamin Ingham's nephew, a dedicated businessman: but 'Pip' Whitaker was not, nor was he drawn to the huge warehouse that was the hub of the family's main business, the Baglio Ingham. For him, the Baglio – the local term for the place where wine was made and matured – meant discussions with associates, sellers and buyers, and Joseph Whitaker was no good at that. His accurate handwriting turned sour when it had to list accounts and details of shipments of the specially fortified wine which was shipped from the castellated harbour. His mood changed, though, when he went out with his gun to spend silent hours by the water of the Stagnone watching the migratory flamingos and the aquatic birds.

As a young man Pip was stuck in Marsala at his tedious work in the family business and lived in the Baglio built by his great-uncle Benjamin Ingham. The villa was furnished with everything anyone could wish for, adorned by gardens with fountains and supplied from a kitchen garden a kilometre long. The Ingham–Whitaker business employed 300 men and ran 30 warehouses; all the wine casks were built in the establishment. Within its fabulous stables, which have collapsed, there lived scores of horses, mules and donkeys. The high walls which surrounded the Baglio served a purpose: Marsala was swarming with bandits who operated in squads.

One of twelve children, Pip was born on 19 March 1850 and christened Joseph Isaac Spatafora. The last of these forenames had been given to him in honour of his godmother, the Duchess Alessandra Spatafora di Santa Rosalia, Benjamin Ingham's mistress. Tina, Pip's wife, was to take great pains in underlining that all those biblical names were *not* indicative of any Semitic blood in the Whitaker family. When they grew up, nine of the Whitaker children chose to live in England and never returned to Sicily. Only Joseph, Joshua (1849–1926) and William (1850–1936) remained to look after the family's Sicilian affairs. But if Pip was not born for business, his two brothers turned out to be even worse.

Pip was gentle and sensitive. With his lean body and shy blue eyes, he couldn't have looked more different from Benjamin Ingham Senior – or indeed from his uncle, also called Ben Ingham. Pip had good facial features and could have been described as handsome had it not been for his lack of self-confidence and drooping shoulders. Reserved by temperament, he was utterly different from his brothers, who could not bear to be away from Palermo and its society. Because of its stunning beauty, climate and harbour, Palermo in *La Belle Époque* had become a meeting place of monarchs and celebrities; from the Kaiser to the Prince of Wales, from the Tsar to Wagner, in winter they all came to Palermo where they were sure to be entertained lavishly and enjoy a good climate. The *beau monde* that gathered around them, which Pip could not appreciate, consisted largely of impoverished dukes and princes trying to marry American heiresses – or, as in the case of Prince Lanza Tomasi di Lampedusa's grandfather, to Mafia heiresses. It was a very empty and snobbish world. A relative of Lanza Tomasi was seen embracing the Jesuit Prince Lancia, the last and only heir of Frederick II. 'Cousin!' said Lanza Tomasi. 'In Christ, yes; on earth, never,' was the dry reply.

Then there were the Florios, who were encroaching on the Whitakers' territory in the Marsala industry, and also in shipping. *Nouveaux riches* like the Whitakers, they occupied themselves building in the *art nouveau* style and making as much money as they could spend – and that was a lot. Ignazio Florio married the beautiful Princess Trigona, and their daughter married the Prince of Trabia; thus they linked themselves with the grandest names on the island. The Whitakers, by contrast, did not marry grandly; they kept to themselves, choosing English girls for their brides.

One day while Pip was still a young man, he was in the Baglio when a *contadino* arrived with some artefacts he wanted to sell. The farmer had found them in San Pantaleo while preparing the ground for planting new vines and he thought that, since *il Commendatore* Whitaker liked old things, he might be interested. Pip recognized these objects as Punic.

As time passed, Pip came under pressure to marry. So he proposed to the girl of his dreams – a young Englishwoman, from Liverpool – and when he was rejected made the mistake of marrying Tina Scalia, a snobbish bluestocking born in London of Italian parents who considered herself to be more English than the English, aristocratic and highly intelligent.

Not everybody shared Tina's high opinion of herself. According to a certain Lady Paget, she was immensely tall and looked like a goat. The wedding, which took place in 1883, was followed by a honeymoon spent in England with Tina's mother: Signora Giulia Scalia was never to leave the young couple alone. After their second daughter was born in 1885, this tyrant of a mother-in-law declared that daughter Tina had had enough. Pip's matrimonial rights were withdrawn and Tina henceforth was to share her bedroom with her mother, not with her husband.

It was impossible for Pip to avoid Tina's father, too. General Alfonso Scalia lived in a separate villa in the park of the Whitaker house where he could receive visitors. He was known for being generous with the ladies and with Pip's money, in spite of his wife's temper and his daughter's puritanical character.

Tina had an acute sense of social position and hated Marsala, the Baglio, the sound of the casks being rolled out in the mornings and the 'vulgar' shouts of the workers. She felt that the low life of the wine trade contaminated her ladylike existence and also that it would damage her daughters' matrimonial prospects. Norina, Pip and Tina's elder daughter, was prettier than her sister Delia, but both girls were neurotic, pale and prone to illness. Social life in Marsala must have been limited, polluted as it was with the worst type of Mafia. But Pip's father insisted that his 'boys' should be at the Baglio, so Tina suggested that the three Whitaker sons should take turns. Pip had married before the death of his father; his brother Joss (Joshua) was the last to wed. He met his wife while training at the Baglio in Marsala: Euphrosine Manuel (Effie), a girl with dark hair who became one of Tina's targets of criticism. The other was Maude, who had married the youngest of the three brothers, William (Bob).

While Pip was in Marsala, he would take one of the donkeys and ride the short way along the coast. The Punic remains at Marsala were more apparent in those days, before the massive bombings of the Second World War. He would then take a coastal road called the Contrada Spagnola, which curves along the old Punic harbour, after which he would continue through the salt-pans. The young man would then tie his donkey to a tree and call one of the men who kept a boat on San Pantaleo to come and fetch him. There were sixteen families living on the island at the time. Once there, he would not only shoot birds but would spend hours looking at the Punic remains which emerged from the earth. He would also collect artefacts, buying them from the local farmers or small dealers. He built up a small chain of informers who would tell him when and where some particular piece was available.

Pip knew about Schliemann's arrival in Motya in 1875, and, since it coincided with his time at the Baglio and with the beginning of his engrossing interest in Motya, it is possible that the two met. Schliemann loved to be flattered and he was a great fan of the

British, so a visit from the young and well-connected Pip would have been welcome. Moreover, Schliemann had to sleep and dine somewhere on the mainland. Maybe he paid a visit to the famous Baglio Ingham–Whitaker where food was prepared sumptuously by three cooks.

Pip's own notes on Motya do not start until fourteen years later, in 1889. The previous year, 1888, had been a terrible one for Marsala wine and the business was struggling; Pip and Bob decided to make Joss the manager but Joss was as hopeless as his two siblings if not more so. Pip was not interested in accounts; his writing becomes wandering and spiky when listing expenses and entries, or writing business letters, which he did in both Italian and English (the Italian contains some small grammatical mistakes). It is, of course, a very different kind of handwriting from the one I encountered in his observations on Motya.

In a way it was lucky that Pip married a woman who was neither attractive nor interesting – even if she thought otherwise, as her diaries, in which she gave full rein to her self-appreciation, make abundantly clear. Had Pip been enamoured of a lovely and loving wife, he might have wanted to be with her more often in Palermo. Instead, he travelled the world over to meet experts in Punic history and read every book he could find on the subject. He began to build up a remarkable knowledge on Punic and Phoenician civilization; but his characteristic modesty persisted. In the preface to his book *Motya, a Phoenician Colony in Sicily*, published in 1921, he wrote: 'The idea of excavating the buried remains of Motya first occurred to me some forty years or more ago, but it was not until many years later and after overcoming innumerable obstacles and difficulties that I became sole proprietor of the little island, and was finally enabled to give effect to the project that I had for so long cherished *in pectore*, and commence the work of exploration.'

In Palermo, the Whitakers' life continued on its accustomed course. Tina found that she had to compete with one of her sisters-in-law, who built a palace in mock-Venetian style. This Palermitan Ca' d'Oro today houses the Sicilian Secret Service, a mix of Mafia fighters and Mafia informers all sharing the same elaborate rooms. Villa Sperlinga, which employed twenty-five gardeners, was where Maude and Bob Whitaker lived; Villa Sophia, which housed Bob's (and Pip's) parents, Joseph and Sophia, was to become the Hotel des Palmes. Tina wanted to live in the best house of all.

The feverish social life of Palermo was isolated from the rest of Sicily. In fact the island was abysmally poor and backward; there were few roads, illiteracy was endemic (this remained true until the mid-1950s), and so was banditry. At that time the Mafia was different from what it has become since, but since its main characteristic is its exploitation of an evolving society, this is not surprising. It was not as powerful as it is today, mainly because it was then not so closely associated with politics. It dug out its niche within the landed aristocracy and the new industry, people like the Whitaker family whom it mimicked.

Exploited by the aristocracy and destitute, the peasantry occasionally rose up in bloody revolts, during which the most appalling atrocities were committed. Tales of *carabinieri* being chopped to pieces and of cannibalism coloured the pages of northern newspapers, published in regions which considered Sicily an alien and barbaric land. Eventually the nobility abandoned their country estates and the *Belle Époque* society left Palermo for Nice, which was both safer and nearer to the main European capitals. Cholera flared up in the poorest districts as often as popular revolts. Every palace, villa or Baglio was therefore enclosed by high defensive walls, in order to protect both inhabitants and property.

High walls were soon to be built around the 22 acres that Pip and Tina had bought in a district of Palermo called Malfitano. They decided that their sumptuous villa would be modelled on the Villa Favard in Florence, which had been designed by a German architect. The interior decorations, in Pompeian style, were painted in dark browns. Brown, so dear to the Victorians, became the dominant colour of Villa Malfitano. Even today, the rooms are so dark in the daytime that they have to be lit by electric light – in Palermo. Hearing that the princely family of the Colonnas were selling their set of Gobelin tapestries depicting Aeneas and Dido, Pip acquired five of them, not so much for their artistic value as for the Punic story that they recounted and for the imaginative Flemish portrayal of Carthage. The nudity of a Rubenesque Venus was tolerated in that prim household because of its historical context. Pip also bought two huge Chinese elephants, perhaps in homage to Hannibal and his great enterprise across the Alps.

For her part, Tina had quickly assembled a collection of highly priced Trapanese corals, stunning Baroque artefacts with which she succeeded in outshining her sister-in-law's collection. Dark oak furniture filled sitting rooms and drawing rooms, and copies of Louis XV furniture added a smooth gleam within so much darkness. The Palermitan nobility and Queen Mary poured scorn on this furniture. 'They are copies,' Pip explained to a horrified duchess. 'I can certainly detect that,' was the answer. One single room exploded with joy, thanks to *art nouveau* frescoes by Ettore de Maria Bergher, festive scenes of leaves and birds that gave the walls the look of a verandah; and indeed, it was referred to as the Summer Room. Villa Malfitano ended up combining the Whitakers' strong core of puritanism with Tina's weakness for pomp and grandeur. This contradiction could not but result in an ugly clash. The *bon ton* which Tina so desperately sought was dreadfully missing from every room of the huge villa, each of which painfully reflected the *nouveau riche* aspiration to appear what it was not.

The Whitaker family moved into the villa on 18 February 1889. Pip was then 37; he was married with two daughters, he was rich, handsome and owned a magnificent house. He led a comfortable life; but he was not happy because something was missing: he was intellectually hungry. Tina, at last, had plenty of room for her garden parties, musical soirées, dinner parties. Meanwhile Pip was left to assemble a good library and manage the grounds. Together with his head gardener Emilio Kuntzmann, he planned Villa Malfitano's park and filled it up with exotic plants and creatures like flamingos, roe deer and a rare breed of chicken. He was to employ fourteen gardeners to maintain the rose-beds and the various species of trees that he had imported from Africa and Asia. *Il Commendatore* Whitaker did not follow the English tradition of using local plants and designing 'rooms', friendly gardens which echo the environment; he opted instead for the exotic and for large spaces, maybe in order to please Tina and *épater les bourgeois*.

When work was finished on the house, Pip started studying ancient Greek and Phoenician. In 1897 he founded the Humanitarian Society for Aid to Abnormal Children and for the Protection of Animals. This had not discouraged him from embalming 11,000 birds, although it is only fair to say that he left children alone.

Eventually the Whitakers began to feel the entrepreneurial competition of the Florios, just as Benjamin Ingham Senior had once imitated the earliest Marsala business started by the Woodhouse family. In the face of this challenge, the Whitakers had to keep up with their rivals' initiatives. Having realized the potential financial gains to be made from *tonnare*, special places where tuna fish were brought in huge numbers and treated, Pip's father sent him to investigate and buy property in Tunisia. Pip went to Monastir ostensibly to look for a suitable spot for a *tonnara*, but instead spent his time observing – and shooting – birds. As a result of this venture *The Birds of Tunisia* was published in London in 1905.

Also on the coast of Tunisia, Pip had found locations uncannily similar to those at Motya. He noticed the same kind of 'harbour' (the cothon) and remnants of walls with stones cut just like the ones on Motya. He knew about the great city of Carthage, and he began to study to increase his knowledge. 'The site of Carthage of the Phoenicians as well as the Roman Carthage appears to be now generally recognised in having been on this projecting cape, formerly a peninsula,' he jotted down in 1912.[1] Imitating Schliemann, he read the *Aeneid* and those authors from whom Virgil had adapted his story. He listed all those who had written either on Motya or on the Punics – Timaeus, Polybius, Cicero, Plutarch, Appian, Pausanias, Herodotus, Philistus – and studied them.

The Whitaker girls were growing pale and tame, as tightly chained to their mother's skirt as Tina had been to that of her own forceful mother. When old General Scalia died in 1894, beleaguered by debts and *cocottes*, an embarrassment to the family, he left his pavilion empty. Tina's father had been engrossed in spiritualism, poker and gambling. (Spiritualism, by the way, was a traditional Sicilian pastime; the poet Lucio Piccolo, Lampedusa's cousin, exchanged several letters with the Irish poet W. B. Yeats, also fond of ghosts, imps and the like.) Pip decided to make the sinful pavilion into an ornithological museum for his collection, to which he added 5,000 new specimens acquired from Lord Lilford.

Tina was not amused. But she was enjoying herself, because Villa Malfitano became the hub of social life in Palermo. Having always tormented her family by asserting that she had given up a potential life as a professional singer, Tina could finally sing for charity during *thés dansants*, musical evenings and dinners. Her soprano voice had been trained; but as for its beauty, we have only her word for it.

Opinions differed, notably that of Richard Wagner. 'Wagner was to compose part of *Parsifal* while staying in one of the palatial Whitaker homes in Palermo,' writes Pip's great-great-nephew Ben Whitaker; 'he was remembered as a very trying guest, since all social conversation had to be suspended if musical inspiration came to him, even at meals, when he asked to be covered with a cloth like a parrot in its cage, less the *leitmotiv* be lost.'[2] On that occasion Auguste Renoir, who was also in Palermo, asked to paint Wagner's portrait; he was received and made a quick and wonderfully evocative sketch of the composer. He also left a very amusing report of this visit, and of Wagner, in his diary. When the season in Palermo waned, Tina and the girls moved to their new villa in Rome – at Parioli, naturally.

Possibly because he longed for a more constructive life, and because he was disappointed in his family ties, Pip became more and more engrossed in Motya. In 1905 he started his archaeological plan. Knowing that Schliemann had bought part of the Hissarlik hill which he was to dig (the rest belonged to Frank Calvert, the British archaeologist to whom Schliemann actually owed the discovery of Troy), Pip conceived the project of acquiring the entire island from the sixteen families which then inhabited it. It was not easy. They were suspicious; some had emigrated; and they began to think that, beneath all the debris, there was a lot of gold. One of the owners declared that he would never sell to a foreigner, so that a new friend of Pip's from Marsala, the Colonnello Giuseppe Lipari-Cascio, bought the plot on Pip's behalf. Tina rarely accompanied her husband to the island: Motya was full of insects, snakes and black crabs called *merda*, shit, by the locals.

Lord Ronald Gower, who was one of Tina's most precious friends, accompanied Pip to Marsala to visit the Ingham–Whitaker Baglio, and he also made a trip to Motya. 'They stayed in the Baglio, "more like a fortress or prison than a wine factory", and were rowed across to Motya,' writes Raleigh Trevelyan,

of which Pip now owned about a third. Most of the island, Gower noted, consisted of vineyards, with olives, carobs and almond trees; Pip had been introducing the agave ('like huge goats' horns') for commercial purposes. The peasant inhabitants, about sixty in all, stood in a row to meet them. Pip told Gower that the eminent excavator of ancient Troy and discoverer of the 'treasure of Priam', Professor Schliemann, who had died in 1890, had been there for a fortnight in 1875, though without achieving very much of importance. He indicated to Gower the weed-covered causeway, only two feet under water, and various other partially excavated ruins. It was at Motya, he said, that the *ballista*, the instrument for throwing stones against beleaguered cities, had first been used, an invention as revolutionary as that of artillery. His story of the sacking of Motya and of the subsequent crucifixions was blood-curdling. Eighty thousand men and 3,000 boats had been used for the attack, and wheeled wooden towers, six stories high, had been used by Dionysius to cope with the high houses, for which the town was famous. [3]

Lord Ronald thought that the Whitakers kept the Mafia at bay because Villa Malfitano employed a mafioso butler. But the Mafia was not really kept at bay; the truth is that the Whitaker clan observed the rule of *omertà*, silence, which they referred to as 'discretion'. Only rarely were Mafia threats recorded in Tina's diary. One of her nieces, for example, was kidnapped; but her parents denied everything and did not want to discuss the affair. On another occasion a severed hand had been thrown inside the walls of Effie's house in Via Cavour.

One of the first political murders was the killing of the Marquis of Notarbartolo, father of one of Tina's friends. An honest man, Notarbartolo, who was a politician, had tried to obstruct the infiltration of the Mafia into the Bank of Sicily. That such an important man could be assassinated with impunity pinpointed the growing power of the Sicilian Mafia. The Whitakers were appalled; but they remained silent.

It is likely that banditry and Mafia activity had much to do with the waning success of the wine industry. Extortion and protection payments must have been heavy for the Whitakers, although there is no mention of sums paid 'to protect'. Marsala production reached its peak in 1870, when the Baglio exported 6,200 pipes (a pipe is equivalent to 412 litres), but with the new century it was falling rapidly. Between 1901 and 1905 the Baglio Ingham–Whitaker was exporting less and less, while the quality was also declining. Other businesses, like that of the Florio family, were diversifying. The fact was that demand for Marsala wine in England was almost over.

In the meantime, every eligible young man in Sicily was calling on the Villa Malfitano to ask for the hand of one of Pip's daughters. Tina thought that Delia was not intelligent and rather ugly – and told her so to her face. Like her mother before her, Tina kept a firm hold on her 'chickens' and discouraged them from getting married, for fear of fortune-hunters. The unfortunate girls seemed to be preoccupied entirely by their clothes, parties, *tableaux vivants* and private theatrical events. Norina was presented at court in London wearing a beautiful dress, but Delia was not. Of their many letters to each other, none mentions Motya or their father's archaeological interests. Norina, though, did write a poem about Motya, which her father typed out under the heading 'Norina's Poem':

I

Dream isle of peace, beneath a Southern sky
set like a jewel in the sapphire sea,
silent upon shores save for the seabird's cry
Where once Phoenicians' glory used to be.

II

The fallen stones around me seem to speak
Of the far days when you were great and strong
But riches, strife and warfare with the Greeks
  mingled with wine and feast and woman's songs.

III

Dream isle of peace beneath a summer sky
Like a fair jewel in the sapphire deep
Silent your shores, where only ghosts now sigh
And ancient glory sleeps its long-lost sleep.

By 1906 Pip had succeeded in becoming the proprietor of the whole of San Pantaleo and had befriended Professor Antonio Salinas, the director of the museum in Palermo and both a scholarly and an enlightened man. A little house had been hastily erected to give shelter to Pip and his guests.

'We spent the day on Motya,' Tina wrote in her diary on 20 June 1906. 'Salinas enthusiastic over two flights of steps which P. has dug up lately. The next morning he told us that he had been thinking of

Motya during the night and hoped that he might be able personally to supervise the excavations during the summer! Motya occupies all our thoughts. We settled about enlarging the house on the island. I am struggling to keep back from extravagant expenses.'[4]

When the Whitakers went to Motya with Professor Salinas, the latter persuaded Pip to build a museum in which to house, study and list his finds. Tina was distraught at the idea, protesting that too much money was spent on Motya and too little on her daughters; she left the island, ill. There had been a major confrontation through which, one can imagine, Pip sat silently, listening. 'This morning I had a look at some of the Lilybaeum fortification ruins at Capo Boeo. NB Another day we must inspect the old port, the necropolis and the sacred well of the Sibyl,' he jotted down in a quick note in 1912.

In 1914 the outbreak of the First World War interrupted excavations. But, having assembled so much documentation and information, Pip was able to record his archaeological work and discoveries in a book which was published in 1921, a fundamental work on the Punics. He drew from his own notes, but consulted scholars and libraries as well. No fewer than 4,050 artefacts, found between Motya and Lilybaeum, are listed in the notebook which he kept.

At Motya, Pip built a larger house on the same site as the first smaller one: this was the 'Vitakre Castle'. He wanted to be able to sleep on the spot, and entertain distinguished guests. He also included the small museum that Salinas had suggested in which were displayed all the best items, each documented with a label in Pip's own hand. A family of custodians were employed to look after the Castle and also to cook for the squad of diggers who were employed during the spring and autumn excavation seasons.

But, as success came, so did trouble. Increasing difficulties were obstructing his progress; even in 1915 the authorities were making life difficult for him, motivated by jealousy, nationalism and greed. The new Sovrintendente, Professor G. Gabrici, was doing his utmost to prevent a 'foreigner' from digging inside the 'beautiful Italian ground': if Fascism was not yet established, nationalism was. Pip himself wrote several letters protesting against official hostility, but only the sketches of such letters have remained; they can be read at the Whitaker Archives at Villa Malfitano.

British royalty was not interested in Motya. When King Edward

VII and Queen Alexandra paid a visit to Villa Malfitano, Tina was beside herself with pride, especially because her sisters-in-law had not had the honour of entertaining the royal couple. Unfortunately, on the day, Pip was seriously ill – perhaps with a psychological complaint, since he hated that kind of exposure. The king had asked to have lunch *al fresco*, which worried Tina more because she would be unable to show off her sumptuous diningroom than because this might aggravate Pip's indisposition. Tina was so clumsy in placing her guests that the king himself took on the task, distributing the company around the table set in the open and decorated with lilies and roses. As related in Tina's diary, the menu consisted of *croustades of maccheroni*, fish *à l'Écossaise*, lamb cutlets *à la Villeroy*, roast turkey, Russian salad, *pêches Hélène*, strawberries, prickly pears (which the king did not trust), melon and *cassata siciliana*.

As the royal couple left on their yacht, news came that an important discovery had been made at Motya. Pip dashed to the island and, on this occasion, Tina and the girls accompanied him. Her diary for 11 May 1907 reads:

They have found a little necropolis on the Northern side of the island, located outside the defensive walls. It was thought earlier that the only cemetery at Motya was the one at Birgi, on the mainland. They had found a large urn and some smaller ones; there were two stratifications, . . . Pip thought that the two strata belonged to different periods, the smaller urns with lids that looked like plates may have contained animal bones or children who had been sacrificed. [5]

He also drew a very accurate map of the island.

In London, where he visited the Phoenician curators at the British Museum, Pip was offered a peerage at a cost of £100,000 and later at a discount: £60,000. But Pip, who was by now acquiring a distinguished appearance with a triangular white beard and a huge pair of white moustaches, was spending a great deal of his money on Motya, on acquiring rare books and on travelling in the interest of his research. Among historians he had become a celebrity, and important men of culture wrote asking to visit Motya.

8, III, 26

Dear Sir,

Perhaps you may remember that last Easter you were kind enough to give me permission to pay a visit to Motya in order that I might see the site of the ancient Phoenician town and the interesting finds made by you in digging on the island.

Since I paid that visit, my interest in Phoenician antiquities, which was already great, has grown enormously. For two seasons I have been associated with the Franco-American dig in the sanctuary of Tanit in Carthage. I have been commissioned by the director of the dig, Prof. F. M. Kelsey of Michigan, to make an especial study of the series of cinerary urns found on that site with a view to publication. These urns seem to date from the earliest period of Punic Carthage down to the Roman conquest and during last summer I was engaged in working out a rough classification of them. And now during the coming Easter vacation the Expedition has furnished me with funds to enable me to make a tour with a view to studying parallel Phoenician funds in those places.

I expect to be in Palermo about the 31st March and I should very much like to show you and discuss with you some of the photographs which I and others took of last year's dig and the objects found.

If in addition to granting me this interview you could see your way to allowing me to make another visit to the island so that I might compare the pottery of Motya with the Carthage series and also, perhaps, take photographs of some of the more important parallels, I should be very grateful.

After the exceeding kindness shown to me by Mr and Mrs Clark [Clark was the Vice-Consul at Marsala] and yourself last Easter, I have hesitated very much before writing to ask you if I might be allowed to make another visit to the island. All the more so as it is so short a time since I was there last. My excuse must be however that the finds at Motya are so extraordinarily important from the point of view of helping to date Carthaginian pottery and also the fact that child burials of a very similar nature have been found by you at Motya and by our expedition at Carthage.

I hope to arrive in Rome on Friday week, March 17th, so if you are answering this letter, would you be so kind as to direct the answer to the Scuola Britannica, Valle Giulia, Roma.

I hope you will forgive my presumption in making so many requests to you but I really do feel that a great many important facts can be ascertained from the point of view of both Motyan and Carthaginian archaeology, from the correlation of the finds in the two places, and I am eager to try to do my little bit towards obtaining that end.

I am, yours faithfully, D. B. Helou (University Assistant, Aberdeen University)

This letter, which is in the Whitaker archives, is one of many similar requests acknowledging the invaluable possibilities of Motya as a source of light for anyone interested in Punic history. It shows that by this time scholars were writing to Whitaker on an equal footing and needed to discuss their discoveries with him. 'Motya probably shows more remains of an old Phoenician town still standing in situ and untouched, save perhaps by the husbandman's plough in the course of agricultural labour, than any other ancient site we know of,' Pip noted.[6]

Whitaker should have been honoured. A title was due to him; Motya was a real achievement. Instead, he began to experience real difficulties as the Fascist regime gathered momentum and its bullish and nationalistic nature began to be felt by Pip and the British community in particular. In January 1927 he had to close down the Baglio; he had no choice as he was an 'enemy alien' (Pip had never given up his British passport). And 'the excavations at Motya had more or less to be halted, particularly as Professor Gabrici, the new Director of the Palermo Museum, had actually gone so far as to forbid them,' writes Raleigh Trevelyan.[7] He goes on:

Pip, normally mild and slow to anger, was furious at such 'petty persecutions'. The visit to Motya by his friend, Dr Thomas Ashby of the British School in Rome, had been virtually wasted. Professor Gabrici now maintained that, since Motya was a site of national importance, any excavations must be done by Italian archaeologists. Useless for Pip to point out that the island was his own property, that he had had the initial enthusiasm, the perseverance and the capital; that he was British and wanted the British School to do the excavating. Among Pip's latest discoveries had been some pebble mosaics of a griffin and lions.[8]

By this time Pip was thin, even leaner than in his youth, and photographs show him surrounded by scholars and visitors to Motya, sitting by that same spot where I had lunch on my first visit to the island. He must have felt a great deal of satisfaction. As he contin-ued excavations, he jotted down in Italian (my translation):

Bronze arms such as arrows and javelins can be found just beneath the surface of the upper level of the necropolis, possibly in preparation for the battle against Dionysius which took place exactly on the North side of the Necropolis since it was near the dam; and where the fortification wall crossed the necropolis there is evidence that during the siege it had been breached. Such a conclusion is suggested by the way in which the city wall was breached and because a great quantity of bronze arrows and spears are to be found near the base of the wall. A large part of the arrows were embedded in the walls on the other side of the breach. The fiercest fighting must have taken place at this point rather than the oppo-site shore.

On 4 April 1921 Tina noted in her diary that Professor Biagio Pace, a distinguished archaeologist who enjoyed good relations with the Fascist Colonial Office, thought that findings at Motya 'were almost unbelievable'. Pace's presence became a necessary condition for Pip to go on excavating; some archaeologists today insist that it was Pace who provided Whitaker with knowledge (and maybe even wrote his book for him!), but the truth is that the Fascist academic was the only means for Pip to continue his work. The publication of his book in London was a success among interna-tional scholars; but it was never translated into Italian. In any case, Phoenician and Punic studies were being discouraged at the time 'because of anti-Semitic feelings', Tusa told me. Nevertheless, the diminutive King Victor Emmanuel III paid a visit to Motya in June 1922, and Pip hoped that royal interest would protect his excava-tions from the Fascists. But it was a hot day, the king, Pip and the courtiers were dressed up and the mosquitoes were atrociously hun-gry: the royal visitor was more interested in swimming, and only absent-mindedly inspected the walls and some new digs.

Norina finally married at the age of 36. She had fallen in love with a 53-year-old general, Antonino di Giorgio. He was shorter than her, a bully and a Fascist at heart (indeed, he went on to be a minister under Mussolini). Pip disliked him intensely, but Tina admired him. Pip thought that di Giorgio was 'destined to emerge in the Fascist era'; the vulgarity of the regime did not escape him.

Eventually, in 1938 Tina met 'the great man', together with her son-in-law but without Pip: that was Mussolini, of course, and she was totally enchanted with him. On the contrary, Pip watched with sadness the turn of events in Italy as all his properties were threatened with expropriation. His adopted country was turning more and more nationalistic, and the English colony in Palermo was encouraged to leave. The Whitakers' charitable institutions were seized by the state; now they are empty and in ruins. Pip's son-in-law, General di Giorgio, once so close to the regime, quarrelled with Mussolini. Di Giorgio's brother was even accused of being a mafioso, and in 1932 the general died during a simple operation; the rumour was that he had been killed. Pip was saddened, in spite of the fact that he had never seen eye to eye with his son-in-law; Tina, Norina and Delia wore black for years, and were mockingly nicknamed 'the three di Giorgio widows'. The fact was that, now that the Fascist regime had weakened the Whitakers, they were perceived as losers. *Vae victis!* In Italy, and especially in Sicily, popularity is assured by being on the winning side. That is still the secret of the Mafia bosses' success, and indeed for the lack of criticism attaching to some of those major Italian political leaders who are known to be crooks.

Pip had stopped his excavation campaigns back in 1927, when the Fascist regime grew more aggressive towards the British. It was decreed that only Norina could own properties since, having married an Italian, she was forced by law to renounce her British citizenship and take on the nationality of her husband (a law which was enforced until the 1970s). But Pip could look back on his work with satisfaction. He had spent twenty-one years in Motya, during which he had discovered the house of the mosaics, the ancient necropolis, the tophet, the sanctuary at Cappiddazzu and part of the north gate. Professor Tusa thought that Whitaker's archaeological work had been 'exemplary'.

Pip had it in mind to write a piece of fiction about Motya; indeed, he jotted down a sketch of a novel in which a beautiful Motyan girl falls in love with a Carthaginian, survives Dionysius' slaughter and, hidden in a grotto, waits for her beloved who, of course, eventually arrives to marry her. I found this outline narrative, laboriously typed by Pip himself; I imagined him having sat alone, dreaming of delivering all the intense atmosphere of what he felt about Motya in fiction, in imaginative prose rather than in a factual piece of archaeological work. As far as I know, he never wrote it.

Pip feared now that 'they' might take Motya itself away from him; and indeed, had it been a Roman or a Greek city rather than a Punic one, the Fascists would have seized it. He began to feel ill, although, unlike his wife and daughters who never stopped complaining about their health, he never mentioned his sickness. 'In August 1928 he had to give an address on Motya to the Royal Association in Cardiff, but at the last moment Dr Ashby had to read his paper for him,' writes Raleigh Trevelyan.[9] 'Such excavations as had taken place since the war had at first been mostly under the auspices of Cavaliere Giuseppe Lipari-Cascio, also a pretty ancient character, with splendid white dundrearies – a son of the Piedmontese Consul.' Pip's whole world was disintegrating; he had to confront a hostile regime and cope with a weakening body. After asking for the return of the busts of his parents, which had once stood in one of the charitable institutions sponsored by the Whitakers, Pip died in November 1936. At least he was spared the Second World War. In 1940 Mussolini stabbed France in the back and declared war on the Allies. One of the many consequences was the bombing of Marsala and the destruction of many Punic artefacts, including several from Motya.

The tame, shy Joseph Whitaker left a touching will in which he praised his wife's goodness and left all his possessions to his three women: but the document, a copy of which is in the Whitaker Archives at Villa Malfitano, makes no specific mention of Motya.

Tina lived for a long time in Rome, and survived both Norina and the war. When Norina died her part of the inheritance was shared between her two next of kin, her sister and her mother, so that heavy death duties had to be paid twice. On her mother's death in 1957 Delia was left with the encumbrance of the huge inheritance. She became old, a dry English spinster, tall and portly. A cumbersome wig, worn even on the hottest of Motya's afternoons, shaded the huge eyes which were Tina's; she had inherited her father's shyness and much of his gentleness, but none of his scholarship and intellectual curiosity. She was easily persuaded into bequeathing the Whitaker estate to a foundation which in due course fell into incompetent hands.

11

MOLTO INGHAM!
THE SOURCE OF THE
WHITAKER FORTUNE

The Tuscans of Leghorn were cunning traders. In a way they were just like the Punics. Since Leghorn was 'invented' late in the sixteenth century by the Grand Duke of Tuscany who needed a harbour and who filled the new city with Jews, the observation is not absurd: as we have seen, the Semitic tie between the Phoenicians and the ancient Hebrews was close.

In the nineteenth century the port of Leghorn was very active: Napoleon had blocked the way out of the Mediterranean via the Pillars of Hercules, so British trade from North Africa, Asia and Greece was shipped to the harbour of Leghorn and then proceeded by land through Austria to the British Isles. That is the route which the Marsala wine took to reach the British market when sherry, port and madeira were no longer available because of Napoleon's temporary blockade. Thus the Livornese enriched themselves. They had plenty of money to spend; and anything that was extra de luxe, exquisite, expensive, was labelled 'Ingham, molto Ingham'. The expression is used to this day. A fine meal, an expensive restaurant, is '*Molto Ingham.*'

'*E' buono?*'

'*Buonissimo! Ingham!*' The expression recalls the memory of the fabulously rich Benjamin Ingham, who built an immense fortune in Sicily and who was the originator of the Whitaker empire.

'The real founder of our family fortune was the remarkable Benjamin Ingham (1784–1861)' writes Ben Whitaker, who started the family firm of Ingham-Whitaker. His family were cloth merchants in Leeds. He himself, as a good-looking youth of 18, quit Yorkshire for Paris in 1802 – having reputedly been jilted by his fiancée because of the loss of a valuable cargo ship – and vowing not to return until he was rich enough to buy up all the district of West Yorkshire. He moved on to Sicily in 1806 and began his wine business in Marsala six years later, as one of a number of enterprises exporting lemons and oranges, olive oil, manna, sulphur, shumac, almonds and other goods from the 'sundrenching nightmare' of Sicily. He also owned several ships (including Sicily's first steam vessel) which traded between Boston, New York, Europe and Sumatra, returning laden with goods including pepper and spices from the east Indies which he sold in Italy and Marseilles as well as later to Australia and Brazil.

On a warm spring day, I drove by the harbour in Marsala, searching for the Baglio that Ingham built and also for some vestige of the past, something that could betray the might of Lilybaeum, the Carthaginian colony. But all I could see were battered huts, peeling cement and disorderly housing estates; the city walls had been rebuilt in the seventeenth century and I never succeeded in finding the Punic walls buried within them.

I ventured along the docks and stopped to buy a box of prickly pears from a sleepy boy who overcharged me. He looked at me with amazement for not having haggled on the price and helped me to put the case in the boot of my car. The docks were deserted; or rather, they appeared to be so because, in that usual Sicilian way, dark eyes seemed to be scrutinizing anything that moved from behind wooden sheds. I could sense the threatening presence of the Mafia, a perpetual ghost hovering over the docks, the supermarkets, the whole city. There were few ships; among them was a broken-down cargo ship from Russia, its past glory unguessable behind its rusty carcass – just like the city of Marsala.

I drove on the old road along the coast, heading towards Mazara del Vallo. The Arabs had started the conquest of Sicily at Marsala, and so had Garibaldi, eleven centuries later. General Garibaldi had visited Motya; in fact, he had spent a night in the little house where Rosa's husband used to live. I don't think Garibaldi had any interest in the Punics, and his visit happened before Schliemann's, but he was an intelligent and intellectually curious man who loved islands.

He finished his life in Caprera, off the coast of Sardinia. But now the Mediterranean was no longer the theatre of battles and trade, of politics and myths. It had become an overfished sea of floating plastic bottles and yachts pissing their way though the litter they left behind.

I drove on, glancing at the Baglios: I passed the Florios' and then thought I saw the shape of the Ingham-Whitaker Baglio, which I recognized from faded photographs. I stopped, took my camera and left the car outside the fortified walls, becoming the subject of investigation from two barking mongrels.

'They don't bite,' a young man shouted and, seeing me carrying a camera, added: 'If you want to take photographs, drive in.'

He spoke with a Sicilian accent and, at times, used words in dialect. His nose was hooked and his skin dark: a good-looking chap. Maybe he had Punic blood.

Was this the Ingham Baglio? I asked, looking at the dilapidated villa standing at the bottom of the alley, flanked by warehouses.

'It was the Vitakre's. You should have seen how beautiful it was! They pulled everything down. Come,' he added, 'I'll show you.'

I parked the car inside the courtyard of the Baglio alongside two huge lorries filled with cases of toilet paper. The dogs followed us, still barking.

'The palazzina is due to be restored, they have promised . . . But nothing happens here. Money just disappears. Ah! if the English would only come back, life would return to Marsala. You see, that was where they stored the grapes and the must, and there was the wine, millions of litres stored in those casks. It was exported all over the world . . . They found that it was the best wine in the world, better than anything else . . . Ah, if only the English would come back! We are no good in managing things here in Sicily, we need the English, the Vitakre.'

I asked whether the Baglio was originally the one that Ingham built.

'It was, Beniamino Ingham, *Creso, pieno di dollari* . . . One day they went away, they sold everything, and we never saw them again; we have no work, no wine, nothing any longer.'

He told me that his name was Erede and that his father and, before him, his grandfather had worked in that very Baglio. He was the custodian now. I started calling him Signor Erede, and he liked that.

He escorted me to visit what once had been the Whitakers' garden. There were a few large terracotta urns, most of them broken, lost among the vegetation, and some timid blossom of wild roses witnessed the past presence of a formal garden.

'The grapes would be carried here, to this spot, and then made into Marsala wine. Ingham and the Vitakre took the wine the world over. Ah! if only *gli inglesi* were here!'

Had his father witnessed those times?

'No, but my grandfather told me. Everybody worked here.'

When my mobile telephone rang and I answered a call from London, Mr Erede's admiration grew; he decided that I was English. I took photographs of the crumbling villa – a whole balustraded terrace had crumbled away and a wing had been pulled down in order to let lorries park in the back yard. The Baglio had clearly been a lovely building once.

'There is nothing inside the villa now, everything has been taken.'

'Stolen?' I asked.

'You can come back whenever you like,' he did not want to answer, 'and take more photographs.' He presented me with an old cork from an Ingham bottle.

As I prepared to leave, the custodian tried to call for my attention. He was enjoying the opportunity of talking about those times he knew about from mythical descriptions. Mr Erede wanted to show me a fountain. Among scattered stones and weeds there were bits of coloured marbles which, with some fantasy, could be attributed to a garden fountain.

'Once this was full of water, it sang and flowed with fresh water,' he said, enchanted. Water was still a magic element in this dry part of Sicily.

'But surely you can't remember any of this?' I asked.

'Me? No. It was a long, long time ago . . . Come back, don't worry about the dogs. You see those towers around the walls? Those were to guard the Ingham and the Vitakre family.'

Had they been in danger of something? I asked. Had there been any episode that his grandfather had described, that he could remember? Maybe the Baglio had been the subject of Mafia blackmail, of racketeers?

Mr Erede froze. That word should have not been mentioned.

Mafia was still a forbidden subject in Marsala. Poor Mr Erede; I had been unfair. I pretended not to notice his embarrassment.

'Well, the Mafia is just part of Sicilian life, especially in this part of Sicily,' I added, smiling.

He nodded, without smiling. 'Come back, I shall tell you about the Inghams and the Vitakres ...' He went on describing a multitude of servants and workers, the Baglio of plenty.

So, that was the Baglio that Benjamin Ingham built and where it all started. It looked powerful and yet elegant, self-contained and well protected from outside, from the sea and from inland. Ingham seldom lived there but his nephews did. The younger Whitakers, as we saw, were not keen on business and their wives detested Marsala; so the living quarters of the Baglio remained a shell. And the whole enterprise was closed down in 1927.

Having told Pip's story, I should recount the extraordinary career of Benjamin Ingham, who arrived to Sicily when he was only 22, having heard of John Woodhouse's success in the production and shipment of fortified wine. Admiral Nelson, who was a friend of Woodhouse and was soon to become acquainted with Ingham, was enthusiastic about the local wines and ordered large quantities of Marsala for his fleet.

Summoned by the Bourbons, who had no fleet and were feeling the hot breath of Napoleon on Naples and Sicily, the British were hoping to extend their colonial presence into Sicily. Indeed, when the French conquered Naples, the royal family was saved by the British navy; once on board the *Vanguard*, Lady Hamilton became the queen's close friend and Nelson remarked that his mistress was the only one who was not seasick. They landed in Palermo, to the populace's initial enthusiasm. 'It was wonderful to see the improvement and resources which started up in Palermo after the arrival of so many strangers,' wrote a Miss Knight. This is corroborated by the gossipy Sicilian, Don Palmieri de Miccichè.

From 1799 to 1814 Sicily flourished. During these years almost continuous war throughout Europe with France and the Court of Naples on opposite sides had caused the influx into Sicily not only of the Neapolitan diplomatic corps but also of wealthy families fond of travel or a change of air like Russians, Germans, English and Spanish (for whom this country was the only outlet of escape, and the only foreign land they could visit), but also of the soldiers and statesmen from Europe who intrigued and plotted with Maria Carolina, who was the very heart of all conspiracies against France. [Maria Carolina was the queen of Naples, daughter of the Empress Maria Theresa of Austria and sister of Marie Antoinette of France.] The affluence of all these visitors stimulated trade and created work. The population increased and everything began to prosper, especially in Palermo.[2]

Ingham landed in Sicily with the British occupation troops in 1806 and moved to Palermo for good in 1809. 'He was outstanding as a merchant and exceptionally enterprising, trying one venture after another but not hesitating to drop those which proved unsuccessful,' writes Ben Whitaker.[3]

Ingham was one of the many young men who, following the good fortune of John Woodhouse and Nelson's victories, arrived in the fabulous Sicilian harbour of Palermo. He was handsome, determined and tough. He quickly understood that in Sicily there was a huge opportunity to trade in fortified wine which, before the French Revolution and the Napoleonic war, had reached England through Madeira, Malaga, Jerez and Oporto. By then Woodhouse was already established in Marsala, where he built a Baglio, fortified to protect it from the pirates raiding from the sea. Nelson advised Woodhouse on different brands, which he had himself named Bronte, Sicily, Madeira-Sicily.

None the less, young Ben Ingham wanted to be in Palermo.

As the air became warmer, Palermo unfolded its glowing, fragrant petals: the valley of the Golden Shell – Conca d'oro – with its groves of acacias, palms and orange-trees, its citron-espaliers and walls of oleander, 'decked with thousands of red carnation-like-blossoms', fully justified its name. The city had not changed since Goethe visited it in 1787. The mode of life of the higher ranks of society, imitated by the lower, differed little from that of the Neapolitans. They rose late, went out for a stroll, dined between three and four, drove or walked by the sea in the evening before going to the opera; then played cards, and retired to bed at daybreak. Since their country villas, in which they spent a few weeks in spring and autumn, were in the near vicinity, the routine was the same as in the city. [4]

The island of Motya. The ancient Phoenician/Punic city was linked to the mainland by a road which is now under water. Its geographical location bears similarities to Tyre and Carthage (Enzo Sellerio Editore)

Salt pans opposite Motya. Salt was farmed by the Phoenicians in their colonies; in Gades (Cadiz) and Motya these salt pans are still part of the landscape and of the local economy (Gualtiero Malde)

Grinning mask probably worn by the victim before being 'passed by fire'. From the Motya's tophet (6th century BC) now in the Whitaker Museum (RCS Libri)

Detail of the bas-relief in the palace of Sargon depicting the transport of cider wood in Phoenician ships (hippoi)(The Louvre)

Heinrich Schliemann aged 60, about the time he visited and excavated in Motya. The famous archaeologist left Sicily in a huff

The Whitaker brothers; only three of them, Joseph ('Pip'), Joshua and Ben (third, fourth and sixth from left respectively), remained in Sicily after the collapse of the Marsala wine trade diminished the family's interest in the western side of Sicily (Fondazione Giuseppe Whitaker)

Giuseppe Lipari-Cascio together with Joseph Whitaker excavating near the North Gate. 'Il Colonello represented local power and was able to fix everything until the arrival of Fascist clans (Fondazione Giuseppe Whitaker)

King George and Queen Mary visit Villa Malfitano for lunch. 'Pip', il Commendatore Whitaker, is to the King's left, and his wife Tina to the Queen's right (Fondazione Giuseppe Whitaker)

A dish for serving fish found at Motya and made by Greek artisans living in the city. The concave centre contained the sauce, while the grilled fish was served on the sloping sides (Gualtiero Malde)

These stairs used to lead to crenellated defensive towers flanking the main gates to the city. Arrows are still found in nooks and crannies, such was the fierceness of the battle for Motya (Enzo Sellerio Editore)

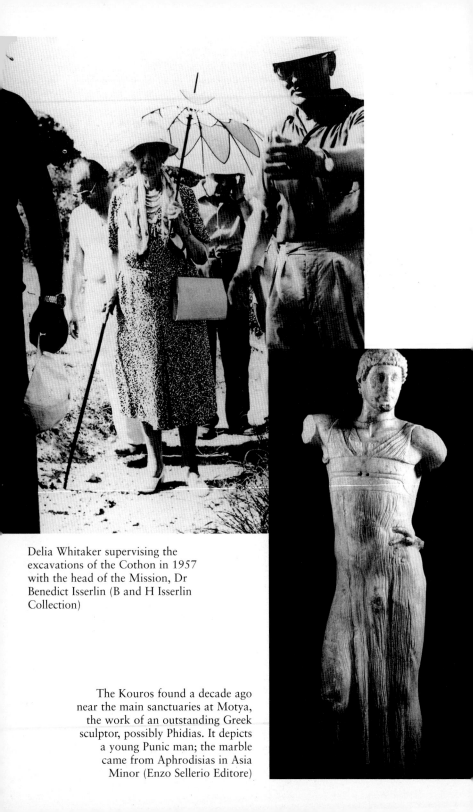

Delia Whitaker supervising the
excavations of the Cothon in 1957
with the head of the Mission, Dr
Benedict Isserlin (B and H Isserlin
Collection)

The Kouros found a decade ago
near the main sanctuaries at Motya,
the work of an outstanding Greek
sculptor, possibly Phidias. It depicts
a young Punic man; the marble
came from Aphrodisias in Asia
Minor (Enzo Sellerio Editore)

The ancient Punic cemetery at Birgi, facing Motya, is washed by the sea, thus revealing the sarcophagi of many generations of Motians in the sand. Most stones bear no inscriptions, since the Phoenicians barely believed in an afterlife (Gualtiero Malde)

The archaeologist Dr Marisa Fama (centre) together with Giuseppe Pugliese, who started work for Whitaker when he was 18, and Pamela Toti, the archaeologist for the Whitaker Foundation at Motya (Gualtiero Malde)

Prof. Vincenzo Tusa worked at Motya after the war and was entrusted with the 'inheritance' of the excavations by Delia Whitaker. His son, Sebastiano, is now in charge of archaeology on the island (Gualtiero Malde)

Harold Acton thus describes a somnolent capital which is not dissimilar to the one I first encountered in the mid-1950s. In this environment somebody like Ingham, hard-working, intolerant and rather crude, felt that he had the field to himself. And so he had. Immediately he summoned his brother from Yorkshire and, the moment he arrived, sent him off to Spain to study the systems used in Andalusia to fortify wines. Paying only a few visits to his Baglio, Ingham would show an almost cruel side in his haste to make money. He could not tolerate sloth and he despised the slow pace of the Bourbon bureaucracy which, thanks to the presence of the British fleet, he regularly bypassed.

With the face of an angel, large eyes and a full mouth, Ingham betrayed his determined character just by a little twist of his nose. All kinds of tales were told about him, all the more as he began to diversify and accumulate more and more money. 'To most Inghams and Whitakers, Benjamin Ingham was a thoroughly alarming person and his temper was supposed only to be equalled by that of his paramour, the Duchess of Santa Rosalia, nearly six years his elder,' writes Raleigh Trevelyan.[5] 'No doubt he treated his family harshly because, being childless, he knew they were after his money.'

As his business became almost unmanageably large, he asked a nephew to join him in order to keep the firm's accounts. William Whitaker, one of his sister's sons, arrived aged 18 and died only four years later. He was rumoured to have succumbed to his uncle's intolerable pace, but it is more likely that William died of typhus. Ingham asked for another nephew. By 1820 Ingham had a considerable network of agents working for him both in banking and in his import–export business. Palermo was torn by civil wars and insurrections against the rule of the Bourbon king. The mob hacked a couple of aristocrats to pieces, and Ingham felt unprotected. Sir John Acton, the Bourbon king's chief minister and the queen's lover, had died and Queen Carolina had turned against the British. Still, the mob left foreigners alone, probably recognizing that they brought wealth and employment.

Meticulous and quite sensitive, Joseph Whitaker was different from his uncle, whom he nevertheless admired, and they got on famously. He had large grey eyes, which his heirs have inherited, and a thin, rather mean mouth. He was a man of his times, looking towards modernization and machinery, a true son of the Industrial

Revolution. Ingham bought a new machine for washing grapes automatically; the must was stored in cellars 150 yards long. Joseph Whitaker was required to remain in Palermo and look after Ingham's many affairs in the capital, while another nephew, Joshua Ingham, was sent to Marsala.

Since 1823 Benjamin Ingham had been living with Alessandra, Duchess of Santa Rosalia. She looked like a peasant, but had the virtue of being a genuine eccentric. With four spoilt children, she formed a conjugal relationship with Benjamin Ingham, who retained his Protestant faith. Neither partner wanted to sanctify or legalize the connection: he did not want to part with his money, and she did not want to lose her titles. So they faked a wedding to satisfy his prim family and the powerful Sicilian clergy. At 57 Benjamin still kept his boyish appearance. A portrait shows him looking slightly portly, with the peaceful expression of a contented peasant, his Baglio and the harbour of Marsala in the background, as if he were a king. In a way he was, since he had become the richest man in Sicily.

He probably grew fond of Joseph Whitaker, who in 1837 married Sophia; in the same year the most virulent cholera epidemic swept Palermo. Traditionally recognized as the capital's patron against cholera, the Holy Virgin Mary found herself demoted, as Palermo decided to replace her with another saint protector. Some children had found the bones of Santa Rosalia, a virgin martyred on Monte San Pellegrino. These bones were in a grotto which was immediately turned into a holy place. Actually, the bones were suspected not to be human at all; but that did not bother the Palermitan populace, who carried statues of Santa Rosalia in procession; and indeed she overcame the calamity and the cholera epidemic was quenched. However, even Santa Rosalia failed to protect Palermo from the next year's cholera outbreak; in 1838 almost 50,000 people died of the disease, excluding assassinations and the questionable revenge taken on those who were believed to have spread the disease.

Ingham began to realize that, what with cholera epidemics and civil unrest, Sicily was not an ideal place for investment. He had started buying cargo vessels which plied the seas of the world carrying freight. The Bourbon king made him a baron; but who cared about the Bourbons? They were finished, they had no political sense and behaved like spoilt children at best and cruel tyrants at worst. British public opinion labelled the regime odious.

By this time Benjamin and Alessandra were living in a house just outside Palermo, but still used the Baglio as their residence in Marsala. However, the Duchess thought it was a bit too noisy and demanded to move to the country. A superb site was acquired at Racalia on the undulating hills facing the Stagnone, just a few miles outside Marsala. The view of the islands – Motya, Santa Maria, Scola and Isola Lunga – was superb, while the Égadi stood out at sunset. Mount Eryx sheltered Racalia from the north winds; this villa, which still belongs to the family, is most agreeable, with shady gardens. As Raleigh Trevelyan shrewdly observes, Ingham was 'almost the only member of the foreign merchant community prepared to mingle with the Sicilians socially and to trust them in business; the British, as usual abroad, kept their distance from the natives, intermarrying among themselves and keeping rigidly to their roast-beef-on-Sundays traditions. It also cut the other way. Again because of the Duchess, aristocratic Sicilians were prepared to accept the bourgeois Ingham on equal terms.'

Ingham's main initiative towards the Atlantic coincided with the revolutionary events taking place in Sicily where social unrest was fuelled by hunger, high taxation and injustice. Benjamin's American money now stayed in America: he perceived the energy of the new nation, the potential of its growing industry aided by new networks of communication. That is where Benjamin Ingham began to invest: a part of what is now Fifth Avenue in Manhattan was his, there were large estates in Michigan, and he bought shares in shipping companies and railways. His Sicilian appetite was sated.

Finally, in 1851, he retired from business, leaving Joseph Whitaker and his nephew Ben Ingham in charge of his affairs; but he did not retire from Sicily. In Palermo he built a new, spacious house for himself and his duchess in which they entertained lavishly. Everybody wanted to meet the 'Sicilian Astor', as Ingham came to be known. When Garibaldi landed in Sicily, touching ground at the Harbour of God, Marsa-Allah, Marsala, Ingham had much to do with the success of the revolutionary landing. The captain of the *Argus*, the warship which had supposedly arrived 'to protect English interests', was called Winnington-Ingham. HMS *Intrepid* also arrived, and both ships were ordered to Marsala while Richard Cossins, the Director of the Ingham Baglio, was also acting as

British Consul. When it was clear that Garibaldi had won the day, an English officer arrived and told Ingham that his villa in Palermo was to become a hospital. Garibaldi's victory loosened existing bonds and associations, and new allegiances were forged overnight with the victors; so much so that Ingham wrote a forceful letter to the local newspaper protesting at the lack of order, the multitude of assassinations, arson, rackets. With Italian unification, the Mafia was triumphant.

'When my grandfather died in 1861 he left over £10 million; if his heirs had not sold the Fifth Avenue area of Manhattan and the 40% share of the New York Central Railroad which their great-uncle and father had acquired as a result of their international trading, the family fortune would have been even more obscenely spectacular,' writes Ben Whitaker. Benjamin Senior's main beneficiary was Willie Whitaker, Joseph's second son; not his first, as had been expected.

Six years later it was the turn of Ben Ingham Junior to die. As was his habit, he was staying at the Hôtel Meurice in Paris. After dinner one night he suffocated, dying almost immediately; everybody whispered that he had been poisoned by his wife.

Ingham had been a pioneer, a character who could have easily taken part in a Wild West shoot-out. He did not try to buy works of art, and his villa in Palermo was plainly built; indeed, he wanted it to look as simple as possible, especially from the outside, so as not to tempt the curiosity of the forever destitute Sicilians. Totally unpretentious, Benjamin Ingham was a real capitalist. Had he landed in America he would have been called Rockefeller.

12

THE JOSEPH WHITAKER FOUNDATION

After Norina's death, and Tina's death, and everybody's death, Delia Whitaker was left lonely and alone. She would walk in the dark corridors of Villa Malfitano, an ash-blonde wig wobbling on her head, an expression of wonderment in her eyes. Every door would open in front of her, pushed by the invisible hand of an otherwise sleepy footman. Villa Malfitano had been closed since her sister died in 1954; but now a few friends were invited to stay. Delia insisted that they accompany her to the cemetery, where she would descend into the family vault clutching a bunch of flowers that had been gathered by her gardeners.

To be known as a rich spinster in Sicily was like curing a ham among a pack of wolves. *La Signorina* was left like a rather mature sacrificial lamb, but as such, she began to enjoy life a little more than when she had been the prisoner of her mother, who had always referred to her as 'not very intelligent, poor Delia'. She started travelling between her Roman villa and Villa Malfitano, visiting Motya once a year. The excavations had stopped altogether, but at least the Whitaker properties had been returned to the family.

The only male heir to the Sicilian part of the Whitaker fortune was Manfred Pedicini, only son of Joss and Pip's niece. Audrey was the girl who had been kidnapped when riding in the park; her father had never uttered a word, either at the time or subsequently. Her husband, General Pedicini, had helped the Ingham–Whitaker Marsala business from plunging into bankruptcy; the wine business was bought by a Turinese firm which made a consortium of the famous Baglios – Woodhouse, Florio and Ingham–Whitaker.

Delia's cousin, Manfred Pedicini, paid dearly for his anti-

Fascism with years in prison; even his mother Audrey had to go into hiding. Tina condemned Manfred's political leanings and was extremely irritated when Audrey frequently pleaded with her to intervene on behalf of her son. Tina, of course, had powerful Fascist friends.

While Manfred inherited Joss Whitaker's side of the fortune, Delia was left with Villa Malfitano, valuable properties in Rome, Palermo and the Sicilian countryside, cash in the bank and, most precious of all, the island of Motya. Motya was very much Delia's concern because, having loved her father most, she understood that the little island was Pip's real achievement. In fact, she was not the fool that her mother had made her out to be. Delia was so paralytically shy that she found it hard to look people in the eye; some Palermitans thought that she was haughty, mistaking her shyness for stand-offishness. Too tall, she carried a kind of aristocratic clumsiness with difficulty, dressed in pastel colours like the Queen Mother, and wore gloves when she had to shake hands because she feared human contact. Aware of the importance of the archaeological research pioneered by her father, she would pay a visit to Motya every May and stay on the island for a couple of weeks. She arrived escorted by her personal maid, her driver, her cook and sometimes a gardener. As she inspected the platoon of local servants lined up on the mole, *la Signorina* would ask each of them as she extended her little gloved hand: 'How have you been? All well?' Every year the same question.

'She did not wait for an answer,' recalls Giuseppe Pugliese. 'There would have been things to show her, problems to discuss, but she did not want to know.' Giuseppe had become one of the custodians and had married. He was grooming his nephew, Vincenzo, to take over when he retired.

Rosina Arini, Giuseppe's sister, remembered *la Signorina* wearing a boa around her neck and an elegant mauve hat as she shook her hand, while her eyes wandered towards the sea. When she was in Motya, Delia would take a walk around the city walls every morning, parasol in hand, leaning on a little stick. Her eyes seemed full of nostalgia. There was no digging at Motya, so history was mute, at least for the time being.

'We would not speak to her again until the day of her departure. There was no chance of talking to her. She knew nothing about the goings-on, she was an innocent; but much was stolen, there were many who were taking advantage of her,' said Giuseppe, her faithful servant. *La Signorina* would retire within those rooms in the Vitakre Castle which had been decorated by her father with dark lithographs on the wall representing the English countryside, shooting scenes in Scotland and tiled mantelpieces from the Midlands potteries. The rooms were dark, sombre, because the many trees that Pip had planted had grown so high and thick that the sun could not penetrate them.

Clearly Delia enjoyed the solitude of Motya. When she walked around the island before the sun became too hot, she was often accompanied by Colonnello Lipari-Cascio, a staunch Fascist who had served in the army and who, like Professor Biagio Pace, was a freemason. Professor Pace came to Motya too; a Fascist in Fascist times, he had kept to his credo and was now a neo-Fascist. With the war, the Germans had arrived in Motya, and Giuseppe Pugliese and his wife were of paramount importance in defending the museum when the Nazis wanted to remove some of its artefacts. Marsala was heavily bombed, but the custodians remained on Motya.

Professor Tusa first visited Motya in the 1930s as a student, together with Professor Pace and Colonel Lipari-Cascio, who had looked after the Whitaker properties in and around Marsala since Pip's death and knew all the digs intimately. When the students were assembled, Delia plucked up courage and explained her father's work to the group of young men. She then led Tusa to the so-called 'house of the amphoras', and asked him to continue her father's work. '*La Signorina* Delia was lonely,' Tusa remembered, 'but she was kind and very English; tea at five o'clock and change for dinner.'

One day, after her mother's death, *la Signorina* and Professor Pace were joined by Vincenzo Tusa. 'I well remember,' he recalled, 'that *la Signorina* Delia said to Professor Pace, "What shall we do, Professor, with our little island? Who will look after it when we are both gone?" Obviously, before my arrival, they had discussed the Foundation because, pointing at me, Professor Pace told Miss Delia: "This is the young man who will look after it."' Professor Pace, Tusa added, was always telling him that '*gli inglesi se la vogliono pigliare*', in short, that the British wanted to get their hands on Motya, so something had to be done, but what?

After this conversation, Vincenzo Tusa accompanied Professor Pace to the Hôtel des Palmes, where they sat down for coffee, and Pace explained the idea under discussion: that of forming a charitable foundation of Delia Whitaker's properties, named after her father. 'Since I was then working in the Soprintendenza per le Antichità in a junior capacity, Professor Pace asked me to help to cut through the paperwork and bureaucracy,' says Tusa. From that day onwards, he saw *la Signorina* more regularly. When he once commented on the beauty of Villa Malfitano's park, Delia pressed him to bring his wife and children to visit it. One day *la Signorina* begged Tusa to continue her father's excavations and offered him 6 million lire (a lot of money in the 1950s) to proceed with one of his digs. 'I said, *per carità*, Signorina, don't give me any money. I will do it and you pay for it, but I don't want to touch any banknotes.' Subsequently Delia visited Motya more often and followed Tusa's excavations of the tophet with interest.

Villa Malfitano was a solitary place, indeed it had become almost ghostly; only Raffaele Pellerito, the butler, could recall the good old days, and now even Raffaele has gone. The running costs of house and gardens were gigantic, even in the 1960s. A British citizen, Delia had always been loyal to her country, and so now she offered Villa Malfitano to the Foreign Office, hoping that it could become the British Consulate in Palermo. But most of the British colony had been expelled from Sicily under Fascism, and British business had declined at the same time; now there was hardly any need for a consulate in Sicily at all to replace the thirty-five that had served the British community in the previous century. So Delia's offer was turned down; Her Majesty's Government decided that the upkeep of such a place would have been an extravagance. But Delia was at least awarded an MBE for her efforts. So she decided – or was persuaded – to leave her fortune to a foundation: the Joseph Whitaker Foundation.

In May 1966 *la Signorina* decided that Rosario Chiovaro, a lawyer of questionable character who had become very close to her, should be her executor. After Delia's death, and with the formation of the Foundation, Chiovaro 'inherited' the position of general secretary. During his ascendancy, both before and after Delia's death, most of the Villa Malfitano treasures disappeared; of course, there was no inventory. But one evening in the 1970s, when Chiovaro was returning home, he was beaten up and left on the ground for dead; he actually died a few days later. No one knows whether this attack was at all connected with the Whitaker affairs, and no one is likely to explain yet another Sicilian mystery. The only intelligence one can glean is that Chiovaro was another freemason and some also say a mafioso. He might have been both.

Delia had come to trust Vincenzo Tusa and would consult him on details concerning Motya. 'Sometimes it was difficult for me; for example, in her will she had left the house in which *il Colonnello* lived on Motya to him, in perpetuity. I said, "It's not my business, Signorina, but you cannot leave him just the house; he has to get to the house, so you will have to endow him with some land for him to arrive, keep his boat and then walk to the house." "You are right," Delia answered. But then I added, "I know that *il Colonnello* will not build on Motya, nor will his son. But who can tell about his grandson? He might build a hotel or sell the land ..." So Delia left the house to *il Colonnello* only for his lifetime. When I saw Lipari-Cascio next in Marsala, he would not even greet me. "What have you done ... you hate me!" I tried to explain that what I had advised *la Signorina* had nothing to do with him or me, just with the future of Motya ...'

It was decided that Villa Malfitano should also be part of the Joseph Whitaker Foundation, and endowed with funds from Delia's personal fortune. In her will she left 68 million lire to charities founded by her family; the house in Rome went to the di Giorgios, Norina's husband's family. The rest of her Italian estate, including Motya, was placed in a non-profit-making fund. The Foundation saw the light of day in 1975, four years after Delia's death and nine after the solicitors had received all the necessary papers. Questions should be asked why so long a period had to elapse before the Joseph Whitaker Foundation was recognized by the Italian state. The villa was to become the headquarters of the Foundation and was to be preserved in the state in which it had been left, with all its treasures and artefacts in place. Pip's museum at Motya, which had been enlarged by Delia, was to be kept intact and looked after as further excavations proceeded.

The Foundation should also have been used to further Pip's botanical interests, but Delia failed to mention her father's ornithological passion which, like her mother Tina, she did not share. She had been delighted to see the last of all those dusty feathers. The various institutions in Palermo having turned it down, she succeeded in finding a home for the extravagantly large collection of stuffed birds in museums in Belfast and Edinburgh, where they can still be seen. The villa at Racalia which Benjamin Ingham had built for his duchess went with its 15 hectares to another branch of the Whitaker family, descended from Joshua's wife Euphrosine, and it is still enjoyed by them.

The Joseph Whitaker Foundation was put under the aegis of the Accademia Nazionale dei Lincei. According to the statutes of the Foundation, the board of trustees was to include the President of the Republic, represented by a delegate. The stated aim of the Foundation was to boost cultural activities, including archaeology and in particular the study of the Phoenician–Punic civilization whose most significant and characteristic centre was the islet of Motya.

'Motya was central to the Whitakers' patrimony,' the Foundation's President, Aldo Scimè, told me. 'The villa was a gift together with all its contents, 8 hectares of garden and some apartments in Palermo and Rome. There is a trust which looks after this patrimony, made up of seven people; I am the president now. Three of the trustees are elected by the Prefect, for life, one is nominated by the Accademia dei Lincei – he is Professor Angelo Falzea of the Institute of Near Eastern Studies. Dr Rosalia Camerata Scovazzo is the Sovrintendente of Fine Arts for Western Sicily.' One of the trustees appointed for life was Eduardo Lipari, son of the Colonel, nominated by Delia herself; but he has fallen seriously ill, and has passed his position on to Mr D'Ali, something which the majority of the Foundation declared unacceptable. Another, Professor Paolo Mathiae, is the distinguished archaeologist to whom we owe the discovery of Ebla. Dr Onofrio Salamone is a nominee of the Sicilian Region, and Dr Francesco Tortorici the nominee of the Prefect of Palermo. The secretary general is the handsome Maria Enza Carollo.

In the 1970s, while the Foundation was struggling its way into existence, many artefacts disappeared from Villa Malfitano. According to Raffaele, the Whitakers' butler, furs and clothes which had belonged to the three ladies disappeared overnight. Some embroideries were found scorched and stuffed inside the oven,

Maria Enza Carollo said. 'Raffaele used to say that these rooms did not need electric light because the silver was so plentiful that it glittered,' she went on. 'Only one silver bowl has survived the looting of Villa Malfitano. Raffaele knew everything, but it was not in his interest to talk.'

Dr Scimè, a solicitor universally praised for his rectitude, was called in to become the Special Commissar of the Foundation in 1987 after the former president had dissolved the previous group of trustees. When he arrived he found a debt of 1,700 million lire. Recently, before falling ill, Mr Lipari insisted that his son Giulio be given a permanent job in the Foundation and, because of the connection of the Lipari family with Motya and the Whitakers, Aldo Scimè eventually agreed. But after a while Giulio Lipari disappeared – literally; so completely, indeed, that Scimè became worried and asked the *carabinieri* to investigate. Finally a fax arrived, through a solicitor and signed by a solicitor on Giulio Lipari's behalf, asking the Foundation to accept his resignation. But nobody has seen the young man anywhere.

As we went on our tour of Villa Malfitano, the sombre rooms still scorched, like Punic Motya itself, by the fire that had torn through it in 1994, Scimè told me that he had decided to lock the best items, the 'treasure', in a room on the second floor. But the treasure, mainly made up of the *coralli trapanesi*, Baroque pieces of bejewelled construction, was in need of repair. The most important items in the villa, the Gobelin tapestries representing the story of Dido and Aeneas, suffered during the fire, but the regional authorities intervened with funds to have them repaired. 'The fire caused 2 billion lire of damage,' remarked Scimè. 'Things had been happening, much mystery . . .'

My first official visit to Villa Malfitano had been arranged by Giuliana Saladino, a writer. She rang up on my behalf to make an appointment with the President of the Foundation and told him that I was particularly interested in consulting the Whitaker archives. I was hoping that I might find some notes by Pip, perhaps jotted-down comments on Motya . . . Maybe I would even find that missing document concerning the future of Motya. Surely Whitaker had known what would happen if he left Motya to chance and to Delia; he knew Sicily, he had been born there.

As we waited for the President, Giuliana and I were entertained by Mrs Carollo, who gave us strong coffee and was quite explicit about the major thefts from the villa, but did not mention any names. Dr Scimè received me cordially, and we set off through the dark rooms of Villa Malfitano which exuded unhappiness and waste: wasted lives, loneliness.

I was introduced to the archivist, Signora Bice Gozzo, who told me that she had been trying to put Joseph Whitaker's papers in order but that she had not finished. What? Had thirty years not been long enough? I asked. In any case, she could not take me upstairs to the archive, because she was in a hurry to leave and collect her grandchild. I was not amused; I had come all the way from London to see Pip's papers. I said I would return on another day. What I did not realize was that Signora Bice had only been working on the archives for three years because no earlier decision had been taken about what to do with Pip's papers. Not only that, but she had taken on the job as an unpaid hobby. Between 1975 and 1995 nobody had done a thing about Joseph Whitaker's papers, which remained on the top floor of Villa Malfitano in a state of total disarray. Many letters had been burnt during the winter to keep the stoves going, maybe out of ignorance rather than mischief.

On my second visit, a few months later, Signora Bice led me up via rickety stairs and an ancient lift to a cold little room that now served as the library. Most of the books belonging to the once fabled Whitaker collection had disappeared. During the last years of Delia's life everything had gone to pieces, the archivist told me. She had done good work, filing Joseph Whitaker's letters, his notes and those of his wife and daughters under different headings according to their subjects. When she thought that she had put the thousands of sheets in order, she had opened another door in the attic and, to her utter consternation, was confronted by another disorderly mass of sheets, left on the floor in total disarray. At least they had escaped the stoves. 'I had to start all over again.'

I asked her if she thought that some of the documents might have been destroyed on purpose.

'Oh, no, I don't think so.'

Signora Bice had been a teacher of classical languages at the Termini Imerese upper school, where she had taught Maria Enza Carollo, 'the best in her class. You should have seen her! She was so good-looking, always tidy, I can still see her in a white ironed shirt . . .' Signora Bice was as proud of the other woman as if she were her mother. 'There, she is the most important of us all, she began to work here when she was eighteen. All the others come and go, but she stays.'

Signora Bice must once have been a good-looking woman too. She was a retired widow, keen to apply her knowledge as an archivist, in which subject she had taken a university degree. 'I have never had a chance to exercise it and I really enjoy it.' As she had worked through the papers she had gradually grown fonder of Joseph Whitaker – Pip, as we began to call him between ourselves – and enthusiastically demonstrated to me his scholarly curiosity, his knowledge of classical languages and his appetite for reading.

I took up a fragile piece of paper, a note written in pencil on the stationary of a St Moritz hotel: 'It is interesting to note how in the early cremation necropolis one meets with proto-Corinthian vases but no attic pottery, thus showing that it was in existence in the VIII Century BC.' I found Pip's sketches of the mosaics which he had drawn as he found them buried along the Motyan beach, and we examined them together. Pip marked the Phoenician letters for Motya on several sheets of paper and learned the Phoenician alphabet so that he could read the carved stones. He was more than just a dilettante; he was a passionate scholar, aware that he had hit on the only surviving Punic city which could reveal the secrets of a forgotten people. Did he know that he was the owner of the best-kept secret in history? Probably yes, otherwise he would not have endured all the difficulties of buying up the plots of land on the little island from suspicious farmers while being harassed by envious bureaucrats trying to block the progress of *l'inglese*.

Signora Bice, portly and neat, enveloped in black widowhood and also in scent, talked about Pip as if the two had met in the distant past, as if only she understood this shy, timid man. At times, Dr Scimè climbed all the stairs of Villa Malfitano in order to join us for coffee and biscuits. His office was on the ground floor, next to the billiard room where two employees sat surrounded by an immense quantity of paper. How come Motya's excavations had virtually stopped? I asked. There was no money, came the answer. The Sovrintendente, on the other hand, had answered the same question by saying that she had decided to spend the money on the preservation of what had already been done, to tidy things up at

Motya. The region gave the Foundation 450 million lire a year, and there was some money from Whitaker properties let in Palermo and Rome, as well as a little bit from entrance tickets in Motya; but they employed fifteen people altogether. 'If the state had to pay for the upkeep of Villa Malfitano and Motya,' said Scimè, 'it would have to pay far more than what the region actually gives us.' The Foundation had also finished assembling the music archive of the Whitakers, which is large and important. 'It will become part of the Beni Culturali [Department of Fine Arts].'

Had Signora Bice found any documents? I asked her one day. Any official letters concerning Motya, for example, or a will? I was still dreaming of finding Pip's Motyan will. She did find two unsigned copies and a signed copy of Joseph Whitaker's will, dated 28 September 1935, in which he gave everything to his two daughters; and on 5 November 1935 he had signed an official *rettifica*, an amendment concerning some plots of land. The notary was Carlo Mercantini from Rome. But there was no specific mention of Motya.

Of course Pip would have written an official document concerning his desire on the future of Motya. Meticulous and careful as he clearly was, Pip would have not left Motya in the hands of those three neurotic women. I had already figured it out. Having sought advice from his friends at the British Museum, Pip would have left Motya to the Archaeological Faculty of Oxford University – or to the British Museum. The last thing he would have wanted was to leave the responsibility of a decision to either his wife or his daughters. Of course the paper had been destroyed.

But who destroyed it?

Tina, maybe. She was a patriot, which in those nationalistic days meant a Fascist. She was, after all, an admirer of Mussolini. Or maybe she did not want to see Motya slip away from her control, even if she had never cared for it. Or had Delia been persuaded to throw away her father's will on Motya and relinquish control to a Foundation? It could have been Chiovaro himself who foresaw the easy plunder ahead; or, more likely, it could have been a masonic deal: a lot of people around Motya seemed to have belonged to the Brotherhood. This had nothing to do with the Mafia, of course. But it did concern national glory, the good name of Italian archaeology and all those Fascistic concepts which stank of Sicilian freemasonry. At least the new President, Scimè, had decided to put the archive in order; and he was an honest man.

One day I went to pay a visit to Salvatore Lamarna, called 'Totuccio', once head gardener at Villa Malfitano, where he had worked since he was seventeen. An old man with North African features, he spoke a lovely Palermitan. I met him standing by the pavilion which had originally housed the sinful General Scalia and then Pip's ornithological collection. It was now Salvatore's turn to live there; and it was there that he eventually died, in early 1999.

'There have been so many changes!' he lamented: 'the staff grew old, some died, some were pensioned off, some were replaced and others were not. When she took a walk in the park, Signorina Delia was followed by her maid, Signorina Antonietta, and a footman. When they went out they always took a coach with two horses and a coachman following. At times they even had four horses. The stables held ten horses altogether.'

When Salvatore first arrived, recruited by the chief gardener Vizzini, Commendatore Whitaker was already dead. 'The three ladies lived at Villa Malfitano and ten people worked for them plus the driver and two nurses for *la Signorina* Dorina. The first car they bought was a Lancia. It was a really noble house. The porter stood there and people were announced to them. I used to wear a dark blue uniform and Pasquale, when he served at table, he wore white gloves and had coral buttons.'

After her mother's death, Delia finally enjoyed some attention. 'Each year in June, as if she were the Embassy, she gave a party to celebrate the Queen's birthday and all the Consuls came, the American and the English, and there was a little band playing in the garden,' Totuccio recalled. 'Now there is nobody ... the Bordonaro, the Princess Maria de Seta, Prince Paolo, they all came to play tennis ... There were the Princesses Niscemi, the Princess di Trabia, and the Butera coming to tea.'

Ben Whitaker remembers visiting his cousin in the late 1950s when, looking at the colourful stuffed birds left by her father, Delia would compare them to the Palermo nobility, giving each an appropriate name. That was the Princess Alliata, that other one the Duchessa Trigona, etc. When her young cousin came to Sicily to work for Danilo Dolci, the social reformer, Delia told Ben that he should not, that Dolci was a Communist; she condemned Ben for his left-wing leanings, and when he became a Labour MP she thought that he had been lost to the family altogether.

The number of gardeners dwindled until eventually Totuccio Lamarca was doing most of the work himself. 'You should have seen the flowers!' His eyes lit up as he remembered the gardens. He had a rugged face and hands like elephant's feet. He described the garden not as we saw it, but as it had been when it blazed with rare flowers and plants, its rose-beds thick with blooms arranged in the initials of the Signorine's names. 'We changed the flower-beds every season and did the vases in the house every day.'

When Delia felt that her time had come, she asked to be moved into the bedroom where her mother had died. The Palermitan nobility came to see her with flowers and prayers; by then they regarded her as one of their own. The idea would have left Delia – but not Tina – indifferent.

Delia left a heavy responsibility which required someone knowledgeable and strong to take it up. Someone capable of fighting like a lion.

13

DR ISSERLIN IN MOTYA

When they talk about Dr Isserlin, at Motya, Rosina and Giuseppe smile with their eyes. They hope that he may return, but they also like to have a chance to talk about him and to recollect the days when he lived and worked with them.

Like most outstanding people, Dr Isserlin is modest about himself and about his work; available to people who want to steal his knowledge and experience. He answered my questions and gave explanations patiently and methodically; I could sense that he had been an excellent teacher. Nor did he think of himself as exceptional, or that his exceptional work was remarkable.

I went to see him in Leeds, where he lives in a dark house, cosily tucked away among his Mittel-European books and papers, watched over by some portraits and photographs evocative of treasured memories. I had heard a lot about him. In particular, his researches had demonstrated that the so-called cothon was not a Phoenician harbour, as had hitherto been believed. It was too small to be used as anchorage for the ships of the time; it was more of a mooring bay, where damaged ships could be refitted in safety without actually removing them from the water, as in a dry dock. The cothon in Motya, as indeed the cothons in Carthage, might also have been used for pre-assembling ships, since the Phoenicians invented the method. Motya could have easily been a centre for making ships. The different pieces of wood might have been shipped to the island already numbered and manufactured; I doubt that the wood was worked at Motya itself, because of lack of space. The industrial district which was near the cothon might have produced the special glues and nails needed for assembling the ships. On the other hand, the now bare hills behind Selinunte and on Mount Eryx were wooded once, and the Elymians – as indeed the Selinuntines – might have sold wood to the Motyans and even to

Carthage; the ships which sailed in that part of the world were not made with Phoenician cedars but with Italian and Sicilian trees.

Dr Isserlin wrote:

One of the features of San Pantaleo which attracted Whitaker's attention was a rectangular water-filled basin, retained by ashlar masonry, situated towards the south-western corner of the island. When Whitaker first began to investigate it, he found that it was connected to the sea by a cutting which formed a kind of street . . . The basin was known as *la Salinella* and had indeed served as a salt-pan during the Middle Ages and after. At times it may also have served as a *piscina* or reservoir for fish, particularly during the period of the Jesuit ownership of Motya from the sixteenth to the eighteenth century. [1]

The Phoenicians were competent engineers, and the cothons or basins in Carthage and Tyre were clearly built for the same reason as the one in Motya.

Dr Isserlin and I had exchanged letters, and I had asked him if I could see him to talk about his time in Motya. His house was on a busy boulevard lined with trees and green with gardens hiding rather sinister Edwardian houses. The door was opened by his son, also an archaeologist and historian, whose own subject was Roman Britain. Father and son lived together, Dr Isserlin having recently lost his beloved wife. I could not help sensing the emptiness he felt without her from almost every word he said. His son was trying to compensate for his father's loss by cooking and providing for him. He too had been in Motya as a baby, when he had been smitten with sunstroke, much to his parents' consternation.

'We took him to Marsala hospital by boat, at night, covered with blankets, and Dr Casciola looked after him very well. That was on the second year of our expedition. After that all the members of our team were looked after by Dr Casciola in Marsala.' This incident apart, Dr Isserlin had very pleasant memories of Motya.

He was Head of the Department of Semitic Studies and Reader in Semitic Studies at the University of Leeds until his retirement in 1981. He was obviously also a Jewish refugee, but we did not share this kind of knowledge although we felt a kind of mutual gratitude because of this tacit recognition. Besides, I could better understand that the stimulus for his interest in Phoenician culture and language was not merely the result of scholarship in the ancient Hebrew language, history and customs, but was also caused by curiosity about the ancient roots of our people. Indeed, I questioned him about what seemed to me to be the extraordinary similarities between the Phoenician and Hebrew languages.

In his youth, Dr Isserlin had worked at the Phoenician city of Sabratha in Libya with Dr Kathleen Kenyon, the daughter of Sir Frederick Kenyon, whom he called 'the outstanding biblical scholar in the late nineteenth and early twentieth century',[2] and Motya, he thought, was an ideal site to work with the stratigraphic method that he had learned from her. 'I was very interested in the Phoenicians and decided that Motya was well worth investigating. It seemed an ideal site to be doing stratigraphic investigation of the type with which I had become familiar with Dr Kenyon. I was at that time mainly concentrating on the Levant, and particularly on Israelite archaeology. I still am, but I have always been interested in Phoenician studies as well and I know my way around them reasonably; when I went to Sabratha it was not a totally new departure. So I decided that Motya was worth further investigation using the Kenyon method, and the idea was well received in Oxford. Donald Harden, author of *The Phoenicians*, was at the time head of the Ashmolean Museum, and Dr T. J. Dunbabin, a leading expert in Greek pottery, also from Oxford, pushed the idea forward. We then mounted a small expedition to test the ground.'

That was in 1955. Dr Isserlin asked the Whitaker family for permission to visit Motya with the object of planning an excavation programme. He met Tina Whitaker and her two daughters, Delia and Norina, who were very pleased by his interest. Dr Isserlin had become aware of Motya not only because of the importance of the site but because he had read Joseph Whitaker's book.

'Delia, of course, was the one who mattered, as it were, and she was quite in favour of our plan; she put the island at our disposal. In particular she told her administrator, the late Colonnello Lipari-Cascio, and he looked after us really wonderfully well and we were put up partly in his farmhouse, partly in the villa; but it took a number of years before a proper expedition could be arranged. We started again in 1961 and that was an expedition mounted jointly with the Institute of Archaeology in London, represented by Miss Joan

Du Plat Taylor, who already had a name of her own as one of the promoters of underwater archaeology; she had been in Cyprus in the Antiquity Service and she joined us as the representative of the Institute of Archaeology. So it was a Leeds–London expedition, at that stage; we were possibly ten or fifteen people, something like that.' [3]

Their early visits were usually by train, to Marsala, where they stayed at the Hotel Stella d'Italia, but later they arrived by air to Palermo or even Trapani, before moving on to Motya. 'In those days, to make yourself known, at the end of the landing-stage you waved a white handkerchief. If they saw you, it was fine; if they didn't it was a bit tedious, and five times over the years I waded across with my clothes on my head and caused a little astonishment at the other end. That is how we conveyed ourselves – or were conveyed – across the lagoon. Later they got a sail and finally an engine, but it was the measure of prosperity gradually coming to that part of the world. Workmen were first on foot and bicycle, then on motor-bicycles, then they had their own little cars.'

From the very beginning, Dr Isserlin's wife Hilda was in charge of the administration, although at the outset she could not speak a word of Italian. However, she learned the language quickly on the job, and got on excellently with everybody, especially with the local ladies. 'I remember a very funny episode,' recalled Dr Isserlin. 'In the local fashion, wives didn't really matter, what the husband decided was what counted. When each morning the breakfast menu was decided, a widow called Maria together with Rosina Arini, who was Giuseppe Pugliese's sister, would arrive and ask: "Professore, how am I to do the eggs? Fried?" Hilda listened to this a number of times and when the question came up again she said, in English – her Italian was still not good: "Never mind what he says, what I say goes!" They understood the meaning and the question was not asked again. So we managed.'

At that time Motya was extremely primitive. Each evening Vincenzo Pugliese, together with his brother Giuseppe and Vincenzo Arini, would patrol around the island with a shotgun and make sure that there were no intruders; the bandit Giuliano had just been killed in nearby Castelvetrano in very mysterious circumstances. Banditry was still a problem. Moreover, Motya was without electricity, except for the batteries which served the custodians' house, where the group of academics would often gather in the evenings to read and to discuss their day's work.

'There was no water fit for us to drink, all water as well as wine and beer had to be brought in from Marsala, and even that was not easy because the water supply in Marsala was often turned off for a number of hours every day. It was years before we had running water. Shopping had to be done in Marsala, and since we usually came to Sicily at the end of June or beginning of July, the hottest part of the year, food could turn bad very quickly. We had to buy ice in the market to keep food without it going off and provisions were wrapped up in ice; even that didn't always help and occasionally things went bad. When the food had got to the kitchen in the farmhouse we put everything inside an old ice-box dated 1860. Each morning the ice had disappeared and there was a big lake under it, but the stuff was edible. We lived passably well. Light at night was a problem. We had a big lamp suspended from the ceiling in the room where we took our meals.'

In the year 1968 a new approach was made to the cothon because Professor Mingazzini had suggested in a report for the Italian expedition that the cothon might have been a 'sacred lake', part of a sanctuary complex. The word 'cothon' or 'kothon' has reached us from ancient authorities like the Latin writer Servius, who described this type of artificial basin as being typically Phoenician. A new phase of the expedition, also organised by Dr Isserlin and specially dedicated to the cothon, started in the summer of that year and continued into 1969 and 1970, 'in three brief campaigns'.

At times Professor Tusa came to see Dr Isserlin and his team. 'He had his representative who looked after us and saw that we did not do anything not in our permit. Some were very nice, I especially remember Mr Affatigato, who came for several years and looked after us very well. Whenever Professor Tusa queried something, I would say, following his advice: 'Ho già parlato con il suo assistente'('I have already spoken to your assistant'); that would be enough. La Signora Aldina Tusa came as well; she is an authority on coins. Once or twice her son came with them and I remember when he had a bit of heatstroke; we had no ice but we had a cool potato, which was sliced and applied to his head. It did the trick.'

That lamp which hung from the ceiling got broken practically every year. On one occasion the group included a particularly tall young professor, a specialist in metal objects who, getting up from the table, hit his head against the lamp and shattered it: 'But not all was lost – there was still a shop in Palermo where we could buy a new lamp to replace it; which we had to do year after year. We made quite sure that the lamp was always there because Colonnello Lipari-Cascio would have not been pleased if his favourite lamp were to be destroyed.'

At night, after supper, individuals found their way back to their rooms with a candle or a torch; but before that they would all be sitting around the large stone in the garden of the Liparis' farmhouse 'for very pleasant evenings, I remember. Gradually civilization caught up with us, there is electricity now ...'

When he first went to Motya, Dr Isserlin decided where he wanted to dig. 'I thought "this would be a good spot", "this other one would be an excellent spot" . . . because locations were keys to questions which needed an answer. One was the cothon region, including the cothon itself, which we excavated in the late sixties and early seventies, and it was one of the most enjoyable things I had the good luck to do. First of all, we drained the whole thing with a pump that we hired in Marsala. This took a day or possibly two, then the area dried and you could dig in it like any dry site. You had to keep the pump there and each morning you put it on for about twenty minutes and that was enough to deal with the seepage, surprisingly little. We blocked it off where the canal meets the sea, simply with a little bit of earth and some sandbags. That kept the water out.'

From their observations on the cothon, Dr Isserlin concluded that a ship on entry would have been guided into position through the canal. A groove built into the paving would have accommodated the keel, and steps on the side of the basin could hold the vessel upright. The channel between the quays would have been used for unloading ships or for repairs; it also served as an entrance from the lagoon into the basin. The team dated the original building of the cothon to the sixth or early fifth century BC. 'Such a sloping basin would have been very useful for beaching ships, and we may suppose that it was intended for careening and other repairs more extensive than the limited facilities in the channel between the quays would allow,' Isserlin concluded in his paper in *Antiquity*.

In 1968–9 the team excavated the whole section 'between the masonry quays ... it revealed a splendid piece of marine engineering, constructed from large blocks of sandy limestone, some smooth faced and some provided with marginal drafting . . . We wanted to investigate the cothon channel which we did, we freed the pavement that had not been seen for many centuries and it is still down there in the water. It was like a piece of nineteenth-century railway engineering, about the width of a single track, 2.70 metres from the paving up to where the stone ends.'4

They made a film showing the channel being freed, which Dr Isserlin still has. 'It really looks like the Great Western Railway being born, it's quite remarkable.'

Another area where he chose to dig was the north gate and its connection with the causeway. They excavated a great deal and found many more cut stones and details. 'We investigated the road for the sake of information and we looked into the various layers of paving and more or less succeeded in dating them. This was a rare piece of analysis, because roads don't usually get the attention they deserve, and to have a Phoenician road which has its history dated is fairly unusual. We also found a little sanctuary nearby. In the other main region where we worked near the south gate we cleared out all the housing and investigated the history of the gate and city walls. We tried a little in the water but that remained a sideline.'

Pierre Cintas, an eminent French archaeologist who collaborated with the Isserlin mission in 1961–2, understood that part of the necropolis discovered by Whitaker was in actual fact a tophet, the sacred precinct for infant and animal sacrifices. In 1964 the excavation was taken over by Professor Tusa and his team, and the Motya tophet with its many objects and inscriptions turned out to be the most important find for deciphering Punic history. During that excavation the Italian expedition dug out a group of masks of a very eclectic type which mixed Egyptian and Greek styles, but also some statues and artefacts which had a unique Motyan/Punic flavour, with grotesque and scaring features. A very important stela which was found at that stage described the number and locations of the offerings, 700 in all starting from the seventh century BC and continuing to well into the middle of the third century BC.

When the Isserlin expedition first arrived at Motya it was a Leeds–London team, with a director and co-director. But this pattern changed. 'First of all we had a Leeds visiting professor from the United States, and he engineered a link with Fairleigh Dickinson

University near New York. Each year we took on a number of American students as trainees to give them some idea of what a dig is like. In return we were given some funds, which were very welcome because our finances were limited. Finally, a visit from Professor E. C. B. MacLaurin from Australia gave us a connection with his Department of Semitic Studies in Sydney. So in the end we had the grand title Leeds–London–Fairleigh-Dickinson–Sydney Expedition. The American students in particular were an interesting bunch and brought in some unexpected characteristics. The young ladies appeared with their best wardrobe, not quite suited for Motya; one young gentleman was bitten by a small dog and was terribly frightened, he thought that he might get tetanus or rabies, and he wanted the dog to be destroyed and its head sent to the forensic laboratory. Fortunately it did not happen.'

Rosina Arini, the mother of the present custodian of Motya, cooked for them. I showed Dr Isserlin photographs of the Pugliese family and of the Arinis. In the evenings, meals became both jollier and important occasions for discussions and meetings.

'The biggest number that there ever was at table was twenty-six, or perhaps twenty-three, all at a long table; occasionally somebody didn't take to the Sicilian menu. In the morning people went out well fed. We started at seven o'clock, breakfast was at eight with half an hour to get people arriving from the site; then we worked until lunchtime at noon and then there was a siesta. At two or two-thirty we went back, and then we went on digging until five. In the evenings there was registering and you name it, we had to do it. But a great deal had to be done back in England. That's the way we worked.'

The Whitaker ladies were not on Motya when the expedition was at work, because they only visited the island in May, while it was still reasonably cool. Isserlin remembered Delia's visits. 'Miss Whitaker usually came for one day every year in order to check on our progress. In early years she walked down to the cothon but latterly she had to be pushed in a little wheelchair. Tina was too old even to do that, but Delia was genuinely interested and very helpful; she made clear from the beginning that we would not receive any funds from her but short of that all help would be available. She did precisely that. Colonnello Lipari-Cascio couldn't have been kinder and more helpful and all paths were smoothed by him. Whatever we wanted, we asked him and if he could possibly help us, he did, he was first class. When he died, his son Eduardo tried to help us similarly but he didn't quite have the same position. Colonnello Lipari-Cascio was a figure to be reckoned with in Marsala, he more or less ruled it. His son Eduardo did his best but he did not have the same stature. He might have now, I don't know.'

But things had changed and the old Mafia had disappeared, giving way to a more thuggish crowd. Colonnello Lipari-Cascio represented the old boy network, a world that the new generation with their Kalashnikovs and Swiss bank accounts regarded as palaeolithic.

Did Motya still have much to yield?

'A lot, I would think; in some ways more of the same. But I think that in the place selected by Professor Falsone (and where he found an outstanding statue) there might be some impressive things. And I have a hunch that if only one could get at it, near the farmhouse and the little village, there would be more. It is a high point and Whitaker built his villa there because it is a pleasant area, it catches the wind. That would have been true in earlier times. On the other side, in the museum, there is a copper vase with two faces, one faces this way and the other faces the other way. And that, I was told, was found near the back of the farmhouse which now belongs to Eduardo Lipari. Things like that don't knock around without a good cause . . . When the extension to the museum was built we asked to be allowed to inspect the earth and the bits of pottery; we saw that there was evidence that it belonged to the eighth century BC. So there is an earlier nucleus there; I would think there is more on that site. There are ways of exploring which can be used now even without excavating. There is a geophysical technique, for instance, where you use something like radar; the electric emissions come back and give you a picture.'

They had tried this at the time when the extension to the museum was being built, but the device was then in its infancy. 'Now much more can be done. I personally have been involved in something of the kind in Greece.' I asked him where in Greece. 'This would be something you studied at school. You will have heard of the invasion of King Xerxes. In 480 Xerxes invaded Greece, he wanted to make it part of his empire, and in order to let his fleet get along without having to round the dangerous Mount Athos, he had a canal dug behind it and his fleet passed safely. For the past few years we have done geophysical measurements about where the canal was and how wide it was and so on. I was led to this by Motya, when I was trying to get an idea of what was the channel like which led from the cothon to the sea. Have we got any parallels? I asked myself, and the first thing that came to my mind was the canal that Xerxes built in Greece and it appeared that nobody was doing a thing about it.'

Of course, the Persians had used Phoenician ships and engineers, and Dr Isserlin must have reckoned on this; he would have found the same know-how in both Mediterranean places. 'After a few years I thought, perhaps I can try to find out. An expedition was arranged and it has been working on and off and is just about winding up. The Greeks are now interested; they were not then, but they are now thinking of doing really big things there. I won't be involved, I'm getting too ancient.'

As we talked in that dark room in suburban Leeds, it seemed to me that Motya had come alive and that suddenly the wide desk, the pile of books and papers, all vanished and the heavy curtains were filtering the blue waters of the Stagnone. There was much nostalgia and pleasure in Dr Isserlin's account of his days in Motya.

I asked him whether he thought that Diodorus Siculus had been accurate in his description of the battle that destroyed Motya. Diodorus actually had a reputation for having copied whole sections of his immense *History of the World*, at times borrowing verbatim from various texts which have since disappeared. Evidence of this can be seen in the way in which his prose style varies. In fact, unlike Herodotus, Diodorus hardly travelled. He might have gone to Alexandria and called on its famous library in order to look up missing episodes, but that was about all. As we know, Diodorus lived three centuries after the fall of Motya. It was as if I were to write an accurate description of conditions and events in the France of Louis XIV, and even that would be much easier because we have more information than the Greeks had. Or have we? We forget how many papyrus documents were available, as well as paintings, inscriptions and monuments. Anyway, I asked Dr Isserlin whether he thought that Diodorus had been accurate.

'I think it is as good as we are going to get. We did find archaeological evidence that proved many things to be true.'

There was another opinion that I wanted to extract from this scholarly man, and that concerned Joseph Whitaker's reputation, which lately has come under attack. At Villa Malfitano, lovingly filed by Signora Bice, I had found the text of a lecture Pip had given at the British Museum in 1919. He introduced it thus:

With the exception of a few articles and letters which, from time to time, have appeared in some of our English newspapers, as well as those of other countries, little has, so far, been published concerning the archaeological work which has been carried out at Motya in recent years. This work was commenced in 1906, but unfortunately, like many other undertakings, was interrupted and almost brought to a standstill by the war of 1914 . . . In the course of the excavations which have been carried out at Motya since 1906, however, a good many discoveries of interest have been made, some of them indeed, according to my friend, Dr Thomas Ashby, being of sufficient importance to be brought before the present meeting, and it is at Dr Ashby's suggestion that I have written the following short paper on them. 5

Whitaker then explained the work he had done on the fortifications, the sandstone staircases, the city garrison. He also talked about the location of the guard-house, the northern gateway with its two towers, the causeway and 'the road or street, leading from it inland, which was also probably the main thoroughfare of the town, extending possibly right across the island to the southern shores'. But Whitaker did not understand the real use of the cothon, which he thought was a small harbour. In the end it was Isserlin's investigation that led to its present attribution. As he explained, 'Within a short distance to the west of the south gateway the important discovery was made of a small artificially built dock connected to the sea by a fairly wide channel and with well-constructed quays on either side. The cothon is of rectangular shape and measures 51 metres in length by 37 metres in width. As in the case of the gateway, here also evidence is to be found of the Motyans' efforts to defend themselves during the great siege, for the channel, in one spot, is blocked by large stones, purposely laid across.'

Dr Isserlin went on: 'Whitaker did things as well as the standard of the time permitted, and the more I saw of his excavations, the more I appreciated the man, his scholarship and his efforts.'

I myself left Leeds full of respect for Dr Isserlin. His work was the perfect continuation of what Whitaker had started in Motya; it stretched through a decade and it achieved really important goals. The cothon was recognized as a dockyard, underlining what high standards of engineering the Phoenicians and the Carthaginian people had achieved.

14

VINCENZO TUSA AND
SELINUNTE

For many Sicilians, Vincenzo Tusa represents the quintessential archaeologist. *L'archeologo-contadino*, they called him, and nobody today can be compared to that energetic man who, in T-shirt and straw hat, used to dig tirelessly under the perpendicular sun. He was a familiar figure as he roamed the countryside, inspecting work in progress and sometimes even appearing at night in order to discourage the gangs of tomb-robbers. When Tusa, with his big head and tanned skin, emerged from behind a bush or a Doric column, unquestioned authority was on his side.

Tusa, who retired in January 1986, belonged to the heroic days of archaeology; these days he lives modestly in a flat near the cathedral in Palermo. It is full of books dedicated to him, photographs and mementos which remind him of the good old days. He had been famous; his thundering voice would echo in the university halls and on archaeological sites. Now that he is old he feels that he has been forgotten and that his achievements have been put on one side.

But only somebody of Professor Tusa's calibre could have put up such a fight against the Mafia in defence of archaeology and lived to tell the tale. On many counts he won, which was probably due to the fact that he is himself Sicilian. He is a native of eastern Sicily, and because of that he could understand the mentality of his opponents. In the defence of archaeology, he fought illegal real estate development and corrupt administrations; and as a result, he made many enemies. There are countries where to have a conscience is rare and to be honest is a choice of life that is often penalized, setting a man apart from his fellows. In Sicily this phenomenon is exaggerated because the individual generally fights exclusively for his own territory and has no concept of the community; and this includes those who administer the commonwealth, who should work to preserve or protect what belongs to the community.

We have already seen how the young Vincenzo Tusa was taken to Motya in a group of students in the 1930s. Delia Whitaker offered them ice-creams and showed them her father's excavations. These young men were the first of a crop who learned from Joseph Whitaker's studies and from people like Professors Pace and Salinas, whom Pip had attracted to Motya. Having taken his archaeology degree in 1947, Tusa worked in Bologna before moving to Solunto, one of the three main known centres of Punic civilization in Sicily – the others being Motya and Palermo (Ziz in Phoenician).

When Tusa became Superintendent of Antiquities for Western Sicily in 1963, he took charge of the Punic side of the island because the western part of Sicily was where the Carthaginians built their cities, as Thucydides tells us in a few lines that speak volumes of history:

There were also Phoenicians living all round Sicily, who had occupied promontories on the coast and the islets adjacent for the purpose of trading with the Sicels. But when the Hellenes began to arrive in considerable numbers, the Phoenicians abandoned most of their stations and concentrated their abode in Motya, Solunto and Palermo, near the Elymians, partly because they were trusted allies, and also because these are the nearest points for the voyage between Carthage and Sicily. [1]

Unlike many Italians, Tusa never felt envy or hostility towards Joseph Whitaker's work. 'Whitaker's book is interesting to read and to study in order to understand how little was known about the Punics at that time. Whitaker was an individual who did something valid. Anybody who today wants to study the Punic civilization must read his book; it all starts from that, it is a great achievement.' As the person in charge of archaeology for western Sicily, Tusa's authority covered an area which was so dense with antiquities that every inch of ground could hide treasures; and he was responsible for delegating the necessary work. This is an almost unknown art to Italian academics, who keep 'their' areas sheltered from possible 'rivals'; that is why they are nicknamed *i Baroni*, the barons. One of the places which fell within Tusa's administration was Selinunte, Motya's neighbouring city. Indeed, Selinunte was so near Motya that he could move between the two in just over an hour. 'In winter, there was a crackling fire in the dining room, it was lovely at the "Vitakre Castle". I had people to stay – I paid for the food and everything – interesting people, who could bring knowledge to Motya. Some said to me: "Do you realize that it is forbidden for you to have guests? You can't do that." "Yes," I would answer, "I know; what are you going to do about it?"'

Let us have a look at Selinunte, the Greek city which was crucial for Motya and its development. At one stage Selinunte even came under Punic control; I will therefore make a historical detour. As we have seen, Greek migrants had established themselves in Sicily around 750 BC and more came in successive waves during the next two centuries. Selinunte was founded by the settlers of Megara Hyblea, the oldest Greek colony in Sicily; so it was in fact the colony of a colony. Like Motya and Palermo, these new colonies were politically independent from the very start and defended their local autonomy. During the sixth century BC most of the main Greek centres were ruled by tyrants, men who seized power and tried to establish dynasties but who were not kings. Like the Punics, once in Sicily the Greeks developed differently from their metropolitan antecedents. They married locally, including among the Punics; they also developed their own style of painting and architecture, which soon became distinct from its Greek provenance and is called *siceliota*. 'When we talk about the marvellous things that the Greeks brought us,' Tusa explained, 'we are really talking about a period of only fifty years. Although the Greeks gradually became Sicelioti, they corrupted the local language, which took a different course; so that soon the whole island was speaking and writing a special kind of Greek, but Greek all the same.'

In the beginning Greeks and Punics lived in harmony, in part because the latter were the stronger, certainly in terms of sea power. The Carthaginian fleet controlled the Mediterranean; indeed, Carthage, which was only 100 miles across the straits, seemed at times on the verge of controlling the whole of Sicily. Indeed Motya began to pay tribute to Carthage only when it felt militarily threatened by the Greek.

The mightiest and richest Greek cities in Sicily were Syracuse,

Acragas and Selinunte. Today, the wreckage of ancient Selinunte lies in a valley heaped with fallen temples, vast columns reaching to the sky with the sea directly beyond stretching to Africa. This is the valley of death that so attracted Vincenzo Tusa. 'In a whole year I went home to Palermo only on three Sundays; my daughter used to complain that she never saw me.' Selinunte was one of the largest Greek colonies in Sicily, a bustling metropolis with a flourishing harbour; it was an important trading centre which did business mainly with Motya and Carthage. But it was built in Punic territory; the creation of seven huge, spectacular temples in that corner of western Sicily should be seen as an act of provocation.

A school of sculptors developed at Selinunte whose extraordinary skill and inspiration can be admired today in the archaeological museum of Palermo. I think that one metope in particular, dating from the fifth century BC and showing the yearning of Zeus for his wife Hera, is a masterpiece. Depicted like a grand man of 'a certain age', Zeus reclines, his face lit with passion for his beautiful wife and grasping the goddess by her wrist with his outstretched arms as though longing to unfold her pleated garment which she, modestly, keeps close to her body. In another, the desperate Actaeon, supine, is attacked by Artemis' dogs while the goddess looks on rather sulkily. There are also earlier metopes of Athena and Perseus, of Apollo in his sun chariot, of Heracles, Demeter and Kore. Many others have been stolen during the two centuries in which Selinunte has been excavated, some probably destroyed. But others perhaps are still buried there, abandoned after the appalling destruction which followed the capture of Selinunte by the Carthaginians. Tusa found three metopes used as building material embedded in later fortifications.

The first Greek settlers named the place after the golden parsley, *selinon*, which they found growing near the rivers Modione and Gorgo by the mouth of which they located the harbour. The parsley still grows there in profusion among the olive trees, in the Mediterranean *maquis* and around the fifth-century Doric temples, among the finest in Sicily. The metopes which made these temples unique, the only ones embellished with sculpture in the whole of Sicily, include an archaic image of Europa, the Phoenician princess. It depicts her abduction, two dolphins carrying the holy bull which is looking towards us as if colluding with the viewer. The princess, whom he carries on his back, is dressed in the Punic way with a kind of round shawl fashioned around her neck. Europa's hairstyle also denotes the foreign origin of the princess, suggesting that the local sculptor must have observed the Punics at close quarters. At that time Punic traders were living in Selinunte and there were many exchanges with Gozo and Malta, Gades and the Sardinian cities, Motya and Carthage. The image of Europa sculpted in local stone and painted in glaring colours was almost prophetic, as if the Punics, provoked by seeing that piece of sculpture high on the temple frieze, would be tempted one day to take revenge on behalf of their abducted princess.

Since the patron gods of the temples in Selinunte are unknown, except for two, they are each identified by a letter of the alphabet; some think the largest temple was dedicated to Zeus, others to Apollo.

A series of earthquakes engulfed the huge columns, splitting some in two before throwing them one against the other and leaving them abandoned on the ground where they still lie, like a huge cemetery of dinosaurs. Some fluted columns smashed against each other, crumbling on impact. The monolithic capitals collapsed on to the remains of the architraves, grounded, frozen in time, stunningly sad and beautiful. Selinunte is so grand in comparison to Motya, and displays such a different approach to life, that one cannot help being surprised by the diversity of these two civilizations which existed side by side.

Selinunte was powerful but it had a rival over the mountains, near Eryx. This rival was Egesta (Segesta), the capital of the Elymians, a people who were close allies of the Punics. Arrogant Selinunte started expanding northwards into Elymian territory where, in the sixth century BC, it even founded a city called Heraclea Minoa. This was a threat to the status quo, to the delicate territorial balance, and could not go unchallenged. At the end of the fifth century, encouraged by the Elymians, Carthage and its allies (which included Motya) moved against Selinunte, even though the latter had once been allied to the Punics. Their commander was that same Hannibal whom we have already encountered in eastern Sicily, Hannibal the Rhodian, who was not related to the celebrated Hannibal Barcas who later fought against Rome in the Second Punic War. This earlier Hannibal besieged and destroyed Selinunte with a cruelty and destructiveness equalled only by the earthquake that followed.

Let's take another step back.

The major conflict which ended with the destruction of Selinunte came about when Athens accepted an alliance with Egesta against Selinus. Thucydides explains the background:

The same winter the Athenians resolved to sail again to Sicily, with a greater army than that under Laches and Eurymedon and, if possible, to conquer the island; most of them being ignorant of its size and of the number of its inhabitants, Hellenic and barbarian, and of the fact that they were undertaking a war not much inferior to that against the Peloponnesians. For the voyage round Sicily in a merchantman is not far short of eight days; and yet, large as the island is, there are only two miles of sea to prevent its being mainland . . . The Egestans had gone to war with their neighbours the Selinuntines upon questions of marriage and disputed territory, and the Selinuntines had procured the alliance of the Syracusans and pressed Egesta hard by land and sea. [2]

The Athenian fleet and army first struck against Syracuse (c.413 BC), suffering a disastrous defeat. So Egesta asked for help from Carthage and, twelve years before Dionysius' attack on Motya, a small army of 5,000 African mercenaries and 800 soldiers from Campania that had crossed on 1,500 cargo ships and 60 warships, under Hannibal's command, overpowered the resistance of the Selinuntines. Selinunte fell after only nine days and the siege ended in the total destruction of the city and the slaughter of its inhabitants. As the Punic army rampaged across other Greek territories, a feeling of pan-Hellenist solidarity was generated, almost a national call to arms, which was something new for the Sicilian Greeks.

Having put the city's inhabitants to the sword, General Hannibal commented that 'since the Selinuntines do not know how to defend their liberty, they deserve to become slaves'. On the other hand, as Diodorus observed: 'People from Selinunte would not have expected to be pushed to such horrors by those whom they had previously helped.'[3] Perhaps that was the reason why the Selinuntines had not put up much of a fight. In fact, seventy-one years earlier the city had sheltered the Carthaginian Gisco, son of Hamilcar, a cousin of General Hannibal.

After the Punics had destroyed Selinunte and their triumphant mercenary army paraded along its streets sporting necklaces of severed arms, the city remained silent and ghostly, witness to Carthage's might. Sixteen thousand had been killed and 5,000 made prisoners and sold as slaves. Selinunte never recovered; and the city's fate was sealed by an earthquake which occurred around the fifth century AD. The colossal white marble columns which now lie on the ground in pieces, where they fell all those centuries ago, are mute witnesses to the existence of what had once been one of Sicily's richest cities. Still, among the ruins life continues in the form of the ubiquitous *selinon*.

Some sixteen years after Selinunte's destruction at the hands of Hannibal, a few Punic refugees returned to inhabit it, possibly survivors of Dionysius' slaughter at Motya. Diodorus Siculus mentions how the Motyans feared a Greek victory because they knew how cruelly they had behaved at Selinunte and anticipated that the Greeks, given the chance, would retaliate in like manner.

Before its destruction, Selinunte had been famous throughout the ancient world, celebrated for its art and wealth. In fact, by 560 BC it was so rich that it could build a little temple at the Thesaurus in Olympia with a statue of the god Dionysus made of gold and ivory. The raw materials were bought from the Punics, but the statue itself was made by Selinuntine artisans.

Vincenzo Tusa and Pierre Cintas discovered traces of Punic occupation on top of the Greek acropolis, and also in some residential districts. They had also built sacred places typically Punic in shape, where Tusa found several engraved signs of Tanit. The Punics probably maintained the harbour of Selinunte so that foodstuffs from its hinterland could be shipped to Motya, which apparently had difficulty in feeding itself. So, for a while, Selinunte became a Punic city; but a few of its Greek inhabitants who had escaped Hannibal's fury occupied one of the acropolises until the First Punic War (third century BC), when the Carthaginians finally destroyed what remained of the city so that it should not fall into Roman hands. 'We found this out,' explained Professor Tusa, 'by a series of archaeological digs. Last century there were two Englishmen who were involved in digging at Selinunte and indeed found some of the metopes which are now at the Palermo museum. They wanted to take them back to the British Museum, but the Bourbons hastily passed a law as a result of which those pieces of sculpture fortunately stayed here.'

In the fifth century AD, just before the huge earthquake which brought the temples to the ground, the Byzantines built a small village in Selinunte, which now lies under the fallen pillars of Temple C. 'For years I lived on the farm nearby; it was important to be present and keep a strict control on the archaeological area. At times there were several of us. There was a French mission digging on the hill on a pre-Hellenistic village and we spent time together, they were very advanced in Punic studies. Indeed we took a Frenchman to Motya [this was Pierre Cintas⁴], and when he saw the tophet he understood what it was. Whitaker had not and nor had I. Then we excavated and found many important objects, and much information.'

The Greeks regarded Selinunte, a city with 80,000 inhabitants at the height of its splendour, as a work of art. Now its gigantic stones are overthrown and the harbours are silted up, adding to the sense of dereliction. I often went there to swim, just below where the main acropolis had been and near where the harbour once was. During the hot summer months, that stretch of sea is particularly fresh since it is open and ventilated. Remnants of columns and buildings are still visible under the sea while, on the distant hillside, shepherds still watch their sheep grazing, just as if time had stood still. Even the newly built Antiquarium, and other buildings intended to provide 'amenities' for visitors, have an abandoned appearance.

For a graphic demonstration of how unexpected the Punic attack was, one should visit the quarries at *le cave di Cusa*, about 10 miles from Selinunte. Half-sculpted columns lie abandoned there as if they had been struggling to emerge from the rock and escape from the quarry, but were left frozen in time when the stonemasons fled in panic at the news of the Punic atrocities. Simone de Beauvoir and Jean-Paul Sartre went to admire these columns, which have not yet escaped from their stony roots and reflected on them. Goethe did likewise.

When Tusa first arrived, the archaeological area of Selinunte was being built over by illegal second homes, and the vast necropolis, known to contain important tombs, was being sacked daily by clandestine gangs. Tusa acted swiftly.⁵ He soon became aware not only that the local authorities were linked to the rape of Selinunte, but that the Mafia and politics were involved in the protection of illegal real estate development and the theft of antiquities. At first, by fighting a bureaucratic battle, Tusa succeeded in changing the status of the entire archaeological site at Selinunte into a national park to be owned jointly by the Italian state and the Sicilian region, 8 square kilometres which were to be fenced. Although the project was enshrined in law by an act of parliament, much patience was required and many battles had to be fought before it was translated into reality. Billions of lire were granted and billions of lire disappeared. The Antiquarium, a building which had been erected originally as a museum and visitor centre, is still closed and used as a warehouse. But Selinunte's popularity with the newly developing tourist trade eventually saved the site. 'On this land the Mafia, building speculation and bad government have ignored the law and only brave action by the Soprintendenza of Antiquities for Western Sicily has prevented housing development taking place among the temples themselves,' proclaimed *L'Ora*, the left-wing Palermitan newspaper, in 1980.[6]

The following year, the same newspaper criticized the regional authorities for preventing work taking place to protect the archaeological park;[7] and Antonio Cederna, a campaigner against illegal building, denounced in a national daily the building of a record number of five to six thousand houses, all of which had been illegally developed near to or visible from the archaeological park. It was war, with Tusa alone on one side and on the other, against him, most of the Italian national and regional authorities, among whom Mafia links were widespread.

'I have saved Selinunte by expropriating 220 hectares.' Professor Tusa began to tell me a story that has never been written before. After planning to create an archaeological park, Tusa succeeded in the compulsory purchase of part of the property on behalf of the state. He then received a visit from a notary, who told him he was ready to sell him further territory and told him what the value of the land was. But, he added, 'We are three.'

'I knew very well what he meant but I decided to pretend not to; and I answered: "I see that there are two of us, you and I, I don't see the third person. Or do you mean that there is a part of the property which does not actually belong to you?"'

This exchange took place in Sicilian dialect which Tusa reproduced for my sake, translating into Italian from time to time. His wife Aldina remembered these meetings and laughed, although, at the time, it would not have been easy to laugh off an encounter of the kind. It was easier (and safer), as Tusa observed, to pretend not to understand. 'I am a Sicilian from the countryside near Catania, another part of the island ...' And he carried it off until, at a later stage, part of the property which was to be purchased by the state was acquired by two cousins who in the 1970s unofficially ruled Sicily. Let us call them Y and Z.[8] In the end the former was kidnapped and died of what is called *la lupara bianca*, which means that records state officially that the body of the victim has never been found. Often these bodies are known to have been concealed in the concrete columns which support *autostrade* in Sicily. I imagine those skeletons inside the vast columns, as big as those at Selinunte, like some horrible *kouros* chuckling within the cement. The mighty Z was lucky enough to die naturally of cancer. Or maybe he did. But we have to go back in time to the mid-1970s, when these people were the big bosses.

'Y and Z owned the land but in somebody else's name,' Tusa continued. 'When I published the plan for the archaeological park of Selinunte, I went to see a mayor because, by law, these plans had to be shown in public for a given amount of time. Instead, they had been kept in a drawer, and I was unable to act until the plans for Selinunte had been exposed to the public. I pretended not to know, but asked the Mayor why the plan for the archaeological park had not been made public since I, the Superintendent, had sent it a month earlier. These plans had already received all the permits from the various ministries in Rome and Palermo. The Mayor finally displayed them on the public board.'

But nobody really believed that the park would see the light of day; continual campaigns were mounted against it, and new obstacles were placed in its path. 'One day the cousins, together with two others, came to see me in my office. I had already been offered a sum of money that would have changed my life, the whole course of my life, a big sum for those days but I had not even answered. Z was the diplomat, he was courteous and so was I.'

They talked for two or three hours; laughing, Tusa remembered that, oddly, he was not frightened. 'At a certain moment, Z said: "What do you think? We keep 30 hectares and 40 are for you." This would have meant that they would have been able to build a holiday village, plus a hotel, right next to the temples as they had planned. I kept to my initial position and then, getting up from my desk, I shook their hands and indicated that the meeting was over. Without showing disappointment, Z said: "At least, Professore, join us for a coffee, let us offer you *un caffè al bar* ..."

'"I would like this very much," I answered, "but after the animated conversation that we have had there is no reason for us to drink a coffee together." And so I did not join them. Because it could have been dangerous. In Sicily it would have been interpreted as marking an agreement between me, the Superintendent, and the Mafia. A coffee drunk together publicly at a city *caffè* after a discussion, has a specific meaning, it seals a promise made, which is the impression my visitors wanted to give.'

In 1975, soon after this incident, Professor Tusa was elected as a local councillor for the Sicilian Communist Party, on a list called 'independent' which meant that those elected did not have to keep to the party line. 'At this stage the right-wing magistrates took their revenge on me.' He received no fewer than nineteen *avvisi di reato*, (non-proven accusations of crime). This type of accusation is of no criminal consequence but still means that one has to defend oneself in court. Vincenzo Tusa would have been broken financially had he not found Nino Sorgi, an excellent and honest lawyer who was also the legal representative of *L'Ora*, the daily newspaper for which Tusa had started writing. At that moment, in fact, we were colleagues, because I too wrote for the same paper.

L'Ora had been started by the once powerful Florio family of Marsala wine fame, and eventually was bought by a group close to the Communist Party, whereupon it became the only opposition paper in southern Italy. In the 1950s and 1960s *L'Ora* fought battles against overwhelming corruption, the Mafia and the Christian Democrats who supported them. When the Mafia began murdering trade union officials, *L'Ora* announced that it was starting an inquiry into their activities; it was the first time that a Sicilian newspaper had even printed the word. On the following day, when *L'Ora* received a threatening warning, it published that as well; and when its printing presses were blown up, it managed to publish all the same, proclaiming defiantly: 'The inquiry goes on.'

It was a small newspaper, but its writers were among the best people in Sicily: people like Giuliana Saladino and Marcello Cimino, Danilo Dolci, Gioacchino Tomasi di Lampedusa and, of course, Vincenzo Tusa himself. Since the paper had very little money, I myself chose to be paid with a month's holiday every year in a fisherman's house on one of the Égadi Islands, where I took my children with me. I would go to a different place every year – and that is how I arrived at Motya in the first place.

'The accusations against me were absurd; but I still had to fight them.' In Tusa's days the modern Mafia had not arrived in Motya, because the island was not a tourist attraction. In a way, a character like Colonnello Lipari-Cascio, who was a Mafia figure of a kind, protected first Joseph Whitaker and his properties in the area, and then Motya itself. It is in fact impossible that the Baglio and the Vitakre 'Castle', as it is still called by the locals, would have been left alone had it not been for Mafia protection. Colonnello Lipari-Cascio was officially responsible for its safe-keeping; in Dr Isserlin's innocent comment, 'He seemed to be in charge of the whole of Marsala.'

As Superintendent, Tusa had invited to Motya Professor Sabatino Moscati, the foremost authority on Punic studies. Moscati's team began to work in the summer of 1971 and Moscati wrote an article about the great Punic discoveries at Motya. In this article the famous archaeologist also mentioned the voracious Motyan midges which had attacked his team. When Tusa next met Colonnello Lipari, he was told: 'That man, Moscati, is not to put a foot on Motya ever again.'

'What do you mean, Colonnello?'

'Have you seen the article today?'

'Yes, but ...'

'You will see to it that this Moscati man is never in Motya again in his life.'

On that day there was nothing that Tusa could do to placate the Colonnello's fury. Later on, he went to see Lipari again. It took him a long time to convince the Colonnello that, first of all, his word of honour had been given to Moscati and that another word of honour, Lipari's own, had been given to Tusa. Tusa had himself invited Sabatino Moscati; so there would have been a breach of trust, of a given word, which was something very grave. He, Colonnello Lipari-Cascio, could not be seen by the public, nor indeed by Tusa, doing such a thing as breaking his word of honour. It was this, and not the fact that Professor Moscati was a great scholar in Punic and Phoenician studies, that eventually impressed the Colonnello.

Tucked away in his Palermitan flat, Tusa lives with his wife and, with sorrow, sees Sicily unchanged in its worst characteristics. Archaeology at Motya has almost ground to a halt, while there remains much to be done that should be done. But at least he has left behind him a group of students who are excellent scholars and archaeologists, like Antonia Ciasca and Marisa Famà, to name only two.

Marisa Famà has been working in Motya for the last twenty-one years and has taken on the responsibility of trying to defend the island from outside attacks – recently with the assistance of Pamela Toti, engaged by the Foundation as their representative and guardian of their interests on Motya. As in a siege, exterior forces come armed with heavy-duty weapons with which to threaten their target. It is a different kind of army from that of Dionysius of Syracuse, and totally unlike the old Mafia, most of whom have disappeared inside columns of cement. It is a more sinister and sophisticated Mafia which is capable of blowing people up if they stand in the way.

15

THE FINDING OF
THE *KOUROS*

Outside, the sunlight was so strong that even insects had taken shelter. We humans had also taken refuge inside the house of one of the present custodians, Vincenzo Arini. His uncle Giuseppe had joined us with one of his best bottles of wine. Vincenzo's wife Ignazia closed the shutters and the sittingroom was plunged into a refreshing darkness. She began to make coffee, but Zio Peppino turned it down with an 'it's-bad-for-me' justification, mumbled between his teeth. I had my little cup, though, and so did Marisa Famà, the archaeologist. The darkened screen of the television set reflected a bunch of flowers in that small room filled with the warmth which radiated from the friendly attitude of the family. Zio Peppino's own house stood on the other side of the courtyard and was equally tiny. He grew luscious tomatoes and the biggest basil plants I have ever seen, a forest of scented green. In the middle of the rectangular table near the vase glowed the bottle of Marsala wine, filtering such sunlight as successfully penetrated the shuttered windows.

Giuseppe's wife had remained at home because she was shy and because, as she repeated many times and with some justification, her accent was incomprehensible. Schliemann had had a point when he had observed that Motya's locals spoke the most difficult of all Sicilian dialects in which, I am certain, are buried Arab words as well as Phoenician expressions. Cassata, the famous Sicilian sweet, for example, derives from *qasadh* in Arabic, and cous-cous is served in Sicily.

Outside, it was too hot to venture abroad.

Zio Giuseppe poured the wine in small glasses, remembering the year and the occasion when it had been made. 'This was made in '42,

before the end of the war. The Germans wanted to take it. Then
also the Americans wanted it, but they were going to pay, unlike the
Germans who wanted to steal everything.' Rosina Pugliese was
young when she became a widow, she told me, still unreconciled to
such an unjust fate; her brother Giuseppe had started working on
the digs in 1950, 'with Isserlin and Dottoresse Ciasca'. But he never
abandoned working his little plot of land with vines, figs, olive trees
and tomatoes. *Il Commendatore* Whitaker had taught him to look
after flowers and vegetables, he explained, and trees as well;
'Vitakre' had had green fingers.

Marisa Famà had a classic face, strong features and, in spite of
an Emilian mother, a pleasant Sicilian accent. She was clearly at
ease with these Motyan people. This little family, in fact, represented continuity. Giuseppe Pugliese was the only person still living who
had met Joseph Whitaker. He had joined a team of labourers when
he was 18 and came to Motya every day on foot, walking along la
Contrada Spagnola. He only started digging when he acquired
more skill. I told him that I had gone to meet Dr Isserlin in Leeds,
which made him happy. He was pleased to know that the doctor
was well, but I did not tell him that his wife was dead; Zio Peppino
would have minded that. He had a gentle disposition, somehow
enhanced by his large, concave eye-sockets, and was beginning to
fear the future; after 80, nothing good is to be expected, he said.
And he was 85 . . .

When we were all settled down, Marisa and Ignazia Arini on the
sofa, the others sitting around the table, I asked them to tell me
what happened when they found the statue.

They each knew what I meant by 'the statue', and all their eyes
brightened at the thought of the white youth who was standing not
too far from us, in another room; handsome, secure, eternal in his
beauty.

In October 1979 there emerged from the Motyan earth the most
beautiful Greek statue, *il Kouros di Mozia*, the Youth from Motya:
an artefact of such superb classical artistry as, when displayed to the
human gaze, unfailingly provokes a flood of emotions. The statue
was not formed by Punic hands, but had clearly been made by a
great Greek sculptor; some contemporary art historians even mentioned the name of Phidias. The discovery of that statue had been
so astonishing that, after I uttered my question – which was directed

to everybody in general – they all took a breath, as if they did not know how to convey the feelings they had experienced. I was addressing all of them, because they had been present at that birth, which must have been as miraculous as the birth of Aphrodite rising from the foam of the Aegean sea.

Finally, it was the oldest who answered. 'When the knee of the statue emerged from the ground, I kissed it.' Zio Peppino, one of the custodians of the island at the time, smiled at the memory. It was in October, on one of those sunny days when autumn begins to refresh the air and the light is golden. One worker saw a corner of white marble appear in the ground and shouted: 'A statue! a statue!' The team who were digging in depth in a preselected square designated area K, near the Cappiddazzu, gathered around the white piece of marble which protruded through the gravel.

'It might be just a fragment,' one of the archaeologists commented. A large fragment, but only a fragment all the same; the life of an archaeologist is punctuated with false hopes. He might spend a lifetime analysing minute pieces of pottery which could tell him much about daily life in ancient times but never unearth a single intact artefact from beneath the soil. It is a chance in a million to hold in one's hand or uncover with one's trowel even one single really well-preserved vase or statue.

News of the discovery spread like wildfire, and soon Professor Gioacchino Falsone, the field director, arrived to inspect the white piece. 'It's likely to be a fragment,' he repeated. 'Let's not get excited.'

The workers continued to dig, carefully but at a more feverish pace than before; the fact was that everybody was infected by barely suppressed excitement. Gradually, as more and more white marble became visible, so that the sculpted muscles of a recognizable leg betrayed mastery of the chisel, the tension became breathless. They tried not to let themselves believe that they might have found an entire masterpiece; but hour after hour and day after day, more of the statue gradually emerged. It lay at a considerable depth, almost 2 metres, beneath nearly 7 feet of soil and debris. Although the original shape of this dig had been planned as square, the team could now imagine the design and shape of the statue, and therefore enlarged the size of the trench accordingly. But they had to work slowly and methodically, painstakingly scraping away layer after layer, carefully removing anything which might be identified as a small fragment of ceramic until they exposed enough of the white marble to identify the rectangle which enclosed the statue.

Vincenzo Tusa, busy at Selinunte, was immediately given the wonderful news. Otherwise the greatest secrecy was maintained and, each evening, the object would be covered up and safely hidden. It was a priceless discovery. Tusa was sceptical: a large statue in a Punic area? They did not go for such embellishments, those Phoenicians; indeed, they hardly bothered to depict their gods, so would they really have had a statue at Motya? Moreover, from the first glimpse it looked as though it were Greek, and what was a Greek statue doing in Motya? It is true that archaeologists were learning something new, the extent of cultural exchange between those peoples. In spite of the fact that the population of Selinunte had been massacred by the Punics, and Motya in its turn had been razed to the ground by the Greeks, there had been close and friendly exchanges, including intermarriage and the borrowing of language, of customs. The Greeks had adopted Melqart and turned the god into a hero – albeit with Zeus as his father – and they had merged Aphrodite with Astarte. The Punics were adopting the Greek language and buying artefacts not only from the local Siceliots but from the Greeks themselves.

'It's marble! it's marble!' they were all shouting.

'We excavated in section and as each section advanced in depth, we prayed, we exclaimed, we marvelled,' Marisa Famà recalls. 'I saw to it that we should not forget the stratifications which were in direct contact with the statue. Little by little, we freed it from the ground; it was practically whole,' she continued. 'In the life of an archaeologist something of that kind hardly ever happens.' Joseph Whitaker almost touched it; he was very close to the statue. Had he not stopped but continued to enlarge his trench by 40 centimetres, he would have found the statue.

The whole process, from the beginning, from that moment at which a corner of white knee had been spotted, had taken a week. An eternity. But patience, Marisa Famà says, is one of the first requirements of an archaeologist. Tusa added that the ground is like an open book which the archaeologist has to learn how to read; he must decipher it slowly and learn history from it. But it is a book with a difference: once a page has been turned, the reader cannot go back; the context of a chapter has been erased. When he was a student of archaeology at Edinburgh, Bruce Chatwin jotted down: 'Definition of archaeology: a series of methods to gather information about the past which depend on the analysis of results obtained by those methods.' Chatwin could not endure the slow pace, the huge amount of patience required; he gave it up and became a writer instead.

Elated, the Sicilian archaeologists dusted the face and the marble pleats of the tunic with a dry brush. And the face. It was a young man with a defiant expression and finely chiselled features. The head was neatly broken off at the neck, but was lying close to the trunk, as if it had fallen as the statue was being hastily hidden.

'When we were convinced that we had found a whole statue, we brought a bottle of champagne to the site and celebrated.' They were, of course, ecstatic. The team which was under the direction of Gioacchino Falsone consisted of himself, Famà, Spatafora, Fresina, Spanò and Calascibetta; they were all young and fresh from their studies. It was an especial thrill to them to have shared this experience, which must have forged an extraordinary bond among them.

'I am in no doubt whatsoever – and the majority of scholars who have studied the statue agree with me – that it should be dated around 470 BC. The head and the dress, which can only belong to the "severe" period of Greek sculpture, clearly prove this,' wrote Tusa.[1] The Punic toga was held by a belt, often hidden under the folds of the tunic, and Sabatino Moscati added that the robe worn by the *kouros* was an exact description of 'the Carthaginian national costume, of Phoenician origin, which used neither toga nor cloak. It consisted of a straight, ankle-length tunic which was very wide.'[2]

It is likely that the statue was erected near the large Motyan sanctuary and the industrial area where it was found. It was probably meant to embellish a crossroads, a piazza or some kind of meeting place. When Dionysius' army was about to enter the city and the Motyans realized that all was lost, a group of citizens must have hastily hidden this most precious of the city's possessions. They laid it in a trench and covered it with gravel; but as they lowered the heavy marble object into the pit, with the aid of ropes, the sounds of battle threatening the city, the cries and screams of the terrified and dying gave their task such urgency that there was an accident and the head of the statue was severed from its neck. It was found next to the body, the fractured edges almost touching. Those who had hidden the *kouros* perhaps hoped that, after the human tempest was over, they would be able to dig up the masterpiece and replace it on its pedestal. But none of them survived; they must all have been killed or sold as slaves in some faraway place, so that the memory of the *kouros* faded with their ashes.

As it now stands, without its feet and arms, the statue measures 1.81 metres, so that, standing on a pedestal, it must have stood at least 1.9 if not 2 metres high. There would also have been a dedication, a written epigraph. Where has that gone? Did some Byzantine monk use it for making lime, or some Arab farmer grind it into a device for irrigating his field? Or was it crushed more recently, by those who worked the land for the Jesuits? That inscribed stone, if it is ever found, holds the secret of the Youth from Motya. In order to be in proportion with the figure, the pedestal, in marble or tufa, would have been at least a metre high; so there is no question but that the statue was meant as a monument for all citizens to enjoy and as a statement of the wealth of Motya, just as Diodorus wrote.

Vincenzo Tusa thinks that the monument depicts a Punic winner of an Olympic race in his triumphant ride. In fact, there are indications that the missing left arm was elevated, as if holding a crown over the statue's own head. The other arm, also partly missing, culminates in a beautifully designed hand which stretches over the pleats of the youth's falling tunic. Amazingly, there are still a few hints of colour among the pleats; the statue, of course, would have been brightly and variously coloured.

When the statue was analysed, it was found that the young man's hair, beautifully rendered around the forehead and the back of the neck, is only roughly sculpted around the crown of the head, which is pierced by five holes. Those five holes would have originally held a metal crown or ornament, probably a wreath of leaves forged in bronze or even in gold. There had been another piece of precious metal holding the strings of the belt just over the youth's waist, in the Punic manner. 'At the level of the right arm, there is a small rectangular hollow, like a stamp impressed a few millimetres into the surrounding surface, maybe a symbol or a motif used as the sculptor's signature,' writes Tusa.[3]

I left the Arinis' house and walked the few paces across the courtyard to the Whitaker Museum, screwing up my eyes against the violence of the sun. I entered the museum and looked at the *kouros*, which has been placed on a plinth in the middle of a specially built room, so that one can walk all around it. The walls of the small room are of the same colour as the statue, and the monochrome tonality of the background does not help the eye.

The haughtiness and confidence of the *kouros*'s expression, and the movement of the statue's body, stress that the youth came from this Punic province and was rich enough to have a horse or two and travel to Olympia for the famous games. He had returned home triumphant, having become the *victor ludorum* and thereby brought great honour on the name of his family and the name of the Sicilian Punics. On his return, he was carried triumphantly into the city. The suffetes, the city's senators, decided to dedicate a monument to the young hero and so they commissioned the best Greek sculptor of the day. The piece of marble used came from Aphrodisia, near Ephesus: it was the best, no money was spared.

Or might this instead be the effigy of Apollo? The statue certainly has a face and a body handsome enough to be that of the sun god, and his arm could have been holding up the reins of his chariot. But why would the Punics erect a statue to Apollo? Unless originally the statue had been in Selinunte at the time of its destruction. Motyan ships must have been carrying supplies for the allied Punic army, so might not some Motyans, enamoured of the beauty of the statue, have decided to remove it as loot in order to adorn their own city?

Even so, why would a youth dressed in Punic robes be in Greek Selinunte? Not unless he represented a Punic athlete from Selinunte who, although representing a Greek city, wore his own customary Punic robes. After all, there were Punic families living at Selinunte, as indeed there were Greeks living in Motya. As we have seen, Selinunte had strong ties with glorious Olympia, where it had paid for the erection of a little temple inside the Thesaurus of the famous Peloponnesian centre. We also know that Phidias worked at Olympia, where he sculpted the great frieze of Apollo; we can even visit his workshop there.

One thing is certain: the handsome young athlete depicted by a master among Greek sculptors is not effeminate. In fact, he is almost macho, and has the same manly grace as the Phoebus Apollo at Olympia. And yet, most unfairly, this virile young man came to

be described as an 'ephebe', an effeminate youth, maybe at the insti-
gation of certain art lovers. Effeminate the youth is definitely not.
Not even the most fertile homosexual imagination could turn this
dignified young man into an effete without indulging in the most
extravagant wishful thinking.

After study and a few repairs, the statue was put on show in that
same Marsala regional museum that successfully hides the Punic
ship. Motya protested; then a request was made for the *kouros* to
appear at an exhibition dedicated to the Phoenicians organized by
Sabatino Moscati and held in Venice, at the Palazzo Grassi. It was
the first time that the *kouros* had been seen by large numbers of
people. Crowds queued, not to see the Punic bits and pieces, the vitreous masks and the frightening gods, but in order to admire this
amazing piece of Greek sculpture. Rarely had something so beautiful as this been shown in public 'for the first time'; there had been
the so-called Riace statues, two bronze masterpieces of Greek gods
found off the coast of Reggio Calabria, in the 1970s, which were
also stunning.

By the time the statue returned to Sicily from Venice it had
become famous. Requests to display it arrived from everywhere.
Eight years later the Motya Youth returned to Venice for another
exhibition, also at the Palazzo Grassi, this time dedicated to Magna
Graecia, which is that part of Italy colonized by the Greeks. It was
a stunning exhibition and the *kouros* from Motya was among its
stars. The statue remained in Venice for six months and then 'it
came back, but this time to Motya; it belongs here, it should be
here.' Marisa Famà is adamant. There followed 'request after
request, even from Tokyo, but it should not travel all the time. It is a
delicate piece, the aircraft could crash and also many people come
here in order to see it, not to be told that it is somewhere on the
other side of the hemisphere for six months or a year. If they want
to look at the Youth, let them take the trouble to come to Sicily.'
Works of art are travelling too frequently and too far, she said.

The statue now belongs to the state. 'There is a 1939 law by
which anything of artistic or historical merit found underground
belongs to the state. This statue was valued at a billion lire. How
could one give a value to such a masterpiece? However, in 1979 a billion lire was a lot of money. The Whitaker Foundation received
250,000 for it, exactly a quarter of the total sum.'

By now I have been alone face to face with the *kouros* many times, in different lights, at different times of the day and also in different places, because I actually went to both the exhibitions in Venice. Of course, when I first visited Motya, the statue was still lying undiscovered underground; but since it has emerged, I have admired it also in the Whitaker Museum. It has never failed to evoke a profound emotion within me, that depth of feeling which pervades one when facing the inexplicable potency of genius; this is an object whose mastery wants to convey something more than an aesthetic message, and calls forth the same emotion by which one is also shaken when observing the Prigioni by Michelangelo or the weeping Athena in the Parthenon museum.

The posture of the *kouros* conveys an elegance of movement; his head is turned slightly to the left and the face, although badly chipped in some areas, has preserved an expression of serene boldness and confidence. The weight of the body is on the left leg, while the other is slightly bent, giving a special rhythm to the body. The pleats of the robe are wrapped tightly around the chest and held in place by a wide sash band, probably made of leather. Two strings cross at the back and are tied in front, and where they cross, there must have originally been a brooch or a clasp of gold, its existence marked by two holes which attached it to the marble. The boy's garment clings to his body as it falls. It has numerous folds which form their own mass but nevertheless reveal the shape of his sinuous body beneath; the live detail is exceptional.

After spending some minutes in the museum, alone with the statue, I returned to the Arinis'. Zio Peppino had left, but I found Marisa, immobilized by the heat, almost where I had left her.

'You went to see him,' she stated.

Shaking herself, Marisa took me to where the *kouros* had been discovered. As we walked slowly along, she told me how, a few years after the statue had been dug up, the Pugliese and Arini families had received a letter insisting that they vacate their houses immediately. These were the people who had been loving guardians of the island, ensuring that there were no fires and no thieves. The publicity created by the miraculous beauty of the statue had led some people to think that money could be made from tourism in Motya. Probably they thought that the little houses in which the old custodian and his nephew's families lived could be converted into bars and restaurants. Holiday homes could be built and tours sold to global travel agents. When this horrifying letter arrived in 1987, the President of the Whitaker Foundation was Giusto Monaco, apparently a weak man, influenced by Rosario Chiovaro who, as we saw, had been Delia's 'Cagliostro'; both men had signed the letter.

'They came to see me, crying,' said Marisa. 'I immediately took them to a lawyer.' There had been the usual intimidation; life was made difficult with telephone lines and electricity supplies mysteriously cut off. There were times when Marisa Famà was scared by the possible repercussions of her opposition to certain plans. In the morning, before leaving home in her car, she would check her tyres. It would have been illegal to evict the Puglieses and the Arinis; but illegality means little to some powerful people. Eventually, the island's custodians succeeded in staying put.

In 1964, over ten years before the statue was found, the same team of archaeologists had been concentrating on excavations of the Cappiddazzu. As we have seen, Whitaker started his excavations there. In his book he wrote:

The name of Cappiddazzu, the Sicilian for Cappellazzo, meaning a large hat, appears to have attached itself to this locality in consequence of the legend of a spectre wearing a large hat, the ghost of a hermit at Motya having been supposed to haunt the neighbourhood. Possibly some scarecrow, put up to frighten off the birds from the corn-fields, may have given rise to the tale.

He continued:

When speaking of the north gateway and road leading into the town, mention has been made of the ruins of what would appear to have been constructions of some importance having been discovered at a spot situated about one hundred metres or so inland and to the south of the gateway. This spot which is commonly known by the name of Cappiddazzu, stands at a comparatively high level and probably formed an important quarter of the town. [4]

So it was natural that the statue of the youth would have been found in the so-called Zone K, an important civic and religious location. A scholar called Maria Giulia Amadasi says that in this place a piece of pottery bearing a few Punic letters could mean that the main sanctuary was dedicated to Astarte, but she is cautious in her conclusions and believes only in scientific archaeological proof. As we know from Diodorus, there must have been temples of the Greek cult in or around that place; it could be that a sanctuary was dedicated to the double deity of Apollo/Eshmun or Melqart/Heracles, or even Astarte/Aphrodite. The fact that the statue of the *kouros* was found near the sanctuary is indicative of the importance that the Motyans attached to it.

If the area under the Vitakre Castle hides the institutional centre of Motya (the mint, the archives, the tribunal and the headquarters of the suffets, for example), the Cappiddazzu, close to the north gate, should have been the marketplace and the centre for worship – the two being directly connected because the temples were used as banks and the market provided food not only for people's stomachs, but also to be used in sacrifices.

Patience had to be exercised; secrets would unfold, slowly. For the moment, most were still underneath Motya's ground.

Modern archaeology has developed since Schliemann's time. The German dug 'trenches' or, as he himself called them, 'pits'.[5] Today the terrain is chosen and then divided into squares which are creamed off stratum by stratum, each 'slice' embodying a specific era. How an archaeologist identifies where one ends and the next one starts is a matter of experience and knowledge. Each slice must be inspected and shelved away before starting a new one. Fires, floods, great upheavals help the archaeologist in reading any one particular slice. Man-made clay, especially if baked and painted, even in the tiniest quantity, reveals age, trade, voyages, customs.

Schliemann studied pottery and used it in his dating system, but he often made gross mistakes, destroying several strata in his impatience to get to what he believed to be the 'right' goal. He got it famously wrong with Priam's Troy, which he bypassed by two strata, thereby erasing the real Ilium of 1200 BC. Whitaker, too, threw away some layers and did not keep records that would have been valuable; but, on the whole, his work is praised and represented the best practice of the time. Moreover, today the archaeological world has been enormously aided by the advance of science; a good team nowadays includes a biologist, a geophysicist, a botanist, while new technology makes it possible to read dates and chemical compositions. We have seen how Dr Isserlin's team included specialists, as did Miss Frost's: a team of specialists who were able not only to conserve but to read the exact dates and places where the artefacts they discovered were made.

Most of the archaeologist's work is monotonous. Fragment after fragment must be examined and understood, because together they make history, the history of mankind: this is the obscure, routine side of the job. Academic discipline enables a scholar to piece together a whole culture out of tiny pieces of old pots. 'I really enjoy the hours which I spend studying the minute pieces and trying to make a puzzle talk: this is my real passion,' Marisa said. Sometimes, though, the monotony suddenly disappears when the work yields some rare piece of man-made evidence that sheds light on our forebears. The enthusiasm and satisfaction are all the greater when the object is a work of art.

The *kouros* is one of the finest examples of genius, in amazing contrast to the severity of Punic artefacts. It also demonstrates the extraordinary cultural exchange which happened in that melting pot that was Sicily, where Motyan women ate out of delicate dishes painted in the Greek style and addressed their own gods in Greek. The Punics called Astarte Aphrodite as often as the Greeks called Aphrodite Astarte. Even if there was much self-destruction among them, their genius has remained, marvellously kneaded within a pastry which made the Sicilians Sicilian, which eventually gave rise to great architecture and literature, as well as philosophical and mathematical thought.

16

THE YELLOW DAISIES

In the summer of 1997 I took a house near Castellammare, between Alcamo and Eryx, in ancient Elymian territory. It was as hot as July can be in Sicily, so we often went to swim at Selinunte; the climate is fresher there because of the breeze and the currents passing through the straits between Sicily and Africa, and the sea is blue, quite cold, full of bubbles, like champagne.

Driving along one of those motorways which are festooned with oleanders in amazingly strong colours, high on a hill above me I passed the temple of Segesta, magical, its golden-pink Doric columns bathed in sunlight, where the Elymians cheated the envoys from Athens, who believed that the hastily built temple was proof of these people's wealth; as we have seen, the Athenian expedition (415–13 BC) ended in disaster. Occasionally, beside the road, there were little shrines where fresh or plastic flowers bound to the safety barriers marked the scene of the many fatal accidents that frequently occur on these empty roads. The only such spot which was neither marked or honoured with flowers was further east, where the car of Magistrate Falcone and his wife were blown up. With him ended the fight against the Mafia in Rome.

I drove on until the deserted motorway forked into two, one branch heading towards Trapani and Marsala, the other to Mazara del Vallo. I took the route towards Trapani, the ancient Drepanum, the Elymians' port, after which one turns off for Motya. Even during the dry summer months this territory was green with the vineyards which produce one of the best white wines in Italy.

On that July day I stood with my son on the jetty opposite Motya, waiting for the boat, just as I had done almost half a century earlier, under the same sun and with the same sense of anticipation. My son Orlando was slightly younger than I had been at the time. But a few things had changed. There were organized tours. The salt-pans looked neat and tidy, and indeed they had been arranged as a museum; even the mills looked spick and span, white-washed, their wings having undergone huge works of restoration. I also noticed that a restaurant had been built nearby, along with a parking lot for cars and buses. There was an attendant who kept to the narrowing strips of shade, unwilling to venture out into the sun until the *Tanit* arrived. The *Tanit* was a proper motor boat, a large vessel, quite unlike the battered fishing-boat that used to take visitors to the island when I had first gone to Motya. In fact, there were two boats now because, the boatman told me, many schoolchildren visited Motya in termtime. The statue of the *kouros* had made the island famous. On another jetty, which is linked to the tour of the salt-pans, there is a new line which belongs to Mr Antonio D'Ali.

When I offered to pay for my ride, the boatman, who is called Michele Arini, told me that I was expected by *la Dottoressa* Famà and that I was a guest of the island. So off we went. By contrast to the mainland shore, not much had changed in the little hamlet on the island, and it was easy to find *la Dottoressa* in the Casa delle Missioni Archeologiche. She was busy among her labelled pieces of pottery, which filled drawers and drawers. She was working on the topography of Motya: how was a Punic city planned? 'The body of evidence regarding city planning and architecture in the Phoenician–Punic world allows the identification of certain constant features that combine to delineate a typical "settlement culture",' writes Professor Bondi.[1] 'One of the basic aspects of this culture consists of the topography of the islet-towns whose peculiarities have made it possible to extract a real Phoenician cityscape, that is, a group of distinguishing features to be found in a great many colonies in the East and in the West.'

It might well be that Marisa – nobody calls her by her full name of Maria Luisa – is establishing an important point: these new cities which were built from scratch appear to have followed a given design, since Carthage resembles Tyre and Motya as well as most of the Sardinian colonies in layout. The tophet, for example, seems to be always on the east side of these cities and slightly outside the centre; the cothon has exactly the same shape in Motya as in Carthage, as if the same engineer had travelled from one city to another to design the new facility. There must have been an overall structure to Motya. There was also a special Punic unit of measurement, which first Isserlin and now Famà are working towards establishing. Famà agreed with Doctor Ciasca that there was an additional man-made harbour at Motya. But only underwater digs could establish the existence on the east side of the island of the mole that would have indicated a sheltered port in exact replica of those in most of the North African colonies.

On that day Marisa was wearing a scarf to protect her head, like a Russian woman, and dark glasses; she was exhausted. The Sicilian summer takes its toll on people, especially during the hottest months. Pamela Toti had arrived from Rome. In spite of the fact that she must have been asked the same questions by all the visitors to Motya, Pamela was enthusiastic and friendly and showed us around. This was Orlando's first visit, and it was wonderful to see his reaction to the dead city. Even for me there were new things to notice; most of the monumental areas had been enclosed by nets and the tophet had been covered by a roof.

First we walked around the perimeter walls which, Pamela explained, were reinforced by a series of towers which Doctor Ciasca had investigated. They had been set at regular intervals near the two monumental gates set into the city walls. The Whitaker museum was going to be partially closed for some time, she added. I did not ask why, but I sensed that she was annoyed about it. She then took us to the residential area, only part of which has been identified. Clearly 'readable' with the help of a learned guide like her was the industrial area. There were a few pottery kilns and two ceramic workshops; a large area of about 600 square metres had evidently been laid out on the northern coast of the island specifically for tanning and dyeing hides, and also for manufacturing bricks and other clay products.

The Motyan tophet, the construction of which started in the eighth century BC, occupied a triangular area beside the northern walls of the city, and had been progressively enlarged as the city grew. It was developed by filling in a depression in the rock that was retained by a wall made of those stelae which had been gradually removed from the holy site. Much more had now been found from excavations in the tophet, which is still partly undisturbed. The only building inside the sacred enclosure was a very small cella with an altar, the front of which had been embellished with Doric columns and Greek architectural motifs. This early use of Hellenistic designs and patterns in a Punic city was unique to Motya.

The necropolis, the early cemetery, quite a different enclosure from the tophet but located near it, extended from the side of the tophet to the north gate; neither Pamela nor Marisa agreed with the theory that from the sixth century onwards the city buried its dead at Birgi. They both thought that the tombs found at the nearby Birgi were used for people from that settlement. The burial places found at Motya consisted of jars containing incinerated remains or of monolithic sarcophagi.

Then we moved to the sanctuary of Cappiddazzu, in the north-east. What we saw here, or part of what we saw, had been erected in the fourth century BC. It consisted of a large building with a nave and two aisles; underneath, the archaeologists had found a much earlier place of worship with typically Punic structural features. I noticed that most excavated areas had been either covered by a rough roof or closed in and fenced. 'Otherwise people steal, whatever, even a silly piece of stone,' Pamela said apologetically.

We went back to find Marisa, who was sitting in the courtyard opposite the Missione with Zio Giuseppe. I could see that there was a bond between those two, and maybe their closeness was the result of secrets they shared to which I was not privy, but which were also shared with the rest of the family. Behind her gaiety and easy manners, Marisa seemed to hide a pervasive worry. Something was causing her concern; something to do with Motya.

I was right to detect this worry in her eyes and even in her gestures; I was to learn that she had recently been informed that the Whitaker Museum was to be restored, which would have meant a sea of cement invading the privacy of that languidly melancholic island. The Soprintendenza of Trapani had commissioned this new extension from their architect, Stefano Biondo. Aldo Scimè, President of the Whitaker Foundation, who was responsible for finding a large EU grant for Motya, suggested the name of another architect, called Foscari, to work side by side with Mr Biondo; but Sovrintendente Camerata Scovazzo had turned the idea down. 'I make no mystery about it,' she said to me; 'between the President and myself there is open warfare.' And while the Whitaker Foundation owns the island of Motya, the Soprintendenza of Trapani has decisive powers on the territory.

'They want to cut down all the yellow daisies,' an alarmed

Rosina told me, referring to the Soprintendenza. I did not understand. There were bushes of daisies in bloom everywhere. Marisa
looked out of the window.

I asked her if she had always been interested in the Phoenicians.
She had taken her thesis on Punic Solunto, she replied. Before
returning to Sicily, where she had studied, Marisa had worked for
six years on the excavation of a Roman villa near Orbetello, under
Professor Andrea Carandini in a joint British–Italian mission. 'He
taught me everything about stratification. We were 130 archaeologists and not one was an inexperienced worker,' she stressed. 'At
that time in Italy everybody was digging as they pleased; it was difficult if not impossible to compare the results of excavations of one
place with another site.'

Carandini, to whom Marisa was introduced by Tusa, was an old
friend of mine whom I hadn't seen for years. He was the son of a
charming man who had been the first ambassador to Great Britain
after the war. Carandini Senior, a convinced anti-Fascist, had
founded an excellent liberal magazine, *Il Mondo*, for years the only
national publication which denounced the corruption of the
Christian Democrats and the enduring Fascist tendencies of the
Italian regime. I myself had started my journalistic life on this
weekly.

Marisa worked with Carandini on this early Roman villa of the
republican era, called Sette Finestre, the Seven Windows. She
intended to stay for just a short time, to study ceramics, but instead
she remained for the entire span of six years. According to Marisa,
the methods now accepted by Italian archaeologists are those established by Professor Carandini.

Archaeology, for Marisa, meant the light which that subject can
throw on the history of mankind. Marisa had also been a pupil of
Tusa's, but she does not agree with him about everything. Besides,
her great interest was in the urban structure of Motya and, since so
little is known about Punic topography, Marisa was almost a pioneer. She lived across the bay with her husband Neil Walker, a
bright and perceptive Yorkshireman who spoke good Italian and
who understood Sicily – and Italy, for that matter – and two stray
dogs which had had the good fortune of finding this young couple.
Their house is simple and betrays Marisa's spartan nature; but it
has lots of books and a friendly atmosphere. There was a newly

built and bare study for Marisa, containing a camp bed for guests – one of whom, I am glad to say, was myself. Colleagues and friends are welcomed by this hospitable couple, both of whom are superb cooks when they have the time. Neil has a little sailing boat with which he sails around the Stagnone, and outside in the open sea. Sometimes he fishes. He also teaches English in Palermo and commutes to Marsala.

Life is busy for Marisa; she has to follow the state's often whimsical decisions on what and how its officials should be employed. She is fiercely attached to Motya, like a ship to its anchor. She is fully aware that Motya is a gold mine of knowledge; the fact that excavations have been limited in these past years annoys and torments her. Maybe so little money had been channelled to Motya because, on the whole, what is likely to emerge from Punic ruins is not glamorous or sexy, as they say now. Perhaps there is an element of envy in the sense that whoever unfolds new areas of ancient civilization might achieve fame and glory; and by now everybody in the field has understood that Motya is the only Punic city in the world which has yet to release its potential treasure of knowledge, even – judging from the finding of the *kouros* – its potential masterpieces. If the city was as rich as the ancient historians related, it is certain that more treasures are hidden underground.

Little excavation has taken place since 1987 and even less is going to take place in the future. The Sovrintendente, in fact, told me that money is going to be concentrated on 'making good and putting things in order' with regard to what has been excavated in the past. 'Anyway, people dig too much.'

However, when Marisa has to gulp down injustice, she puts up a fight by means of articulate telephone calls, letters and, if necessary, the assistance of lawyers. One would not like to cross her as she fights for her rights. Marisa is passionate about her job and believes in it. Whenever she is not at Motya, studying the tiny fragments which convey to her dates and links, she is in an office at Trapani. The ancient Drepanum, that very important harbour of Eryx, Motya's ally, is another Mafia centre, where honest magistrates have been ferociously opposed, even assassinated.

Where would she start an excavation were she able to do so? I asked her. 'I would do it at once in the area designated "A", where there were houses. In ten years I have only worked on four campaigns, few for an area such as this. The ground here reveals more and more secrets.'

When Marisa arrived in 1984, she was immediately asked by Tusa to be in charge of excavations on the island, she recounted. 'I had dug at Motya even before taking my degree. Since 1987 there has been a new Superintendent at Trapani and she doesn't show any interest in Motya. Since she has arrived funds for excavations have almost dried up.' In fact, in the new era of Dr Rosalia Camerata Scovazzo who, unlike Tusa, the *archeologo-contadino*, belongs to the Sicilian aristocracy, there have been few digs. 'With Tusa in charge there were three campaigns a year and research progressed. Now in eleven years there have only been ten digs, less than one a year. They have showered money on Segesta, Selinunte and some prehistoric sites but less than 5 per cent of the budget is allocated to Motya,' says Marisa Famà.

When I returned to Motya with Orlando on that burning July day, I found Vincenzo Arini with his wife custodians of the island. Once again I met Zio Giuseppe, his wife and his sister Rosina, now grown old, still very attached to Motya and its history; and then there were Marisa and Pamela, of course. This group of people was instinctively known as 'us'. Sometimes one felt as if 'we' were under siege, not as ferocious a siege as that of Dionysius, but unleashed for the same reasons: power and money. The enemy – 'they' – are many and armed; they are better equipped and more numerous. Precisely who 'they' are is difficult to say. The 'us' front has been joined by Salvatore Lombardo, a good mayor in Marsala, who wants to maintain the delicate ecological balance in the Stagnone – although that has already been severely damaged by a barrage on the River Birgi and countless illegally built houses which dot the shore of the lagoon.

Since Marisa has been in charge, a programme of excavation has been impossible because of lack of funds, although 4 billion lire – £1.25 million – had been destined for Motya. But Marisa has resorted to a clever tactic. Every time 'they' want to build something new in Motya, she halts them whenever archaeological remains are accidentally uncovered. This happens invariably. For example, a new device for producing electricity had to be installed in the central part of Motya. When the topsoil was removed, Marisa could see that under that very point there had been crossroads. This enabled her to add another piece to the still vague topography of Motya. 'When you think that only 4 per cent of this city has been excavated ...!' she laments. 'They' were going to build behind the house where Colonnello Lipari-Cascio lived and dug the foundations; but the walls of an ancient building alongside a paved road were uncovered. The remains belonged to the eighth century BC, establishing the fact that Motya had been inhabited as a city from its very beginning and suggesting that it might have begun life as a Phoenician settlement, like Malta, and not as a colony of Carthage. It also confirmed Motya's links with Ischia, another old Phoenician colony called Pithecusa rich in metal ores with which Motya traded.

The road, flanked by two important buildings, ran diagonally between the two main arteries which divide Motya, one running from the north gate to the south and the other from around the tophet to the west. The area which Marisa had put under observation belonged to the part which Isserlin had identified as a possible institutional centre including buildings housing a mint, an archive and those Greek temples mentioned by Diodorus. There were also ovens dating from the sixth century BC used for baking pottery exactly like those used in Phoenicia.

In Marisa's opinion the Motyan houses were not made of wood, but of unbaked bricks, which do not last, layered on top of a base made of large stones. Gardens and orchards grew among the tall houses. The roofs of the houses were probably made from branches or seaweed; because of this few roof tiles have been found. Floors were either covered with plaster or made of beaten earth, apart from the sumptuous *Casa dei mosaici*, the House of the Mosaics.

Marisa had found out that as late as 1741, that is, during the Jesuit ownership of St Pantaleo, the ruins of Motya were regarded as a source of building materials, as a quarry, so much so that the Marsala Senate was alarmed and the Senators issued a preventive order. Contemporary salt-pans were built entirely with stones cannibalized from Motya. That explained why whole sections of city walls which, it had been calculated, were two metres thick and six metres high, had disappeared and why only the steps which climbed the defensive towers have remained as evidence of their stocky presence.

While a pattern of 'institutional buildings' was beginning to emerge, little evidence of domestic buildings was uncovered. Whitaker had started to dig on a site called the *casermetta* facing Cape Boeo which might have been, as its name implies, a little barracks. Its rectangular slabs, interspersed with smaller rocks, are a trademark of Punic building techniques. The *Casa delle anfore* housed vessels, and suggested that private houses were not all made entirely of wood.

The House of the Mosaics had been partly excavated by Whitaker. It was built around a central yard on a Greek model, and its floors were decorated with river pebbles rather than real mosaics. The black and white pebbles formed a Greek key pattern framing scenes of fabulous animals attacking each other; all very Asiatic in style. The most interesting 'eastern' figures are the ones which Whitaker discovered; in one of the mosaics a bull is attacked by a lion, and in the other a gryphon bites a gazelle. In 1991 new excavations conducted by Marisa on the House of the Mosaics uncovered more panels, one showing a bull, another two deer, and others a tiger and a horse. The design of the deer is black on white, while the others are white on black, as if in a photographic negative. In order to protect them from the rain and from the visitors (who seem to throw picnic remains on top of them), some of the mosaics have been covered by sand and therefore are not visible. Aldo Scimè suggested that they all be housed in the museum, but his proposal was turned down.

The date of this villa is still disputed, with no two archaeologists agreeing. Some experts think that it was built after the destruction of Motya, when a group of survivors returned to live on the island. But this is unlikely, because those few who had escaped the Syracusan slaughter were moved to the new city of Lilybaeum which, as Diodorus and others tell us, was built to replace Motya. It is also hard to imagine that a grand villa would be built in a ruined city which stank of death. Perhaps some of the poorer people might have made shelters for themselves using parts of the destroyed buildings; but they would have lacked the means to embellish it with such rare and beautiful mosaics. Besides, the river pebbles are not local; they were transported in an expensive and organized operation. Moreover, as Marisa Famà stresses, this floor is a one-off: nowhere else does one find river pebbles used in a mosaic in the Punic style within Greek architecture. After the revelations of the

1991 excavations, one is tempted to think that the House of Mosaics has yet more surprises in store.

When Joseph Whitaker sketched the plot of a novel which I found in the Whitaker archives, he set the story in this house. Ataliarte, the protagonist, had a Greek mother and a rich Punic father who was a merchant. She was known, Whitaker wrote, as 'the lily of Motya'. One day a young and handsome prince from Carthage came to visit the city. Ataliarte and the Carthaginian patrician fell in love and, after the three months that he spent in Motya, exchanged marital vows. Erga, Ataliarte's governess, sacrificed to Astarte. But soon after the Carthaginian fiancé's departure, the Greeks stormed Motya. Erga – a name which has more of a Wagnerian than a Punic ring – saved her charge from Dionysius, hiding her in a grotto. A year went by, and when Ataliarte's lover came back to Motya together with Himilco's Carthaginian fleet, he shed tears on the ruins of Motya and in memory of his betrothed. But, just like one of those charming operettas in which Delia and Norina sang and Tina acted, Ataliarte was found alive, preserved in all her beauty. 'I shall rebuild your house with mosaics and Greek columns,' he told her, 'but now we sail to Carthage where my people wait for you.' [2]

One can see where Pip's sympathies lay: certainly not with the Syracusans. But happy endings are very rare, especially in those days, and his novel was never written. Nevertheless, his short outline of the plot makes it plain that Whitaker thought that the House of the Mosaics had been built after the siege and destruction of Motya when Ataliarte comes back to Motya with her Carthaginian husband and lives happily ever after among the cinders and corpses. Unlikely.

Partly conscious of Pamela's comment about the possible closure of the museum, I decided to go and see it again, in spite of the oppressive heat which turns it into an oven. A new room had been built behind the original Whitaker building in order to accommodate the *kouros*. But the first room had remained more or less as it had always been, full of objects neatly labelled by Whitaker himself, including jewels and amulets dating from the seventh to the fourth century BC. Many of the items were reminiscent of ancient Egyptian culture, and some indeed represented Egyptian deities, such as Anubis and Horus-Ra. There were also scores of arrowheads which Schliemann had found in and around the areas where the struggle between Punics and Greeks had been most desperate. The ones in the museum bear signs of having been used, and were also found by Whitaker embedded in the defensive walls of the north gate. In addition the museum contains objects of no particular beauty, but moving in their representation of domesticity: small artefacts like sewing needles, weights for spinning yarns and aids for the beautification of the Motyan ladies, including containers for creams and scents. There is a really fine bronze censer in the shape of the double head of a woman, which Dr Isserlin mentions. There are also Greek vases and Etruscan artefacts. (The Etruscans and the Punics were allies.)

When her father died, Delia had an extension added to the side of the primitive building in order to accommodate the increasing size of the collection. She brought to Motya the lovely vitrines in polished oak which had housed her father's stuffed birds, once the dead creatures themselves had been safely disposed of in Edinburgh and Belfast. Twelve of the labels were written by Delia herself; the others had been added by Marisa, who kept to the 'home-made' formula using pen and black ink. Outside, the simple courtyard is watched over by Pip's bronze bust, which is an excellent likeness.

The sculpture of the two lions attacking a bull, which crowned the north gate, is in Delia's extension, and there is also a fine female head from the fifth century BC, much superior to the average Punic style but not, in my opinion, the work of a Greek hand. Motyan artisans were learning. An ostrich egg, cut in half to make a cup, was found by Pip Whitaker in a tomb in Motya and bears witness to the many exchanges with Africa. These ostrich eggs, painted in strong colours and designs, were highly prized.

In the Whitaker Museum one could also see some examples of stelae from the tophet. As I have said, almost a thousand have been dug up, but others remain underground. Some of the most interesting are on display. Many bore a dedication in Punic letters to Baal-Hammon; others were sculpted with mysterious symbols or figures. The Motyan stelae are considered particularly interesting because of the variety of their styles and influences; some bear colouring which is still visible. Also on display, and much more sinister, are some terrifying laughing masks in terracotta, also found in the tophet; their function is still debated. The pots and dishes that the local Punics used had none of the flamboyance of Greek pottery. They were simple, utilitarian and often moving in their modesty.

The last boat was leaving, so I hastened out of the museum, thinking I would inspect it more carefully on my next visit. But when I returned the following spring most of the museum was closed, as Pamela had feared. Delia's extension remained barred for the next two years, and most of the artefacts stayed packed up in parcels somewhere in the cellars. The yellow daisies survived the threat to their existence: it had been decreed that they were to be expunged, but they remain to colour the island gold in the springtime. So far. At the time of writing, as they say.

17

MOTYA TODAY

It was nice to stay with Marisa and Neil and to be able to look at Motya from the other side of the lagoon, almost all day if I so wished, and under a changing sky. Motya sunsets were flaming red, with that orange African tinge which spelt heat. In the afternoons, a breeze usually tinted the sky pale azure, while the dawns were lilac and blue.

I drove to Birgi, six or seven kilometres away towards Trapani, and parked my car. The new Birgi was built in the exact location as the old, which had been wiped out by malaria; the cemetery lay outside it, towards Motya and linked to it by the road whose point of arrival was visible at a small platform by the beach. I walked around the small hamlet, disturbing the local dog population which barked at me hysterically. I continued walking through the clumps of reeds to the shore; by the sea and in the fields there were ancient stones, tokens from Birgi's ancient cemetery. That place was magically peaceful. From that angle, the islands of the Stagnone looked completely different: a mass of floating green patches, as thin as lotus leaves and as green, on the dark water. A farmer observing me screwed up his eyes suspiciously; what was I doing there?

At Motya the museum was still partly closed, as anticipated. I felt frustrated: I wanted to study the artefacts collected by Whitaker or scooped from the earth after his time because now, after reading many books and meeting scholars and archaeologists, objects which were once mute had begun to speak to me. And, as always happens when one conquers a new field, I was enjoying it. So I was disappointed to find that, after many previous visits, those artefacts were nowhere to be seen.

The first room of the museum, containing some of the objects collected by Whitaker, and the room of the *kouros* were open, but the bulk of the collection was still in cases and drawers. Even the hamlet no longer looked the same; Giuseppe had lost his little courtyard in which he used to dry his tomatoes and sit in the shade. The cement, apart from sucking in so much of the original atmosphere, had also consumed all of Motya's water. After two years the builders were still building, the cement mixers were still working and the noise was still atrocious.

Would it still be the Whitaker Museum, or would Pip turn furiously in his tomb? The interior of the new extension was scarcely lit by several round windows, like the portholes of an old liner, a feature that was presumably meant to indicate that the Punics were navigators. But it looked more like a set for the film *Titanic*. Apart from the lack of light, the interior was almost uglier than the exterior, and did not take into account the pleasantly bucolic atmosphere that had pervaded what Whitaker had built. There had been a touch of innocent simplicity about the way in which the building recalled some Punic elements and used the same stone as that from which Motya had originally been created. Even the residence had been made to look contemporary, with modern floors and wallpapers, and thus had lost its Edwardian flavour.

Worse still, there was no allowance of space to study the debris which comes in during a dig. As we have seen, the soil has to be filtered, studied, divided up carefully, put in special drawers and labelled. All this needs space. Even before the extension was restored, the space available for study was meagre, and when Marisa showed us some pieces – those wonderful dishes for serving fish, for example – one could see how cramped everything was. And yet the so-called Vitakre Castle is empty most of the time; available for important guests who never visit and archaeologists who cannot dig.

In the saga that has been the story of Motya after 'Pip' Whitaker died there are many gaps, and nobody is keen to fill them, although every person connected to Motya is, I think, in the know. Vincenzo Tusa says that he has been defeated; he is over 80 years old and no longer has the power to fight. There is no longer a newspaper, national or regional, which can argue on the side of honesty like *L'Ora* did. Even ecologically Motya is under stress. At the moment Marsala has a good mayor, but the Stagnone is ecologically dying. The river Birgi was blocked in 1971; illegal second homes dot the countryside around the lagoon, and plastic greenhouses have improved the wealth of the owners at the expense of the landscape, which at times resembles a painting by Schwitters or a dustbin.

'So little of this island has been excavated! There is a lot to come,' Marisa sighs. Others know this too, but perhaps do not understand that what will come out of Motya will be mostly of scientific value, a short cut towards understanding history. Instead, what many think is that the soil might suddenly eject scores of statues like the *kouros* and that Motya might turn into a kind of Pompeii, and therefore a money-making machine. Tickets could be sold and restaurants filled while the ecology – already teetering on the brink of disaster – is ignored.

Perhaps Marsala could profit from this sudden twist, offering tours of the city to see the Punic ship, which is virtually hidden anyway and apparently disintegrating, and the main sanctuary of St Mary of the Grotto, which has been closed for years.

A candidate for the transformation of Motya into the Punic Disneyland is Mr D'Ali, a notable from Trapani nicknamed the 'Berlusconi of Trapani' (he is a politician active in the Forza Italia Party). He is the owner of the salt mounds and has turned them into a destination for conducted tours; he is also the owner of the local airline. 'I have nothing against Signor D'Ali,' the President of the Foundation told me, 'but I do not see why he wants to hold a monopolistic position in Motya. It's a bad thing to mix state property with your own, it does not work.' On the other hand the Sovrintendente for the area, Dr Camerata Scovazzo, told me that 'D'Ali is a person of respect. He put himself forward and I think the two sides could collaborate, I am all for that.'

When Eduardo (nicknamed Uccio) Lipari, the Colonnello's son, suffered from a stroke, 'he nominated D'Ali Junior[1] to take his post at the Fondazione as his heir,' the Sovrintendente explained to me, 'but the council was opposed.' When it came to a vote, the majority of the members of the Foundation voted against D'Ali. Signor D'Ali consulted a lawyer from Trapani who insists that D'Ali is already part of the council because 'Uccio' Lipari, being a member of the Foundation's board for life, a privilege which came directly from Delia Whitaker, can do what he wants with his position. Another lawyer, representing the state, takes a different opinion. The position is still vacant and the Whitaker Foundation is still one man short; moreover, there are those who doubt that Uccio Lipari, being so very ill and in no condition to speak, has been in a position to articulate his questionable inheritance. In the meantime, Uccio Lipari's son is still nowhere to be seen.

The Pugliese family seemed fatalistic. They had accepted the noise of drills and the cement reducing their liberty. But now they see the death of Motya as they knew it.

When the sun's rays were oblique instead of being perpendicular and the heat less ferocious, Marisa took me to see some houses which she had uncovered. She had published a paper about them, demonstrating that they were as early as the seventh century BC. She had also shown that the roads of the city centre were not straight, but curved, almost as if they followed the coastline.

'When we come back, Zio Peppino wants to offer you a glass of his best Marsala.'

'With this heat?' The feeling was that I had joined the camp of 'us' and that the Pugliese family wanted to show it.

'You can't refuse, it is quite an honour. He wants to talk about Whitaker.'

Of course, I was delighted to sip the Marsala wine which, at its best, is a dry, strong, scented wine, similar to sherry. It is drunk in very small quantities, slowly, to savour its taste and aroma.

Zio Giuseppe and his wife were indeed expecting me in the shade of their small room which looked directly on to the courtyard. Outside, the tomatoes drying for the winter had been moved to another wall.

Zio Giuseppe started by shaking his head and smiling. 'I was so young! So young!' He could not quite believe how young he himself had once been. 'I came to Motya in the 1930s, to work in the fields. The *Commendatore* had gone into a business of planting agaves which were going to be sold for making ropes and cloth. I had been engaged to collect the spiky leaves and take them to Acquadolce where he wanted to start a factory. He was a good man. He used to chat with me and did not give himself airs. Once my father Ciccio had cut his arm on the agaves, the Commendatore Vitakre was really worried.'

The Marsala arrived at the table with only two glasses; *la Signora* did not drink. the last time she did so was on her wedding day when she had become drunk, she recollected with a giggle.

Il Commendatore Whitaker was shy and used to wear a Sicilian cap. He walked elegantly with a stick which, as the years wore on, he began to lean on, Giuseppe recalled. 'I was born in the country-side, at Farfarello, near Villa Ingham at Racalia, and my father was already working here at Motya. They called me Peppino, because there was another Giuseppe whom they used to call Peppe Grosso because he was fat and I was always like this, thin as a rake.' The *Commendatore* was modest, Giuseppe added, and did not really like to discuss with people – by 'discuss' he meant to talk. 'His Italian was good but he could also speak dialect,' Giuseppe Pugliese reminisced, his eyes half-shut in the shade of the room.

'I arrived here on 7 June, I remember; I was 18 . . . time goes by quickly. They used to say that Whitaker's father had enriched him-self deeply.' That is exactly what he said: *si era arricchito profonda-mente*. 'I am 85 now, but I have never met anyone who was such a gentleman. Certainly these new people are no gentlemen, I can say that. I was employed by him at 8 lire per day while others paid 3 lire; it was an extraordinary amount, big wages in those days for a lad like me.'

One day, Giuseppe Pugliese had been called up for military ser-vice. His father Ciccio, together with him and with Whitaker, sailed their boat to Marsala. The south-west wind was terrible. 'It was a sailing boat, so there was nothing we could do. "Take courage, Vossia," my father told the *Commendatore*. On the island, under the pine trees, my mother and my sister Rosina were very worried, they could not see brother and son, they already thought that we were under the waves . . . but Vitakre was not afraid.' Today they no longer made gentlemen like that, he shook his head. Now there were this other sort of people . . .

'He used to come in May, when the yellow daisies were in bloom, they made him happy. "Don Vincenzo," he asked my father, who was nick-named Ciccio but was also called Vincenzo like my nephew, "are you happy to live in Motya?"'

Giuseppe became so good with the agaves and with pruning that Whitaker took him to Palermo to work in the gardens of Villa Malfitano. But Giuseppe preferred to live on the island; he did not like the big city. So he came back. 'When I was back here, Tina came only once while *la Signorina* Delia liked the yellow daisies as much as her father. Once her coat got torn in the wire which fenced the field . . . also Garibaldi came to Motya . . . he slept here.'

They used petrol lamps and they made wine every year. 'In 1967 I made a wine of 18 degrees, every year we filled a cask of 500 litres.'

Now there is an added pest around Motya. Mosquitoes? I asked. No, no: rabbits; and while in the past Giuseppe and Whitaker would shoot a few and roast them, it was now forbidden. 'They eat everything, but if one takes a gun out, the police are around in a flash.'

When the *Commendatore* came to shoot duck, Giuseppe followed. Whitaker travelled from Palermo with a footman, a cook and his driver, Giuseppe recalled. 'When I was 20 or 25 he rode on a coach with two horses and we shot ducks.' There had been times when the lagoon became so exceptionally cold that at night it froze; one sailor died. In winter the cuttlefish come to deposit their eggs in the lagoon; when it gets too cold they die and float on the surface. 'Then we go and gather them. I once personally gathered 120 kilos. You should see the seagulls and ibis feasting!'

Whitaker worked on his excavations until 1922, by which time he was very old and could not dig any longer. From 1968 to 1972 Giuseppe Pugliese became part of the Isserlin mission. Now he felt that his world at Motya had been eradicated like the yellow daisies and, although he did not express any opinion, he clearly deplored what was happening.

Tusa, by contrast, was outspokenly very angry. 'The works at the museum cost 4 billion lire' (about £1.75 million). 'They' want to control housing estates, tenders, tourism. Marisa Famà thinks that Motya would have been better off had the island been left to a member of the family, not to a Foundation. The fact is that '*Motya fa gola a tutti*,' as Pamela put it: everybody would like to have something to do with Motya because it could mean money. Or glory. Or both.

In the meantime, the plan of cutting down the yellow daisies is going ahead, I hear. [2]

18
CHARON IN MOTYA

Five-thirty

Gently, I launched the boat into the lagoon; it danced as I stepped into it. I untied the rope which attached it to the jetty and pulled one of the oars towards me; I pressed the other against the slimy bottom of the sea bed and pushed. The boat slid away from the shore of the island and glided out into open water.

Motya was behind me.

My quest for Motya had reached its conclusion; but although my thirst was quenched it had been replaced by a curiosity to learn more, to understand – and by a deep sadness for what was happening and what was not happening. While I had walked on the road that began in Phoenicia and eventually carried me to the north gate of Motya, I noticed things that I had never considered before. I understood, for example, that the memory of the Punics had been deliberately suppressed by history; that fashion and history are first cousins; that success and history are brothers. Had their story been forgotten because they were Semites? If so, their roots, which are common to mine, made me all the more sympathetic towards them. Anyway, who doesn't love an underdog? And if ever there were underdogs in history, they were the Phoenicians and the Punics.

The Phoenicians were disliked in ancient times. The Greeks scorned them because they preferred to make money rather than wage war, and also perhaps because they were small, ugly and smelt of fish. Or is there something endemic in the West as a result of which the Semites have always been and still are abhorred? The Semites represent Asia, the ancient continent which exported rats, cholera, most human migrations and the alphabet. Indeed, that holy bull that abducted Princess Europa also brought in Semitic Asia, and along with it all sorts of evil, but also life, culture and inventiveness. The search for the Phoenician princess by her brothers typified the burning curiosity of the Phoenicians, their need to explore, to find new sources of metals, new harbours, new places. Forever onwards and onwards.

Those Pillars of Hercules which marked the end of the known world also indicated mystery and unknown dangers beyond. Indeed, the currents which push in from the Atlantic and out from the Mediterranean were a threat to navigation; but the Phoenicians studied them and chose the time and season of their voyages accordingly. The word for pillar, column, in Phoenician is the same as that for stela. In fact, the Phoenicians did not have columns, they only had stelae, that is rectangular cut stones, which were holy. Often these 'betyls' represented the god who, in the first phase of the Phoenician religion, could not otherwise be depicted. The 'Pillars of Hercules' were really the 'Stelae of Melqart'. As the Punic triremes or the Phoenician merchantmen pushed through the perilous waters of the straits, they were expressing that people's driving need for knowledge.

When Virgil took Dante to a deep circle of hell, they met Ulysses, who had been punished for daring to aspire to be superhuman. Ulysses recalled that as his ship approached the Pillars of Hercules, his companions were frightened, reluctant to venture through the straits and into the unknown; but he vanquished their fear with a speech which could just as well summarize the philosophy of the Phoenicians. Dante changed the personality of Ulysses from the one we know in Homer, converting him into a 'Joycean' character, in the sense of an individual who deliberately avoids returning home. Home means boredom and demands on personal freedom. Neither the sweet remembrance of his old father, nor the anticipation of a joyful encounter with his son, nor the dutiful love he owed to Penelope tempted him to return to Ithaca. He wanted to explore. He was bitten by the Phoenician fever, the compulsion to seek adventure.

Alone with his small group of companions, those who had not deserted him, Odysseus sailed beyond Mediterranean Spain and '. . . *Morocco e l'isola de' Sardi e l'altre che quel mare intorno bagna*'. Those Greeks from Ithaca had grown old by the time they reached '*quella foce stretta, dov'Ercole segno' li suoi riguardi*'.[1] They quivered with fear. But Ulysses addressed them harshly; how could they refuse the experience of seeing the other side of the world? Did they not feel a burning curiosity? What was the point of being human, if they missed the risks and rewards of experience? This is a Phoenician speaking, not Ulysses the cunning king from Ithaca. This is a daring hero driven by the desire to discover what lies beyond.

> O frati, dissi, che per cento milia
> perigli siete giunti all'occidente,
> a questa tanto picciola vigiglia
> de' nostri sensi ch'e' del rimanente,
> non vogliate negar l'esperienza,
> diretro al sol, del mondo senza gente!
> Considerate la vostra semenza:
> Fatti non foste a viver come bruti
> ma per seguir virtute e conoscenza.[2]

What of it if they risked a premature end to what remained of their natural lives on earth for the sake of seeing the unknown?

I knew these lines by heart because my father had recited them to me since my earliest years. In his opinion they expressed the value of being human. I know better now: they express the essence of being a Semite, which my father was.

We find these same lines in another text. In one of those amazingly funny episodes – amazing because of the place and times they describe – recounted by Primo Levi in *If This Is a Man*, he tries to remember Ulysses' speech and translate it to French inmates of Auschwitz:

> Fatti non foste a viver come bruti
> ma per seguir virtute e conoscenza.[3]

Poetry, great poetry, was the only way to be isolated from the horror of Auschwitz: by taking a Pindaric jump into the adventures of the mind, freedom, however abstract, could be achieved.

Six o'clock

The lagoon, that day, was slightly ruffled by tiny waves which made my rowing easy; their crisp white crests broke urgently on the rocks, boldly. Behind me, as I turned, I saw Motya lying flat and green.

The boat's name had nothing to do with the world I was leaving behind; it was the name of a girl, shivering – the other way round – inside the dark lagoon.

MARIA
MARIA

The characters trembled every time I pulled on the oars and became disorderly, dissolving in pieces of varnish, of the sun and of the sky.

God was of no help at Auschwitz; indeed, had there been a god, would he have allowed mankind to behave like that? Would Auschwitz have been possible? God was of no use to Primo Levi even after Auschwitz, when he witnessed the refusal of others to believe what had happened to him and millions others.

The Phoenicians had a practical concept of the afterlife. After death, they thought, there was nothing. There was fog, there was boredom, there was the opposite of life, there was no adventure.

But hardly any literature survives from which we can draw knowledge of these beliefs. Unlike Greek writings, some of which were copied throughout the ages, the Phoenicians and the Punics were ignored; their thoughts were not retained. Their language was forgotten until, two centuries ago, it was cracked and understood once again.

Understanding the Phoenician god or gods also presents a problem; the moment one thinks one has captured the mechanism of their mysticism, the Punics' concept of deity, the picture changes. There is no doubt that the earliest Phoenician religion was monotheistic. Canaanites and Hebrews came from the same stock, migrated from the same regions and probably were neighbouring tribes in the Negev Desert. Deserts, which are inhospitable, have always been the source of great migrations, giving birth to powerful civilizations and great upheavals. This is not so peculiar if one pauses to consider that the desert supplies little food and little water: so that, the moment a tribe became too numerous, it had to move on, taking over its neighbours' sheep and water.

From the Gobi Desert came the Mongol hordes who became masters of much of India, Persia, Russia and Turkey. From the deserts of Arabia the Islamic scourge invaded Mesopotamia and North Africa, Andalusia and Sicily; it was not so much religious fervour that moved them as thirst for greener pastures. Don't we see the same happening today? From the hungry east, rich Europe has been put under siege. At night the Albanians land on the Italian Adriatic coast. Tunisians, Sudanese and Moroccans have occupied the Sicilian coast. Mazara del Vallo, for instance, has three mosques. Along German autobahns and French autoroutes the poorer Europeans press forward, in an endless wave of hungry humanity.

New laws have tried to stop the new barbarians, although these invasions are far preferable to the wars that used to take place in order to achieve the same aim. New waves of migration once meant devastation, burnt cities, nations sold into slavery and entire populations dragged away in chains. Now, at least, the devastation is ecological rather than human.

People migrate all the time, wave upon wave, like the waves lapping against the planks of my boat.

Seven o'clock

The breeze pushed me towards the road which the Motyans had built to link them to Birgi, to the mainland and to their cemetery. I could see it, under the transparent waves which now reflected a turquoise sky. I felt like Charon, rowing my boat towards the ancient Motyan cemetery. It was now the time of the cormorants. They flew low, coming back to their retreat after their banquets out in the lagoon, on their way to rest and sleep. The mournful screams of the seagulls signalled that they saw the approaching black flotilla with despair. Under the seaweed there moved unquiet beings. My oars turned the stones and disturbed a mass of crabs and pulverized creatures; there was plentiful succulent food under there.

The Phoenicians themselves had been the outcome of devastation and migrations. When it was their turn to migrate, a group of people left Tyre for the greener coasts of Africa. There were already Phoenician settlements on that coast, but the new city built by patricians from Tyre evolved its own new rules and regulations.

Carthage had a 'Spartan' philosophy, profoundly religious but fierce. Its deities probably changed as a result of internal warfare. Carthage expanded and became a metropolis; like Tyre, it boasted houses rising to six floors. It was the New York of antiquity, a vast market where goods were conveyed from all over Africa.

Within a century of its foundation, the arrival of new peoples from the interior and intermarriage had produced a race that was no longer purely Semitic or Phoenician – whatever a pure Phoenician might have been. These were the Punics. They were probably darker, perhaps better built than their predecessors the Tyrians. If we look at the *kouros* in Motya, we see that the hooked nose, long curly hair and beard depicted in the Assyrian bas-reliefs are no longer evident. We are confronted by an extremely good-looking and well-proportioned young Punic.

I could see in the distance to my right people riding bicycles along the road towards Marsala which followed the shoreline of the lagoon. They were moving in the opposite direction to me and looked like bundles of cloth bobbing up and down on the fragile wheels. Against the church bells ringing in the background their distant voices were just erased by the sound of the sea against the oars. As I listened, my thoughts returned to ancient Motya and I imagined those who belonged to those far-off times.

Those figures across the water were, like my thoughts, going in the opposite direction; they were like passing ideas, like time fleeing, disappearing silhouettes in the fading light. The colours were changing as the afternoon wore on, breaking into fragments of deeper blue, receding into strokes of turquoise, drawing a contour against the trees and the hills.

Who were the Motyans? Were they really Carthaginians? The fact is that we do not know for sure, so we can only imagine. What we can say for certain is that those who first found the island of Motya in the lagoon must have been Phoenicians. It would have been an ideal stopping place; the lagoon, with its protected opening to the sea, provided shelter, and the island was in itself a natural defence. Then these early settlers mixed with the Elymians, the Sicans and even with the Greeks. They became Punics; but probably of a different mix from those in Carthage, Gades or Sardinia. Their guttural language softened into something which employed more vowels; it became Hellenized to such an extent that they adopted Greek writing and speech. Their religious belief was dark and intense and, like the Carthaginians, they changed their deities. Interestingly Tanit, Carthage's powerful goddess, is almost absent in Motya, although I found her sign sculpted on one sarcophagus lashed by the sea at Birgi.

Their belief in the supernatural, in magic, was also strong. They would have gone to the grotto of the sibyl at Cape Boeo where, under the church of St John, there are still ancient stones. They believed in the magical powers of the spring of fresh water which gushes from the bowels of the earth beneath the church and the sea. The whole site was a place of spiritual power, so different from what we see today: a bare promontory covered in cracked cement, swept by a wind carrying plastic bottles and dirty Kleenexes. No sea voyage was ever undertaken without consulting the Punic Pythia, the sibyl of Lilybaeum. Pythia is the Greek name for the oracle, the woman with occult powers who went into paroxysms during which she would utter words which had to be interpreted by priests. We know very little about that other sibyl in Gades, the one presiding in the temple of Melqart, the sanctuary built in honour of the Tyrian god. Those Punic temples would have been completely empty inside and the god was represented by a mere stone, a betyl, a flame. The rare statues of Punic divinities were not located inside sanctuaries.

What was the Phoenician word for a sibyl? The Hebrew language does not help us although, as Isserlin points out in his book,[4] the Israelites honoured Baal, Astarte and many of the Phoenician gods. The populace was apt to disobey the diktat of the elite about the existence of the one and only Jehovah, who was a difficult god to serve, without an image and usually in a bad temper. It was difficult to believe in one god alone, as the Phoenicians had originally done, when they shared the dry desert with the Jews. After they migrated and when agriculture became the focus of their lives, together with sex – both being needed for procreation – one god could no longer provide help and consolation for a larger range of needs. Later still, seafaring required gods of the oceans and of the winds. Therefore the sky was watched and studied as well as the moon; the eclipses and the guiding constellations were all personified as minor gods.

Women in the pains of childbirth needed goddesses who understood their problems, and the nature of their particular sexuality. A woman's lot was wretched in Semitic societies. Sacred prostitution in the cult of Astarte was a means to ensure women's subjection from the very beginning, and we know that this rite was followed by the upper class in particular. As it had to be performed in the premarital state, it follows that these females must have been mere teenagers, probably even as young as 11 or 12, considering that the average life expectancy was only around thirty-five years. The system also relieved husbands of the bore of initiating their young wives.

Since women had to endure the experience of sacred prostitution before they were married, it becomes clear why the life of the firstborn, who might be suspected of being the son of some casual client, would have been offered to the god in sacrifice by being 'passed through fire'. This society of men would therefore humiliate womanhood twice over. The tears and sorrow, the cries of pain and loss, would have belonged to the mother and not to her husband. The sacrifice of infants was a form of abortion, undertaken having proved that the bride was fertile, an important point in ancient societies.

Maybe Carthaginian society, initially ruled by a matriarchy or at least by powerful women – the queen who founded the city symbolically – transformed sacrificial prostitution and burning the firstborn into a system in order to subjugate women. The clergy were almost all male; perhaps this misogynist coup can be linked to the change in the religious nature of the Carthaginians.

Seven-thirty

As I pondered, the sea turned from blue to green, then to dark green, and tentacles of straggling seaweed brushed under the wood of my boat like snakes; the colours of the bow were reflected and magnified in the water before losing themselves among those wriggling sacred monsters.

I was examining the bottom of the sea with care because I was searching for the section of the road which the Motyans had pulled up in order to hinder the advance of Dionysius and his war machines. When they saw the huge catapults approaching, the Motyans must have thought they were monsters, like the ones which had attacked Laocoon and his sons. Monsters emerging from the sea.

Again I removed one of the oars from its rowlock in order to use it like a punt-pole, forcing it with both hands into the muddy bed of the lagoon. Time was passing quickly by, towards the approach of dusk. Soon the sunset would ignite the lagoon into one of its famous fires which gave each ripple a vermilion liquidity.

I found the underwater road; it was still visible. Leaning on the blade of my oar, I made the boat glide along the stones until I reached the spot which had been breached. I felt a great sorrow and pity for those ancient people whom, somehow, I felt that I had come to know. I felt like praying, but to whom?

The 'Vitakre Castle' was dark, confused among the trees; it would soon disappear in the distant gloom. 'Pip' had saved Motya, I thought. Had it not been for him buying it all and starting excavations, it might by now be littered with villas built at random with no permit or proper sanitation. Punic Motya might have been converted into the San Pantaleo Hilton. Pip had been a modest man, dedicated to study. The publication of his book relaunched interest in Phoenician studies. Today some people say that *Motya, a Phoenician Colony in Sicily* was written not by him but by Professor Pace; and yet the style of the book is unmistakably Pip's, and so is the scholarship. It is enough to spend some time at the Whitaker archives in Palermo to understand the extent of Joseph Whitaker's knowledge. The tendency to discredit Whitaker's achievement is possibly attributable to a latent vein of nationalism and posthumous envy. And yet he was not honoured as he should have been, nor did he receive the recognition to which he was entitled for his achievements in a field that he pioneered.

Several boats left from the other side of the lagoon: small boats, fishing boats. Their motors made a peculiar noise, a mournful noise, as if those departing vessels had all simultaneously started to cry.

Perhaps polytheism is needed by more advanced societies. Monotheism is too simple. Our own religions have evolved in several ways, but they are all basically the same. The Egyptians and the

Mesopotamians believed that the sacrifice which the son of God made was for the sake of humanity. The son of God – in Phoenician worship, Eshmun or Baal or Adonis – dies and is reincarnated with the cycle of the seasons. The Greek world believed differently; they had a sunnier religion and a polytheistic credo; but our religiosity and mysticism come from the Semites. In religion we are Asiatics. Without doubt the Greeks' religion was more enlightened. Abandoning monotheism was symptomatic of a developing civilization. No rich races have inherited a monotheistic religion. Women need a female deity to address when in pain or distress; peasants need a god to invoke for rain or sun and more abundant crops.

Although we call ourselves monotheistic, in reality we are not: we actually have a whole range of gods from which to choose. We have saints of all genders; the Pope makes new saints from Poland or South America, deities which people can address easily, who speak their languages and who can be perceived to share their problems. The more spartan north, which is generally more attentive to the Bible, has fewer gods, in some cases none. But who says that this is more civilized? The exaggerated use of psychoanalysis among the Anglo-Saxons and other groups who have few deities suggests that perhaps it fulfills a need. It seems to me that most of those who cultivated psychoanalysis, and those who sought it out in the first place, were practising or non-practising Jews, people who were groomed in monotheism.

Who, then, are the Semites? They included all the major tribes which from 3500 BC onwards migrated from the deserts of the Arabian peninsula towards the green pastures of the Euphrates and the coast. Alas, we know nothing about their literature. The Romans destroyed Carthage's archives and the Greeks destroyed those of Motya. The Arabs burnt down the library of Alexandria where presumably there were scrolls of Phoenician writings bearing their legends and poetry. There must have been many examples stored in Alexandria, if for no other reason than the thirst for knowledge and the Ptolemaic pride of possession.

The Motyan archives might have been written on clay rather than papyrus, because papyrus only grew around Syracuse while Motya possessed several kilns. Maybe they still lie under the 'Vitakre Castle'.

Sunset

I carried on rowing as the sun prepared to plunge into the sea. It lit the lagoon which was a sea of fire, almost frightening in its intensity. Time was running away and it soon turned dark.

Time passes so rapidly. All those years had gone by, while on a different scale the bicycles on the road had also gone. Years had passed since I had first come to Motya, knowing nothing about the Punics or about the years ahead of me. Since then four decades had vanished, gliding away like those little waves which reflected the golds and crimsons of the setting sun. The figures in the distance, like the trees, were fading into the dusk.

Dusk

It seemed to me that the new devastation, the second destruction of Motya, was now beginning. I agree with Marisa Famà that Motya should have been left to the Whitaker family. Or it should have gone to a scientific institution like the British Museum or the Ashmolean. Motya is not a place to show indiscriminately to hordes of tourists and schoolchildren who cover it with Kleenexes and Coca-Cola cans. Groups should be shown around, because those stones of Motya need explanation, they are not 'beautiful' like great Greek temples or Roman forums. Besides, Motya is the most important place for scientific Phoenician studies and it should be treated accordingly. Famà denounces the transformation of the Whitaker Museum. How could it happen? Will more cement cover Motya in the near future? Sadly, the Whitaker Foundation, which is now headed by a man who understands the problems, has difficulties in facing them. Too much power lies with the Soprintendenza, which has almost dictatorial powers. Sicilian art authorities have total autonomy, they do not respond to the Italian central Beni Culturali. The Sicilians complain about this, about the autonomous status of the region; indeed, independence has gone sour. But whose fault is it? Aosta, which is also an autonomous region, has been a social and financial success.

Joseph Whitaker must have known what might happen to Motya

because he understood Sicily well. Somehow, his will concerning Motya in particular was destroyed. The will whose copy is at Villa Malfitano does not even mention Motya, speaking only of 'his possessions'; and yet it is impossible that Joseph Whitaker would have casually bypassed the mention of Motya. Motya was specifically the property of an English subject, as well as being an asset of world importance. As things stand today, it is in danger.

The history of the Whitaker Foundation has been so scandalous that in 1987 the Prefect who, in the name of the state, has the power to do so, had to appoint Aldo Scimè as Commissar to put the house in order. Scimè was then elected President of the Foundation in 1992. It has all happened in such a short time and so recently. Were misdeeds covered up? The fire which devastated Villa Malfitano might have been arson, carried out to destroy written evidence. Was documentation from Motya burned in that fire? Is it likely that Joseph Whitaker would have transferred nothing from Motya to his villa in Palermo?

Punic objects are of great interest because of the gap in our knowledge of that subject. Greek or Siceliot artefacts, like those delightful fish plates, can easily find a home in the museums or private palaces of the world. And there is the *kouros* as well. Did anything else comparable emerge from the earth at Motya that we do not know about? Some say that it did.

If only 4 per cent of Motya has been excavated, so that the greater part of the city still lies hidden underground, is it possible that there should be no other *kouros* or *korai*? The same exquisite standard of craftsmanship might be too much to expect, but there are certain to be more Greek artefacts buried in the city which the historian Diodorus, repeating Timaeus who saw it with his own eyes, described as 'most beautiful and richly adorned because of the wealth of its inhabitants'.

There are serious archaeologists who refuse to return to the area even though they are well aware of the important discoveries the site could yield. Professor Tusa no longer has the energy or the influence to continue his fight. He has changed his mind about the Punics. For years they were not studied by historians or archaeologists, because of anti-Semitic feeling. 'In the twenties and thirties, there was no chair of Punic or Phoenician studies in the whole of Italy. In fact Punic studies were actively discouraged, especially in

Italy and Germany, because of endemic anti-Semitism.' At the same time, Tusa thinks that something of the Punic cruelty has stuck to the Sicilian territories once dominated by them. He emphasizes that the eastern region of Sicily, once in Greek hands, is not so brutal as the Palermo–Trapani–Marsala triangle which has developed a ferocious criminality.

The French rediscovered the Phoenicians and the Punics under Napoleon III in Lebanon, and through French colonial power in Tunisia. In 1860 the Druzes of Lebanon massacred 30,000 Christian Maronites and Napoleon III sent a punitive expedition to the area. He saw to it that an Orientalist team accompanied the expedition in order to study the civilization of Phoenicia, as his uncle Napoleon I had done when he went to Egypt, and as a result of which he had filled the Louvre with Egyptian treasures. Without Bonaparte's initiative we would have no Champollion and no Rosetta Stone.

Napoleon III chose Ernest Renan, the author of a study on Semitic languages, to accompany the expedition which provided yet more artefacts for the Louvre. Renan was particularly interested in Byblos, which was not only the name of the Phoenician city-state but also the Greek word for papyrus. From it came *biblion*, book, and also our name for the book on which Renan founded his scientific belief, the Bible. When Renan reached ancient Byblos, he found nothing except for the typically Phoenician shape of a harbour and a crusaders' castle. After laborious excavations, several 'columns' of granite emerged within the walls of the castle, and slabs inscribed with hieroglyphs were found embedded in the structure of some wretched Arab houses. There was also a bas-relief of a goddess which, Renan thought, represented the Egyptian goddess Hathor. He was wrong: it was the image of Baalat-Gebal, the lady of Byblos, the Phoenician queen of heaven.

In 1919 another Frenchman went to Byblos to continue Renan's work and two years later, at the same time as Whitaker's book was being published in London, the Arab workers spotted a cave revealed by a landslide. It was a burial chamber. Inside a sarcophagus was found, and offerings. The first chamber opened into several others. In one of the burial chambers there were obsidian vases set with gold, silver sandals and looking-glasses, bronze and pottery jugs. One of the sarcophagi in particular was different from the

others, bearing an inscription in Phoenician alphabetic script: 'This
coffin was made by Ittobal, the son of Ahiram [or Hiram], king of
Byblos.' The world of archaeology gasped; this find stimulated
study of the Phoenicians, which until then had been ignored. In
1933 the French mandatory powers in the Lebanon were used to
pull down all those houses that had hindered the progress of the
archaeologists, and the history of the ancient Phoenicians began to
emerge from where it had lain buried all those centuries.

Carthage was less fortunate because, in spite of its glorious
history, the great capital was viewed with contempt by its rivals and
enemies; it had been one of the losers of history. The
Carthaginians' reputation for brutal savagery is changing only now.
The French dug on the hill of the Byrsa at Carthage, around the
harbour and the cothon. Soon they came upon the tophet, which
was immense. It inspired Gustave Flaubert to describe the sacrificial automaton Moloch.

To satisfy him, they heaped sacrificial victims in his hands and laid a
chain round them to bind them together. To begin with, the pious had
wanted to count the number of the victims to see whether it correspond-
ed to the days of the solar year, but more and more were added, so that it
was impossible to recognize individual bones in the vertiginous movement of the horrible arms. It lasted for a long, an endlessly long time,
until evening. Then the inner walls grew darker. It was possible to see
burning flesh. Some even thought they recognized hair, limbs, entire
bodies.[5]

Night

The fishermen's night lights, the *lampare*, pinpricked the horizon
outside the lagoon. They grew stronger, dancing on the sameness of
the horizon like glow worms; and as the night turned darker, they
punctured it like the lights of Italian cemeteries, a lugubrious sea of
tombs. That light, a symbol of life, killed the fish underneath. It
was a symbol of life but also marked the end of it.

I had to hurry now; it was becoming dark and I was gliding
towards Birgi, towards the Motyan cemetery: by now arable land
from which slabs still emerged as if in a *Dies Irae* by Berlioz. I felt

like Charon rowing my boat in the dark world of Hades, heading towards nothingness. The sea was turning black.

Another interesting piece of the puzzle was set in place by Schliemann, who thought that the Mycenaeans were Phoenicians. In Motya, he looked for that link. Contemporary studies point to the fact that the successive waves of invaders called the Sea People, who swept the eastern and southern coasts of the Mediterranean, were Mycenaeans. They were armed with Phoenician bronze arrows and helms; their kings wore gold cuirasses and carried huge shields. They attacked the rich harbours which led into the Black Sea – and that is how Ilium fell; the Trojan War was merely an episode in this prolonged period of disruption. The Mycenaeans with their army and fleet reached the richest of countries, Egypt, celebrated for its monuments, its women and its temples. On their way, the Sea People devastated the cities of Phoenicia. Some of them settled there.

Therefore Schliemann was right in seeing Mycenaean stock in the Phoenicians, because the latter are the outcome of a blend, an intermingling of the previous Canaanites with this new input. However, there is less Mycenaean blood in the Phoenicians than the other way round. It is from this date, around 1200 BC, that modern scholarship dates the birth of the Phoenician 'nation' which developed its impulse for navigation and adopted polytheism.

The Phoenicians called themselves Canaanites, and so did the Punics. They – Phoenicians and Punics – retained a consciousness of belonging to a single culture; they shared the same language, they dressed in the same way, they belonged to the same stock, they followed similar customs.

I landed into the night. I beached my boat and pulled the oars on board. A dog barked in the blackness.

Motya, behind me in the distance, was a dark, mysterious mass.

Chronology

	near Motya and attacks Motya. Carthage sends General Malchus who defeats the Cnidians
535	Battle of Alalia in Corsica. The Carthaginians and their allies the Etruscans beat the Phocaeans who are trying to challenge Carthage's command of the sea
520	Doriaeus, brother of a king of Sparta, founds a colony near Eryx in Elymian territory; the Carthaginians, their Punic allies and the Elymians defeat him
509	First treaty of friendship and cooperation between Carthage and Rome, detailing their respective territorial spheres and sea routes
c.500	First Motyan coins struck
480	Syracuse and Agrigentum attack Punic territory in Sicily. Battle of Himera. Hamilcar is defeated
450	Himilco, Carthaginian captain, reaches the coast of Cornwall
415–413	Athenian expedition to Sicily
409	Destruction of Selinunte and Himera
397	Battle and siege of Motya
396	The Carthaginian Senate votes for the introduction of Demeter and Persephone (Kore) into the Carthaginian cult
392	Dionysius makes peace with Carthage
348	Second treaty of friendship and cooperation between Carthage and Rome
332	Capture and destruction of Tyre by Alexander the Great
310	Agathocles, tyrant of Syracuse, attacks Carthage in Africa
264–241	First Punic War
241	Hamilcar Barcas signs a peace treaty, losing Sicily and being required to pay a tribute to the Romans
240-237	The mercenary rebellion at Carthage; Hamilcar Barcas quells it and saves Carthage
221	Hannibal Barcas acclaimed General of the Spanish army
217	Battle of Lake Trasimene (northern Umbria)
216	Battle of Cannae, in Puglia; the Romans are defeated by Hannibal
201	Victory of Scipio Africanus at Zama (Africa)
149–146	Third Punic War

| 146 | Carthage is destroyed by the Romans. Salt is spread on its ground so that it should be barren |
| 46 | Julius Caesar decides to build a new Carthage |

Year AD

1850	Birth of Joseph Whitaker
1875	Heinrich Schliemann comes to Motya
1885	Birth of Delia Whitaker
1921	Publication in London of *Motya, a Phoenician Colony in Sicily* by Joseph Whitaker
1936	Death of Joseph Whitaker
1971	Death of Delia Whitaker

Glossary

Acragas	Greek name for Agrigentum
Baal	Lord: designation used by Punics of their gods
Baglio	Wine factory/warehouse: from *ballium*, yard. Related to Old French *bail* and English 'bailey', as in Old Bailey
betyl	Bet El (Punic) = house of the god. Bet (= 'house') is also the second letter of the Phoenician alphabet
Canaan	The land of Phoenicia in Hebrew and all Semitic languages
Can'ani	Designation used by Phoenicians and Punics to refer to themselves
cella	sacred enclosure
cothon	Greek, 'harbour': the Punic dock-basin
defixio	Latin, a black strip in lead that the Punics nailed near a grotto or a pit where the infernal gods would be able to read the curse inscribed on it
El	Master
Eshmun	Our appellant
Gubal	Byblos
kouros	Greek, boy or young man
Libya	Africa
Mel, Malik, MLK, Malco, ML, MLQRT	
	Phoenician, 'king' (Assyrian: Mil Qartu)
metu	Akkadian: low level of waters
murex (*pl.* murices)	The shell from which the Phoenicians made the colour purple
obed	Phoenician: 'slave, servant'. Obad-iah = servant of Jah, of Jehovah, a (Hebrew) prophet
omertà	From the Spanish *hombredad*, 'being a man': silence, enforced by Mafia intimidation
Ophir	a place 'full of gold' in the Far East
poenus, poeni, phoenix	
	Latin transcriptions of the Greek noun *phoinix*, from which was derived the adjective *punicus* used to refer to the North African Phoenicians

Pygmalion	Greek equivalent for names Pumgaton, Pumaigaton (from the god Pumay)
Qart	City, great city, capital. Qart-Hadash = New City: hence Carthage, Cartagena, and other forms of the name
selinon	The yellow parsley after which Selinunte was named
Selinus	Greek for Selinunte
Sor	Tyre
stela (*pl.* **stelae**)	Slab of stone, sometimes inscribed
suffet, suphet	Hebrew (pl. *sophetim*): governor, a kind of magistrate who embodied the monarchical power and ruled for two years. In Carthage they were called to office by the Upper House of patricians
thalassocracy	Rule of the sea. Following the Mycenaean thalassocracy, after the twelfth century BC the Phoenicians established their thalassocracy of the Mediterranean
Tarshish	Fabulous land of rich metals
Tartessus	Andalusia, centre of tin extraction
tophet	Hebrew: a biblical term meaning the place for sacrificing live creatures
Ziz	Punic name for Greek Panormus = Palermo

Notes

CHAPTER 1

1 The Phoenician alphabet was deciphered in the eighteenth century by the Abbé Barthélemy, a French priest. At more or less the same time, in 1750, Bishop Pocock brought back to Oxford some inscriptions from Kition (Cyprus) which were translated by John Swinton, keeper of the university archives, using the close connection of Phoenician to Hebrew.
2 Xenophon, *Oeconomicus*.

CHAPTER 2

1 *Murder by Neglect*, 1959.
2 Polybius, *Historiae*, III, 22.
3 Note dated 25 May 1917; Whitaker Archives, Palermo.

CHAPTER 3

1 M. I. Finley, *The World of Odysseus* (London, 1991).
2 Robert Graves, *Ancient Mythology* (London, 1953).
3 Arrian, *The Anntasis of Alexander*, II, 17, 1–4.
4 Strabo, *Geographia*, III, 5, 5
5 Pausanias, *Hellados Periegesis*, VII, 25, 6; II, 27, 2.
6 'On the fall of Ilium, some of the Trojans escaped from the Achaeans and came in ships to Sicily and settled next to the Sicanians under the general name of Elymi, their towns being called Eryx and Egesta . . . the Sicels crossed over to Sicily from their first home in Italy, flying from the Sicans as tradition says and, as seems not unlikely, upon rafts . . . Even at the present day there are Sicels in Italy; and the country got its name of Italy from Italus, a king of the Sicels so called. These went with a great host to Sicily, defeated the Sicanians in battle, and forced them to remove to the south and west of the island which thus came to be called Sicily instead of Sicania, and after they crossed over they continued to enjoy the richest parts of the country for nearly 300 years before any Hellenes came to Sicily; indeed, they still hold the centre and north of the country': Thucydides, *The War in Sicily*, Book VI, 1.
7 Pliny, *Historia Naturalis*, Book VII, 57, 199.
8 Strabo, Book III, 5, 11.

9 Ancient Greek travellers described Phoenicia, and Byblos in particular, as rich in wine, places where 'wine ran in rivers'; and in the Bronze Age it was shipped in Canaanite jars.

10 Thucydides, *The War in Sicily*, Book VI, 2.

11 A. N. Wilson, *St Paul* (London, 1997).

12 C. A. Garufi, *I documenti inediti dell'epoca normanna in Sicilia* (Palermo, 1899).

13 The details of the sale are to be found in the Bibliothèque Nationale in Paris. A notary was sent to the salt-pans to make an inventory of the salt accumulated by the Jesuits. Captain of Justice Alberto Lombardo Morana was in charge of the expulsion of the Jesuits from Motya and Marsala. One of the aims of the Tanucci ministry was to offer the citizens a lay school, but on 15 December, when the schools re-opened, no lay teacher could be found and tuition fell once again into the hands of the priesthood.

14 Harold Acton, *The Bourbons of Naples* (repr. London, 1998).

15 Pliny, *Historia Naturalis*, Book V, 19, 76.

CHAPTER 4

1 Diodorus, *Bibliotheca Historica*, Book XIV, 42.

2 Ibid., 41.

3 Olympic I, for Hiero, tyrant of Syracuse 487–467 BC, from *The Odes of Pindar* (518–438), trans. Richard Lattimore.

4 Diodorus, *Bibliotheca Historica*, Book XIV, 45.

5 We do not know where Alicie was, or how its name has evolved.

6 Polyaenus (*Stratagemata*, Book V, 2, 6) recounts that Himilco tried to distract Dionysius by burning those ships which had stayed behind in Syracuse, but, having failed in this, he sailed back to Carthage and then, re-armed with 100 battleships, returned to Cape Boeo, where he destroyed all the Syracusan ships which were anchored at the mouth of the Stagnone and waited for Dionysius to move his ships out of the lagoon. Dionysius realized that, since the mouth of the Stagnone was small, his ships could only leave it one by one, and if they did this they would be picked off by the Carthaginians. So he pulled them overland back to the open sea – Cape Teodoro being then linked to Isola Grande, which was part of the mainland. The initial position of advantage was lost and, since the Greek fleet was numerically superior, Himilco, taken by surprise by the catapults which spread havoc among his ships, decided to withdraw back to Carthage.

CHAPTER 5

1 Vitruvius was the first-century AD author of *De architectura*, a ten-volume work based on Greek texts and dedicated to the Emperor Augustus.

Vitruvius covered the whole problem of structure; his work was reprinted in the Renaissance (Editio Princeps, 1486) and was followed by many, Alberti and Palladio in particular.

2 R. Canfora, *The Library of Alexandria* (London, 1997).
3 Virgil, *Aeneid*, Book IV, 81, trans. David West.
4 Ibid, 102.
5 G. Cervetti and L. Godard, *L'Oro di Troia* (Einaudi, 1980).

6 *The Odyssey*, XV. pp. 415–417.
7 B. S. J. Isserlin, 'Schliemann at Motya', *Antiquity*, vol. 42, 1969.
8 These papers are held by the Gennadius Library, American School of Classical Studies, Athens, from 'Schliemann at Motya', op.cit.

CHAPTER 6

1 Pliny, *Historia Naturalis*, Book XXXII, 22. The best Tyrian cloth was called Dibapha (twice dipped) and to produce the buccinum (shell) was used on the first dip and murex on the second.
2 Fernand Braudel, *Les Mémoires de la Méditerranée* (Paris, 1997).
3 Ebla is not far from Aleppo; it was discovered and excavated by a mission under the direction of Prof. Mathiae, and its language was deciphered in the 1970s.
4 Joseph Whitaker, *Motya, a Phoenician Colony in Sicily* (London, 1921).
5 M. I. Finley, *The World of Odysseus* (London, 1991).
6 Apicius, *De re coquinaria*. Pliny writes: 'Marcus Apicius, who was born with a genius for every kind of extravagance, considered an excellent practice for mullets to be killed, a sauce would be made of their lot, hence the name *garum sociorum*' (*Historia Naturalis*, Book IX, 30)
7 Translation by John C. L. Gibson.
8 Herodotus, Book II, 44, trans. George Rawlinson.
9 It has been suggested that the name 'Motya' derives from the name of this Phoenician god, because of the muddiness of the Stagnone.

CHAPTER 7

1 Herodotus, Book XIII, 54, 2–4. idem.
2 Virgil, *Aeneid,* Book I. idem, 21.
3 As related by Menander, Flavius Josephus, Timaeus and Justinus.
4 Maria-Eugenia Aubet, *The Phoenicians and the West: Politics, Colonies and Trade*, trans. Mary Turton (Cambridge, 1993).
5 'It was probably assimilated by the Greeks on hearing the pronunciation of the Semitic word Byrsa, which means "fortified citadel or fortress" ': ibid.
6 Virgil, *Aeneid*, Book I. idem, 78.

7 Aubet, *The Phoenicians and the West*.

8 Virgil, *Aeneid*, Book III. idem, 79.

9 From the museum in Marsala; original in Greek.

CHAPTER 8

1 Plutarch, *De superstitione,* xiii

2 Maria-Eugenia Aubet, *The Phoenicians and the West: Politics, Colonies and Trade*, trans. Mary Turton (Cambridge, 1993).

3 Joseph Whitaker, *Motya, a Phoenician Colony in Sicily* (London, 1921).

4 St Augustine, *Confessions*, in *Patrologia Latina* he wrote '*Unde interrogati rustic nostra quid sunt, punice respondenti chanani . . .*' (When one asks our peasants who they are, the Punics answer that that they are Canaanites).

5 Whitaker, *Motya*.

6 Jerusalem Bible, 1966.

7 Ibid.

8 L. Delaporte, 'Phoenician Mythology', in *Encyclopaedia of Mythology*, intr. Robert Graves (London, 1959).

CHAPTER 9

1 According to Velleius, Gades was founded 80 years after the fall of Troy in 1220 BC, which would make it contemporary with Utica. According to Strabo, Utica was founded 287 years before Carthage, in 1100 BC (Velleius Paterculus, *Compendium of Roman History*, I, 2).

2 Maria-Eugenia Aubet, *The Phoenicians and the West: Politics, Colonies and Trade*, trans. Mary Turton (Cambridge, 1993).

3 According to Italian law, everything found underground belongs to the state; but the finder or the owner of the ground is granted one-quarter of the value of the object(s) found.

4 Honor Frost, Navis 1, n. 056 (Internet home page), *The Marsala Punic Warship*.

5 Honor Frost, *International Journal of Nautical Archaeology and Underwater Exploration*, 1973, 2: 1, pp. 33–49.

6 Dr Camerata-Scovazzo has since been promoted to Palermo (summer, 1999).

7 Polybius, I, 9–10, 20.

8 Pliny, *Historia Naturalis*, Book XVI, 192.

9 Frost, Navis 1, op. cit.

10 Polybius, I, 47, 59.

11 Frost, Navis 1, op. cit.

12 Piero Bartoloni, 'Ships and Navigation', in *The Phoenicians* (exhibition catalogue; Milan, 1991).

CHAPTER 10

1 From the Whitaker Foundation archives.
2 From a manuscript that the author has kindly allowed me to quote.
3 Raleigh Trevelyan, *Princes under the Volcano* (London, 1972). Actually, by that time the Whitaker Palace had been sold and was the Hotel des Palmes.
4 Ibid.
5 On the following day, Pip was to jot down, in Italian, the following note: '12 maggio 1912 Scavi di porta Nord. Yesterday we removed the first stratum of earth 1.40m high from both corners' (from the Whitaker Foundation archives). Whitaker was not aware that he had found the tophet.
6 Whitaker, *Motya*.
7 Trevelyan, *Princes under the Volcano*.
8 Ibid.
9 Ibid.

CHAPTER 11

1 From a manuscript that the author has kindly allowed me to quote.
2 Harold Acton, *The Bourbons of Naples*, vol. 1 (repr. London, 1998).
3 Ben Whitaker, manuscript.
4 Acton, *The Bourbons of Naples*.
5 Raleigh Trevelyan, *Princes under the Volcano* (London, 1972).
6 Ben Whitaker, manuscript.

CHAPTER 13

1 B. S. J. Isserlin, 'New Light on the Cothon at Motya', *Antiquity*, vol. 45, 1971, pp. 178-186.
2 'Her model has come to be adopted almost universally since then, sometimes in combination with locus registration. Essentially this "stratigraphic" method is based on the systematic distinction and separate excavation and registration of all individual soil layers visible and documented in carefully drawn sections. These may be along the sides of single search trenches, but to cover larger areas a grid system or square digging areas divided by baulks is used. Running sections along these allow the sequences across the whole excavated area to be read. To be employed successfully this method needs well-trained staff. It has proved most helpful in establishing the history of sites, provided always that sweeping conclusions about these are not based on isolated small trial excavations': B. S. J. Isserlin, *The Israelites* (London, 1998), 17.
3 'After World War I, Whitaker was unable to continue his excavations at Motya and the investigation of the cothon complex was left incomplete. It was not until 1961 that some additional fieldwork was carried out here by us,

especially by Miss J. du Plat Taylor of the Institute of Archaeology of the
University of London, assisted by a team of divers from Imperial College,
London, led by Mr Brian Matthews, as part of the programme of the
Leeds–London expedition of which the present writer was director and Miss
du Plat Taylor co-director': Isserlin, 'New Light on the Cothon at Motya',
Antiquity, vol. 178.

4   'A set of Petter pumps held by no. 38 Engineering Regiment in Ripon was
made available to us on hire by permission of the British Ministry of
Defence; together with another pump obtained locally they were set to work
under the direction of Mr J. Fox, a lecturer in the Department of Civil
Engineering in Leeds University, assisted by two lance-corporals on leave
from the same regiment. After the channel had been closed off from the sea
with a wall of sandbags, strong jets of water from the pumps were directed
on to the mud surface, turning the soil from sandy mud into liquid sludge.
This was then pumped out to sea, and the operation repeated until most of
the top deposits had been removed'. The deposits lower down were then
pumped dry and excavated: Isserlin, 'New Light on the Cothon at Motya',
Antiquity, vol. 178.

5   Joseph Whitaker, *Recent Archaeological Research at Motya* (London, 1919).

CHAPTER 14

1   Thucydides, *The War in Sicily*, Book VI, 11. trans. Richard Cowley.

2   Ibid., 1 and 6.

3   Diodorus Siculus, *Bibliotheca Historica*, Book XIII.

4   Pierre Cintas was investigating whether Selinus had been a Phoenician settlement before the Greeks arrived. With its two harbours and rivers, it could
have been a natural choice for the Phoenicians; and it almost certainly was.

5   Just to give an idea of the richness of the Selinunte necropolis: when the state
excavated with official finance from the Bank of Sicily, about 5,000 tombs
were dug up, from which over 20,000 objects were extracted. Some of these
are now in the Archaeological Museum at Palermo, others with the Bank of
Sicily at Villa Zito.

6   Giovanni Ingoglia, *L'Ora*, 10 November 1980.

7   In the first instance Professor Tusa gave me all the names of the individuals
involved in this story and insisted on relating it to me in the presence of several other people. I recorded his narrative on tape; however, when I showed
him my manuscript he asked that I leave out names and some elements of the
story for fear of reprisals by their heirs.

CHAPTER 15

1 Vincenzo Tusa, 'The Youth of Motya', in *The Phoenicians* (exhibition catalogue; Milan, 1988).
2 A new interpretation dates this statue to 476 BC, and says that it represents Nikomachos, the youth who won the 76th Olympics in a victory celebrated by Pindar.
3 Tusa, 'The Youth of Motya'. op.cit.
4 Whitaker, *Motya*. op.cit.
5 Heinrich Schliemann, *La scoperta di Troia,* ed. Wieland Schmied (Turin, 1962).

CHAPTER 16

1 Sandro Filippo Bondi, 'The Phoenicians, City Planning and Architecture', in *The Phoenicians* (exhibition catalogue; Milan, 1988).
2 Joseph Whitaker, manuscript, Whitaker Foundation archives.

CHAPTER 17

1 There are two Antonio D'Alis, uncle and nephew. D'Ali Senior is the owner of the saltmines Ettore. D'Ali Junior was senator for Berlusconi's Forza Italia Party and owns the local airline.
2 During the summer of 1999 Marisa Famà was moved on to become the director of the Museo Pepoli at Trapani. Professor Sebastiano Tusa, the son of 'our' Professor Vincenzo Tusa and also an archaeologist, took over, while Dottoressa Camerata Scovazzo went to direct the Archaeological Museum in Palermo.

CHAPTER 18

1 'Morocco and the island of the Sardinians, and the others bathed by the sea'; 'that narrow mouth where Hercules marked his signs'.
2 Dante Alighieri, *Inferno*, Canto XXVI.
3 'You were not made to live like brutes, but to explore and acquire knowledge.'
4 Isserlin, *The Israelites.*
5 Gustave Flaubert, *Salammbô* (1862)

Bibliography

A Note on Sources

I have often claimed that, when writing a book, I follow a self-imposed academic discipline. I mean this in the sense that every time I write a work of non-fiction I read, reread, memorize and try to expand my comprehension. I cram information and ideas into my brain, which is growing older and less adventurous but simultaneously richer in experience and knowledge of different fields.

I must declare my fear of Vestals, of the keepers of the Holy Grail who will not allow anybody else to enter the sacred area. This is a difficulty encountered everywhere by writers who are just writers, not specialists in any specific field. Do I consider myself a historian? No, but my appetite for history is unquenchable. Do I know more than others? It depends on how much and what I read, what I study and retain, on my capacity of linking notions and, to some extent, on my intuition.

Luchino Visconti, the Italian film director, once told me how frightening Proust's Vestals were. He wanted to make a film about *La Recherche du Temps Perdu*, and was discovering that everybody who knew about Proust was the carrier of the torch of truth. 'Some self-elected Vestals protect their subject as if it were their own territory. If somebody like me wants to step into it, they are ready to commit murder,' he added. When it was my turn to pry into the Visconti sacred area – I wrote his biography – I encountered some dangerous Vestals there as well. In investigating the Phoenicians, I am aware into what a perilous nest I am putting my nose.

And yet, as a writer, I believe that the accumulation of knowledge in different fields is invaluable and I despise the tendency towards specialization. People who know everything about, say, Renaissance art and nothing of what came before and what went after it have knowledge but little understanding. When writing history, it is vital to have a wide vision. When I asked Professor Gombrich: 'What is history of art?' he thought long and hard. So apparently simple a question was not easy to answer; and his reply, when it eventually came, was that of a man of profound understanding: 'The history of art is history.'

This is one of the reasons why in the course of this book I use artefacts to explain some of my arguments. My other sources are archaeology, modern and contemporary scholars, and my own eyes. But the core of my story about Motya, the Phoenicians and the Punics is related by the ancient historians. In particular, I chose to tell the story of the siege and fall of Motya in the words of Diodorus Siculus, otherwise known as Diodorus of Agyrium; a historian who lived in Rome between 60 and 30 BC. The scene of Motya's tragedy is described by him in a translation which owes much to my husband Hugh Myddelton.

Since Diodorus is so important to the whole of this book, I will say a few words about him. He took thirty years to write forty volumes of a history of the world intended for a Roman readership. But, in the words of M. I. Finley, Diodorus 'used scissors and paste to compose a universal history'. On the other hand, since Diodorus copied texts of authors who were contemporary with the events described in this book and whose texts have for the most part disappeared, he is by far my most important source. Indeed, as Dr Isserlin says, Diodorus is the best description available.

This historian has been studied by many scholars who often disagree about the sources he used. I am not going to pronounce on any of them; but, on the whole, everybody agrees that Books XIII–XV are based on, and some passages may even be copied verbatim from, Ephorus of Cyme, a pupil of Isocrates who was a historian of the fourth century BC. Ephorus lived at the same time as the events he described and had himself written a history in thirty volumes which has been lost. Scholars also agree that Diodorus used Timaeus, a Greek from Sicily who loathed the tyrant Dionysius, as his source in describing the Sicilian wars which are fundamental to this book. Timaeus also disliked Philistus, a fellow historian who wrote four books on the same subject and who, before they quarrelled, was the companion and close friend of Dionysius the tyrant. We know that Philistus' books were available in Rome, but because of his friendship with Dionysius, Timaeus was prejudiced against him.

Other historians wrote about the western Greeks but, in spite of the fact that Syracuse was part of Hellas and, as it turned out, became one of the most powerful cities in the ancient world, not much was written about it.

Thucydides is an illuminating and enjoyable historian. He is concise and exact and, although he never mentions Motya, he is a marvellous source for understanding what was happening in Sicily (and Greece) at the time. However, his popularity as a historian dates only from Roman times. He was in his late twenties at the time of the second Peloponnesian war between Sparta and Athens, in 431 BC, when he consciously decided that he would write its story. Unlike Herodotus, he was writing about contemporary events, and while previous historians had used myths and traditions in their narratives, Thucydides was careful to keep to facts and rational deductions. He was an Athenian of Thracian aristocratic descent, born around 460 BC into a family which owned a gold-mining concession, and was later exiled for twenty years. A genuine intellectual, Thucydides admired and read Herodotus.

Herodotus was born around 480 BC in Halicarnassus in Asia Minor (now Bodrum, in modern Turkey), but we know practically nothing about his life although he spent much time in Athens, where he became a friend of Sophocles. For some unknown reason, late in life he migrated to Thurii in southern Italy and probably travelled to Sicily and Cyrene. He died around 430. His first book starts in this way: 'According to the Persians best informed in history, the Phoenicians began the quarrel . . .' Herodotus describes the Sidonians, and mentions Tyre and the Phoenicians a great deal, so that one feels their importance in his historical world. His method was pioneering and unique at the time in the sense that he decided to write about past events by investigating personally, visiting people and places, questioning witnesses and reporting what they said.

Another source is Polybius, a Macedonian who wrote in Greek. His father was a wealthy landowner and politician who died in battle against the Romans in 168 BC. The young Polybius became a hostage in Rome and, because of his scholarship and intelligence, he was soon part of the circle of friends around Scipio Aemilianus, with whom he spent twenty-five years. He was with Scipio when the latter destroyed Carthage in 146 BC. Polybius travelled very widely and consulted most important archives and rare documents; consequently he was particularly well read.

For the translations of these authors I have used that of Richard Crawley (1874) for Thucydides, that of George Rawlinson (1858) for Herodotus, and various references for Polybius. Some translations are mine.

Virgil too used historical texts, because he wanted to be credible in order to justify the Julian family's ancestry, which was to be linked to Venus/Aphrodite (Astarte), Aeneas' mother. Many of Aeneas' journeys (see chapter 7) are derived from earlier texts which have disappeared; hence their geographical and historical precision – apart from the great literary quality.

But if the literature on the western Greeks and the Siceliots is not massive, what is available on the Phoenicians is even scarcer. Phoenicia's history was written in Greek by Ezennius Philos of Byblos, a contemporary of Hadrian; his work was preserved in fragments by bishop Eusebius of Caesarea in the fourth century AD; at the same period St Augustine wrote of the religious practices of the Carthaginians. The Punics seem to have attracted attention only lately (though the historical research behind Flaubert's novel *Salammbô* is impressive). Carthage was also feared because it was considered to have a 'spartan' soul and a determination to succeed.

Nobody starts with innate knowledge, and the trick of writing is reading, learning, rereading, trying to work towards the creation of a wide picture in one's mind. Historians like Steven Runciman or Eric Hobsbaum seem to have not only a broad vision but an encyclopaedic mind from which they can pick dates and episodes. Runciman writes in a way that makes some think that it is all very easy. Nothing is, of course; but that ease merely signifies that reading history by Runciman becomes a great pleasure.

A Note on Terminology

I have taken liberties with some words; notably I use 'Punic' as a noun, not only as an adjective, as is customary in the English and Latin languages. But to talk about the Carthaginians when I mean the Motyans would have become too confusing – also for me. So I write about 'a Punic ship' but also 'the Punics did this and that'.

Despite warnings from several archaeologists, I call the Greek statue which was found in Motya a *kouros*. In archaeological convention, this word actually describes a statue of the archaic period and of a naked pubescent body. On the other hand, as Professor Nicosia reassured me, the word *kouros* in ancient Greek means exactly what I want to convey: a young man.

Sources Consulted

I have listed here the texts I have used chapter by chapter, as in this way this bibliography might be more useful for consultation, keeping in mind that the writings of all the previously mentioned historians form the basis for this entire story (and are all quoted).

1: RETURN TO MOTYA

I used Diodorus Siculus, otherwise known as Diodorus of Agyrium, *Bibliotheca Historica*, Books V and XI–XV (Palermo, 1988); for this chapter I also read B. Pace, *Arte e Civiltà della Sicilia Antica* (Milan, 1958) and *I Whitaker di Villa Malfitano, Atti* (Palermo, 1995; Fondazione Giuseppe Whitaker e Regione Siciliana). Maria-Eugenia Aubet's magnificent *The Phoenicians and the West: Politics, Colonies and Trade,* trans. Mary Turton (Cambridge, 1993) guided me through the whole story; and I also read F. Coarelli and M. Torelli, *Sicilia, Guide Archeologiche* (Bari, 1990).

2: MY FIRST VISIT TO MOTYA

I used Sabatino Moscati's *I Fenici e Cartagine* (Torino, 1972) and the beautifully written *Sicily: A Traveller's Guide* by Paul Duncan (London, 1992), as well as Gerhardt Herm, *The Phoenicians*, trans. Caroline Hillier (London, 1975). I also read an article on Motya in *Airone* ('Airone Mare', April 1988) by Manuela Stefani, which the magazine kindly sent me in photocopy.

3: THE MAGIC OF MOTYA

I used the *Encyclopaedia of Mythology*, intr. Robert Graves (London, 1959); the chapter on 'Phoenician Mythology' is by L. Delaporte. Also G. Battista Caruso, *Storia di Sicilia*, vol. 1 (Palermo, 1875); M. I. Finley, *The World of Odysseus* (London, 1991) and the same author's *The Greek Historians* (London, 1959); and

Harold Acton, *The Bourbons of Naples*, vol. 1 (London, 1998), which has fortunately been reprinted. I also used Thucydides, Book VI, *The War in Sicily*;
Herodotus, Book 1, *The Truth about the Trojan Wars* (London, 1959); and
Giovanni Alagna's very useful *Marsala: la città e le testimonianze*, vol. 1 (Marsala,
n.d.; presumably a reprint from volumes published in 1890).

4: THE FALL OF MOTYA
I based this chapter on Diodorus, *Bibliotheca Historica*, Books XIII, XIV, XXIV
and XXII; I also read *Motya–Lilybaeum* by Philologus (see XXIV 51–81).
Dionysius I, Warlord of Sicily by Brian Caven (New Haven, 1990) is a very excit-
ing book. I also used Antonio Sorrentino, *Da Erice a Lilibeo* (Bergamo, 1928), and
J. Innes Miller, *The Spice Trade of the Roman Empire* (Oxford, 1969).

5: THE MOTYA FEVER
L'Oro di Troia by G. Cervetti and L Godard (Einaudi 1980) is one of the many
books I read about Heinrich Schliemann, besides his own Trojan diary which I
read in the Italian translation (edited by Wieland Schmied), *La scoperta di Troia*
(Turin, 1962). The best is Michael Wood's *In Search of the Trojan War* (London,
1985), a thoroughly fascinating work. I. Coglitore's thesis of 1883–4, 'Mozia:
Studi storico-archeologici' in the Archivio Storico Siciliano, n.s. VIII–IX, pin-
points San Pantaleo as Motya. W. H. Smith's *Sicily and its Islands* (London, 1824)
is a useful book for its views. I also used Dr B. S. J. Isserlin, 'Schliemann at
Motya', *Antiquity*, vol. 42, 1969. As for the vicissitudes of the library at
Alexandria, the famous Ptolemaic repository of knowledge, I read Roberto
Canfora's admirable *The Library of Alexandria* (London, 1992). The episode of
Eumaeus comes from the *Odyssey*. Giovanni Alagna's *Marsala*, mentioned above
under Chapter 3, was a source of original documents.

6: WHO WERE THE PHOENICIANS?
Throughout this book I drew from Maria-Eugenia Aubet's *The Phoenicians and
the West*, mentioned above under Chapter 1. Fernand Braudel's unfinished *Les
Mémoires de la Méditerranée* (Paris, 1997) contains some wonderful ideas and
views. I have also used Pliny's *Historia Naturalis* and of course Joseph Whitaker's
Motya: A Phoenician Colony in Sicily (London, 1921). I consulted John Kendrick,
Phoenicia (London, 1855) and George Rawlinson, *Phoenicia* (London, 1899). At
the London Library I found George Smith, *The Cassiterides: Commercial
Operations of the Phoenicians in Western Europe, the British Tin Trade* (London,
1863). Also useful was J. Innes Miller, *The Spice Trade of the Roman Empire*
(Oxford, 1969).

Flavius Josephus, who wrote on Tyre and the Phoenicians, makes occasional
references to texts now lost such as the *Annals of Tyre*; I also read Gerhardt
Herm, *The Phoenicians*, referred to under Chapter 2 above. Sabatino Moscati,
Chi Furono i Fenici? (Identità storica e culturale di un popolo protagonista del-

l'antico mondo mediterraneo) (Torino, 1992) was also a source of information. Dr Isserlin sent me John C. L. Gibson's *Textbook of Syrian Semitic Inscriptions*, vol. 3: *Phoenician Inscriptions*.

7: WHO WERE THE PUNICS?

In this chapter I used the *Aeneid* by Virgil in the excellent translation by David West (London, 1990), where the Punics are depicted as enemies worthy of the great Rome. M. I. Finley, *The World of Odysseus* has been a fundamental text. Unsurprisingly, given the French colonization of Lebanon, Syria and Tunisia, there are many good books in French on Carthage: for example, Serge Lancel, *Carthage* (Paris, 1992); M'hamed Hassine Fantar, *Carthage, la cité punique* (Paris, 1995); and Alexandre Lezine, *Carthage, Utique. Etudes d'architecture et d'urbanisme* (Paris, 1968). I also read the excellent *I Fenici* by A. Parrot, M. H. Chehab and S. Moscati (Milan, 1976) and John Kendrick, *Phoenicia*, referred to above under Chapter 6, and drew much of my information from Sabatino Moscati, *I Punici* (Milan, 1986).A very interesting and useful book is M'hamed Hassine Fantar, *Les Phéniciens en Méditerranée* (Tunis, 1997). Gustave Flaubert's *Salammbô* (Paris, 1917) is well worth reading.

8: RELIGION AND HUMAN SACRIFICE

Here again I have used Moscati, *I Punici* and Maria-Eugenia Aubet, *The Phoenicians and the West*, referred to above under Chapters 7 and 1 respectively, as well as the Bible and Joseph Whitaker's *Motya, A Phoenician Colony in Sicily*. I also read the very interesting B. S. J. Isserlin, *The Israelites* (London, 1998) and Gerhardt Herm, *The Phoenicians*, referred to above under Chapter 2. A. Caquot, 'Le Dieu Melk'ahshtart et les inscriptions de Umm el Amed' (*Semitica*, XV, 1965) was an important source. Donald Harden's *The Phoenicians* (London, 1962) contains important maps and illustrations. The catalogue of the exhibition *Liban* (Lebanon) at the Institut des Etudes Arabes in Paris (1998) was beautifully produced and informative – though the artefact from Motya which should have been in the exhibition did not appear because the bureaucracy to allow the piece to travel took so long that it did not reach Paris in time.

9: SHIPPING

The catalogue of the exhibition *The Phoenicians* at the Palazzo Grassi in Venice (Milan, 1988) is a massive tome which includes essays on Phoenician and Punic shipping by Piero Bartoloni. Miss Honor Frost sent me two of her papers from which I quote. They are 'Navis 1, n. 056' and 'The Marsala Punic Warship', both in the *International Journal of Nautical Archaeology and Underwater Exploration*, 1973, 2: 1, pp. 33–49. Petronella Russo, *La Nave Punica* (Marsala, 1998) includes new material. I found some details in *Marsala Arte Cultura Tradizione*, (Marsala, 1995), a detailed guidebook of the city, and of course I again used Whitaker, *Motya*. I quote from *Oeconomicus* by Xenophon and from the *Compendium of Roman History* by Velleius Paterculus, I. 2 and Pliny the Elder, *Historia Naturalis*. M. Gras, P. Rouillard and T. Teixidor, *L'Univers phénicien* (rev. edn, Paris, 1995) is an excellent and absorbing book. I also read M. Famà, *Il porto di Mozia*, estratto da *Sicilia Archeologica*, vol. 28, 1995, nos. 87–9.

10: IL COMMENDATORE: PIP WHITAKER
In addition to Whitaker's *Motya*, I also reread Raleigh Trevelyan, *Princes under the Volcano* (London, 1972) Giuliana Saladino sent me *Carissima Mamma: Lettere di Norina e Delia a Tina Whitaker*, ed. Giovanna Fiume (Palermo, 1986) which contains evidence of the lack of interest in Motya felt by Joseph's family. Vincenzo Tusa's *La famiglia Whitaker* (Palermo, 1995) incorporates interesting details. The best book on the Whitakers is R. Trevelyan's *La storia dei Whitaker* (Palermo, 1987). There is also Francesco Brancato's *Villa Malfitano* (Fondazione Whitaker, Palermo, 1992). Ben Whitaker sent me part of a manuscript from which he gave me permission to quote in this and the next chapter.

11: *MOLTO INGHAM!* THE SOURCE OF THE WHITAKER FORTUNE
Once again I used Trevelyan, *Princes under the Volcano*; I also quote from Harold Acton's *The Late Bourbons*, vol. 1, which has fortunately been recently reprinted (London, 1998).

12: THE JOSEPH WHITAKER FOUNDATION
Whitaker, *Motya*, is one of the bases for this story. I also used *I Whitaker di Villa Malfitano*, Atti a cura di Rosario Lentini e Pietro Silvestri (Palermo, 1995) and Tusa, *La famiglia Whitaker*; Trevelyan, *La storia dei Whitaker* (Palermo, 1987).

13: DR ISSERLIN IN MOTYA
I read again the many entries from the wonderful catalogue of the exhibition *The Phoenicians* at the Palazzo Grassi in Venice (Milan, 1988) reprinted as a paperback (Milan, 1989); also B. S. J. Isserlin, 'New Light on the Cothon at Motya', *Antiquity*, vol. 45, 1971.

14: VINCENZO TUSA AND SELINUNTE
Vincenzo Tusa, *Greci e non Greci nella Sicilia arcaica* (Palermo, 1997); Sabatino Moscati, *Chi Furono i Fenici?* (*Identità storica e culturale di un popolo protagonista dell'antico mondo mediterraneo*) (Turin, 1992); Vincenzo Tusa, *Greci e non Greci nella Sicilia antica* (Caltanisetta, 1993).

15: THE FINDING OF THE *KOUROS*
I consulted again Alagna, *Marsala, la città e le testimonianze*, which reprints documents on the history of the city; also Tusa, *Greci e non Greci nella Sicilia anti-*

ca; but this chapter is based mainly on personal observations and conversations with the archaeologists.

16: THE YELLOW DAISIES

Marisa Famà gave me several volumes in which the results of her researches have been published: *Actes du IIIe Congrès International des Études Phéniciennes et Puniques, Tunis 11–16 November 1991* (Tunis, 1995); Maria Luisa Famà, *Il porto di Mozia,* estratto da *Sicilia Archeologica,* vol. 28, nos. 87–9 (1995); Kokalos, *Studi pubblicati dall'istituto di Storia antica dell'Università di Palermo,* vol. 11, 2 (Palermo, 1993–4); Maria Luisa Famà, *Il diritto allo studio dei dirigenti tecnici archeologic dei Beni Culturali,* estratto da *Sicilia Archeologica,* vol. 28, nos. 87–9 (Palermo, 1995), *Gli scavi recenti nell'abitato di Mozia* (Atti, Pisa-Gibellina, 1997) and *Mozia: La collezione archeologica G. Whitaker* (estratto del Volume Marsala). She has also written the following essays: 'Appunti per lo studio dell'urbanistica di Mozia', *Actes du IIIe Congrès International des Études Phéniciennes et Puniques* (Tunis, 1991); 'Gli scavi recenti di Mozia', *Giornate Internazionali di Studi sull'area Elima* (Gibellina, 1994); and, with M. P. Toti, 'Mozia, gli scavi della Zona E dell'abitato', *Forschung zum Thema Wonbauborschung* (Zurich, 1996). 'The Phoenicians, City Planning and Architecture', by Sandro Filippo Bondì, is in the catalogue of the exhibition *The Phoenicians* (Milan, 1988).

17: MOTYA TODAY

Maria Luisa Famà, *Mozia: La collezione archeologica di Whitaker* (1995); Gerhardt Herm, *L'avventura dei Fenici* (Milan, 1980); G and C. Picard, *La vie quotidienne à Carthage au temps de Hannibal* (Paris, 1958). Tommaso Spadaro, *Motya* (Marsala, 1998) makes some interesting points. Mr Spadaro is a local citizen in love with Marsala and its history and art. I heard him talk to a group of northerners about the Punic ship with great enthusiasm, ignoring the din of a local orchestra.

18: CHARON IN MOTYA

B. S. J. Isserlin, *The Israelites* (London, 1998); Thucydides, Book VI, *The War in Sicily*; Herodotus, Book I, *The Truth about the Trojan Wars*, (London, 1959). op.cit.

Index